KRYSALIS

KRYSALIS

JOHN TRENHAILE

1817

Harper & Row, Publishers, New York

Grand Rapids, Philadelphia, St. Louis, San Francisco
London, Singapore, Sydney, Tokyo, Toronto

FIRST EDITION

Designed by H. Roberts Design

Library of Congress Cataloging-in-Publication Data

Trenhaile, John
  Krysalis/John Trenhaile.—1st ed.
    p. cm.
  ISBN 0-06-016390-9
  I. Title.
PR6070.R367K95 1990
823'.914—dc20   89-46123

90 91 92 93 94 CC/HC 10 9 8 7 6 5 4 3 2 1

AUTHOR'S NOTE

The reference on page 294 is taken from Corbett Thigpen and Hervey Cleckley, *The Three Faces of Eve*, Chivers Press (Library Association of Great Britain), 1985, page 165, where the authors ascribe it simply to "Bernheim," without further elucidation.

Anna Lescombe, one of the characters in this novel, is a barrister of some standing. I practiced at the Chancery bar for thirteen years. Past professional colleagues (and, I hope, present friends) who think to find themselves within these pages will be committing the crime of deceit, albeit only of self-deceit.

Anna Lescombe was adopted shortly after her birth, as indeed was I. But members of my immediate family who likewise imagine that I have represented them here will fare even worse than my former colleagues, for they will be making a mistake.

EDITOR'S NOTE

References in this novel to "Five" and "Six" as institutions mean England's domestic security service, MI5, and her foreign security service, MI6, respectively.

Beware the fury of a patient man.

—John Dryden,
Absalom and Achitophel

BEFORE

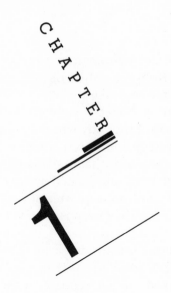

CHAPTER

1

David Lescombe did not look like a man about to face a make-or-break interrogation. Only the churning in his stomach gave the game away; and only to him.

He walked up and down the corridor, hands clasped behind his back. At one end was a high window overlooking London's Whitehall; whenever he reached it he would pause for a few moments to examine the busy scene before resuming his steady progress to and fro.

On every sweep of the corridor he passed a leather-padded door above which hung a sign: COMMITTEE ROOM TWELVE. Soon he would have to go through it. Whenever David thought of that, his stomach knotted and he walked on a little more quickly, as if by doing so he might escape what lay on the other side of the innocent-looking door. He glanced at his watch. Did he have time to run to the lavatory? No, don't risk it, this morning of all mornings, don't risk *anything.*

He was about to be subjected to the process known as "positive vetting."

He came to a halt by the window. Outside it was a cold, bright winter morning, but David no longer saw it. Eager to escape the present, he remembered his youth: another passage not unlike this one, with busts of former statesmen on pedestals, and heavy-framed oil portraits hanging from the walls. His public school, the headmaster's study, waiting for judgment.

Seventeen, then. A prefect, someone in authority. Someone *liked.* In his class was another boy whom nobody liked. David took a good-natured interest in him, protecting him from the worst excesses of bullying. Hamilton, that was his name.

David folded his arms and leaned against the window embrasure. Why think of Hamilton, a quarter of a century later? Ah, yes, of course. This morning, they proposed to vet him as a precaution against betrayal. . . .

The class had been waiting for a math lesson to start. Their master, "Beaky" Tozer, came in, took one look at the floor beside David's desk and barked: "What's *that?*" "That" was a pool of black ink, flowing in glossy abundance over the classroom's parquet floor.

David didn't know who had spilled it. His desk was next to Hamilton's, however, and he deduced immediately that one of Hamilton's enemies (they were legion) must have sluiced the ink as a frame-up: not the first time that had happened. For a moment there was silence. Then, from somewhere at the back, had come the drawl: "Oh, Hamilton, what *have* you done *now*?"

"It wasn't me!" Hamilton's pale, freckled face grew taut with fear. A brawl developed, with accusations and countercharges flying. David couldn't believe the stupid childishness of it all. He and several others ended up in front of the headmaster, part of a long-drawn-out inquiry as to who had spilled the ink.

David had weighed up the pros and cons, assessed the risks, and embarked on his first attempt at what years later he learned was called "crisis management." The headmaster would expect him to name the guilty party. Instead, he'd confessed to the crime himself, pleading carelessness.

"Why?" the headmaster had asked. "I mean, why own up to something we both knew you didn't do?"

David wasn't sure.

Standing by the window overlooking Whitehall, he to this day couldn't be certain. Part of it was a feeling that Hamilton had suffered enough and should be protected from false incrimination; more, perhaps, had to do with David's inner promptings of how best to deal with the ridiculous. If he confessed, there would be a swift end to an incident that was sapping house morale to an extent he regarded as nonsensical beyond words. . . .

The adult David laughed out loud. He was remembering how, after he'd taken his punishment, a fine as he recalled, the headmaster had said to him, "There's something I want you to know, Lescombe. It may affect how you handle this kind of thing in future. Hamilton claimed that it *was* you who spilled the ink."

David had stared at him, uncomprehending.

"He blamed you for doing it," the headmaster said impatiently. "Because he's a coward and a sneak, and he knew that since you were sitting next to him he had some pathetic chance of making it stick. But you've tied my hands, Lescombe. You and your silly, quixotic confession . . ."

David moved away from the window, still smiling at the memory of the daft things he'd done in adolescence. Then the leather-padded door swung open, bringing him fully back to the present with a lurch. "Mr. Lescombe?" he heard a voice say.

"Yes."

A man stood on the threshold of Committee Room Twelve, holding open the door. He was wearing an old thick tweed jacket over flannel trousers, very large in the bottom, and brogues that had been polished almost red. Two jowls hung suspended from either side of his ruddy face, ending in little pockets of dead-looking flesh. He succeeded admirably in his aim of not looking like anyone's idea of a member of the British intelligence fraternity. He could have passed for an altogether different kind of vet. "Would you come in now, please?" he said.

As David followed him his mind was busy making connections. Because he'd done his homework, deliberately seeking out others who had undergone this process and survived, he knew this man to be Jeremy Shorrocks, assistant director of MI6. Genial, that's what they said about him. A pushover. Brewster, he's the one you've got to watch. . . .

There were three people in Committee Room Twelve: Brewster, a deputy permanent secretary within the cabinet office's security hierarchy; Shorrocks; and a woman wearing a police commander's uniform, who David guessed must be from Special Branch. There were no introductions. David swiftly identified the chair he was meant to occupy and sat in it.

During the silence that followed he tried to still the beating of his heart and concentrate on working out how they would see him: a tall, lean man in his early forties wearing a good suit and a calm expression. Yes, fine; stay with that.

"Mr. Lescombe . . ." It was Brewster, the chairman, who spoke. "Thank you so much for agreeing to make yourself available this morning." His smile turned conspiratorial. "I know how these things interrupt schedules."

"Not at all."

David crossed his legs at the ankles and languidly rested his hands on the arms of his chair, the fingers unclenched. He prayed that any connoisseurs of body language who might be present would notice and approve.

"You know why we're here: to consider whether there are any security *objec*tions to your admission as a member of the Krysalis com*mit*tee." Brewster combined a slight stutter with a liking for mid-word stress.

David cleared his throat, and instantly wished he hadn't. "Yes indeed."

"You appear to be clean," Brewster said, but reluctantly, as if a man without blemish was an oddity.

Shorrocks pushed back his chair and removed a pair of heavy spectacles. "Boringly so," he agreed with a smile. "First vetted in 1985, no-shows on all subsequent repeats, nice wife, nice boat down at Brighton, no other hobbies, no vices . . ." He closed his spectacles with a snap and tossed them onto his papers. "Glad I'm not married to you."

"I'm glad you're not," David said. "They'd have to sack us both."

Shorrocks guffawed.

"There's just this *one* thing," Brewster continued; it was clear that any humor would be lost on him. David resolved to keep a tighter grip on himself. "Just one query."

"Hardly worth raising, really," Shorrocks put in.

"This is Krysalis." Brewster's voice had turned acid. "It's not just your common or garden in-depth vet, now is it?"

"Sorry."

"Lescombe will understand, I'm sure, that we don't want to overlook anything." Brewster's irritation was unappeased. "With the Vancouver summit less than three months away, and Washington breathing down our necks."

"Quite," David said. "Please ask me anything you like."

His polite smile signaled that he did not anticipate any disasters, but inside him fear was gathering. If he could but pass this, he would become a member of the élite Krysalis committee, that select band of Englishmen and Americans whose job it was to prepare ground plans for the next European war. It would mean more money, more prestige, but above all it would mean that he belonged. That at the impossibly early age of forty-two he'd become a major power player. For a second he let himself imagine that moment of bliss when he would say to Anna: "I've done it!" Next second he had levered himself back to reality to hear Shorrocks say, "Your wife, Anna."

With an effort David somehow managed to keep his face under control.

"At one time she seemed to be rather friendly with a German chappie."

"Indeed?" David forced himself to produce an unruffled smile. *Say something!* "Am I allowed to ask, what does friendly mean, in this context?"

"Just that. Our informant . . . let me see . . ." Brewster flipped through several pages. "Ah, yes . . . this is a couple of years back, although it only surfaced recently. . . . A Treasury man, went to his favorite restaurant, there was your wife at the next table, didn't seem to notice him although they'd met before . . . her companion talked fluent German to a passing acquaintance, obviously his native language. . . ."

"So it's linguistics in the Treasury now, is it? I often wondered what they did."

Idiot! They don't like fun and games. But Shorrocks laughed; and this time even Brewster permitted himself a smile. Only the female commander continued to sit there, flintlike. Shorrocks wrote something on a scrap of paper and slid it in front of Brewster, who affected not to see it. David would have given three years' pension to know what it was.

"I think that must be Duggy Atkinson," he said quickly. "Your source."

"I'm afraid we're not allowed to disclose—"

"Oh, quite. Do excuse me."

Brewster cleared his throat. "Then it would appear that the same thing happened the next week and the week after that."

"I see. Two years ago, you say?"

"Yes."

David looked up at the ceiling, as if pursuing some elusive memory. In truth, he was trying to quell the apprehension that had begun to undermine him. What on earth had Anna been up to? No,

don't think about that, just *deal with it.* "But not since then . . .
however, the restaurant sounds all right." David was seized with a
sudden inspiration. He took out his diary. "What's it called?"

Shorrocks chuckled. He produced the restaurant's name and
even, after further research, a phone number. "According to our
source, you should try the salade Niçoise."

"I see." David's forehead creased in a frown. "I'm sorry, I feel
I'm missing something terribly obvious but . . . it hasn't been made
a crime to have lunch with Germans, has it?" *Wonderful! Keep
going!*

"Do we know which Germany?" the woman commander
asked; and David turned to her. "I think we can safely assume West
Germany," he said.

"Why?" she asked.

David raised his eyebrows. "East Germans having lunch with
lady barristers, well . . . ha ha. That *would* be in the file, now
wouldn't it?"

"Ha ha," Brewster agreed. "But you can see our problem, I'm
sure. Do you recognize this man, from our informant's description?"

David shook his head. "Anna's circle of friends doesn't totally
overlap with mine. Possibly a client? She's always had quite an
extensive Euro-practice."

"Possibly." Brewster made a note. "Now you *know* the next
question, and it's a frightful bore, I realize that, but—"

"How's the marriage?"

"Ah . . ."

"Sound as a bell, I'm happy to say."

"You're surprised by this information but not perturbed by it;
would that be a correct summary?"

Damn right! David thought; but what he said was: "As to the
second part of your analysis, yes; the first part gives me pause. I
don't find it surprising that my wife should lunch several times with
the same man. What were they discussing, do we know?"

"We don't."

David shrugged. "She's a barrister, very successful. Quite a lot
of wining and dining goes on at the bar, from what I hear."

"When you next see your wife, will you put this to her?"
Shorrocks asked.

"Something that happened two years ago? I suppose I might. If
I remember, which I probably won't. Why, would you like me to?"

"Noo . . ." Shorrocks shook his head with a smile. "And for the record, let me just say that Lescombe does have a point: the Germans—half of 'em—are on our side now, you know. Not like last time."

Big Ben struck the quarter, affording Brewster an excuse to crush his ebullient colleague with magisterial silence. "Can I take it, then," Brewster said at last, "that you have no objections to the admission of Mr. Lescombe to the Krysalis Committee?"

"You can."

Brewster opened a plastic-backed folder at the last page. David drew a deep breath. Brewster was uncapping his fountain pen, was actually on the point of appending his signature, when Shorrocks cleared his throat and David's chest tightened. Surely there could be nothing else, *surely*? But Shorrocks merely nodded toward the far end of the table.

"Commander?" Brewster's face was flushed.

"No objections from Branch, sir."

Brewster signed.

————

David sprinted through the arch into Whitehall as if competing for a place on the Olympic team. He did not pause until he came to a phone booth on the fringe of Trafalgar Square. It seemed like an eternity before Anna's clerk put her on the line, but then there was that wonderful, musical voice: "Darling! How did it go? Did they . . . ?"

"*Yes!*"

"Oh *David!*"

"It's all right. It's all right." Memories of his wife having lunch with mysterious Germans fled from his mind, leaving only a heady mixture of love and exultation: Let Anna have lunch with everyone and anyone, who cared?

"I knew it," she cried, "The champagne's already in the fridge; damn it, I'll put another bottle in to chill the minute I get home."

David was trembling; he could scarcely hold the receiver steady, but one thing he must say and the words came rushing out, "I'm too ill to drink—"

"Ill! What's wrong?"

"Nothing that a few hours in bed with you won't cure."

He ran out of the booth, leaving the receiver to swing at the end of its cord. When the next caller in the queue picked up the phone he was astonished to hear a woman's joyous laughter still echoing down the line.

CHAPTER

2

When Jürgen Barzel turned the key in the lock of his Köpenick apartment that evening he had no idea that he was opening up the end of the world. Then he entered, caught sight of Hauptverwaltung Aufklärung's Colonel Huper perched on the kitchen table, swinging a bamboo swagger cane against his leg, and he knew. Twenty years of heartache, gone for nothing.

"Books," Huper said mournfully. "Why, Jürgen?"

It was the use of his first name that told Barzel how serious things were.

"You were the best HVA had," Huper went on, coming out to meet Barzel. They stood face to face opposite the door to the huge living room. Huper gestured with his cane. Barzel looked. They had taken up the floorboards. All of them.

There was nothing for them to find, but still he wanted to vomit. Something rose out of his stomach and he swallowed it down hard, repelled by the awful aftertaste. His teeth chattered with cold. Somehow he managed to keep them clenched together. It was all right as long as he averted his eyes from the carnage that once had been his living room.

"Four thousand books, and more," Huper went on. "You're the

best we have. And you make a library for yourself."

Barzel became aware of others in his apartment: gray men in macintoshes, who now seemed to come slithering out of his carved oak paneling like rats from a sinking vessel.

Barzel looked down to find the tip of Huper's cane planted against his breastbone. "You *are* a library. You know that, mm?" When Barzel said nothing, Huper continued: "Every secret service has two or three like you. 'Why use the computer; Barzel's in the building?' A walking library. Twenty years of knowledge. Secrets. Connections. Cross-references."

Huper sighed. He was short and stout and he had little hair left: his face was that of a schoolmaster who has uncovered a drug ring in his honors class. Now he removed the cane from Barzel's chest and said, "Let's talk."

He raised his voice and ordered the apartment emptied. The gray rats scuttled. Moments later the two men were alone.

Huper eyed Barzel. "Want a drink?"

For the first time since entering his domain, Barzel felt strong enough to speak. "There's whisky . . . but of course, you know."

Huper nodded lugubriously. "I know."

They sat in the kitchen and drank. "Shakespeare," Huper said between fastidious sips. "Proust." Sip. "Böll." Sip. "Orwell."

"Who told you?" Barzel asked.

"One of your bookseller friends. Someone you'd tried to help get over the border, in exchange for a handful of first editions."

That must have been Ratner, Barzel supposed; Ratner who was so good on the Romantic poets. He did not feel resentment toward his betrayer, any more than he hated Colonel Huper, who had been a humane boss over the years. Rather, he felt a bizarre kind of gratitude toward this man, who at last had set him free. Perhaps in prison they would allow him to keep some of the books. . . .

Yes, that was it, Barzel told himself: Concentrate on doing a deal to keep the books with you in jail. Even if it's only ten of them. *The Analects*. And Ovid, no, not Ovid, oh dear God in heaven, *which* . . . ?

Huper started to speak, sighed, tried again. "I know why you did it, Jürgen. Retirement. Old age. These books are worth a fortune on the black market, aren't they?"

Barzel stared at him, keeping his face expressionless. What was Huper talking about? Books were beyond price. They took you far away, into a world circumscribed only by your own mind, your own imagination. A world of civilized values, rare sensations, exotic scents. A world, above all, where the Communist party of East Germany, and its secret service, the HVA, occupied none of the space.

Barzel looked into the colonel's eyes and knew a moment of hope. "They're worth a lot," he admitted slowly. "In the right hands."

Could Huper be bribed?

"We have a problem, Jürgen. Don't we?"

Hope died.

"We have a problem . . . more than one. Does the name Krysalis mean anything to you?"

Barzel thought the colonel must be referring to a book title. He frowned, shook his head.

"We have a little problem, we have a little opportunity. The KGB invites our cooperation in obtaining a British file entitled 'Krysalis.' It must be done before the Vancouver summit."

Barzel, knowing himself to be at the end of his career, could not understand why Huper was telling him this. Might as well show interest. . . . "Why have we been singled out for this . . ." The two men's eyes met briefly. ". . . privilege?"

"One of your agents in place has a connection with this file."

"Who?"

"Gerhard Kleist."

Barzel had been struggling with the realization that Huper might offer him some kind of deal. But on hearing Kleist's name, his hopes fell again. The steam had gone out of that one, long ago.

Huper leaned forward to rest his elbows on the table. "Jürgen. Listen to me. You can keep the job. The car. The apartment. Even the books."

Breath rushed through Barzel's lips, his heart jolted against his ribcage, he felt dizzy. "The books?"

"Yes. All of them. Even the banned ones, the ones you stole on raids. But . . ."

Barzel scarcely heard the "but." "Thank you," he breathed. "Thank you, thank you, thank you . . ." He could not stop speaking the meaningless phrase.

"But it won't be *easy*."

Barzel's lips continued to move; now, however, as he caught sight of the glint in Huper's eyes, they moved soundlessly.

"You have to get that file, Jürgen. *Soon.* Otherwise . . ." Huper spread his hands, shook his head. "Finish. Sorry."

Barzel stared at him, his heartfelt elation dwindling rapidly now.

"Gorbachev needs that file for Vancouver, you see. So the KGB must have it. So they're leaning on me. I'm leaning on you." Huper smiled, made a pathetic attempt at humor. "The only person nobody's leaning on is Gorbachev." His expression had turned painful. He wiped his face with his hand, then said: "I don't like screwing you. Really. But we do have to have that file." He paused. "Or I'll make a bonfire, Jürgen. A four-thousand-volume bonfire."

As Barzel stared into the older man's eyes he felt such an implacable hatred, such rage mixed with terror, that the colonel must have seen it, for he sat back, turning away as he did so.

Barzel looked down to see that the hand holding his glass was dead white. Very slowly he made himself relax his grip; but his hand shook long afterward.

"Just tell me one thing, colonel," he said, and the calmness of his voice surprised him. "How long have I got?"

———

One week later, almost to the hour, Jürgen Barzel caught a whiff of smoke from some nearby domestic log fire and again felt ice penetrate his bone marrow. A bonfire, Huper had promised him. Unless . . .

It was twenty minutes past midnight. He stood concealed behind a cypress in the garden of a large house in Hampstead, a wealthy area of London where property owners valued their privacy; hence gardens like this one contained numerous trees and shrubs. Barzel had been waiting here for over an hour. During that time he had chewed all ten fingernails down to the quick. Now there was blood in his mouth, and his thumb hurt where his teeth had scraped the flesh raw.

Movement. Lights coming on in the hallway . . .

A group of people appeared at the front door, twenty feet or so away. He drew back into the shadows. Three silhouettes against the house lights: Kleist and two guests. Barzel ground his teeth. *Why don't they go?*

He heard them speaking a language he didn't know. Ah yes, Spanish: his contacts had told him Kleist would be entertaining friends from the Paraguayan embassy. Kleist's late wife had been half American, half Paraguayan; he still kept up friendships in South America. Sometimes Barzel wondered whether he shouldn't have checked that out long ago: a man could hide in Paraguay, or Peru, even from the East German secret service. . . .

Barzel heard feet crunch along the gravel drive; a gate swung on rusty hinges; the noise of the departing guests died away. He peered through the foliage. Gerhard Kleist, the man who owned this imposing residence, was resting his back against the door frame. He lingered a moment, scanning the night sky, then closed the front door and turned off the light.

Barzel hesitated no longer. He glided up to the now-darkened house and laid one ear against the front door, his hand resting on a brass plate to one side. He could not read the plate in the dark, but he knew well enough what it said: GERHARD KLEIST, MA, ABPSS, CONSULTANT PSYCHOLOGIST.

Barzel reached up to unscrew the light bulb, and rang the doorbell.

Nothing happened. Then he heard footsteps approaching. The hall light came on to reveal a shadow through the glass-mullioned upper half of the door. But the shadow's hand froze on the latch; for despite its having pressed a switch, no exterior light came on.

"Who's there?"

"Gerhard," Barzel said; his tone was imperative, urgent. *"Gerhard, lass mich rein!"*

"Barzel?"

"Ja. Mach schnell!"

Kleist turned off the hall light. Only then did he slip the latch.

"What the—"

"Ssh!"

Barzel ran inside and held the door open while he surveyed the driveway. "Clear," he said after a long minute. "Here, you'll want your light bulb back."

"You're mad! To visit this house—"

"If I had a choice, believe me, I wouldn't come within a mile of you."

"Then why—"

"Time! This can't wait one hour, let alone a day. Let's get out of sight, for the love of God!"

The two spoke rapid German, keeping their voices low from habit, but Barzel knew his fear showed through, in every clipped, breathless syllable.

Kleist escorted Barzel into his living room. He made sure that the curtains were drawn before switching on the desk lamp, then

poured two large whiskies. Barzel dropped into a leather armchair
with its back to the windows. He still was breathing fast.

Kleist sat at one end of a sofa. "You haven't changed," he said,
a touch of envy in his voice.

Barzel, though in his early fifties, knew he'd maintained the
face and figure of a younger man. His sandy hair had kept its youthful texture, like his mustache, and his pale gray eyes were free of
broken veins. With his cultivated German accent, slim figure, and
understated manner, he prided himself on passing for a well-to-do
member of one of the modern Euro-professions: publisher, perhaps,
or financial consultant. Certainly no one taking a casual glance
would have been likely to fasten on his real job, deputy chief of
Directorate One/A of the Hauptverwaltung Aufklärung, or HVA:
East Germany's secret service.

"You're not quite the same, I think," Barzel remarked at last.
"Fatter—a little. More lines in the face." He drank a slug of whisky.
"You should try a few early nights."

Kleist looked away. Barzel studied the drawn face opposite and
felt his heart sink. Kleist had once been his best mole, the man he
called on when all else failed, an ingenious spy. Since Clara, his
wife, died of breast cancer a year ago, however, things were not the
same. Barzel knew that Kleist had long ago ceased to love Clara, but
he'd relied on her to keep his life running smoothly. When she died,
it was as if an inner spring had broken. Barzel, obsessed with his
future, silently cursed the fate that made him now so utterly dependent on this man.

"I have to be out of here *fast,* so listen to me," he said. "I need
some information. Hypnosis. You're an expert, yes?"

Kleist shrugged. Barzel took it for confirmation and swiftly
moved on. "You once told me that a person can be hypnotized to
remember things that the conscious mind has long since forgotten,
is that right?"

"Yes."

"Even things that the subject doesn't know he knows: events
that he once witnessed without realizing, things like that?"

"There's no particular magic about it. The human memory is
ultra-retentive. A lot of the things we're privy to get shunted into
the equivalent of a back file, that's all."

"But you can retrieve that back file." Barzel leaned forward
eagerly. "Can't you?"

"Usually. What's the point?"

"Suppose a patient of yours had watched somebody open a safe. Could he—or she—have retained the memory of the combination, subconsciously, in such a way that you could dredge it out of her?"

"Her?"

Barzel chewed his mustache. Now or never, he told himself; no choice . . . "You once had a patient, Anna Lescombe."

"Haven't seen her for years. If you came here just to say that—"

"Shut up. I'm here to give orders, not listen to a dissertation. You were in love with her, once."

When Kleist stared at the floor, Barzel exploded: "Weren't you in love with her? *Answer!*"

"Yes. But I was married." The look in Kleist's eyes struck Barzel as far from pleasant. "You ordered me to stay married. Remember?"

"You were too valuable in those days for me to lose you."

"And then you ordered me to point Anna in the direction of the man who married her. And I'll . . ."

Yes, Barzel thought, *say it*! Say you'll never forgive me, Kleist; show me you've still got some spunk inside that gone-to-seed body of yours; show me you're willing to *fight*! For you, for me . . . But Kleist stayed silent. "So when did you last see her?"

"Two years ago."

"Professionally?"

"No."

"When did you last treat her, then?"

Kleist thought. "Five years ago, I suppose. Minor counseling, nothing serious."

Barzel concealed his disappointment. "No other contact?"

"I phone her every other month, to chat: one friend calling another. What's the point of all this?"

Barzel hesitated. The task facing him was near impossible, yet he had no option other than Kleist, and that maddened him. "You know about the Vancouver summit, perhaps?"

"Who doesn't?" Kleist scoffed. "Arms reduction in Europe, my God! Bush and Gorbachev between them will put you out of a job."

"No, they won't. David Lescombe, the husband of your one-time patient, has just been appointed to a committee that has only one job: to maintain a file called Krysalis."

"What's that?"

"*Listen!* Never mind what it is, just take it from me, this is urgent, like in *panic*! If we can lay hands on Krysalis before Vancouver, we are going to change the balance of power in Europe. So heads are on lines, Gerhard; mine, yours . . ."

Mine, Barzel thought savagely. I don't give a toss for yours, my friend, but if I can't swing this I'm going to jail, and my precious books, the only friends that make life worth living, will be burned, and that's if I'm *lucky!*

"I do as I'm told." Kleist turned sulky. "You've no complaints."

"If we don't get Krysalis, we shan't complain, we shall, well . . ." Barzel laughed, and glanced around the room. "We both know that this oh-so-pleasant lifestyle requires more than professional fees to keep it going."

"Just tell me what you want and get out."

Barzel experienced real anger at being spoken to thus by an inferior, but he reminded himself of what was at stake, swallowed his rage, and said, "You have to contact the wife, Anna. Bring her under control, *before* the summit meeting. *Long* before."

"In two months' time? No, I can't help you."

"Kleist, I am telling you—"

"You don't understand. I haven't seen her for two years. I can't just force her into psychotherapy. There's professional ethics to consider."

Barzel tipped his head back and found himself laughing at the ceiling. "Ethics!" he said, suddenly bringing his head forward again. "You wouldn't know an ethic if it got up and spat at you!"

Kleist flushed. "How the hell do you think I manage to—"

"I don't know and I don't give a shit. Now listen. David Lescombe is going to be away for the coming weekend and for some days after that, too."

"How can you be sure?"

"How am I sure of anything? Just accept that he *won't be home.* You will use that opportunity to contact Anna Lescombe— you said you phoned her sometimes?"

"Yes, but—"

"So she won't be surprised to hear from you. Good. Now listen. Every member of this Krysalis committee has a safe installed in his house. They're allowed to take the papers home, as long as everything's kept locked in the safe when not being used. You will put Anna Lescombe under your control, just as before. You'll program her to open her husband's safe and bring us what's inside. Then she will take the material back. You will ensure she remembers nothing. Then, Gerhard, and only then, you can relax."

"Barzel, allow me to tell you something." Kleist's voice was restrained, even polite. "Understand that I speak purely in a professional capacity now, and what I must tell you is that you are insane. Just that. Insane." He stood up. "If that's all you—"

Barzel's hands moved with dazzling speed, and Kleist flinched. But Barzel held only a photograph. When Kleist looked down at the image, his face turned white.

"Sit down."

Kleist hesitated.

Barzel shouted, *"Sit down!"*

Kleist obeyed, very slowly. "Please . . . My housekeeper, you'll wake her. . . ."

"To hell with your . . . your *servant!* You forget, in the Democratic Republic there aren't many servants." Barzel poured acid into his voice. "Your sister Ilsa, for example." He jiggled the photograph. "She does all her own housework. Cooks for the kids. And for Walther, that layabout husband of hers."

He saw with satisfaction that Kleist could not take his eyes off the photo, which showed a blonde woman, her face lined and unremarkable, standing beside a man a full head shorter than herself, with her hands resting on the shoulders of a small boy. The man was holding a baby.

"The hospital has given her a raise." Barzel flipped the photo over so that he too could look at it. "They are considering taking a bigger apartment. Four rooms instead of three, think of that!" He let his eyes roam around Kleist's richly furnished living room. "You no longer have a wife, but you have money. This house. Reflect, Gerhard: those are things that can *change*."

"I'm a naturalized citizen. No one can throw me out of England."

"Naturalized, yes . . . on the strength of Institute 631's forgeries. A phone call, that's all it takes."

"You wouldn't risk that. I've run too many of your people."

Barzel looked into Kleist's eyes. They belied his confident words. "My orders are to procure Krysalis forthwith," Barzel said. "For that, I am both authorized and prepared to make *any* sacrifice."

"Why can't you just burgle the house, steal this Krysalis thing, and have done with it?"

Kleist's voice had become a bleat and Barzel, hearing it, felt hope stir. "Because we can't risk leaving the slightest trace, that's why. When the General Secretary leaves Moscow to go to Vancouver he wants Krysalis in his pocket, but no, repeat *no,* fingerprints on it."

"And if Anna has never seen her husband open the safe, so that there's nothing for me to discover even under hypnosis?"

"Then you'll have failed." Something clawed at Barzel's guts as he spoke those words. "But at least you'll have tried."

"Suppose I do get the combination out of the wife, which is by no means certain, let me tell you, and the safe turns out to be empty?"

Barzel sensed that his host's breathing was slowing, calming. Yes, he was hearing a new note in Kleist's voice. Interest. Attentiveness. Why? Could it be that Kleist missed Anna Lescombe?

"Then you'll have to do it again," he said. "And again. As often as is necessary until the safe is *not* empty."

Kleist lowered his head, but Barzel felt increasingly certain what was going through his mind. The man feared exposure and disgrace, yes; but more than anything he wanted to see Anna again, and here was the opportunity he had secretly been praying for.

In better times, the thought of that anguished paradox might have moved Barzel to pity. Now, the only emotion he felt was fear and a pain in his gut: Could Kleist handle it?

"I'll need time," Kleist said at last. "It may take months to reestablish that kind of trust, the necessary degree of dependence. . . . I need at least three months."

"I know. And I feel sorry for you." Barzel studied the photo one last time, flicked it, put it back in his pocket. His heart was beating very fast. At the start of this conversation he had felt it was hopeless, but somehow he'd succeeded in igniting a spark. Don't weaken, he reminded himself; you could still end up in a Berlin jail. . . . "Sorry, too, for Ilsa."

"Why?"

"Because instead of three months, you have only a fortnight."

THE FIRST WEEKEND

CHAPTER

3

"How did you do?" Duncan Broadway, Q.C., inquired of Anna Lescombe as she trudged into the clerks' room.

"Oh, lost."

"Bad luck. The judge got it wrong, did he . . . ?"

"Bless you, darling; you're better than a large scotch any day. Roger . . ."

The senior clerk looked up inquiringly.

"Roger, am I still okay to take the first three days of next week off?"

"Yes, I've kept the diary clear."

"Thanks." Anna skimmed through the messages waiting for her. "Who's this, Roger?"

"A Mr. Christ phoned."

"I knew things were bad, but—"

The clerk was too busy sorting out next week's schedules to acknowledge her attempt at humor. "Said would you ring him back, not urgent, social."

Then it clicked. "Did he leave a first name? It wasn't Gerhard by any chance?"

She looked at the number Roger had scribbled down on the

yellow Post-It slip. *Yes!* Anna felt a marvelous upsurge of energy.
She went to her room, where she paused only to fling wig and gown
onto a chair before snatching up the phone. Thank God it was
Friday; the two men who shared an office with her had already gone
home for the weekend.

"Gerhard? Anna. I can't be-*lieve* it!"

"Hello."

He sounded a touch bored, she thought; no, don't think like
that, snap out of it, something's going right today. "God, you pick
your times to call! I wasn't expecting you to ring till next month,
at the earliest."

"Am I early? I can always ring off."

"Don't you dare!"

"Something wrong, lovey?"

"Oh, Gerhard!" She perched on the desk. "It's years since you
called me that."

"Mm, two. How's tricks?"

"Shitty. More shitty than usual. Juliet's being a pain." She
paused. "I've just lost a case."

"You should know how difficult children can be, by now. And
as for the case: you have to lose some. At least, I thought you did."

"My fault, this time."

He laughed, a rich blend of mellow sounds that still had the
power to loosen all the muscles in her stomach, his roller-coaster
laugh . . . "Always your fault, yes? Anna Lescombe, the big failure."

"Oh, you . . . !"

"Sorry. Look, I've got some time off at last and so I took my
courage in both hands and thought—"

"That you'd phone. I'm so glad you did." Anna simultaneously
took a deep breath and a momentous decision. "What are you doing
this weekend?"

"I'm free most of tomorrow. But it's a Saturday, aren't you and
David—"

"He's off on one of his seminars, bless him. He often is, these
days. He won't be back until the end of next week, I shouldn't
think."

The pause was a long one. "Gerhard? Hello, are you there?"

"I'm here. You sound . . . I'm concerned."

Another jagged pause. Anna stared out the window. "Things
have been better," she said at last. "You know . . . ?" And she
laughed, trying to pass it off as nothing, because she always made

an attempt to be cheerful nowadays, when there was so much to be cheerful about.

"We can talk tomorrow. Come to the house. Come early. Lunch. At the usual place."

"Oh, *Gerhard.*" How had he guessed what was going through her mind? "Will you phone Seppy or shall I?"

Again that wonderful laugh, pulsating down the line. "Leave everything to me. Until tomorrow, then . . ."

As Anna replaced the receiver she gleefully told herself that as well as a much-needed holiday she had tomorrow to look forward to now. One whole day in the presence of Gerhard, without distractions or worries.

No, there would be worries. As she steered the BMW through London's rush-hour traffic, so her mind wove its way through a maze of potentially disastrous conversations that might evolve when she met him.

It would be their first meeting since Clara's death. She could not picture Gerhard as a widower, somehow. What would it be like, going to the Hampstead house and not feeling that it was another woman's domain?

By the time she reached Islington, however, she had the thing under control. Spending the day with him might be a mistake: if they hadn't met for two years, that was for a reason. Each moment she spent away from him represented a tiny moral victory, further proof that she could do without his therapy, and without him, too. But by going to his house tomorrow, and remaining untouched, at least she would prove to herself just how far she had come.

Anna liked to remind herself how far she had come, and grown. A matter for quiet pride.

As she went up the steps to the front door she savored an anticipation that had nothing to do with Kleist. The first thing she did was flick through the mail. Circulars. No Cornish postmark, no familiar hand. Nothing from her daughter. Anna, experiencing the sullen letdown of disappointment, made a face. There was something terrible about the power mail had. It got to the point where she was afraid to look.

She had sent her daughter a sweater. A month ago now.

Anna checked the answering machine, then made herself a large gin and tonic before deciding to have a bath. As she lay in the foam, glass conveniently nearby, she found herself dwelling on the day's events. She had lost a case and she was to blame. This year, she'd lost more than she'd won. Not all of them were her fault. This one was, though.

And what about the other case—the one where the clients were suing her for negligence? *No.* This is *wrong.* Think positive. Tomorrow is another day. Everybody makes mistakes. You can only do your best. Look forward to the next *good* thing: a weekend followed by three whole days off . . .

Gerhard had taught her the tricks, how to cope, when all of life had been one long cope.

By the time she'd finished dressing there was a smile on her face again. She looked at her watch. David had promised to ring at eight: forty minutes away. How she longed to hear his voice again! But . . . I'll put the time to good use, Anna thought. Juliet's my daughter, by God, and if she doesn't care about me, I love her, and she's only sixteen, and if I want to phone her I will. Even though—oh God, admit it—the only person I really want to talk to is David.

But it was such a rigmarole. That dreadful girl who ran the commune and always answered put up so many barriers. At last, after much negotiation and some old-fashioned pleading, Anna heard the familiar snuffly voice.

"Lo."

"Hello, darling. Mummy." The pulse of sheer, naked love that flared through Anna rendered her breathless for a second. "How are you?" she managed to say at last.

" 'Mall right."

Pause.

"I hadn't heard from you for such a long time, I just thought I'd ring to see how you were getting on." *Help me, darling.*

Silence.

"I sent you a sweater a few . . ." (she was about to exaggerate and say "months," mentally altered it to "days," then compromised) ". . . weeks ago. Did you get it?"

"Mm."

"Is that mm yes or mm no, darling?"

"Yes."

"Is it all right?"

"Mm."

Sometimes Anna wanted to scream at Juliet when she was like this, but tonight she just felt sad. She was trying to think up a way of salvaging things when Juliet said, "Dad came down."

Anna heard the note of accusation in her adolescent voice and for the second time today knew herself to be on trial; this time, not as a barrister, but as a mother.

"Oh, yes? How is Eddy, then?"

" 'Sall right."

"Good."

"Why don't you phone him?"

"Did he say that, darling?"

Silence. Then: "You never phone him. Never. Why don't you?"

"There's not much I really want to say to Eddy, I'm afraid." Anna gritted her teeth, but before she could stop herself the words were out: "Why don't you phone me, darling? You know how much I worry." She moved the phone from one hand to the other, wiped her forehead. "Couldn't you just once—"

"The sweater's too big. I gave it to Fergie. Look, I can't talk anymore now."

"Juliet, please don't—"

But the purr on the line meant that her daughter must have hung up. I will not cry, Anna told herself. And I must not drink any more, either, because that will . . . *not* . . . *help.*

She kept to her resolve until eight-thirty. By that time David still had not rung, so she poured another double, to give herself Dutch courage, and called him.

While the phone rang she entertained herself by planning all the things she was going to say. How was he? How had his day been? Were things going well? Yes, they *must* be going well because his seminar was so important and he had to triumph . . . then she would tell him about losing the case, but lightly, not in such a way as to worry or distract him. . . . And then he would say . . .

Someone picked up the phone. Anna asked to speak to Mr. David Lescombe. It seemed ages before he came to the phone. She was aware of a comfortable buzz of conversation in the background; something about it told her that David wasn't going to be pleased and the longer she waited the more chance her heart had to sink from its euphoria of a moment ago.

A clung; then a brisk voice said, "Hello."

"David? Anna."

"Hello, love. Yes?"

"Have I interrupted anything? Are you busy?"

"I am, rather. Sorry. Can you make it quick?"

"You promised to ring me, that's all. When you didn't, I was worried."

A long pause. "Oh, damn." He sounded dispirited. "I am sorry. I forgot."

"Not going well?"

"So-so."

"Me too."

"What's up?"

"Oh, I lost a case today, that's all."

"I'm sorry."

"It doesn't matter. Not important."

"I see. Look, Anna . . ."

"Yes?"

"Can you do something for me? I've made a hash of things, rather."

"Yes, of course." She picked up a pen. "Shoot."

"It's the marina. They're expecting us tomorrow. I ordered fuel and one or two other things before I knew about this blasted weekend. Can you phone in the morning after nine-thirty and cancel? Only I don't want them to charge us, you see."

"No problem." Suddenly she felt so happy to be of use. "Anything else you'd like me to do?"

"No, that's it. I'm really sorry I forgot I was supposed to phone you." His voice seemed softer, the tension in it had faded somewhat. "But . . . well, it's a bit embarrassing to be called out of committee by one's wife, actually."

"Mustn't keep you, then. I love you, David."

"I love you too, darling."

"Bye." Anna quickly put down the phone, even though she knew he had started to say something else. She was worried that it might take away from the power of "I love you too, darling," and she couldn't bear that, not tonight of all nights, so she cut him off.

Afterward, there didn't seem to be anything to do except make herself a cup of soup and go to bed. Lying propped up on the pillows, she reran her conversation with David, savoring it, wishing she could have brought him greater comfort. She needed to cushion him. Why did she always feel that way?

Anna had never told David that she'd spent years in psychotherapy. She'd wanted to, but Gerhard had always talked her out of it. Tonight she felt the habitual vague feelings of guilt that beset her whenever she considered the omission. Perhaps tomorrow she would ask Gerhard about it again. Yes. It was time David knew.

The last thing she did was appropriate Juliet's pajama case, the one in the shape of a pussycat with a zipper up its stomach, and lie down hugging it to her. She liked its smell. Juliet's smell.

On Saturday she got up early and agonized over what to wear. In the end she chose a dark blue suit and—an impulse, this—a rather bold hat, hoping that the contrast in styles would end up transmitting only nonsensual messages.

She felt virtuous about her early start, but she soon discovered that virtue, as well as being its own reward, can also exact a special kind of price. She parked the car and was just stepping onto the pavement when she glanced up in time to see a girl who looked scarcely older than Juliet walk out of Gerhard's front gate, shouldering a tote bag as she did so.

Anna folded herself back inside the BMW and watched the teenager slouch off down the road. God, he likes them young now, she thought savagely. *God . . .*

The intensity of the pain surprised her. That was all over so long ago. The thought of another woman in Gerhard's arms still had the power to affect her like a blow to the stomach, and she hated herself for that.

But it wore off quickly, she found. The past might be able to hurt her; it could not keep her in thrall. She had David now—David whom she loved more than any other man in the world. If she closed her eyes, she could imagine his strong arms around her, hear his patient voice whispering in her ears.

She got out of the car again and went up the path. When she rang the bell, to her surprise June opened the door: loyal, efficient June, who had been Gerhard's receptionist ever since he put up his brass plate, but whose hair sadly no longer matched the plate's sheen. June, untrue to her name, had turned autumnal.

"Hello, my dear," she said.

"How lovely to see you again. I wasn't expecting that, at the weekend." Suddenly a great light dawned across Anna's horizon. "Does he work Saturdays now?"

"Not often. There's this kid he's been assigned by the court, you know, one of *those.*"

So Gerhard wasn't into teenagers yet, then. Why be relieved about that, Anna thought? *Idiot!* But: "Oh, yes," was all she said. "Those . . . Can I go up?"

"Of course."

She knew her way; she had visited this aggressively red-bricked house off Keats' Grove many times. Gerhard refused to be separated from his beloved Hampstead; even when young, and comparatively poor, he had found an attic somewhere under the eaves of Fitzjohn's Avenue to practice as a psychotherapist. She had known her way there, too. She felt as though she had always known where to find Gerhard Kleist.

Anna climbed the oak stairs, relishing their dull gleam as a sign of homecoming, and pushed open the door to his room.

It was like entering the studio of a seventeenth-century master: Pieter de Hooch, perhaps, or Francken the Younger. Anna knew those names because Gerhard had used them to describe the effect he was after. Light poured into this south-facing room through high windows, onto a herringbone parquet floor the color of honey. Beneath the windows stood a long table of pale oak, on which were the half-finished model of a Spanish galleon and the canvas-backed plans for it, weighed down by a lump of abura, Gerhard's favorite carving wood. Gauge, pinchuck, callipers and glue were neatly aligned, as always. The priceless Laux Maler lute rested in its usual place, against the side of the floor-to-ceiling bookcase that ran the length of one whole wall. Yes, everything was just so; she had time to absorb that comforting knowledge before his voice coiled out to caress her:

"Hello."

———

Anna walked toward him, her shoes tap-tapping across the varnished wooden floor; and Gerhard rose. He had decided to wear white today, wanting to project the cleanness of new beginnings: linen shirt open at the collar, white shoes, even the belt holding up his white slacks was white. He stood with legs slightly apart, hands in pockets, watching her. His casual stance belied the stew of intense, conflicting emotions that sluiced around inside him, but he was already sensitizing himself to the nuances of her mood.

"You look like Coco Chanel," he said. "In those photos of her when she was young." His voice broke. For a moment he could not go on: she seemed so beautiful still, so much the woman he'd always wanted. "Chic personified, only softer."

All the breath went out of her and then she laughed. "You really know how to lay it on, don't you!"

"Yes." He smiled, hoping his nervousness wouldn't manifest

itself in a tic. "But it takes practice."

"It's been rather a long time." Her voice sounded artificially bright in his ears, like that of a bereaved widow preparing to say, "Won't you come back to the house after the service . . . ?"

"I've been terribly busy," he confessed. "And—"

"No apologies. Not today. But June said you'd been working, are you sure I'm not in the way?"

"Of course not. Relax."

"Oh dear. Now you'll be categorizing my insecurities again." She surprised him by raising a hand in the solemn gesture of one who intends to take an oath. "Freud said . . . or are you Jung? I never could remember."

"I'm Pisces, actually."

"Two fish swimming in opposite directions, how appropriate."

And they laughed, glad to find the spell broken, although, yes, of course she knew he was Pisces, and what's more, Gerhard knew that she knew: his birthday fell on March 3; there were some things Anna would inevitably transfer from one year's diary to the next, no matter how redundant they might seem to her, and that indisputably was one of them.

"What's been happening?" He tried to sound, in his own word of yesterday, concerned. *He had to win back her confidence!* But there were other, less tractable factors at work. He had not been prepared for the reality of her loveliness, her subtle charm; he had forgotten how much he had loved Anna, once. Yet now his duty was to manipulate her, bend her to his will, and he found himself loathing the necessity.

"When we spoke, I sensed a regression," he said quickly. "We seem to have lost some ground."

"Ah, *we* do, do we?" Anna made a rueful face. "Yes. You're right. Give me, us, give *we* a drink, will you?"

"Good idea. Wait a moment . . ."

He retreated to a small kitchen at the back of the room, leaving the door ajar. The adrenaline was flowing now. The prospect of imminent action buoyed him up, which was as well, because if he failed, Barzel would ruin him. Nothing, *nothing* short of the prospect of imminent ruin could have induced Kleist to tangle with this woman's psyche again.

"What's the holdup on the galleon?" he heard Anna call. "You're still stuck on the rigging."

"Time. The enemy of everything."

Gerhard took three deep breaths in succession, holding the last one as long as he could, then carried in a tray on which stood two flute glasses and a bottle of Laurent-Perrier's Ultra Brut. He poured two frothy glasses, allowing them to settle a moment before he touched Anna on the shoulder. "Here . . ."

"You're like an elephant, you know that? You never forget."

"Of course not."

"I hardly ever drink Laurent-Perrier now."

Gerhard smiled, raised his glass. She was inclined to be sentimental today, he saw that at once. Well, the champagne would help that. "Here's to you."

"And to you. To your perfect taste. As always."

She sat on the special posture chair he used, the one with no back. For a moment he watched her rock to and fro while he read the evidence and tried to analyze it. Then he said, "How far down have you gone?"

"What do you think?"

"A long way."

"No." Anna tossed her head, sweeping strands of hair out of her eyes, and knocked back the drink. "Things have been getting on top of me, that's all."

"At work?"

"At work, yes. And . . ." She heaved a long sigh. "Juliet's being tiresome."

"In the usual way?"

"Yes."

So Anna had problems. Good! "How many times do I have to tell you? The fact that someone happens to be your child—"

"Doesn't guarantee she'll turn into a wonderful human being. I know. She's just so difficult."

"Some people are. It's almost certainly a phase she's going through." Yes, he thought; reassure her. Our old roles; nothing has changed. *Trust me, Anna.* Help me to help myself. "Adolescence is such a bore, especially for the adolescent."

"Especially for those around her, you mean."

"She'll grow out of it."

When Anna said nothing, Gerhard felt a brush of panic return. He was too fond of Anna to want to go through with this thing. But he knew that life in prison, Barzel's ultimate sanction, would swiftly, surely kill him. So he took another deep breath and set out on the next stage of his reluctant journey across the tightrope.

"What else is wrong?"

"Oh . . . David's never *there,* somehow. Not like he used to be."

Ah, better! Gerhard refreshed her drink.

"He got this wonderful promotion last month. There's some standing committee, ultra hush-hush, you get onto it and you're like God. The trouble is, he has to fit it in with all his other work, and the committee meets every day. Or it seems like every day. Some weekends they troop off to the country, and . . . oh, I don't know. I love him so much."

"Still?"

"Yes, still. He's so fine. So perfect." She paused; then, as the sense of his remark filtered through to her, said, "Why the surprise?"

Good, things were definitely starting to drift his way. All she might need now was a subtle prod. "You understood what you were getting when you married him," he said smoothly.

"You never really approved of David, did you?"

Gerhard repressed a twinge of jealousy that was suddenly more than any mere twinge. "I thought you could have done better."

"I could have, then. Before I got to know David properly." She smiled affectionately at him. "But you weren't free . . . oh, God, I'm sorry."

"It's all right."

"I mean, with Clara . . ."

"Dying."

"It was tactless of me. Sorry. I haven't seen you since she . . ."

"No." Mention of Clara induced in Gerhard a resurgence of the desperation that had haunted him ever since Barzel's visit. One minute he seemed in control, the next he had lost it. There had been a time when he loved this woman opposite: loved her enough to want to divorce Clara and begin a new life. . . . *Christ!* The last thing he could afford today was nostalgia.

He watched Anna casting around for a change of topic. "What did Seppy say when you rang?" she said at last, the words tripping out too quickly.

"He was thrilled." Gerhard forced himself to smile. "He's keeping us the usual table at the usual time."

"You're an angel." She paused. Something about her expression told him that the dice were about to roll again and inwardly he tensed. "I need to talk to you, Gerhard. I hope I'm not using you—I've kept my distance over the past two years, haven't I?"

"I always assumed you had a valid reason."

"In a way. I never told David I'd been in therapy. You advised me not to and so I never did, even though I often wanted to. And somehow keeping my life in watertight compartments just became . . . well, too difficult. Can you understand that?"

God yes, he thought. *God!* "Easily."

"I think that really the only reason I've come to see you is that David's gone away, you see. And I feel a bit cheap. As if I'm carrying on behind his back."

He saw that she was waiting for him to prompt her, but he knew when to keep silent. At last she said, "I need help."

Gerhard managed to keep his smile intact, but he imagined she must surely see the relief in his eyes. "My dear, whatever is the trouble?" he made himself respond at last.

"I'm worried. No, not worried. Frightened."

"Of?"

"Losing the man I truly love."

CHAPTER

4

David Lescombe let the phone ring twenty-seven times before hanging up, which he did by replacing the receiver on its rest with almost excessive respect, seemingly anxious to preserve British Telecom's equipment for as long as possible. Behind him, people were emerging from the refectory in ones and twos, their chatter an irritant. What was Anna up to? Then a hand descended on his arm, and he turned away from the phone booth, remembering just in time to fashion a neutral smile.

"I suppose I really ought to ring mine up. You romantic types give the rest of us a bad name."

The speaker was a fat Welshman in his upper fifties who derived obvious satisfaction from being obliged to spend most weekends away from the demands of family and garden. While David was trying to think of something to say they were joined by a woman, much younger than either of them.

"Leave him alone," she said tartly. "I think it's beautiful. We need more like him. Come on, you old romantic." She put one hand through David's elbow and clasped it with the other. "I want to hear all about NOCC."

"Thanks, Sylvia," he murmured, as she shepherded him away.

"No problem. I rode to the rescue because he's right: you *are* romantic, and I love it."

David flushed.

"Is everything okay, though? You look a bit upset."

"I'm fine. Seems my wife forgot an errand I asked her to run, that's all." His voice was tight. "Well, here goes . . ."

"Good luck. I envy you, incidentally."

"Heavens, why?"

"No one's offered me a shot at Vancouver."

"Nor me."

"Don't be too sure. Your specialty is exactly what they need. Pull out all the stops today, and who knows—a place on the touring eleven could well be yours. See you."

David laughed, but his heart was beating too fast. His third Krysalis weekend, his first paper. He did not relish facing the high-powered types who awaited him in the lecture room, especially since his mind was less on the 1983 Montebello Council and its long-term effects on NATO's Nuclear Operations Command and Control than on where Anna might be.

Sometimes he wondered what he would do if anything happened to her. What would life be like without her? But he could never imagine such an existence for more than a few seconds. She *was* his life.

As he queued at the electronic door, waiting for the guard to scrutinize his pass, he anxiously ran through the possibilities. A girlfriend. A shopping expedition. An urgent case, necessitating her presence in chambers.

On a Saturday? But even then, why hadn't she telephoned the marina, as he'd asked her to? It was so unlike her.

He remembered her saying quite specifically that she would stay at home all weekend to work.

Last night, he'd found himself repeating how much he loved her, the kind of declaration that did not come easily to him on the phone, when others might overhear. But Anna had put the receiver down before he could finish, as if there were something more important on her mind, something worrying her. He felt concerned.

Also—admit it—let down. He could do without this hassle.

Here he was on probation: attached to Krysalis yet not quite part of it. The Soviet Politburo had "candidate members," which struck him as a useful phrase. The paper he was about to deliver could change his own status to full voting committeeman. He knew how these things worked. If he performed well, there would be a subtle change in the atmosphere. Suddenly he might belong. And although he had demurred, he felt sure that Sylvia's words were true: he might even find himself going to Vancouver as an observer of the most crucial superpower summit this decade. But for now he was still only a spectator.

The guard examined David's pass, compared it with the face, and handed it back. David entered what had once been a large classroom and made his way to the rostrum. As he placed his notes upon the lectern, he hoped that the audience saw him as he projected himself: a calm, professional, hard-working civil servant, accelerating through the fast lane. *The Krysalis Committee . . . and he, David Lescombe, was on it!*

Nearly.

Where could Anna have gone?

He cleared his throat. "Ladies and gentlemen . . ."

As the buzz of conversation died away David found himself the cynosure of some very hard eyes. He hesitated a moment, then began.

"The purpose of this paper is to examine several implications of the Montebello Council's decision to cut stockpiled warheads, having regard to recent developments in the so-called bottom-up command structure. My intention is threefold. . . ."

Were they listening? Would he be able to answer their questions afterward?

". . . First, to examine what has happened to the AirLand Battle concept in the light of the so-called Gorbachev revolution . . ."

What was the matter with Anna? How could he help her?

Not now. Somehow, he had to eject her from his mind.

CHAPTER 5

After lunch the weather turned cold, making them hurry back to Hampstead, eager for a log fire. When Gerhard dug out a bottle of Rioja the color of black plums Anna at first protested, but he overruled her: "on medical grounds," as he jocularly put it.

While they drank, she rounded off the story of the past two years. Because of the Rioja's strong, oaky taste she failed to notice the mild sedative in it.

"I can see why you're feeling low," he said when she had finished.

"But pulling myself out of it . . . ."

"Ah, yes, that's another thing."

He paused. Despite the excellent rapport they'd reestablished over lunch, he did not know what to do. He felt torn beyond endurance. If he wanted to stay out of jail and continue his beautiful life here in England, he had to manipulate this woman. He had to mangle her and wrench her mind; and then he would have to let her go. Again.

The last time he'd let her go he'd known that he was throwing away whatever chance of real happiness life held for him. Yet here he was, on the brink of the same mistake.

If he obeyed Barzel, he would keep his freedom. But he would destroy the one person he had ever loved.

He remembered the time when, as a child, his father took him to the aquarium. In the largest tank he saw a shark. All that power, confined in a space less than the family living room . . . and the shark, too, had a theoretical choice. It could swim to the left. Or it could swim to the right. But instead it chose to hang suspended, facing the spectators as if paralyzed, without hope. Looking at the shark, he'd had his first inkling of what happened to someone when life became pointless.

"Have you considered becoming a patient again, for a short while?" Would she notice the catch in his voice?

"I really don't think it's a good idea. Just chatting with you is enough."

"Didn't you find therapy helpful?"

"Helpful!" Anna laughed gaily, making him tingle. "When you first met me, I was a total wreck. And look at me now: successful barrister, married, going to work every day like any normal person." She stifled a yawn. "You did that."

"No. You did it."

"Oh, come on! You saved me, Gerhard. And you ask if therapy was helpful!"

She looked so beautiful to him, sitting there; a little tired, maybe, but sparkling with inner life.

"Then surely a few sessions could be just the thing. After all, you've been back for refreshers in the past. Most patients have, there's no stigma attached."

"No, Gerhard."

He swallowed. Things were drifting off course again. She had to come back. *Had to!* "Look, you've got three days' holiday next week, that's more than long enough for me to—"

"I was planning to go away, actually. Paris, I thought Paris. Or I might get around to the chores I've been neglecting. The car needs a service, my wardrobe's at an all-time low, I . . ."

"You sound frightened of therapy. Are you?"

She shook her head, without meeting his gaze.

He studied her face for several moments before trying again. "How are the relaxation exercises going?"

"Not well." She sighed, giving him hope. "I do miss them."

"Oh, why? I taught you how to self-hypnotize."

"Yes, you did. It was so refreshing. That more than anything else was what transformed me, you know. Whenever I was feeling down, knowing I could retreat into a beautiful world all my own . . . but . . ."

"But what?"

"It faded." She yawned again. "Sorry. Tired all of a sudden."

He allowed the silence to continue, desperately wanting her to see that there was only one solution. But she didn't speak. At last he was forced to say, "I suppose I could . . . ginger it up for you again? Only the self-hypnosis, I mean: the relaxation exercises."

Her face lengthened. "I don't know."

"Think of one good reason why not."

"I'm just giving self-reliance a chance, that's all. Though to be honest . . ."

"Yes?"

"It's the trances I do miss the most." She half turned toward him, refusing to cover the final inch that would have caused their eyes to meet. "If I did say Yes, could you pep it up for me in just one session? No repeats?"

Gerhard made a supreme effort and mastered his breathing. "No repeats; you can still go to Paris on Monday. I'll come with you, if you like."

"Part of the therapy?" Her smile was arch.

"Definitely." When still she hesitated he said, "We'd better go upstairs," and rose.

This sounded like an invitation to bed and so it was, after a fashion. In his consulting room Gerhard had a Z-shaped Corbusier chair, perfect for inducing the relaxation that led to forgetfulness.

Anna took a moment to sit down in that painfully familiar chair, but then the routine seemed to come back to her without thought or effort, like riding a bike again after years of driving a car. She settled back and arranged her limbs until they were comfortable. Once she was at her ease she looked around, taking pleasure in each little detail. She had never expected to see this place again.

The room was beautiful, not just because she had helped create it but because he lived here and it was him. Wood, everywhere. He had become an expert carver; she remembered how he could carve a perfectly straight line without the help of an edge, his eye was that good and his hand, of course, obeyed him, because everyone, everything in the world, obeyed Gerhard.

Gerhard pulled a chair up close beside her. "Look at me."

Anna did so. Within seconds she had no limbs, no body, no

head; just eyes. She was floating, no, that was the wrong word, she was suspended in amniotic fluid, weightless, and she, meaning her pair of eyes, was being pulled into another pair of eyes the color of pale blue Curaçao.

He began the soft, lilting incantation that had fallen on her like the summer rain of evening, poignant and sad, a threnody; apart from dear David, the one constant in her tired existence since he had first taken her by the hand nearly sixteen years before and said, "It will be all right. It will."

"You are falling deeper and deeper into a refreshing, restful trance, deeper, lower, falling, until your eyelids are so heavy that you cannot raise them, cannot open your eyes, and when you reach that point of heaviness I want you to indicate it to me by raising the middle finger of your right hand . . . yes, good . . . and when I say so I want you to open those heavy, heavy eyelids in a blink, just one, now . . . and again . . . now . . ."

So long since she had felt herself falling, falling, Alice in the white rabbit's burrow, the fantasy amused her, soon he would begin to count . . . so normal. So reassuring. It hadn't been a mistake to come back, after all. . . .

"You can open your eyes, Anna."

She lay still, staring into the liqueur-rich pools, which now were lit from within. When at last he stood up quietly and moved out of her vision she remained immobile.

Her head was placed so that she could see another of his lutes, in a glass-fronted case beside the door. He had made it; for Gerhard, as well as being a lutenist, was also a luthier. She knew this instrument. He had explained it all to her, long ago. Spruce for the body, sycamore for the neck; a sound board of cedar and fingerboard of rosewood; for the bridge, pearwood, and plum for the pegs; strings of gut; assembled with pearls of skin glue, a jewelers' piercing saw, dedication and love. The beautiful lute expanded to fill her vision until she was aware of nothing else.

Sometimes, as now, he used the instrument to focus a patient's attention, but he'd also played it to soothe her, in the old days, before her perceptions of him had changed. Anna wondered dreamily if Gerhard guessed how much she'd come to loathe this lute, which had sent her dear friend Robyn into such ecstasy. . . .

Solid bars of golden light angled through the windows, telling her that the sun was out. Suddenly the rays were blocked and she heard Gerhard say, "Can you see my wristwatch, Anna?"

She looked. "Yes."

"It's an Omega."

For an instant nothing happened. Then all her limbs seemed to relax, as a body settles after losing its struggle with death.

———

Gerhard slowly let out a sigh. The worst obstacle, the fear that had kept him awake every night since Barzel's visit, was behind him. Two years away notwithstanding, she remained his creature.

Now he had to focus her.

"Anna," he said quietly, settling himself at her head. "Can you hear me?"

A long pause. "Yes."

" 'Omega' is the same now as always. When you awake, you will not remember anything of what happens between my having spoken the word Omega and my speaking the other word known only to you. Do you understand?"

Half a minute passed. During that time Anna neither moved nor uttered a sound. Eventually Gerhard rose and took a few steps around the room. "Anna," he murmured. When still she failed to respond, he removed a handkerchief from his pocket and wiped his hands with it. This had to work. *It had to!*

"Yes."

He stopped in midstride and wheeled around, not sure what he had heard. Anna's eyes remained shut; her lips were parted. Gerhard hesitated no longer, but again took his place at her head.

"Everything I say now you will record, deep inside your mind, and you will obey the instructions I shall give you, answer the questions I shall put. Do you understand?"

Her brow slowly furrowed into a frown; she opened her mouth, closed it again. "Yes." A whisper.

"David has a safe in the house. It was delivered three weeks ago. Do you know how to open that safe?"

After another of those nerve-racking waits she shook her head. The silence went on. And on. Gerhard ground his right fist into his left palm. His breathing had become shallow; he could feel sweat trickling down his back.

I can't do this, he told himself. I can't destroy another human being, not one I love—

You don't love Anna. *Think of Ilsa!*

Think of what it's going to be like in prison, if you let Barzel down. . . .

"There is a problem," he said hurriedly. "A serious one. For some reason, no one can now open the safe. David says there is a fault with the lock. But the Foreign & Commonwealth Office believe that he must have forgotten the combination. We both know that is ridiculous, don't we? David would never do a thing like that."

He paused while studying her face, but could not tell how she was taking it. Please, he mouthed. Please, Anna . . .

"David's superiors urgently need to open the safe, right now. Our country depends on it. You are our last hope. Have you watched David open the safe?"

Nothing.

Gerhard wrestled with a mounting desire to pounce on her, pummel her with his fists while he screamed meaningless words. Eventually, to his unutterable relief, she nodded. But it was several minutes before he could speak again.

"Then it is possible that, under hypnosis, you can throw some light on what has gone wrong. There is a square keyboard on the door: the nine digits and a zero, plus two other electronic keys. Go back to the day when you are watching David open the safe. Describe to me what his fingers are doing to the keyboard."

Anna said nothing.

"Let me assure you, I would not ask you to do this if it were not important. Outside the room, important officials are waiting to find out if you can help."

Still she did not respond.

He was fast approaching the end of his tether. This could not go on.

"I'm not supposed to tell you this, Anna, but David's career is in the balance. His superiors are very angry with him." He was speaking quickly now, and his voice had risen in pitch. "They blame him for forgetting the combination. We both know that they are wrong, and that David is right. So you can save him. But between us we *must* somehow find a way to open that safe."

"Yes."

Her voice was low, although this time it sounded firmer. Gerhard, hearing a note of acquiescence there, wiped his forehead. He needed a few moments to adjust. Barzel would let him keep this house. His sister, Ilsa, still had a future. He no longer would become that pitiful shark.

While he waited for the memories to surface from Anna's subconscious, he opened a note pad and drew squares representing a keyboard, ready to record the safe's combination.

CHAPTER

6

A s Anna opened the front door the phone began to ring
and she rushed to answer it. "Yes?"
　　　"Darling? Is that you?"
"David! Oh, I—"
"Where've you been?"
"Out. Why, what's the—"
"I've been ringing you all day. The marina people told me you
didn't phone them, you forgot to put the answering machine on,
I've been worried sick. Darling, what is it?"
Anna leaned against the wall, trying to clear her aching head.
". . . Only you told me you'd be working at home this week-
end."
"Okay," she said. "Keep calm."
"I am calm."
"I've got a headache."
"I'm sorry. A bad one?"
"Dreadful."
"Poor darling. Try not to drink too much this evening, then."
"Why not?" she flared. "It is Saturday, you know. Are you
going to tell me you don't drink, you and the rest of them down at
bloody Midhurst?"

"Anna! Please don't *ever* say things like that. This isn't a secure line."

"Sorry, love. Wasn't thinking. No, I forgot the marina." *Damn, damn, damn!* "Sorry. Is there anything else I've done wrong?"

"Hey, listen, it's me? Remember me—David, your husband, the one who loves you most? What's going on?"

"I don't know. I think I need a break." She paused. "I might go to Paris on Monday." When David did not respond at once she hurried on, "What's going on with you, come to that?"

"I don't—"

"You sound as if forgetting one phone call's the end of the world. Well, I've got problems here, too. I lost a case on Friday. Juliet's being a total little bitch." The tears were flowing freely now. "You're drifting away from me, you pick on my failings. . . ."

"Sweetheart, that's just not true."

"Well, why did you phone me just now, then? It was because I forgot to phone the marina, wasn't it? You wanted to carp—"

"Listen, Anna, I've had a lousy day. I—"

"I, I, *I!* David, I'm telling you: there are two Is in this house! I'm miserable. And I can't make you care." Was that her talking? What was going wrong? She didn't mean to come down on him like this, she *loved* him . . . but before she could think of the right words to retrieve the disaster opening up in front of her, David had rushed into the breach:

"*You're* miserable! Successful barrister, good-looking, rich, a husband who loves you . . . what else do you want?"

"*Time!* Time to be with you now and then, like in the old days." Anna's warmth for him had somehow become a flood of resentment.

"Next weekend. I promise. Assuming you're back from . . . Paris, or wherever it was you—"

"You promised this weekend."

"Anna . . . Anna, please, just try and pull yourself together, will you? And when I ask you to do something, would—"

Anna found herself slamming down the phone. It fell to the floor. She stepped over it on her way to the kitchen, where she made herself an almost fatally anemic Bloody Mary. Part of her knew that it would make her feel worse, but another part craved the kick. She'd have just one drink, then she could attend to whatever it was that seemed so important. Oh, yes: the safe . . .

Anna had a second drink without noticing. What possessed

David to talk to her like that? She had been cradling her head in her arms, but now she raised it and shouted at the ceiling, "How *could* you?" before dissolving into tears.

"How could *you*?" a voice murmured inside her. "You've been drinking too much, you're feeling rotten . . . but it won't mend matters if you snap at David, will it?"

Strange. There wasn't only this one voice inside her, there were others, too, all speaking at once. . . . a sense of weirdness stole over her. She remembered hearing how people felt when they lived on Valium. . . .

She knew she had to do something. But she couldn't remember the whole of today. Again—another of those fearsome blanks. One moment she was in the kitchen, the next she found herself entering the study, without any recollection of going there. Of course, the important thing. The safe.

Why was the safe so important? David's safe. Surely she ought not to touch it without his permission?

Anna was swaying. She raised a hand to her forehead. Sleep. What she needed was sleep. Forget the safe. Tomorrow.

Bed.

The safe.

Her hands knotted themselves into fists; she raised them to her temples in an attempt to drown out the monotonous drumbeat that was pounding in her head.

David, where are you?

Why aren't you here?

Sitting on her bed, she found she had made herself coffee. *How could she have done that without remembering?* She took the cup back to the kitchen, washed up, dried her hands, folded the tea towel neatly.

She recalled knocking over the phone when David rang. It was suddenly important that she put it back on the hook. For a long time she sat on the lowest stair, gazing at the telephone, trying to work out why it meant so much to her.

Then she was in her bedroom again, putting on her nightgown. But it was all wrong, because she ought to be dealing with the safe, for David's sake, only she didn't much care for David, right now. Yes, of course she did, she loved him. . . . Tomorrow. Everything could wait for tomorrow.

Once in bed, however, her mind remained active. Outside in the darkened square a passer-by, or perhaps it was an animal, knocked over some empty milk bottles. Anna raised her head to listen, but the sound was not repeated. London seemed oddly silent beneath the faint, familiar sigh of mingled traffic and voices.

Her vision blurred. She squeezed her eyes tight shut, then opened them and strove to focus on the window. She must be getting sick, she supposed; this wasn't just alcohol. Flu . . . just when she was planning a few days off. No, worse than flu . . .

Her mind strayed again, along with her eyes. The orange street lamps made bars of shadow out of the window frame, gridding her bed with black, so that for an instant she felt herself inside a cell.

Fear gnawed at her. She was sick, all alone inside this big house. Helpless.

She was so tired. Why, then, couldn't she sleep? If only her head would stop *pounding!*

Take a sleeping tablet.

The pills were in the top drawer of her bedside table. She tipped some onto the sheet. David's words were reechoing in her brain. *Successful barrister, good-looking, rich, a husband who loves you . . . what else do you want?* Anna picked up one of the tablets and chewed it, unable to face going to fetch a glass of water.

She couldn't hold her head upright. It kept falling forward. But still her brain wouldn't let her rest.

She absent-mindedly took another tablet.

Tomorrow, first thing, she would attend to the safe. If only her headache would go, perhaps she could do what she had to do to-night, before she slept?

No. Too tired.

Her fingers made contact with something small and round lying on the sheet. A pill would help. . . .

———

If Saturday had been a nightmare for Gerhard, Sunday was to become living hell.

He'd given his housekeeper a couple of days off, anxious to ensure privacy for the likely period of the operation, so once Anna left on Saturday evening he was alone in the Hampstead house. At first he tried to stay awake; then, as the hours dragged by, all desire for sleep left him, to be replaced by insomniac terror.

She was supposed to open the safe, bring him Krysalis, wait while he copied it, then take it back. A couple of hours' work at the most. But of Anna there was no sign.

Where was she? What was holding her up? Had she been

caught? Perhaps David had come home unexpectedly. . . .

He dozed fitfully, a prey to lurid dreams. Sunday dawned, still without contact. Gerhard somehow managed to put off calling Anna until eleven. No answer. After that he dialed every fifteen minutes for three hours. Once he got the busy signal, and his heart soared, but next time he dialed, although the line was free, no one picked up the phone. He realized that someone else must have been trying to contact her and felt his legs go weak.

David.

What would Lescombe do when he got no reply from his own home?

Kleist got into his Audi and drove to Islington. He circled the peaceful square several times, noting how the curtains of the Lescombes' house were closed, despite the hour, then accelerated away back to Hampstead. He let himself into the house and poured himself a large Scotch. While he was still trying to work out which was more dangerous—to alert Barzel or leave him in blissful unawareness of the catastrophe looming—he fell asleep.

When he awoke it was to discover that the clock read nearly six A.M. Monday already. His stomach felt nauseated. Disgusting gray matter coated his tongue. His skin was clammy, his hands shook. He tried the Islington number again. Same result.

He sat staring at the wall, afraid to imagine what might have befallen Anna. *"How could you?"* he burst out suddenly, shocking himself. "How *could* you . . . ?"

He knew he must go and find out what had gone wrong.

Had Anna set the burglar alarm. *Had she?*

When she left on Saturday evening, she had seemed dog-tired. He'd fretted about that at the time. Would she have preserved enough presence of mind to go home and set the alarm before . . .

Before what? Collapsing? Calling David? Calling the police?

Gerhard tore a piece of cuticle from his thumb and swore. He was shaking. He was also reacting like a fool. Why on earth should she call the police?

There was only one choice now. He had to go and find out for himself.

He prepared carefully, selecting a flashlight, a tight-fitting pair of gloves, and—not without a great deal of hesitation—a gun that he had kept concealed in his house for many years past. Barzel's idea, that. At last he was ready. He drove to Islington through deserted streets, parking a quarter of a mile from the Lescombes' house and hugging the shadows for the rest of the way. There was no easy means of access from the back, so he was forced to descend to basement level in full view of the square, only at quarter to seven in the morning there was no one about.

Masking the butt of his gun with a corner of his overcoat, he smashed a pane of glass. It made surprisingly little noise. As he lifted the casement window, no bells went off. Gerhard heaved a sigh of relief and swung one leg over the sill. His heart was beating terribly fast. Until this moment, he could have talked his way out of trouble. Now he was a housebreaker.

It was pitch black inside the cellar, but he dared not risk a light. Slowly he groped his way upstairs. He had never visited this place as a legitimate visitor. He had no idea where Anna slept. Second-long bursts of light from his torch showed him over and over that he was in the wrong place.

Then suddenly he was in the right place, the torch was shining onto Anna's face, and already it was growing light outside.

"Anna," he breathed.

No response. Her face was marble-white.

"*Anna!*"

As Gerhard shook her for the first time, the phone rang.

He froze, staring at it in horror. He had to find a way of somehow making her answer that and get rid of the caller.

She stirred, groaned, made an attempt to turn over.

"Anna!" he cried. "For God's sake, *wake up!*"

The phone rang again. Anna changed position and uttered a groan. She looked terrible: her long blond hair tumbled in rats' tails to frame a narrow oval face whose principal features were black circles around eyes that opened but a slit. She opened her mouth again, and this time the groan turned into a gag. "Head . . . hurts. Blind . . ."

"Anna! Wake up. *Anna!*"

Gerhard dragged her up to a sitting position and slapped her cheeks.

The phone kept ringing.

He folded her right hand around the telephone receiver. Her head lolled on her chest. "Answer it," Gerhard hissed.

"He . . . herro."

He heard pip-pip sounds, the caller was in a phone booth. "*Anna! Anna, for Christ's sake, is that you?*" It was David.

Anna stared at him. Her mouth fell open. In the split second before she could speak he raised a finger to his lips. "Speak . . . to . . . him," he mouthed. And when she continued to stare at him, he snatched up her right hand to force the receiver against her mouth.

"*Anna . . . why don't you answer?*"

"Hello."

Gerhard sat on the bed and held his head close. Anna's breath stank, but this was life or death.

"Oh thank God, thank God. What the hell's going on? Are you all right? Anna? *Anna!*"

"All righ . . ."

"What?"

"Must have . . . overslept."

"Darling, do you know what time it is?"

Anna continued to stare at Gerhard as if she were a moron. "Sunday morning," she whispered mechanically.

"*Sunday!* It's Monday! Monday morning, seven-fifteen. Anna, what is *wrong* with you?"

She sat up and transferred her gaze to the alarm clock. She was struggling, Gerhard knew, to come to terms with the knowledge that she had lost an entire day. His face tightened.

"I'm sorry . . . Monday, how silly. I was working till all hours last night."

"I phoned the house, no answer, I couldn't sleep for worry . . . Anna? Darling, please *talk to me!*"

"Tired, that's all. Just very tired."

"I've left the seminar. Wait there until I come, we'll get a doctor—"

"Where . . . are . . . you?" Gerhard articulated soundlessly.

"David . . . where are you?"

"Still in Sussex. Anna, you're ill. I'll be back in a couple of hours, less."

Gerhard held up both hands and waved them frantically. Anna understood. "No. I don't want—"

"I love you."

"*David!* You mustn't—" But she was talking across the purr of an empty line.

She just sat there, staring vacantly. Then she threw back the duvet and slid out of bed. "Going to be sick . . ."

She could make it to the bathroom only on her hands and

knees, like an animal. Once there she began to retch; she seemed
to be throwing up endless amounts of bile and she couldn't stop.
When Gerhard turned on the bidet's cold-water tap she somehow
slurped a drink. After she'd brought that up and drunk some more,
the spasms began to abate.

Gerhard threw open the cabinet. Aspirin. No, Alka-Seltzer: he
found a packet and mixed it into a glass of water. Down it went.

The one cogent, coherent fact that kept Gerhard thinking
straight was that David would be home soon. They had time, but
only a bit.

Anna turned away from the basin, ever so slowly. "What are
you doing here?" she asked suddenly.

"I . . . I phoned you but you never answered. I came around,
rang the bell, but I couldn't make anyone hear. In the end I had to
break in. Thank God you hadn't set the burglar alarm."

As far as he could see, she accepted this. Her eyes unfocused
again and she muttered, "Dreams . . ."

"What?"

When she did not reply he shook her. "What did you say?"

"Terrible . . . dreams. Nightmares. Safe."

Gerhard's skin turned cold. "What about the safe?"

"Opened David's safe . . . took papers. Must look. Now."

Gerhard tried to restrain her but she pushed him aside. *"Now!"*

She made her way to the study, Gerhard following, and sat
down in David's swivel chair. She could not take her eyes off the
electric-blue safe in its niche over by the window, but neither did
she approach it.

"Wrong place."

"What?"

She seemed to know exactly where to go next. As if sleepwalk-
ing, scarcely aware of Gerhard's presence, she led the way to the top
of the house.

Nothing matched in this cramped, untidy room. The chaise
longue was faded, the curtains too new-looking, the Singer sewing
machine almost antique, the old, jumble-sale desk . . .

Anna snatched open the desk's bottom drawer and reached
down.

"It's there."

She was holding a bulky spiral-bound file in a gray plastic cover.
Gerhard looked over her shoulder. The rubric in the upper right-
hand corner caught his eye, "Top Secret"; then, opposite, the type-

written formula "This is copy number . . . of seven copies" and somebody had written "5" in the blank space. And halfway down the page was the single word "Krysalis." Just that.

"Oh, *Anna* . . ." The file, *the file!* He had succeeded beyond all hope; elation burst into his bloodstream like the aftermath of fine champagne; he could scarcely formulate words. "What have you done?"

His mind was working furiously now. He mustn't let her see him rejoice. Anna must think he had come to help, that's all.

"Why should they do that?" She had begun to speak coherently at last. "Thieves . . . how did they find out about my precious drawer?"

"Precious—"

She gesticulated at the open drawer. "The one where I keep Juliet's letters."

Gerhard looked down and saw a thin bundle of childishly addressed envelopes.

"No, not thieves . . ." She was staring into the middle distance, still half in the real world and half not. Then suddenly knowledge must have flooded through her, for she cried, "Gerhard! You've got to help me. I've broken into David's safe and I've got the papers. I stole them. I stole David's file."

"*You* stole . . . ?"

"It must have been me. Help me."

"But the safe door was shut when we saw it a minute ago. . . ."

He couldn't afford to have her go around confessing. She obviously didn't understand anything of what had happened. He felt helpless. "Anna, listen to what I'm saying: how can you have done anything of the kind when the safe is still shut?"

"That's how I found it. Locked."

"But the papers . . . ?"

"That's how I know it was me." Her mouth slackened into a round O of horror; for a moment she could not speak. "In the dream . . . I saw myself do it. Me. A barrister."

Gerhard was aware of the minutes ticking by. How long now before David got home? What to do for the best? Nothing seemed to work. "I was afraid of something like this," he muttered. "On Saturday, you were deeply, deeply distressed."

"Was I?"

"You don't remember?"

Anna shook her head.

"It only came out during the trance. I told you to forget everything, but I was very worried. The resentment you'd built up toward
David . . ."

"Gerhard, why did I do this?" She was obviously frightened.
"*How* did I do it? Tell me. I don't even know the combination to
the safe."

"Why do you say it was you who opened it, then?"

She spread her hands helplessly. "Who else could it have
been?"

"Burglars. Spies."

"They wouldn't have put the papers here, they'd have taken
them."

"Anna, are you *sure* you don't know the combination?"

"Absolutely."

Hang on to that, he told himself. There's hope. . . . "Then how
can you say it was you who stole them?"

"But I . . . I dreamed it all. I can see myself now. I heard this
voice inside my head. . . ."

"You've been hearing voices?"

The face she turned to him betrayed growing wonderment.
"Yes."

While he was desperately thinking how to retrieve the situation, "Gerhard," she said, "I think I'm going to be sick again."

She ran down to the toilet. Gerhard waited a moment; then he
closed the door and, mindful of fingerprints, drew on his gloves.

He sat down and read the file quickly. As he came to the bottom
of the last page, he unconsciously allowed Krysalis to fall onto his
thigh, feeling like a man who has heard Mozart for the first time,
and recognized the voice of God, and known that life has changed.

NATO's General Situation Plan. A detailed description of
where the forces were, in what strengths, able to call on what
reserves. Inventories, capacities, lists . . .

But there was more, much more. The second section of the file
told the generals what to do with their lists, if war broke out. It
specified targetings for warheads. Counterstrikes. Counterstrikes to
counterstrikes. Deployments.

Lescombe was planning the first phase of the next land war in
Europe.

And that was not all. The file disclosed a British assessment of
America's attitude toward her supposed allies. Contempt. Mistrust.

A deep-rooted feeling that Europe was of scant importance, that its tinpot armies could be relied on to do only the wrong thing at the wrong time and in the wrong way.

Gerhard now knew why Barzel had been in such a funk.

Footsteps in the passage. By the time Anna opened the door Gerhard had placed Krysalis on top of the desk and was staring out the window.

"Oh, Anna, my Anna . . ." He gestured dolefully toward the file. "What have you done?"

"But how *could* I have done it? . . . I don't even know the combination to the safe!"

He thought he might go mad. He could not let this file go, not ever. It represented more than wealth, more than safety; if he could somehow hold on to Krysalis, that meant a new start abroad, new life. Somehow, *anyhow,* he had to neutralize Anna's half memories.

"The only possible explanation," he said slowly, "is that it's in your subconscious. Dreams, voices . . . does anyone know, suspect, that you might have this?"

"Of course not!" His expression terrified her.

"When will David be coming home? Christ, why didn't I think of that before—*when?*"

She darted a look at her watch. "Soon. Gerhard, I think it might be best if I went away for a while, what do you think?"

He gaped at her. It was so exactly what he wanted her to do, and so much the very opposite of what he'd expected her to say, that for a moment he could only sit in silence. "Perhaps . . . but it's a . . . a little difficult to just, well, run away from something like this," he temporized.

"Running away is the last thing I mean to do. But listen. I'm a barrister, I've done enough cases to know how these things work. People panic, because they talk first and think later. I've got a solicitor and tomorrow we'll call him, I'll make a statement, but the first, only thing I need is *time!*"

"But . . . but wouldn't that seem like running? To the police, I mean?"

"You don't understand. Look at me."

"Anna, I—"

"No, just look at me." She laid both palms against his chest. "I'm calm, yes?"

Reluctantly he nodded. There was something terribly wrong

with Anna but he couldn't put his finger on it yet.

"I'm a trained lawyer. You can't tell me how things appear and don't appear to the outside world, because I understand better than you do. Now. The first thing to face up to is that David doesn't know anything about you. He doesn't realize I've been in therapy, or why I went into therapy in the first place or anything about my problems. Right? *Right?*"

He nodded again. At last he was beginning to understand. She was scared out of her wits, but determined not to show it. She wanted to run away, she *had* to run away . . . but first someone, an outsider, must provide her with corroboration of *rational* reasons for flight. Somebody had to give approval.

"Maybe it was a mistake not to tell David," she went on. "None of that matters. All that counts is that *David doesn't know!*"

He could not but admire her. She was talking it through calmly, like a true professional. All she needed now was gentle encouragement.

". . . If I'm going to save my marriage, we need to prepare David. Hearing everything at once could knock him out."

The time had come to test his theory. Oppose her. Force her to step up the argument. He drew a deep breath: "But if you let me talk to David . . ."

"After nine years of marriage? Suddenly tell him I've been in therapy before and after I met him and he never knew about that, about *you!*"

"He'd understand."

"*No!*" She clenched her fists and began to pound his chest. "He *wouldn't!* Gerhard, I live with that man and I'm telling you: he would not. So I have to go. Just for a day, maybe two, while we sort out what to do."

"But you'll be incriminating yourself!"

"You *must* keep a sense of proportion. This is serious, but not a major crisis. The file hasn't disappeared, it's *there,* on the desk. David knows that I was thinking of taking a few days abroad; he won't be totally surprised to find me gone."

It was working. Don't stop, he told himself. "But, Anna, he's bound to call the police when he finds the file out of the safe."

"Of course."

"They'll discover your fingerprints on it, they'll assume you've taken a copy."

They argued it back and forth for ages, but Gerhard forced

himself to ignore the passage of time, knowing that this could not be rushed, that every long minute spent reasoning with Anna was an investment in his own, uncertain future. All the while his brain kept leaping two, three moves ahead, anticipating how to meet his objections and overcome them, until at last Anna found the words that signalled she was ready.

"Gerhard," she said; "Gerhard, do just think for a moment. *Think!* All these things are true whether we call the police ourselves, now, or David does it later. They've only got my word for it that I opened the safe last night, not weeks ago. Forty-eight hours won't make the slightest difference to either the file or my chances in a criminal court. But they *could* just save my marriage."

He hesitated, pretending to consider. Suddenly Anna surprised him by saying, "I know what you're thinking."

Stricken, he raised his head and stared at her.

"You want me to wipe my fingerprints off the file and the safe, don't you? Then there'd be nothing to connect me with either of them. I could just say I came down to find the file lying on top of the safe."

Gerhard swallowed. It was perfect; so perfect that he couldn't think of a way to knock it down.

"No." She shook her head with a smile. "I couldn't do it."

"Why?"

"First, I'd trip myself up. I'm not a good liar. And second, if they believed me, it would mean that David had been almost unbelievably careless. Mean the end of his career. My fault. Do you think I could live with that?"

He was tempted to tell her that since Saturday's hypnosis session he already knew how to open the safe, that they could put the file back and no one would know. But he had to have that file.

"There's another reason why I have to come clean, eventually," Anna said; and he looked at her fearfully, as if she really could read his mind.

"What?"

"You're assuming this file was the only thing in the safe. I don't know what David kept in there. Suppose there were other papers, I've taken those as well, hidden them somewhere else?"

"I have to think." Gerhard began to stride around the room. At last he came to rest by the window and stood there looking out over the square. Muscles twitched beneath the skin of his face, turning it into a restless sea of anger. Now it came down to it, he genuinely did not know what to do.

Anyone with Anna's best interests at heart would persuade her to stay, be utterly frank, and face the music. But what about him, his best interests?

There'd be interrogation. She'd tell them about the sixteen years of on-and-off psychotherapy. In other words, about *him*. Then, suppose she admitted to hearing voices, *a* voice? What if, under someone's hypnosis, she identified that voice?

She wanted to run away. She'd persuaded herself that that was the only course. It was pointless to try and influence her further. A few moments ago he'd felt he was facing disaster. But now he thought that fortune might be presenting him with the kind of once-in-a-lifetime prize that leaves a man breathless. If only he could stay cool enough to plan the next move. . . .

He became aware that Anna had stopped speaking and was looking at him expectantly. He dithered a moment.

It was the need in her eyes that finally decided him.

"You're right," he said. "It's best if you get away for a while. But I'm not taking you to Hampstead."

"Why not?"

"Because if they find you there—and by God! but they'll be looking hard—they can take you on the spot, won't even need a warrant. Abroad's different. And didn't you say you were planning a trip to . . . where was it, Paris? So that would be the first place he'd think you'd gone. . . . I have a villa in Greece. They won't find you there, not easily." His voice had grown steadily more decisive, until at this point he was all but issuing orders. "And I can treat you, while I prepare a report on your mental condition."

"That makes sense to me. If you set everything out, the . . . the history . . ."

"Give David a chance to adjust, without pressure."

She smiled at him. For the first time he noticed a tic at the corner of her mouth. "I knew you'd understand."

"I want you to think back. Who knows about us? Who could trace you, through me?"

"No one."

"*Think*. Of course there's someone—who first referred you to me?"

"My doctor. But that was years ago, he's dead."

"There'd be no record of your consulting me since that time, because you never had another referral. . . . Is there anything informal, say a diary entry, a—"

"Nothing. I never told anyone about us."

"Except Robyn."

"She's in America. I haven't seen her for two years."

"All right. Now listen. I want you to get your things together . . ."

Gerhard looked at his watch. Nearly nine o'clock, *shit*! It seemed ages before Anna came back upstairs, carrying a suitcase.

"Do you have your passport?" he asked her.

"In the study."

"Let's get it."

"The file . . . ?"

He picked it up from the desk. "I'll leave it on top of the safe." Wonderful, he thought, how convincingly a man can lie when he has to. "Here, give me that case. And for God's sake, hurry!"

They'd got as far as the door to the second story study, when down below they heard keys jangle on the pavement, followed by the sound of one being inserted in the lock.

"Darling," a voice cried. "I'm home."

Gerhard eased the study door shut and held a finger to his lips.

As Anna looked at him she felt queasy. She could risk telling David everything, throw herself on his mercy; it was not too late. Tell him that she had been in and out of therapy, describe the horrors that had led her to Kleist. But *no, she couldn't, not about the awful thing she'd tried to do to baby Juliet, no, no, no . . .*

Gerhard, mastering his terror, put his mouth close to her ear. "Get the passport," he whispered. Anna obeyed. When she returned from the desk, Gerhard held her close. "Stay here until he goes upstairs," he breathed. "Then, you go out. Here are my car keys . . . wait for me *inside* the car, where he won't see you."

"What will you be—"

His face contorted into a scowl. *"Ssh!"*

Footsteps were approaching. David tramped past the study on his way upstairs. Gerhard waited until he could no longer hear him, then looked out. The landing was empty. "Ready?" he mouthed.

Anna nodded. A quick look up the banisters, and she was running.

David called: "Anna! Is that you?"

She had nearly reached the front door. But if she went out that way, David, she realized, might see her, and follow.

Hide. *The cellar.* She raced on, passport clutched to her breast, until she reached the stairs to the basement. At the bottom she stopped and raised her head, listening. Above, all was quiet. What could David be up to . . . ?

Gerhard, meanwhile, had folded up the Krysalis file and stuffed it into an inside pocket of his overcoat. Now he moved silently to the windows to position himself behind one of the wall-length drapes. From there he could keep an eye on both the study door and the street below. Still no sign of Anna.

He took his Colt .45 out of another pocket and silently checked the magazine. Seven rounds. This gun had not been fired for a long time; there were traces of rust on the breech. Gerhard stared at it, conscious that sweat had broken out on his forehead. The shot would make a noise. A lot of noise.

Barzel made him keep a weapon always ready; but this would be the first time he'd had to use it.

He tried to swallow, couldn't. He was afraid of the gun.

Where the hell was Anna?

He'd deliberately chosen to send her on ahead, almost as a decoy, because if either of them was going to be caught he wanted it to be Anna, and if the worst came to the worst he might be able to use her interception as cover for his own escape. But she hadn't run into David and she hadn't left the house. He stared down into the street. Empty.

What would Lescombe do next? Where would he go?

Gerhard wiped away the sweat with the back of his gun hand. The Colt weighed heavily in his palm; the jerky movement all but caused him to drop it. He was shaking. Would he be able to pull the trigger?

Footsteps overhead.

Gerhard stared up at the ceiling, trying to map David Lescombe's movements. A door closed. That meant . . . *what did that mean?*

Someone was coming downstairs. Gerhard's throat ached as if with tonsillitis. Now the steps had almost reached the study door. Now they were outside, on the landing.

Now they had stopped, and silence filled the house.

Gerhard tried to release the safety catch. It was stiff from disuse. He jabbed at the lever, accidentally knocking the gun barrel against the wall. The noise of metal meeting plaster sounded impossibly loud; breath forced itself between his teeth in a gasp. Another second and he'd be gibbering. He clenched his lower lip between his teeth and somehow managed to stop the shakes.

"Anna," he heard David shout. "Anna, where are you, love? Come on, darling, stop playing games!"

The safety catch was off, the Colt ready to fire. Gerhard raised the gun until it was pointing at the door. But he couldn't hold it steady. He squeezed even further into the embrasure, and held his breath. A hand rattled the door knob. Movement in the street simultaneously dragged Gerhard's gaze downward. Anna had emerged onto the pavement and was running toward his car. Then the study door opened, and Gerhard convulsively tightened his grip on the gun, refocusing all his attention on the room.

"Anna!" Very loud . . . "Anna!"

A long pause. From where he was standing, Gerhard could not see whether David had actually entered the room. What if he crossed to the window? *Suppose he looked out and saw Anna in the street?*

Gerhard closed his eyes. By now he was shaking so badly he'd become terrified of dropping the gun, the floor was parquet, no carpet to deaden the sound, Lescombe couldn't fail to hear *that.* But if he tried to move . . .

The study door closed. More footsteps . . . now outside, on the landing. Gerhard let out all the breath in his lungs. *Move!*

He tiptoed to the door, opened it a crack. David was upstairs again. Gently, gently . . . out the door, close it . . . listen, wait . . . silence.

Gerhard bent to take off his shoes. Next second he was running. He had almost reached the hallway when, to his horror, someone rang the front doorbell.

He went rigid. Then hasty footsteps sounded overhead and almost without realizing what he was doing he sped to the back of the house.

The cellar.

Gerhard slithered down the back stairs and made his way through the utility room, past the boiler, and so into the scullery, where he tiptoed carefully around the remains of the pane of glass, shattered during his recent break-in.

What was happening up above? Gerhard slipped the outside door open and listened. A delivery man; David having to sign . . .

" 'Ere, guv," he heard the man say. " 'Scuse me."

"What?" David's voice.

"Did you know you'd 'ad a burglar, then? Broken glass, and that."

Gerhard closed his eyes. Now he was done for.

"*Shit!*" David said.

"Thought you'd like to know. Ta-ra, then."

Wait for David to come down the street steps, knock him out, *you can't do that . . .*

But then the front door slammed, no one clattered down to the cellar, Gerhard opened his eyes, *Go!*

Anna was in the driver's seat. She had the engine started. Gerhard flung himself into the car beside her. Then they were being borne along by the tide of traffic and there was no going back.

MONDAY

CHAPTER

7

As David threw his raincoat onto the bed he heard a noise downstairs. "Anna?" he shouted.

Something terrible had happened to her. He just knew it. But he couldn't imagine what. It was driving him mad.

He called again: "Anna? Is that you?" The sound of a door closing somewhere below made his tense expression soften a little; that meant she was at home. Sounded like the study . . . but when he found no one there, he began to panic.

He was interrupted by a delivery. Wine. He signed the chit while his eyes scanned the square. There was Anna's red BMW; wherever she'd gone, she hadn't taken the car; she hadn't been involved in a car crash, thank God, thank God. . . .

The delivery man pointed out a break-in. David's first impulse was to run down and look. Then he thought again. Disaster hovered somewhere on the fringes of his consciousness. Don't do *anything* on impulse, he ordered himself. Think first.

Phone the police. No, wait. Search the house. Start at the top.

He raced up the stairs two at a time. As soon as he entered the master bedroom, something seemed not quite right, something that he had sensed earlier but been unable to identify. His eyes darted into every corner. Anna's suitcase no longer sat in its usual place on top of the wardrobe. He dashed across to the bed. Her nightgown had gone from under the pillow.

The sheets were soft, and still redolent of Anna's night scent: a mélange of warm aromas full of associations he loved that made him want to cry. He flung the duvet back and turned away. As he did so, his eyes lighted on two images of himself, giving him a shock.

A black-and-white photograph of a much younger David stood on the stripped pine chest of drawers between the bedroom windows; it showed his face three-quarters toward the camera, with a narrow tie and white shirt. In those days his hair had been lighter—the photo was fifteen years old—and there was more of it, but the preoccupied smile was the same. Not quite . . . Above the chest of drawers hung a mirror, disclosing David's contemporary face, and he was startled to see how extensive a network of lines had eaten into his skin. He was forty-two, but looked five years older; a reversal of the state of affairs disclosed by the photograph, which was of a man in fact aged twenty-seven who appeared to be scarcely out of his teens. The new-style David was sallow, etched with the tension that comes from long, midnight-oil-soaked hours of labor in the service of his country. And today there could be no mistaking his haggard expression of dread mixed with exhaustion.

What next? The hospitals, the neighbors . . . Phone somebody, *anybody*.

Call the police.

Not yet, not yet.

Why not?

He rested his head against the door frame and closed his eyes. Usually he kept his imagination well in check, but today it seemed that the rooms were smirking at him, as if they'd witnessed some scene which had left behind this extraordinarily unpleasant atmosphere.

Maybe Anna had collapsed and was incapable of speech, a stroke. . . . He cursed himself for stupidity, for not thinking of that before. It took less than five minutes to hunt through every room, look under bed, check closets. Then he knew for certain that she was not in the house.

He sat at her desk in the first-floor study, and stared down at the blotter while he tried to work out what to do. But it was impossible. Visions of Anna stretched out like a corpse, Anna maimed, kept thrusting their way into the front of his brain, obscuring thought.

At last he squeezed his hands into fists and banged them down on the desk. This was no way to go on. Stop fretting, start *thinking*.

First: what did he know?

He found it hard to take seriously her passing mention of going to Paris: too unlike her. But . . . why had she left just as he arrived home, and without saying a word? He felt sure he'd heard a door close somewhere in the house and that must have been she; it couldn't have been anyone else.

Yes, it could. Maybe when he'd got home the burglar was still in the house. . . .

Yes, good, now you're using your brains . . . don't lose your grip again.

The police would ask questions. He ought to come prepared. He drew up a list of names on Anna's scratch pad, and frantically started to dial. He misdialed the last digit, slammed down the phone, tried again.

"Hello . . . David Lescombe here, I'd like to speak to my wife, please. Yes, it's still early, but could you just . . . of course, I'll hold . . . She's not in? Yes, I knew she was due to take a few days off, I just wondered if she'd been into chambers, or contacted you. . . . No, I see. Thank you."

Now he knew something: Anna hadn't gone to work that day and she hadn't phoned her chambers.

Next: Anna's parents.

Mrs. Elwell answered with her usual note of querulous aggression. "Hello . . . hello, who is this?"

"Uh . . . me, David. I'm so glad to find you in, Lydia."

"We never go anywhere."

David recognized this as the prelude to a critical résumé of his and Anna's most recent holidays, with overtones of extravagance and want of application, and he had no time for it. "I was wondering if Anna had been in touch," he said, more brusquely than necessary.

"We haven't heard from her in ages."

"You're not expecting her, then?"

"Certainly not. Why—don't you know where your own wife is?"

David's heart gave a thump. He'd gone too far too fast and now would have to give some explanation. But how to do it without complicating a situation that was already labyrinthine? "You may dig a hole for your minister," they used to teach, tongue in cheek, at Civil Service College, "as long as you cart away enough soil to ensure that he can't be buried." David had no idea of his hole's dimensions.

"David? David, are you still there?"

"Yes, oh Lord, I see what's happened. I got onto the junior clerk at Anna's chambers and he must have scrambled two messages. It looked as though she was going to her mother's, he said."

"I don't know how Anna copes with her staff. They'd never have put up with it in my day. How is she?"

"Fine, thank you. Look, someone's pushing a message under my nose and I've got to rush. . . ."

"Oh, mustn't hold up running the country."

Sometimes when David talked to Lydia Elwell he wanted to explode, but now was not the moment. "No, well, nice to talk to you." He put down the receiver while she was still in the middle of the string of polite codes you were supposed to use when terminating a conversation.

Where was she? *Where had Anna gone?*

He looked at the scratch pad. Who to phone next? His civil servant's brain began ordering the known evidence. One, Anna knew he was going to be at a residential seminar for a long weekend; two, she had sounded distraught on the phone; three, she sounded as if she had been drinking; four, her suitcase was gone; five, she was gone. . . .

He consulted his list and decided on a long shot. Cornwall.

For what seemed ages he listened to the peculiar rasping tone generated by the St. Mary Abbott exchange. At last he abandoned the call. They were probably feeding the pigs, or weaving, or doing whatever communal types did with their days. Besides, Anna had never got on with her daughter. She would hardly have confided in Juliet.

The options were fewer now. David added another name to the list, at the foot of the page, to indicate that it was a last resort and that there might be alternatives he had not yet considered. Then he rang two local hospitals, drawing a blank in each case.

Perhaps she really *had* gone to Paris . . . ?

The final entry on his list appeared to have been written in darker ink than the rest. He could not take his eyes off it. He imagined himself already talking to the person, trying to anticipate the questions. . . .

There had to be a simple explanation. But he encountered only this hole where perceptions of his own wife ought to live and did not. Something that a more sensitive husband might have noticed had passed him by, leaving him with this guilty void.

They had tickets for the South Bank the coming weekend. Brahms, the Second Symphony. It enraged David that at this crucial juncture the thing he remembered was that Anna shared his love of Brahms. Unless she really didn't like Brahms at all . . . Oh, don't be stupid, she wouldn't walk out on you to avoid going to a concert! No, but—how had her voice sounded when he proposed the outing? David could not remember. He was starting to experience an eerie kind of nausea. Nothing could be taken for granted any more.

It occurred to him to search Anna's desk. At first he rejected the thought. When you loved someone, trusted her, adored her, you didn't rifle through her private papers. But sometimes you *had* to do a small bad thing . . .

David opened the top drawer. Anna's diary. He hesitated before opening it. There were few daily entries, but the last section overflowed with names, addresses, phone numbers, none of which meant anything to him. Who were these people? Professional colleagues? Friends? More than friends . . . ?

The memory of his interview for the Krysalis committee came back to him: *At one time she seemed to be rather friendly with a German chappie.* But none of the names in Anna's diary sounded the least bit foreign. He slammed it shut and tossed it back inside the drawer, now angry with himself as much as Anna.

David clasped his hands on the lip of the desk and rested his weight against them. Only one number left to ring now. Before he telephoned, however, there was something to check. He rose and went to open the safe.

For a long moment he stared into the cavity. Then he reached out behind him and groped his way back into the nearest chair, where he slumped down, still keeping his eyes on the safe. He couldn't breathe. There was an ache in the pit of his stomach, a devastating mixture of colic and a punch from a prizefighter. Blood throbbed inside his head until he felt it would lift off his shoulders.

Krysalis gone.

He could not believe it. He *refused* to believe it.

David stood up. For an instant he staggered, his legs not supporting him. At last he summoned up the strength to go and pick up the phone.

The man he was calling answered on the second ring. "Yes?"

"My name's David Lescombe. I'm deputy head of department, defense department, FCO."

"Yes? Could you speak up?"

"My wife's disappeared."

This time there was a long pause before the inevitable "Yes?"

"My copy of the New Testament appears to have gone as well."

"Are you at home?"

"Yes, I'm at—"

"We know where you live. Stay there."

The line went dead. David replaced the receiver. He was back in the maelstrom of a moment ago: his head ached with tension, his stomach churned, terrible visions of the coming interrogation swamped his mind. But through it all, like a poisoned spear, thrust the knowledge that the woman he adored most in all the world had gone away, no one knew where.

David rested his head in his hands. And the spear pierced his heart.

CHAPTER 8

Albert had just finished his lunch when he heard the phone.

"Hi," said the voice at the other end. "Guess who this is?" And they laughed, so that anyone listening in would think that they were just a couple of high-spirited men enjoying a joke, instead of two extremely professional people covering their tracks.

"How are you?"

"Fine, fine," said Albert. "What's up?"

"Sorry to bother you, but your father's been trying to get hold of you."

Albert, whose father had been dead for five years, examined his fingernails critically and said, "Oh yes?"

"I explained you'd been out of town."

The adjutant enjoyed acting out this little charade with the British army's youngest lieutenant colonel; Albert could tell from his voice. "Ah."

"So he might want to ring you later."

Albert was pleased to hear this news, although when his thin mouth extended in a smile, it came nowhere near his eyes.

"I said I didn't know if you'd be going out or not," the adjutant continued.

"No, not. Did he leave a number?"

"Sorry."

"Never mind." A pause. "Anything else?"

"No, except it looks as though we'll have to cancel tonight."

"Yes. Bye, then."

Albert replaced the receiver and stood in thought for a moment. Then he went over to his bag and unpacked it again, knowing he wouldn't be going back to the regiment for a while. With the phone staying silent, he embarked on his fifteen-minute routine for cleaning the flat: not the full "churn-over," as he called it, but a real dust killer, all the same. Albert had a horror of dirt.

Still no call.

He straightened his tie, turning his head first to the right, then to the left. The suntan from a recent skiing holiday had already begun to fade, but in the mirror he still looked every inch the taut, fit army officer that he was. His hair needed cutting—Albert liked to keep it unfashionably short—but that would mean going out and he didn't want to miss the expected phone call. There were some shirts to iron: he never looked less than spruce. The wine cellar was seriously depleted. He could take a chance, sprint to the delicatessen and buy olive oil; they'd sworn the first pressing would be in by Monday and that was today. The deli people were fairly reliable, for Eyeties; which meant little enough, of course.

When the phone obstinately remained silent, Albert began to resent it. Good news was on the way, he felt sure of it; his horoscope for the past two days had promised financial gain. He took up the *Financial Times* and retreated to the living room. As he opened at the stock-market page, something furry brushed against his thigh and absent-mindedly he reached down to stroke it. "Hello, Montgomery," he murmured; and the stout tortoiseshell cat purred in reply.

Four SAS officers shared the expenses of this apartment, a base for their frequent London furloughs. Montgomery, however, belonged to Albert; there was nothing communal about him. Albert operated in watertight compartments. There was the regiment; and there was everything else. Because his parents were both dead and he had no brothers or sisters he felt the need for something alive to call his own. Montgomery was a thorough nuisance: he required feeding and grooming and letting out, which made huge organizational demands whenever Albert went away, which he did often. But Montgomery was worth it. He loved Albert. One day soon, when the time was ripe, Albert would retire to the West Indies with him; Montgomery had all the laidback style required of a successful Caribbean cat.

Albert consulted his stocks. London, following a surge in Wall Street, had risen; it was time to sell a few shares and salt away the profit. At today's prices he reckoned he needed another fifty thousand. That, together with what he'd inherited, would be enough to buy this dilapidated hotel he'd discovered on tiny Carriacou, not yet a tourist spot. He was going to refurbish the place. Then he and Montgomery were going to run it with the kind of manic fervor that would make a typical Swiss-managed hotel look like an unruly, fly-blown pizza parlor.

Fifty thousand pounds, that's all he needed now. Albert folded up the paper and stared at the phone. Fifty thousand, and it was goodbye to the regiment and the executions he carried out efficiently in its name, the best of the best. To use the SAS's time-honored phrase, he would have "beaten the clock." Survived, in other words.

The phone rang. Albert didn't give it a second chance; the receiver was in his hand and up to his ear in a trice.

"Hello, son," said the familiar voice.

———

"Isn't it a bit early for me?"

Albert's miraculously resurrected "father," an MI5 officer whose name was Fox, rested his arm on the car's window sill and blew a cloud of smoke at the windshield while he considered this. "Not exactly *early*," he said at last. "At least . . ." he took another drag on the cigarette and added one more line to the several that already disfigured his forehead. "Not so much early as . . . um, what's the word I want now, prophylactic, no that's something else, isn't it? Something to do with that horrible disease . . ."

"Preventive?"

"Ah, preventive." Happiness reigned, but only temporarily. "Not *exactly*, no."

Albert sighed and leaned back, stretching his arms as far as the car's interior would allow. He admired Fox and on the whole enjoyed working with him, because he had a knack for getting things done on time. He was conventional, right-wing, honest—qualities that commanded Albert's respect. But he found the older man's circumlocutions tiresome, and he couldn't stand the way Fox chain-smoked. Albert regarded nicotine as a drug for those who could not master their own lives but felt a need to pollute the lives of others.

Smoking, in his view, was a mixture of weakness and sin.

"What I think you must understand, what I would like to convey to you . . ." Fox leaned forward to stub out his cigarette, spilling a light shower of ash over his suit ". . . is that this is probably nothing at all. Trivia." He nodded his head in an attempt to give his statement weight. "But on the other hand, it could be *the* big one. In which case, the woman has definitely got to be stopped."

"On the usual terms?"

"Yes. Well, then again, no. You see, there's rather a lot at stake here. America's likely to turn nasty."

Albert's pulse quickened. "We're talking about a fee, then, in the upper range?"

"Yes. And if you have to play a part, we'd like you to disappear afterward. For a little while."

By now Albert was excited, but he did not let Fox see this. "Twenty grand."

Fox blew out a long, long breath. "Well," he said. "That *is* at the upper end of the scale. Isn't it?"

"Twenty."

"We could have it done a lot cheaper, you know."

"And a lot worse." Albert shrugged. He prided himself on the surgical precision with which he carried out his contracts for the state. "Suit yourself." He grasped the door handle, but Fox reached out to restrain him. "Come inside; form a view. Then we'll talk."

"All right. But the risk is yours."

"Risk?"

"The price can only go up." Albert had worked with Fox before. He knew he had to put down his marker early, then ensure it stayed in place. "Not down. Up."

Fox sighed.

"By the way . . ." Albert seemed to be troubled by a speck of dust; he kept wiping one eye. "Will it involve a sea op.?"

Nobody knew about his single weakness. He fought it continually, keeping it hammered down hard, surrounded by a steel chamber deep inside him where no one might even guess its existence. Albert was wary of the sea.

"I can't say," Fox replied. "Why?"

"Nothing."

As Albert got out he studied the square with interest. A pleasantly middle-class oasis in a difficult part of north London: the word ghetto sprang into his mind. The tall, terraced houses had a well-kept air about them, and if there was money to splash on the exterior it followed that there would be more inside, where wind and rain could do no damage.

"What's the time scale?"

"Very tight." Fox pushed on the Lescombes' front door, which he had left ajar when coming down to greet Albert. "Vancouver's so close, that's the problem. I want you to pick it up as we go along. You have to realize—"

He was interrupted by a loud crash from some upper region. Fox grimaced.

"You're doing a search?"

"Category one."

"Looking for?"

"Whatever it is that we find."

They climbed the stairs. At the top of the first flight Fox turned left into a drawing room. Albert had a fleeting impression of Liberty fabrics and large bookcases. Then a man was rising to his feet and Albert concentrated on him.

"Mr. Lescombe, can we resume where we left off . . . ?"

"What the devil was that crash I heard?"

Albert could see that the householder was furious and in the circumstances found it hard to blame him. He liked things to be neat and tidy.

"We have to do a search, Mr. Lescombe, you know that," Fox said placatingly.

"Search. Not smash the place apart. Who's going to pay for the breakages?"

"We can discuss all that later. Now I really must ask you to sit down and get back to what we were talking about when I left you."

It was clear that Fox did not mean to introduce him, so in the pause that followed Albert held out his hand and murmured, "I'm Albert," with that quiet amusement which both forgives and covers up for an absent-minded host. David shook hands; then his eyes connected with Albert's face and instantly narrowed as if in recognition. Albert found that intriguing. He was sure they had never met.

"Please, Mr. Lescombe: sit down."

Albert felt glad to hear Fox take charge. A moment more and Lescombe would have asked what his function was in all this. He quite liked Lescombe for the way he stood up to Fox, and Albert certainly didn't want to start out by lying to him.

Loud bangs echoed through the house. Two sets of footsteps

thundered down the stairs. As they passed by on the landing there was a burst of crackle, followed by a quick exchange on a walkie-talkie.

Fox sat in the dead center of a Chesterfield and twitched the wings of his waistcoat before resting his hands on his knees. His suit was as near black as made no difference, he wore a white shirt and dark crested tie, a signet ring squeezed the flesh of his right little finger. The sartorial image of a churchwarden was belied by a suspiciously dark head of hair, which had plainly been boufféd with the help of a dryer. The bottom-line impression was of a successful if rather close-to-the-wind nightclub owner. Albert had it in mind to employ someone of Fox's general appearance as his Caribbean maître d'.

"Mr. Lescombe." Fox gave his waistcoat another little jerk. "As I was saying earlier, we have considered your preliminary statement. It is very clear and we thank you for that, but we find certain aspects of it unsettling."

"Oh?" David said. To Albert's ears his tone sounded a trifle supercilious, implying that Fox found the statement unsettling only because he was too thick to understand it. Albert wandered over to the window embrasure, his liking for Lescombe on the increase. Somewhere above him he could hear floorboard being prized up.

"Yes." Fox was not to be deterred. "The seminar you were attending was important, was it not? Yet you departed in a hurry, leaving behind an impression of considerable agitation?"

"What I can't seem to get you people to understand is that that is the perfectly normal reaction of a husband who's fond of his wife."

Albert flicked a fingernail against his upper teeth while he thought about that word "fond."

"All right, we'll move on for the moment. Mr. Lescombe. Your wife is a busy professional woman. She has a career of her own and it's a distinguished one. She is, if you'll forgive the phrase, free, white, and over twenty-one."

"She's thirty-nine."

"Leaving aside precise numbers, she's an adult. She mentioned the possibility of going to Paris, I believe?"

"Yes, although she sounded so tentative I didn't give it another thought."

"Nevertheless, her passport's missing and she may have gone abroad, mm? I take it she's not done anything like this before?"

"No."

"No history of mental instability?"

"Of course not. She's a barrister."

"She is a barrister. Not the sort of person who goes off the rails. Furthermore, we have your categorical assurance that she does not know the combination of your safe. Yet, when she drops out of sight, your first reaction is to connect her disappearance with the missing file. Why?"

"I've told you, we'd had a tiff. I was worried for her. I still am, worried out of my skin, and nobody seems to care."

"When you quarreled, did she mention the possibility of going away?"

"No. And I said tiff, not quarrel."

"In any case, what you're giving us is merely your interpretation?"

"If you like."

"What do you think has happened to her?"

Albert waited with great interest to hear the answer to that one. He sensed that Lescombe was angry with his wife, as well as with Fox.

"How the hell should I know? Kidnap, murder, anything's possible. Perhaps she came in while whoever it was burgled my safe was on the job and they made off with her, to make sure she didn't talk."

"Oh, come, come. Taking her passport for good measure?"

"It happens! We know there was a break-in, that cellar window was smashed, that's how they got in."

"We know that, do we?"

"What the hell's that supposed to mean?"

When Fox declined to answer, David rushed on: "These things happen!"

"If you say *that*, I have to tell you that your experience of these matters is greatly superior to mine."

"That wouldn't surprise me in the least. You've got a bloody nerve, coming in here—"

"Mr. Lescombe."

"Accusing me of lying."

"Nobody's—"

"Destroying our house. Have you any idea what we've spent on this place? And what are you doing about finding her?"

"Her? Nothing. Krysalis is another thing. Your stewardship of that file appears to have been rather less than perfect, does it not?"

Fox tilted his head, awaiting an answer; but Albert, whose

instincts were ultra-sharp, sensed that David had begun to eye him sideways, as if trying to fathom who he might be and what he was doing. Lescombe seemed very acute. He did not look to Albert like a man who was guilty of anything.

"Mr. Lescombe?" Fox prompted.

"I . . . you're referring to . . ." David lowered his eyes. "Am I allowed to name it? I mean, I don't know who this—"

"You may speak freely in front of this gentleman; indeed, I hope you will do so. I beg you to do so."

Somewhere up above glass shattered. Everyone froze into silent, embarrassed immobility. Then a distant voice shouted, *"Fuck!"*

David ran toward the door, but—"Krysalis, yes," Fox said smoothly, as if nothing had happened. "For the benefit of my colleague, perhaps you would be so good as to outline what Krysalis is."

David reluctantly stopped his headlong progress and half turned so that his gaze could embrace Albert, still tapping his teeth over by the window, as well as Fox.

"Krysalis is a file that's updated once a quarter," he said to Albert, as if the words had to be dragged out of him. "It contains a lot of things, but what's troubling your excitable colleague here is that at the moment it's got in it the entire NATO General Situation Plan, plus the formulas for identifying S and T SP's on time spans one, two, and three. . . ." He shook his head, angry with himself. "I'm sorry. It gets to be a habit, after a while. It sets out current NATO thinking on strategic and tactical sacrificial pawns in West Germany in the twenty-four-hour period following a Soviet conventional attack."

As David expounded Krysalis, Albert became conscious of euphoria billowing within him. But instead of revealing his joy he merely raised inquiring eyebrows, and Fox produced a mumble in which the word "pawns" could be heard to end on a high note.

"They're the places we'd be prepared to see go before using our nuclear weapons."

Albert's expression did not change, but his exhilaration continued to expand. Fox had said this might be the big one, *the* big one. Albert now recognized that for what it was: a negotiating tactic. Nothing came bigger than this.

"Krysalis contains . . ." Fox had trouble finding the right word. "Shall we say, sensitive material?"

David snorted. "Top secret, sensitive . . . enough to bring down more than one government if it got out. Krysalis actually uses the phrase sacrificial pawn; can you imagine what the gutter press would do with that?''

. ''And the list of sacrificial pawns is quite specific,'' Fox said to the room at large, before reverting to David. ''You brought it home,'' he said; and Albert stopped molesting his teeth.

''Yes.''

''Why?''

''I had permission. Once the safe was installed.''

''We'll come back to the safe in a minute; can we for now just establish why you had it at home?''

''All members of the Krysalis committee keep a current version of the file with them at all times.''

''Why?''

''Discussions frequently take place out of working hours in members' private homes.''

Until this point Fox had been allowing the conversation to proceed at a brisk trot. Now he dropped the reins and sat back. There was a long silence. David fidgeted; his legs seemed to be too long for his liking.

Albert turned back to the window and resumed his study of the square. The thrill inside him was growing all the time. This was ugly. *Very* ugly. The stupid people who pretended to run England had been more than usually careless, probably in the names of Freedom, or Trust, or some such nonsense. This interrogation was just the beginning, the tip of a horrendous iceberg. And Fox, he admitted to himself, was running it with the style of a true master.

''I have to tell you frankly,'' said Fox, ''that we in MI5 were not aware of the cavalier attitude which the London end of Krysalis has displayed. We hope to God that Washington will never find out.''

''Washington's exactly the same as London.'' David heaved an impatient sigh. ''We ring up our American opposite numbers at home. You can do that now, you know; it's called International Direct Dialing.''

Albert's positive feelings toward David were starting to wear thin. A little contrition wouldn't come amiss, he thought. A slight sense of shame, perhaps?

Upstairs, the banging, which had ceased since the accident with the glass, resumed with double intensity. When the doorbell rang Albert murmured, ''Shall I . . . ?''

''If you wouldn't mind.'' Fox looked at his watch. ''It'll be Leadbetter.''

A few moments later Albert escorted a man of about his own

age, say thirty-five, into the drawing room. Fox again took charge. "What have you got?"

"Well, we've oiled the wheels and put them in motion." Leadbetter, a thoughtful man, obviously liked to set his own pace. He opened a notebook and tugged a couple of times at his undernourished mustache, as if a little pain might stimulate him. "Usual alert at all ports and so on. So far, we can't find anyone who remembers seeing her after teatime Friday."

Fox turned his head a fraction. "Did you see your wife on Friday before leaving for Midhurst?"

"No. She was off at the crack. I left later than usual, because I wanted to go to Albemarle Street, to pick up a compass. I'd ordered it specially. They don't open till nine-thirty."

"Ah yes, you sail. . . . Where was Krysalis when you left?"

"In the safe."

"Yet your wife doesn't have access to it?"

"Of course not. It was installed by your department."

"Has she ever been present while you've opened the safe?"

"Possibly. I can't remember."

"But she might have seen you open it?"

"Yes."

"And remembered the combination?"

"Oh, *really*!" David stood up and began to pace around the room, while Albert looked on with what he hoped came across as a sympathetic smile. Fox was never less than good. At times like this he could be inspired.

"Mr. Lescombe, all I'm doing is pointing out that your wife could have had access to the safe without your knowledge."

"She could."

Albert had a sudden empathy for what was making David angry: being compelled to face what he could not endure. He turned away from the window and began to study his unwilling host with real care.

"Did your wife know you were in the habit of bringing home confidential papers?"

"I didn't tell her, if that's what you mean."

"But did she *know?*"

"She might have guessed, I suppose."

As David stalked up and down the room, he kept meeting Albert's eyes, again giving the impression of believing that the two men had met somewhere before.

Fox cleared his throat. "Mr. Lescombe, tell us about your wife, please. What's she like?"

David willfully chose to misunderstand. "Like that," he said, pointing. "It's recent."

His finger indicated a framed photo standing on an ebony Steinway grand. Albert examined it while Fox made a production-number apology for not having expressed himself with sufficient clarity and what he had really meant to ask . . .

So that was Anna Lescombe. She looked younger than thirty-nine, Albert thought, and the blond hair pulled back tightly into a bun would equally well have suited a girl half her age. Lovely, outdoor coloring: the kind of face you saw bobbing behind a horse's head midweek, when most of the men were at the office and the hounds were working double time because it was a treat for them. . . . Rounded features. A firm chin that stopped just the right distance short of aggression. Cheeky smile. Twinkling eyes that spoke before the mouth opened, giving it all away. Eyes like those could never keep a secret. And this inquiry, Albert realized sadly, is almost certainly a waste of time. He sighed. No twenty thousand. So close and yet so far.

God, though, she'd look fabulous in pink. She grew on you. It wasn't until you'd been studying her face for a few moments that it suddenly dawned how beautiful she was. Those luminous eyes . . .

There was, he realized, a potential problem. For professional reasons, he preferred to hate his quarry. Hating the person in the photo would not be easy.

Albert had one favorite fantasy and it was only mildly sexual: a woman on a horse, galloping, with her hair pulled back like Anna Lescombe's. And here she was. Living with . . . Albert glanced at David . . . the kind of prat Whitehall seemed to favor these days, who nevertheless was nobody's fool and wasn't sure how much he trusted his wife.

Yet who was *fond* of her. Odd expression. Did it represent Lescombe's attempt to distance himself from her and so save his career? Was he, in effect, acknowledging that his wife might be guilty of something?

That tingle of hope, stilled a moment ago by Albert's study of Anna's face, resurrected itself with greater fervor.

"She's the usual sort of professional woman, I suppose." David was speaking again. "She had to work twice as hard as the next man, who because he was just that, a man, would always get on, you know what I mean? Conventional, middle-class upbringing.''

Ah, interesting, Albert thought, because you're not middle-class upbrought, are you, my man? In the army we can spot that a mile off. Your accent's marginally wrong and your habits of thought are impure. You smell like a liberal, Lescombe, and that's a dangerous odor. . . .

''Won a scholarship to Somerville, went on to superb corporate law chambers, top-flight. Goddamnit, she makes six times what I do, why on earth would she want to spy . . . ?''

He stopped with a strange look on his face, the kind the hero wears when he's been slugged from behind by his best friend.

Albert's excitement erupted in a sudden burst of restlessness. He saw why Fox had asked for him, now. The road to Anna lay through David. Albert was going to have to make friends with him. Fox needed a nice-guy executioner.

Nice guys were rare. Expensively so.

''As an adult, however, her life was *not* entirely conventional.'' Fox was choosing to ignore the word ''spy,'' but his voice hardened. ''There was an unfortunate first marriage, I believe? A child?''

''Oh, so you know about Eddy, do you?''

Before Fox could respond, someone rapped on the door and entered. ''Sorry, chief, can you come?''

David glared at this tousle-haired ruffian: part of the crew that was busily taking apart his house.

Fox rose. ''What is it?''

''Empty bottle of sleeping pills under the bed, with a clean set of prints matching those on the safe.''

''Mr. Lescombe, do you know anything about these sleeping tablets?''

''No.'' David's voice trembled slightly. ''Nothing,'' he added, as if to cover up the momentary weakness.

''You'll come in straightaway,'' Fox said. ''You can tell a neighbor that the house may be empty for a while, if you like, but keep it general.''

David was so astonished he scarcely noticed when Leadbetter's hand descended on his forearm. Albert, seeing the look of fear on his face, now knew for sure that his earlier misgivings had definitely not been justified.

There was something in this for him after all.

CHAPTER

9

The hell-for-leather journey from London to Greece took up all of Monday, but Anna retained little impression of it. Most of that time Gerhard kept her sedated. She did not really begin to recover until she found herself in a taxi, absorbing impressions of many trees, a dusty road fringed with convolvulus that glowed pinky-white in the dying sun, olive groves, a gearbox whose synchromesh had gone, glimpses of royal blue sea, smell of Papastratos cigarettes overflowing from the broken ashtray . . . then they were jolting down a rough stone track toward a white single-story villa.

Gerhard got out and spoke Greek to an old man, who stood in the doorway nervously twisting his faded straw hat and putting it on his head for a few seconds before jerking it off to give it another few turns. His soft, sad eyes were contradicted by a thin mustache, which, together with his beaky nose, gave his face the severe look of an old soldier. There was also a boy in his late teens, who helped Anna out of the car. She wobbled a little, steadied. When she took a deep breath it was rich with the smell of some pungent herb, rosemary perhaps, that sluiced through her mind, cleansing it.

Gerhard introduced the old man as Yorgos, the caretaker; the youngster turned out to be Iannis, his son. Yorgos produced a scratched and dented tin from which he took a cigarette, hesitantly offering it to Anna. She shook her head, but the sight of that tin lured her away to another time.

Her father had always kept his smokes in a tin. She could see his pudgy fingers struggling with the airtight lid and her nose wrinkled at the vision of those nasty stains, the color of ginger biscuits, which had polluted her nostrils whenever he kissed her. How strange that the acrid smell of spent nicotine could become the odor of love to a child.

While Gerhard talked with the two Greeks she drifted through the spacious house. The main room gave onto a terrace. There Anna sank down into a wicker chair and rested her head in her hands.

Gerhard finished typing a document. He rattled it out of the machine and hesitated while he mentally ran over the plan again. He couldn't afford to take any chances, not when he was embarking on the outright sale of Krysalis.

If he went ahead with this, it meant the end of life as he knew it. No more East Germany. No more Ilsa and her family. Well, it had been a long time since he'd cared a damn about either of the Germanys, but Ilsa . . . He squashed the guilt with a shrug, then looked at his watch, calculating. He stuffed the paper into an envelope, along with some banknotes, and beckoned Iannis, Yorgos's son.

"Let's go through it one more time," Gerhard said. "You leave for Athens, now. Tomorrow, first thing, you'll send this fax."

The boy took the envelope and nodded.

"Afterward, you'll keep checking to see if there's any reply. There's plenty of money for you in the envelope. Remember, keep moving; never stay in the same place two nights running."

Patiently he went through the instructions yet again, dinning each detail into the boy's head, until he felt sure Iannis understood exactly what was required of him.

Looking up at the boy, Gerhard realized that now it was just a matter of time. By the weekend, it wouldn't matter a damn what Anna thought or believed. *But he must have those four days!*

It was going to be a nerve-racking time. What if Barzel somehow managed to find them? He would know by now that Anna had disappeared, along with his prized agent. . . . No, don't think about that; besides, there's only one answer: if Barzel finds you, he will kill you. So there's absolutely no need to think about that at all.

Gerhard reached up to clap Iannis on the arm. "Good boy. See you Sunday, then . . ."

He waited for father and son to leave before going to find out what had happened to Anna. He was relieved to see her sitting quietly on the terrace. Her eyes were closed. Since she had not heard him approach, he left her undisturbed, allowing himself the luxury of reacquaintance with the villa. He always experienced a sensation of homecoming when he returned to the island, but this evening it seemed particularly strong. He knew why: Anna always enhanced everything she touched.

As he looked down at her something clicked into place within him; he knew he wanted her to stay with him forever, if not here then wherever their destinies might entice and entwine them. With that realization faced, he found himself breathing more easily.

The house itself nestled half hidden in a grove of dark conifers. On a patio below the terrace where he was standing the land sloped away steeply as an overgrown garden, littered with spiky, strawlike grass and several huge ribbed pots, still full of last season's dead flowers. The property ended with a wall and a metal-rod gate. Beyond that, a path wound down to the bay, some fifty feet below, where there was a small beach, for all practical purposes a private one.

The bay was wedge-shaped, with the house perched halfway up the bluff to one side of it. Gerhard's domain faced a densely wooded hill on the other side of the wedge. His gaze swept the bay's far shore, seeking his favorite landmark: a chapel. Its white cupola gleamed in the fading light, a bell hung outside in the tower at one end, and Gerhard wished it would ring. This evening he could imagine nothing more beautiful than its clean, clear note summoning to prayer. But since his last visit the chapel had fallen into disuse; Yorgos had told him that, apart from himself, no one ever went there now.

He knew he could not afford to go on drinking in the landscape indefinitely. There was work to be done: hard, finicky work, as dangerous as any he had ever attempted in his long career.

"How are you?" he said quietly; and Anna slowly lifted her head.

"Wretched. Why do I feel so ill?"

Gerhard said nothing.

"I can't remember much about today. Just like yesterday. There're these . . . gaps."

He knew he must reassure her, but not too much. "Things will come back to you, once you've rested. Yorgos has left now. Hungry?"

"I don't want anything." She rubbed her upper right arm. "Gerhard, did you give me one injection or two? It aches so much, but I can't remember . . ."

"One mild sedative, that's all." He had given her two shots of narcotic, but the lie slotted seamlessly into their conversation. "You were looking green and I thought you could probably use some sleep."

She rummaged in her handbag, looking for a tissue. Something bristly grazed against her hand; she pulled it out with a wan smile, her first that day. "Miss Cuppidge."

"What?"

She held up a tatty corn dolly, some three inches long. "Juliet's. Do you know, I put this in my bag six years ago; she'd left it somewhere and I meant to take it to her, but somehow I never managed to part with Miss Cuppidge."

Gerhard was glad to see her spirits lift a little. "What a funny name," he said.

"A raspy name for a raspy toy, that's what I used to say." Again the tired smile. "Pathetic, aren't I?"

He perched on the balustrade wall and studied her. The ravages of flight had done a bit to mar her beauty, but pathetic was not a word to describe Anna Lescombe. Normally there was something helpless, a little wistful about that childlike face, which brought men to her side at parties, bearing tacit promises of love, although as far as he could tell she never appreciated them. Unwitting loveliness was, he felt, one of the most attractive human qualities.

Looking at her now, he remembered why he had fallen in love with Anna. More than that, he understood why the love had never died. No, you mustn't dwell on that, he reminded himself. She can destroy you. Take your life, without even thinking, or knowing what she's done.

He followed her gaze to where two elfin boats progressed calmly toward the yellow horizon, tiny puffs of foam at the stern. "Sailing . . ." he murmured.

"Do you remember that weekend at Yarmouth?" Anna grimaced. "Our one and only sailing trip."

"A disaster."

"You'd never *been* sailing before, you told me afterward."

"I'm a believer in trying out new things. And at least you did meet one real sailor—David."

"Yes. There's that. Gerhard, where are we?"

"This place?" He felt secretly pleased that she didn't know. "The island of Paxos."

"It's so peaceful here."

"I don't even have a phone. The nearest one's in the port."

"But I thought I saw wires . . ."

"Electricity."

Another lie. No way to win her to his side, but she would never understand the truth. "There's a small tourist trade," he went on. "I hope it won't grow too big."

"It won't. This island's too hard to get to."

"Like you?"

Anna nodded. Gerhard pulled up another wicker chair beside her and sat down. Now he had to begin the infinitely perilous operation that had consumed him totally ever since reading Krysalis. But how? What words to use?

"If we use the time wisely," he said, "perhaps we can do something to solve your problems."

She allowed her head to loll around until she could see him properly. "I'm cured, that's what you told me. Often."

"I believed you were."

"Even though I kept coming back to you?"

"I've told you many times: patients frequently come back. There was nothing unusual in it."

"But we became lovers. Sometimes I wonder if maybe you cured me of depression but not of Gerhard Kleist."

Good, good, he told himself. "Ah, no—you love David now, not me. But professionally you've become a major challenge. So what about it, Anna? A spell of intensive, one-on-one therapy here, while I arrange things in London?"

"No time. First I must sort out what I'm going to say, then get back to London. Start putting things right."

He felt his fear come back. "But why? Are you changing your mind?"

"Changing . . . ?"

"You asked to come." He paused, trying to still the rapid beating of his heart. "And when David agreed it was a good idea, that was obviously the logical—"

He could see how he'd shocked her. Her vision clouded while

she gaped at him. "David . . . *knows* where I am?"

"Of course. When I explained what had happened, about your breakdown and so on, he agreed. . . . Look, Anna, just how much *do* you remember?"

But she continued to stare at him as if he were a phantom, making him tremble inwardly. "No, wait," she said. "Please wait. You . . . you've *met* David? Actually talked to him?"

"Yes."

"When?" she wailed.

"He found me in the house, after you'd left to go and sit in my car. Of course, I had no choice but to tell him everything. The three of us sat in the car and talked; don't you remember?"

She shook her head violently. Don't stop, Gerhard told himself; don't hesitate, don't falter, *press on!*

"You got very upset at one point. That's when I gave you the sedative. David held your hand while I did the injection, you must remember that, surely?"

Her face was bloodless. "No," she whispered.

"Well, you went out like a light, so perhaps that's not so surprising."

"Gerhard." Her voice suddenly turned hoarse, as if all her saliva had dried up. "Tell me the truth. Please. Am I going insane?"

He laughed. "Good God, no. Whatever gave you that idea?"

"I can't remember anything about today. You . . . you really talked to David?"

"Yes. I had to. It's utterly inconceivable that I should bring you here without his consent."

"What did you . . . I mean, did you tell him anything?"

"Only what was necessary for professional purposes. Your taking the file, of course."

Anna made a strange sound, halfway between a groan and a croak; but by now Gerhard was too far in to retreat.

"I had to tell him that, when I gave Krysalis back to him. I didn't attempt to cover your entire history, but he did understand what you needed to be cured."

She banged the arms of her chair and cried: "Why can't I remember? *Why?* There's this voice inside my head . . ."

"Voice?"

"More than one. Telling me such strange things . . . I think one of them's David's . . . yes, maybe he did say that I needed a holiday, I'm almost sure. . . . David *knows?*"

"Yes."

"How did he take it?"

"Very well. I'd say that, of the three of us, he was the keenest on your going abroad while he and I sort things out."

"I must phone him. Talk to him."

"Certainly you must; it's essential." Oh dear God, he thought frantically, no, don't worry, *keep going!* "But it's far too late for that this evening."

Gerhard watched her closely. Had the suggestions that he had hypnotically implanted in the course of their journey taken root? He couldn't dare let her go, now. "How much of today can you actually remember?" he asked casually.

Anna made a great effort. "I remember . . . oh, I don't know . . . a ship?"

"That's it. We drove out through Dover." Anna asleep on the back seat, lax passport officers, harassed by thousands of tourists passing through every day, yes, Dover had been an inspiration. "And the flight here?"

"No."

Once in France, he'd chartered a plane, which had cost him the earth, although from the moment he'd opened the Krysalis file he'd seen a way of doing far more than just cover his expenses. His plan was so ambitious that at times it made his stomach churn, but he'd committed himself to it and now he thought of how much, of how *everything* depended on keeping this woman quiet. . . .

"Gerhard, did you say . . . I'd had a breakdown?"

He nodded heavily. "I'm afraid so. A very serious one. As David was quick to appreciate, what you need now, more than anything, is rest."

"But . . . my work."

"You'd already arranged to take a few days off, remember? David will see to that side of things. And he'll be coming here at the weekend."

"He will?" She eyed him anxiously, wanting to believe his reassurances.

"Yes. It's Monday now, so it sounds a long time, but if you rest and don't worry, it'll pass quickly, you'll see."

"Is he angry with me?"

"Not at all. Just concerned for your welfare."

"I always wanted to tell him about you," she said, after a pause. "Right from the start." Some of the lines had been smoothed away from her face; she looked less troubled. "If only you hadn't—"

"Ah, yes, well, plenty of time for that tomorrow. Now, shall we go in? I can't hypnotize you out here, and I think that would do you good, don't you?"

To his immense relief, she nodded; if she'd refused he would have been obliged to use drugs, possibly administered by force, and he dreaded the thought of that.

A fire of olive logs crackled on the hearth of the largest room, filling the air with its pungency. There was a lute here, too. Now Gerhard picked it up and sat by the fire, tuning it. What to play? Ah, yes, Dowland's "Forlorne Hope."

He watched her from under lowered eyelids. The music, coupled no doubt with the realization that David at last knew everything, seemed to have given her a lift. After a while, when she was peaceful, he laid aside the lute and brushed the top of each hand in a gesture he knew she would recognize as comforting, familiar.

"Close your eyes, why don't you?" he murmured; and soon he was counting her down to oblivion, "Deeper and deeper, more and more tired," then she was under.

"Tonight, I want us to go back to the beginning."

"No. Please . . ."

But Gerhard could not afford to let her dictate. When she was under, he likened their link to elastic: one day it must lose its tension, its effectiveness, and then his power would be gone. If that happened now, he was finished. He urgently needed to test how far she had built up resistance, so it had to be the event she dreaded most, the adoption. If he could take her back and hold her *there*, he could do anything with her.

"We must take a fresh look at the moment when the pain began," he emphasized, "so that we can make yet another attempt to heal it. Then later, on other evenings, we shall come forward until we arrive in the present."

She stirred uneasily.

"How old are you, Anna?" Sensing her unwillingness to answer, he prompted her gently. "How old . . . ?"

"Six months." A childlike voice, unnaturally high.

"What are you doing?"

"I'm lying in my pram."

"What can you hear?"

"Voices."

"Do you know the voices, who they belong to?"

Another long pause. "One."

"Yes. And that one belongs to . . . ?"

"My . . ."

"Yes?"

"Mother."

"And the other voice?"

"Another woman."

"They're talking about . . . ?"

"Me."

They had been here many times before. The scene had no surprises for Kleist the skilled physician, although Gerhard the man sometimes found it a touch fey, this easy backward transference almost to the gate of the womb.

"And so, Anna . . . what are they saying? About you?"

"My . . . mother. She says, 'She's adopted, you know.' "

The pause was again a long one, but Gerhard said nothing.

"Then . . . then the other woman, she just walks away, I can hear her footsteps."

The last word came out on a rising tone, halfway to a gulp. Anna chewed her lower lip to stop it from trembling. He watched her face carefully, waiting for the crying to begin. But today there were just two tears: she was letting him look inside so far and no further, so as to give him the most meager satisfaction, enough only to ensure he did not delve any deeper.

He knew then that his instincts had been right: she would be difficult to control. His heart sank and he felt the cold fear begin to creep through him. But he made himself go on.

"Why did the woman walk away, do you think?"

"Because I'm illegitimate. A bastard. No good."

"And do you think of yourself as no good?"

"No. Then I was a baby. But now I'm strong. The woman who spoke to my mother has no power over me. She was bigoted, deliberately unkind, but above all she was jealous."

"Wait a moment . . ."

"Because no one had ever loved her enough to pick her up and say, 'Even though your own mother doesn't want you, even though she's thrown you away like—' "

"Anna."

" 'Though she's betrayed you, I won't betray you. I won't leave you.' " Suddenly the monotonous child's voice changed. It began to fall, become mellow, adult. " 'I won't . . . *ever* . . . let you go.' "

"Rest. Peace . . ."

Still distraught, he waited until she had once again become calm. "Deeper and deeper now," he managed to say at last. "Into the cool, dark depths, where all is stillness, down and down, further down, you can feel your shoulders becoming lighter, all that weight, all that burden, falling, falling . . ."

Eventually she was on the verge of sleep. Everything seemed to take twice as long as usual, and that too worried him.

"Anna," he said softly. "Can you hear me?"

She was breathing very deeply and slowly; Gerhard had to repeat the question before her lips moved. "Yes."

"Omega."

One long, mute exhalation . . . now she resembled a corpse for tranquility.

"I want you to remember certain things. It's dangerous for you to be seen by anyone. No one must know where you are. All right?"

After a long wait, to his immense relief she nodded.

"Do not go out unless I am with you, to look after you."

She did not react, but he hurried on. "Remember, David wants you to be here. He cannot find the time to come to you. His job is important. But he wants you to be here. He is happy that you are here. You should stay in this house for your own protection, and for his."

She was frowning in her trance; he did not know how to interpret that. "Forget your troubles. Trust me."

"I trust you."

He had already risen to his feet, not expecting her to speak. Her words startled him. After a few moments he regained enough assurance to leave her and do the rounds of the villa, ensuring that every door was locked, before going to his bedroom.

On a table next to the window stood a telephone.

Gerhard unplugged the instrument. Anna's noticing the overhead wires leading to the house had unnerved him, one more sign that, despite the injections he had administered, she was neither as sick nor as subservient as he needed her to be.

There was scarcely room for the telephone in the special cavity behind his bed, along with Krysalis, the hypodermic, ampules, and the Luger that were already there, but at last, after a struggle, he made it fit.

TUESDAY

10

Louis Redman, the CIA's chief of London Station, received Albert in his palatial suite of offices immediately above the ambassador's, overlooking Grosvenor Square. "I'm so very glad you could come," he murmured as he rose, buttoning his jacket. "You know Bill Hayes?"

"Of course." Albert extended his hand to another American who was coming around the desk as he entered.

"Hi, Albert," said Bill. "I'm glad to see they've had the sense to bring you in early for once."

"Ah . . . I'm not exactly in, yet. That's why I've made a point of inviting myself for morning coffee." Albert looked around and sighed. "I detect a generous budget, don't I? All that paneling, it's new."

"Rats," Redman said dramatically. "We need wainscots for our rats. Take a seat, Albert."

And while they ranged themselves around the low coffee table, laughing pleasantly, Albert studied his hosts to refresh his memory.

The two men had little in common on the surface. Albert conceived of Redman as an untypical, anglophile American, of quietly efficient appearance: a transatlantic Jeeves with that gentleman's gentleman's tendency to "shimmer." His clothes were reasonably priced but always looked immaculate: here was a man who brushed cloth and shined leather. He also kept his manners polished, something that counted in Albert's eyes.

Hayes he thought of as a mess: someone who wore expensive clothes and let them go to pot. The lenses of his immense rectangular spectacles were so thick that he had to have the frames specially made. When he sported a bow tie, as he did this morning, he reminded Albert of a student in some amateur play, dressed up for the part of Mr. Boffin the Scientist. Or Mr Golliwog, as certain members of the British contingent privately called him; for Hayes had accelerated into the fast lane from a New York public housing project, and he was black.

"You both know and I know what's wanted here," Albert murmured as he accepted a cup of weak Colombian blend from Redman; but it was Hayes who answered: "A quick kill."

"Correct."

"Let me get this clear," Redman said in a low voice, "before we get embroiled in politics. We asked for a briefing on the disappearance of Krysalis and you've been sent in response to that, right?"

"I drew the short straw, yes." Which wasn't strictly true, thought Albert; he'd fought hard to ensure that his name was chosen.

"From which, are we to assume that you've been brought in by our opposite numbers in the British fraternity on the usual specialist terms?"

"Not quite. Neutralization of Anna is merely one option being studied at the moment. I'm to make my preparations, but I'm being held in reserve."

Hayes and Redman exchanged glances. "Then, forgive me," Redman said, "but ought we to be dealing with you at all? At this stage, I mean?"

"That depends on what you want. I thought it might help if I—as opposed to my more peaceable colleagues—could establish what you've been told and how you propose to tackle this mess."

Redman grunted. "As to the first part: a woman's missing with her husband's copy of Krysalis. She hasn't made contact with the Reds yet, as far as the indications go—is that right, Bill?"

Hayes nodded.

"As regards the second question: we want the file back, soonest."

"The file?"

"Yes."

"And the woman?"

"We're indifferent." Redman smiled. "But as far as Anna goes, your vote's for hunt and destroy, right?"

"Emphatically so." Albert reached out to pocket a couple of shortbread biscuits. He did not eat sweet things, but Montgomery did, which went a long way toward explaining his corpulence.

"Tell us who stands where, Albert."

Albert pursed his lips while he considered how best to answer Redman's question. "Brewster's been put in charge," he began cautiously. "He's huffing and puffing as usual. Doesn't want to decide anything."

Hayes coughed, and made a scornful face.

"What about Six?" Redman asked.

"Shorrocks very reasonably won't make up his mind without some hard intelligence. Five have assigned Fox to this case—know him?"

Redman nodded.

"I've got a lot of time for Fox, and on our side he's the one whose point of view most closely resembles mine. Given the choice, he'd let me run."

"Why are you here, Albert?"

"You asked for a briefing and I—"

"Why are you really here?" Redman's expression had turned less genial. Albert met his eyes, and for a long moment held him transfixed.

"I've been doing my homework," he said at last, in a quiet voice. "She's lethal."

"Anna Lescombe?" Redman seemed to have trouble believing it, but his manners still held.

"She's shit."

"Damn right," interjected Hayes. "Albert's a class act, Louis, you should listen to him."

Albert had begun with his own, private reasons for wanting to see some action. Twenty thousand reasons . . . but things had moved on since his first meeting with Fox, at the Lescombes' house.

"If she's bad," he said, "and I'm convinced she is, she might have picked up a hell of a lot from her husband, over the years. He's only been on the Krysalis committee for a few weeks, but his positive security clearance goes back years. And she's corrupt."

"Explain that," Redman said.

"She's got a lot of money, a lot of success at her back. Which means that if she's a spy then it's because she's got contempt for society. She's doing it for the fun of it. For sport."

Suddenly Albert's eyes met Hayes's, and he remembered that here was a kindred spirit. They could both see a way into Anna Lescombe. She was rich and she was free; she celebrated her privileges by undermining those of others. Albert could tolerate genuine ideologues, even when they were opposed to him. But he had no time for discontented traitors without excuses for doing what they did. Hayes felt the same way, he could sense that.

"Right," said Albert. "You asked me why I'm here? The purpose of this meeting is to establish—informally, for the moment—how we're going to set about retrieving the lost Krysalis file and clear up the mess generally in time for the Vancouver summit. I take it we're all agreed about the importance of this?"

"Shit, *yes!*"

The interjection came stinging across the coffee table. Hayes's face was hard.

"Krysalis is deadly for us," he said. "That file contains Pentagon-originated vote-sensitive material, some of it highly critical of our pro-Europe, pro-NATO lobbies." He rested one elbow on the table and jabbed his forefinger at Albert. *"You . . .* are going to have to be pretty damn quick on your feet."

"You sound a mite worried, Bill," Albert commented.

"Bet your ass. Bush and Gorbachev are about to face each other across that table at Vancouver. What's on the agenda? *Everything!* Reduction of nuclear weapons across the board, reduction of conventional armor and artillery, reductions in manpower. You name it, they'll cut it. *If* NATO can manage to keep its General Situation Plan to itself, that is. But once Krysalis goes over the wire, our President will be playing poker with a mirror behind him and that is *out.*"

"Oh yes, indeed. Especially since Krysalis makes it clear that, if D-Day was tomorrow, West Germany would be left to its own devices."

"Look." Redman spread his hands, palms upward, like a priest invoking the Holy Ghost. "Bill and I don't make policy around here. So please . . ."

"We want that file back, safe, intact," Hayes said. "We're going to use any means we have to." He smiled at Albert. "We'll shoot your woman on sight. I mean that."

Albert sighed. "I was afraid you'd take that line."

"Well, no one else is going to." Redman sounded touchy. "Bill, you're off base. There's no question of anyone getting shot, not yet."

Hayes sat back, without apologizing.

"We don't need an assassin right now, Albert. If you've come here today to whip up a little support, I'm afraid you've come to the wrong place."

Albert was nettled. Redman had put his finger on the spot. Why wouldn't anyone see how dangerous the Lescombe woman was? She looked so innocent, that was the trouble. No one wanted to believe ill of her—Brewster, Shorrocks, even Fox himself. (By now, Albert had conveniently forgotten his own favorable reactions to Anna's photograph.)

"So talk to us about David Lescombe," Hayes said.

"Not sure," Albert replied. "There's no proof—"

"Do you *believe* him when he says his wife didn't know how to open the safe?" Hayes snapped. "When her fingerprints were on the keys, actually *on* them! A hundred gets you five she kept her pearls in there along with their code books."

"Given our present state of knowledge, that's a bit steep," Albert replied. "Brewster's words, in case you're wondering."

"Yeah, whatever. Just remember: we want to be there when Five grill Lescombe. What've they got in mind?"

"Their intention," Albert said, "is to let Mr. Lescombe run."

"*What?*"

"Now, Bill." Albert raised one hand; he might have been a traffic policeman, or Hitler saluting. "See it from Fox's point of view. There's no evidence against Lescombe at this time. So why not let him lead us up the line, see where he goes? Who he talks to?"

"That's your risk," Hayes put in sourly. "None of ours."

"Well, of course; he's their man!" Redman let his impatience with Hayes show through.

"Was, you mean," Hayes yapped. "Not any longer."

"How can you be sure?" Redman was angry now, it showed in his face as well as his voice. "You're pointing the finger at someone who has an impeccable record. Brewster and the rest of them have a point: you can't just light a fire under your best people on suspicion of—"

"Oh, I don't believe this!" Hayes rolled his head around in an exaggerated gesture of despair. "Great spies I have known . . . look, please look, we know that Krysalis hasn't made it back through the Iron Curtain, right?''

Albert, delighted by the way things were warming up, was quick to nod.

"We'll know if it does, right?''

"Probably. There's certain steps the Warsaw Pact would have to take if they knew what was in Krysalis. Assuming they didn't just make it public, of course.''

"Which might well be the most effective thing they could do,'' Redman observed.

"So she's gone into hiding,'' said Hayes. "Who's this woman working for, someone tell me?''

"Bill, be reasonable,'' said Redman. "She may not be working for anyone. She's a rank amateur. Fingerprints everywhere. . . . And the empty pill bottle Five found points up someone under strain, possibly terminal strain.''

The funny thing, Albert thought morosely, is that Redman actually believes it. Not good.

"Fuck that; Albert, what are your people *doing* about her?'' Hayes's voice was barely controlled.

"We're having the airports and so forth watched around the clock. All our embassies and consulates have been briefed to look out for her, particularly Paris.''

"She's not in Paris. She *told* the world she was going to Paris, so Paris is where she's *not*. Suppose she left England before Lescombe called you, had you thought of that?''

"Certainly. But because Mrs. Lescombe has a British passport, immigration won't be holding any record of her departure.''

"Jee-*zuss!* What about foreign immigration services, have you alerted them?''

"If she went to Europe by train or boat, she probably wouldn't even have to show her passport,'' Albert replied. "That's one of the things that makes me think she may not be as amateur as all that.''

"Well, at last someone's talking sense.'' The look Hayes gave Albert contained a certain admiration. "She's as professional as they come.''

Albert assumed a modest expression, although secretly he was pleased. "We shall, of course, be checking all airline passenger lists,'' he said. "It'll take a little time, but—''

"Time is exactly what we do not have,'' Redman interjected. "Albert, there is a question I would like to ask and it bears on what

Bill was saying about the foreign immigration people. Your people haven't alerted any European intelligence service about this, have they?''

"Well, no. We wanted to ask you first, you see, Louis. Having regard to what's in Krysalis . . .''

Redman blew out through rounded lips. It took him a long time to empty all the air from his lungs. "Great.''

"But I don't know how much longer we can go on handling this alone. The question I've been asked to put is: Will you cooperate, Louis?''

"Strictly on our terms. You see, I endorse every word Bill said about Vancouver. If the Russians get their hands on Krysalis, there simply can't be a summit. And then we'd have to explain to the world why we were the ones to back away from peace talks.''

Hayes opened his mouth. Before any words came out, however, the intercom squawked. Redman, glad of the interruption, reached out to press a button.

"Yes, Sam?''

"Six on line four.''

Redman retreated behind his oak desk and began to murmur into the telephone. Albert was vaguely aware of his switching over to the scrambler. He examined his fingernails, but they told him nothing he didn't already know.

Hayes, predictably, wanted to eliminate Anna, but Redman, his boss, was playing cautious. So Albert needed to work on Redman, bring him around to his own point of view. But there was a problem: the CIA had a corps of marksmen at their disposal and some of them could shoot almost as straight as he could. Albert wanted CIA support, but only as long as it was *his* finger on the trigger.

At the moment, London had a tight grip on the reins and Hayes lacked both the authority and the excuse to order his own hit team onto a trusted ally's turf, thank God, so Albert was still in with a chance. But first he had to convince his employers that Anna Lescombe needed blowing away; and the British traditionally fought shy of assassination.

Albert was going to have to change that. For the present, however, he could not for the life of him see how. And if he'd hoped to win support at this meeting it was plain that he was in for a disappointment.

Redman had started to take notes. His expression became increasingly agitated. When his eyes met Albert's he shook his head disbelievingly. "Get me a copy," he said at last. "Would you do that, Jeremy?"

He allowed the receiver to drop back onto its rest from a considerable height, and slowly sat back, folding his hands behind his neck.

"Jeremy Shorrocks has received a fax." He laughed. "Ain't that nice?"

"You going to tell us about it?" Hayes inquired.

"Addressed to MI6 Liaison via the generic blue line. Sent from Athens."

"Yeah?"

"Some crackpot is asking one million sterling for the return of Krysalis and Mrs. Lescombe. Any attempt to trace the seller will result in the ending of negotiations as well as the permanent disappearance of the document. And of Anna, too, by the sound of it." He consulted the notes that he had been taking throughout the call. "Deadline for close of negotiations, Saturday noon."

There was a long silence. Albert stared out the window. The weather in London was overcast and cold. A trip to Greece, Athens . . . that could be fun.

"How the hell did whoever sent it know the Liaison number?" Hayes asked.

Albert started to speak, then thought better of it. "Do you intend to negotiate with whoever sent that?" he said at last.

"No," said Hayes.

Albert sought and found reluctant confirmation in Redman's eyes. He felt a *frisson* of pleasure: was that the first sign of a conversion?

"And Mrs. Lescombe sent it," Hayes went on. "She's got Krysalis and it's up for sale. We're not buying. With Vancouver seven weeks off, plenty of others may. How soon before we get a photocopy of that fax?"

"Jeremy's having it biked around."

"Great. Albert, when you see Jeremy, maybe you'd like to suggest he get himself a new fax number?"

Albert's smile was grim.

Hayes took his leave. His departure provoked a deep silence while the other two exchanged those ironic, meaningful glances that said: "How tiresome our teenage children are getting, but what can you do . . . ?"

"What can we do?" Redman said to the room at large.

"You know damn well," Albert replied.

CHAPTER

11

E arly on Monday the duty officer gave Barzel a room under the eaves of the German Democratic Republic's embassy in London's Belgrave Square and left him alone with a phone. He sat at the table, enfolding the instrument with his arms, waiting for it to ring.

He'd been there for the best part of a day now. At odd intervals, nothing capable of giving rise to a pattern, he would dial Kleist's house in Hampstead. Sometimes the housekeeper answered and sometimes it was the receptionist. Never Kleist himself. Mr. Kleist, they told him, more than once, is not available.

Barzel could not begin to guess what had gone wrong. He was terrified.

Colonel Huper said little when Barzel finally summoned up enough courage to make his report. His main concern was to establish the extent of the threat to established lines of communication, agents in place, dead-letter boxes—the trivia of espionage, as far as Barzel was concerned. Huper had been remarkably uncommunicative about the immediate future, Barzel's in particular.

Sometimes Barzel would walk up and down the attic room, smoking, or chewing his fingernails. For the most part he simply sat, staring at the phone cradled between his forearms, waiting for it to ring. He did not know why. No one was likely to call him. Guardian angels were in short supply.

Kleist had vanished, taking Anna with him; that much seemed clear. Heavy MI5 activity at the Islington house showed up routinely on HVA's daily stat sheet, and was capable of only one explanation.

Who possessed the Krysalis file?

What had happened in those lost hours after Kleist made contact with Anna? Could he have managed to program her to open the safe? Barzel had only a half-hearted belief in hypnosis. He wished he'd taken the trouble to study the subject before approaching Kleist. And of course, he'd been mad to reactivate Kleist in the first place.

What had gone wrong? Where were they?

Had Kleist fallen in love with Anna again? Yes. Barzel cursed himself over and over again for failing to see the signs, now so obvious in retrospect. *You fool . . .*

Who had the file?

How much longer would Huper give him?

Questions. Countless, unanswered questions . . .

When his electronic pager sounded at lunchtime on the Tuesday, Barzel stared at it uncomprehendingly. He was short of sleep, he was hungry; it took him several seconds to retrieve reality. Agent contact. Number . . . ?

He held up the pager to highlight the caller's number. That was . . . who was it?

Margaret.

Barzel leapt for the door.

The Soviet KGB had managed to install two moles in the CIA's London headquarters flanking Grosvenor Square. Barzel long ago made friends with the best of them: a middle-aged woman codenamed Margaret. She worked in Bill Hayes's outer office.

Twenty minutes later, Barzel, following a long-established routine, steamed into Hatchard's bookstore on Piccadilly. He loped down the stairs to the basement, where they sold paperbacks. This area was crowded with browsers taking their midday office breaks. Barzel's eyes flickered here and there. Within seconds he'd placed a familiar woman wearing a blue coat, deep in some book taken from the philosophy section.

Barzel had to force himself to ignore his surroundings. He loved this shop. Many an hour had he spent here, gazing with awe upon the ranged volumes, each of which could be purchased for the price marked on the back cover. There were no hidden costs, no extras: the knock on the door in the middle of the night, interrogation, jail here played no part in the simple transaction known as buying a book. Today he had to forget all that. Today was business of a grosser kind, although perhaps it could save his life.

He bided his time, approaching Margaret in stages: a pause by the table to turn over two or three of the latest novels; glance over the shoulder; not being followed, nothing suspicious, move on . . .

At last he was standing beside her, somehow managing to control his breathing. She did not appear to notice him. She replaced the book she had been studying and moved toward the cash desk.

Barzel looked to left and right. All his instincts were at peace. No one was following him. He took down the book he'd last seen in Margaret's hands and opened it at page two hundred. The single sheet of flimsy paper was all he needed to see. Moments later he had bought the book and was making his way along the pavement to St. James's Church.

He sat in a pew right at the back and opened the book again. The sheet of paper he'd noted in Hatchard's was typewritten. He unfolded it and began to read.

> Text of fax sent around to R this am by 6. From Athens. Everyone v. mad. Yr tag Krysalis.

Barzel sucked in a deep breath. Some weeks ago he had routinely "tagged" Krysalis, telling all his contacts to look out for the name; now he blessed his foresight. He read on, eager for the text of the fax itself.

> The document called Krysalis, a sample of which is sent herewith, was brought to the author by a lady who is suffering considerable distress. Arrangements can be made to return both it and her, intact, and without copies of the document having been taken, provided the author is rewarded for his trouble to the tune of one million sterling. What do you propose, please? Fax your reply to the agency named below, where it will be collected. Any attempt to trace the author via that agency must inevitably result in the termination of these negotiations as well as the permanent disappearance of the document; and the shock would be such as to give rise to fears for the lady's health.

For the same reason, maximize security concerning this fax. Deadline for close of negotiations, Saturday noon.

There followed an address, presumably that of the fax agency. Barzel saw that Margaret had added a handwritten postscript:

Ref. to sample: glossary page. Not available, sorry.

"You're forgiven," Barzel muttered. A passing priest glanced at him with a mixture of curiosity and approval.

Barzel sat in silence for a moment longer, mastering his elation. He needed to make one phone call, to HVA's station chief in Athens. Then . . . he glanced at his watch and remembered: Olympic Airways had an office in Piccadilly.

A ticket to Athens, that was the first thing. He could make his call from the car, on the way to Heathrow.

Barzel's headlong rush for the exit was not a seemly way to leave a church.

CHAPTER 12

In 1968 the Duncan Committee reported that moving the Foreign & Commonwealth Office from its Florentine museum off Downing Street to a new building would save five hundred people and a million pounds a year. Nobody can now remember who the eponymous Duncan was, but over twenty years later the FCO stands where it always did and is not likely ever to move.

It was two-thirty on the day after Anna's disappearance when Albert walked through the arch opposite Number Ten Downing Street, into the grand square courtyard, and made for the tower at the northwest corner. He had indulged in a taxi from MI5's Curzon Street headquarters, not wanting to miss the next act. It was time for a private word with David Lescombe.

He showed his pass, climbed the ornate staircase flanked by ancient statues of the Earl of Clarendon and the third Marquess of Salisbury, and walked along the passage until he came to the end, where he did a right wheel into the longest stretch of linoleumed floor the civil service could boast. Here the gloom was only slightly alleviated by sunshine pouring—dribbling would perhaps be a better word—through the tiny windows in the European corridor, each stationed exactly halfway between the bevel-paneled doors opposite, as if to avoid any risk that someone emerging from an office with all of England's diplomacy in his head might conceivably be blinded by a ray of light.

At the far end he came to a grand door, surmounted by a florid representation of two angels and bearing a gothic-lettered name panel, SUPERINTENDING UNDER-SECRETARY SIR ANTHONY FORBES-ANDERTON KCMG. Albert looked at his watch. He was still a little early. He settled down to wait.

He knew that the job of killing Anna Lescombe was worth all of twenty thousand pounds—to the Americans, if not yet to the British. What he had to do now was find a way of convincing the paymasters that this was the logical solution to their problem. He resented the necessity. To Albert, it was perfectly clear that Anna Lescombe had gone to the bad. She represented all that was rotten about twentieth-century society, everything that Albert and his brother officers most virulently opposed. Yet no one wanted to see it.

Albert rested his elbows on the nearest window sill. April. It would be a balmy seventy-five degrees on the west coast of Carriacou today. If he closed his eyes and concentrated he could smell red snapper grilling over a barbecue, taste rum, feel a warm wind drying droplets of salt water on his skin. Fortunately Montgomery loved the heat, although he did *not* love going into kennels: Albert, who sympathized, had devoted a lot of spare time to investigating the quarantine regulations in depth. There would be bribes to pay, but on the island that was nothing new. If he landed this job, it would leave only another thirty thou' to find. And then . . .

And then the door behind him opened to reveal David Lescombe standing there with a dazed look on his face. Albert came upright and turned a smiling face in his direction.

"Hello again," he said.

"Oh, it's you. I . . ." David stared. "Sorry. It's just that . . ."

"Yes?"

"There's something about you, something so familiar it's driving me mad."

"Ah."

Albert turned sideways, toward the light. David's face changed, he even produced a half smile. "Got it."

"Tell me."

"Gustav Mahler."

"Good lord!"

"You've got this high forehead and a studious face, you see. And with those spectacles . . ."

"How extraordinary. Well, there's one mystery solved, then."

"What are you doing here?"

"Hoping I'd run across you." A look of genuine sympathy softened Albert's intense expression. "You've been suspended. Bad luck."

"Yes." David stared at him. "How did you know? They've only just—"

Albert knew because he had been present when Brewster gave the order. He had also been privy to the loud and long telephone protests put up by the Superintending Under-Secretary, outside whose office they were now standing. Words like "brilliant," "outstandingly gifted," and "the most extraordinary brain of this generation of high fliers" had been used, often more than once. Brewster had been left in no doubt of the official Foreign & Commonwealth Office view: that he was making a particularly stupid mistake.

Albert did not see it in quite that light. He needed a lever. This amiable and, Albert suspected, essentially harmless civil servant was hardly likely to help supply it unless put under intolerable pressure. He regarded David's suspension as regrettable, but also as ground for hope.

"I think it's time we had a talk," he said, deliberately overriding the other man's question. "Look, it's a nice day, we could go for a stroll . . . ?"

David looked at his watch. "I've got an appointment later. At six."

I know, Albert thought. And I wouldn't want you to miss that for the world. But what he said was: "Oh, it won't take long. Let's go."

They walked across Horse Guards into St. James's Park under a watery sky, half gray and half blue. It was just warm enough to enable them to sit in deck chairs, not far from the bandstand, where they could enjoy an outsider's view of David's former domain. Albert spent the walk trying to gauge how he must appear in David's eyes—apart from apparently being a dead ringer for Mahler, that is. In the end he concluded that the simplest way of finding out was to ask.

"I expect you're wondering what I'm up to," he said.

David wrenched his gaze away from the Palazzo's rock-solid facade. "Frankly, yes."

"It's tough for you chaps when security marches in wearing hobnail boots." Albert spoke with apologetic concern, as if it were all his fault.

"So you're with security?"

"No, I'm an army officer. Well, yes *and* no's the answer to your question: military intelligence. My regiment would be first in the firing line if your file surfaced in the East. We'd have to hold the fort—literally."

"I see. What's your rank?"

"Oh, just a humble captain," said Albert, who in truth had been the youngest officer ever to be promoted to lieutenant colonel by the British army, because he was that good.

"But what are you actually . . . doing?"

Albert interlaced his fingers and extended both hands in front of him, palms outward. "Blowed if I know. Bloody waste of time, if you ask me." He cast a sideways look at David, who, to his relief, was plainly swallowing it. "You're worried to hell about your wife, aren't you?"

"I'm worried, yes." David stared at the ground. "And I'm angry, too."

"Why?"

"Is that meant to be a serious question?" David burst out. "She goes off, the file's missing, my career's ruined, wouldn't it make you angry if all that happened to you?"

Albert thought that on the whole it would; especially if strangers like himself insisted on asking questions about it. He found himself coming dangerously close to liking David Lescombe again. "You're assuming she took the file," he said quickly.

"I'm assuming nothing. My wife, my file, they're both missing, that's all I know. I can't believe Anna would . . ."

Spoken like a man who doesn't *want* to believe, Albert told himself. "Aaah . . ." He made a scornful face. "None of it hangs together."

"But she's gone, hasn't she?" David's voice was bitter. "So's the bloody file."

There was a long pause. Albert had to induce David to come up with a lot of answers very quickly, there was room for neither failure nor error, and he was stuck for a way in.

"What do you want to talk to me about?" David asked at last. "Look, I'm sorry to keep on, but who *are* you?"

"I'm muscle." Albert smiled bleakly. "Not-very-chief cook and

bottle washer. Typical, of course. Minor public school, undergradu-
ate cadetship to Oxford, a first in English, posting to Northern
Ireland, and now here I am. You've no idea how these things work,
have you?''

"Not much.''

"MoD has a policy of putting square pegs in round holes and
calling it flexible response, also known as shambles. When a file as
vital as Krysalis goes missing, when somebody really important goes
over the wall, lots of people are affected. So everyone wants a finger
in the pie, to check their interests don't get overlooked. That's
where I figure. Because there isn't much for me to do at present,
they're using me to run around and do odd jobs.''

David stared at him. "It's so different from what I would have
expected," he said at last.

"It always is." Good, Albert told himself. But this won't bring
quick results. *Move!* Try anything, try intimacy . . . "Look,
David . . . may I call you David, incidentally?"

"If you like."

"I know what you're thinking. You watch the telly, you read
the posher spy books, and you think: 'So that's what it's like, on the
inside, really like. . . .' But the truth is, the people who work for MI5
are civil servants. Which means they're fully stretched at the best
of times, and when there's a panic, there's one chap for every ten
jobs. So they bring in part-timers.''

"And your job is to talk to me." David's voice became defen-
sive. "They *sent* you."

"Of course." Albert took off his spectacles and polished them
with a silk handkerchief. They were shallow, shaped like a double
sycamore seed flattened across the top, and tinted with just the
merest tinge of pink. Cellophane-thin, they gave the impression of
being more a protection against light than an aid to vision. In fact,
they were a minimal but highly effective form of disguise.

"If I talk to you, will it help them to find my wife? Or only the
file?''

"Both, I hope." Which are you most concerned about I wonder,
Albert mentally added: your wife or your career? Let's find out. . . .
"I'd like us to discuss the personal aspects, I'm afraid. The difficult
bits.''

"Personal?''

"Love and death and sex. The Woody Allen things. You a fan
of his?''

David shook his head.

"They're kind of tricky. The problem is that at some point you're going to have to provide the answers to certain very embarrassing questions about your life with Anna. You can wait for the board of inquiry, if you like. But you just might find it easier to talk about them to me, sitting here, in the fresh air. I'll pass on the answers, and then there's a good chance you won't have to cover the same ground again."

David hesitated. "Go on," he said at last.

"Let's start with a real tough one." Albert suddenly wasn't sure how to go on, finding it an unexpectedly joyless task to manipulate this distressed, pleasant man. "Do you love your wife?"

"Of course."

"No." Albert made himself sound infinitely patient and understanding. "No, I'm sorry, you haven't quite got the flavor of this yet. I'm going to ask you some serious questions and you're going to answer them in the same way. It's not Trivial Pursuit."

"But of course I love my wife!"

"How long have you been married?"

"Eight, nine years."

Albert waited. He knew that David's brain would now inevitably serve up the question: *How can you love her if you don't even know how long you've been married?* Sure enough—"Nine and a quarter years," David said sheepishly.

"No children."

"No. We couldn't. The doctors never found out why."

"Yet she had a child by her first husband."

David laughed in spite of himself. "Yes. Juliet."

"So perhaps you didn't really want children?" Seeing David open his mouth Albert sharply interjected, *"Think."*

A pause. "There were six of us kids in my family. It put me off."

"Did she know you weren't keen?"

"I was careful never to let her know."

Neither man spoke for a long time. Albert guessed what David must be thinking: these questions had begun to give off a sickly aroma: children, impotence, his sex life, Anna's sex life, the antics they got up to in bed . . .

Now, looking squarely at David, Albert had an inkling that it wasn't just Anna's loving personality and warm smile her husband missed at night. They had a real sex life. They did remarkable things together in bed. Perhaps . . . yes, perhaps if David had read about those things in a book before meeting Anna he'd have been fascinated, even a little repelled, thinking anyway that they were nothing to do with him.

Anna had changed all that. Suddenly Albert felt sure of it. And the perception changed his view of what David might now be capable of doing to help and protect her.

To his astonishment, Albert felt a twinge of wholly uncharacteristic jealousy.

"What's the point of this?" David suddenly rasped.

"You see, we need to build up a profile of your wife, then use it to project her probable actions." Albert spoke softly, using his voice to massage David's ruffled feathers flat again. "One thing that could affect her is how she sees you. Do you understand?"

David nodded unwillingly.

"I warned you the water would be a bit choppy. Now. Does she love you?"

"I'm sure she does."

"Does she ever tell you?"

"Yes." A smile stole across his face. "Oh yes."

Albert waited.

"My wife and I, we . . . we found each other rather late in the day. I don't think either of us really expected . . ."

"No. I see."

"I met her on a sailing weekend. She was with a party moored in the next berth. . . ."

Albert could sense that David's mind had drifted back to something that mattered to him even more than his present quandary.

"We got talking. Exchanged addresses. Next weekend we went to a concert together." David drew a deep breath and expelled it in a shuddery sigh. "Beethoven. After that, we started to go out together regularly."

When he fell silent, Albert knew better than to speak.

"Opera. Movies. Dinners. And then . . ." David looked down at his lap, *"Turandot."*

"Ah." Albert almost felt annoyed with David for complicating things so. "My favorite," he reluctantly admitted.

"Really?" David treated the other man to a mingled look of shyness and liking. "There's this wonderful moment when Calaf sings: *'No, no, Principessa altera'* . . ."

" *'Ti voglio tutta ardente d'amor,'* 'I would have you aflame with love.' "

David gazed at him in astonishment. "Yes! And I . . . I was sitting six inches above my seat, you know that feeling? And I reached out for her hand and she took it between both her own and I couldn't breathe." David swiveled until he was facing Albert, as if appealing for, *demanding*, empathy. "And then I knew . . . I knew I loved her," he said simply. "And the feeling never went away. It never left me. Whenever I've been with Anna since, I've been . . . been sitting six inches above the chair. All the time." His voice slowed, subtly telling Albert that he had given up all hope of ever explaining to another human being how he felt.

A memory came into Albert's mind, astonishing him with its singular inappropriateness.

The worst four days of his life, spent undercover in Teheran. For a mercifully short few minutes he had been forced to stand within a foot of one of the Ayatollah Khomeini's most powerful clergymen. Looking into his eyes, Albert saw something that he ever afterward styled "the sacred flame." It had been his job to extinguish it, which he'd done, but he never forgot the sight. He hadn't seen anything even remotely resembling it. Until this moment.

Examining David from under lowered lids, Albert realized that perhaps the memory was not so anachronistic, after all.

"When was the last time?" he ventured at last.

"Mm?"

"The last time Anna told you she loved you, when?"

David wiped a hand across his face. It was as if Albert had addressed him in a foreign language and he was still catching up. "Last weekend, on the phone. Saturday."

"Three days ago . . . So you expressed your affection to each other often, is that right?" *Interesting . . .*

"Yes."

"She didn't have anyone else?"

"A lover, you mean?"

"That's right."

"Don't be ridiculous."

This response nettled Albert; he'd been doing well up until then. "You can answer me straight, or you can have it wrung out of you, under oath."

David breathed in and out sharply, once. "No lover that I'm aware of."

But Albert, sensing blood, couldn't leave it alone. "There may have been, in other words?"

"That's not what I said."

"But it was a cagey answer, 'no lover that I'm—' "

"Oh, this is insane! All I meant was, I didn't spend every second of every day in Anna's presence. Of course she *might* have had a lover; it was logistically feasible. But I don't believe it for a moment. Besides, the things you're asking about are purely personal."

"In a case like this, nothing is purely personal."

"I've got nothing more to say." David's voice was stony, matching his expression.

"At the inquiry—"

"I'll cope with questions then."

David's limbs were trembling. He suddenly stood up and moved a few steps away from Albert, keeping his back to him. When he turned around again, the water was clearly visible in his eyes.

"Sorry." His voice came out uneven. "Not the emotional type, usually."

Albert saw that he wasn't going to get any further, and suppressed his resentment with difficulty. "It's understandable," he conceded.

"Yes." A shiver interrupted David's next words; after a pause, he tried again. "If you want the truth, I miss her . . . too much."

Albert frowned. *"Too* much . . . ?"

"I can't manage without her. Childish . . ."

Albert allowed the pause to go on a little longer, again pitted by that odd flash of hitherto unencountered jealousy. Then he said, "I think you've answered my question, but just for the record, did you or do you have a mistress?"

"Certainly not. To *both* questions."

"So." Albert tilted his head backward until he was staring at the sky. "Whatever she was running away from, it wasn't an unhappy marriage." No easy answers here. *Damn!*

"I don't get that." David had recovered from the weakness of a moment ago; his tone was harsh. "What makes you so sure she ran away?"

Albert brought his head forward again. "You seemed to be saying that yourself."

"Oh, look, I'm sick of this. My wife's missing, the police don't want to know, your people don't care, it's like a nightmare." David's voice cracked. "What has to happen before someone does something? Eh? You just tell me, *what?"*

He was shaking. Albert looked up at him with detached professional interest. "What are you going to do?" he said.

"I'm going to find her. In my way, and without any help from you."

"I think that's an excellent idea."

David had already stalked off, but on hearing those words he stopped and wheeled around.

"You know a lot more people it might be worth talking to than we do," Albert said, standing up. "Eddy, for example. Anna's first husband. Unless, of course . . ." He appeared struck with his own flash of brilliance. "Unless you felt like letting me share the labor."

He already had a hand through David's elbow and was guiding him toward the Mall. "We should talk about that," he said. And then suddenly his resentment at liking this man against his will boiled over into needless brutality, making him show more of his hand than he'd intended: "There's still time," he rapped, "there's still time for a discussion of that before your appointment with her head of chambers this evening."

David's expression of shock on realizing how much the other man knew about his private affairs was Albert's only real consolation for a drawn match.

CHAPTER 13

By lunchtime on Tuesday, the day after their flight, the BBC world service still had nothing to say about Anna Lescombe's disappearance. Gerhard, in a peevish mood, turned off the radio with undue vehemence, toppling it over.

Iannis must have sent the fax by now. How much did London want their file? What would Barzel be doing?

Barzel didn't know about this villa, no one did; Gerhard, who had dedicated half his life to finding out other people's secrets, knew how to keep his own. But given enough time, enough resources, HVA would find him.

How long before MI6 made up their minds? *How much time before Barzel came here and killed them?*

Gerhard, needing a distraction from the terror that had begun to grind in his guts, got up and went to stand by the balustrade.

Anna had found something to intrigue her in the rocks clustered at the foot of the cliff below the church. From his vantage point on the terrace, Gerhard could sometimes see her, sometimes not, as she swam in and out of his vision. It was ever so: she had always presented herself to him in fits and starts.

He remembered the first time he'd met her as if it were yesterday.

Sixteen years ago she had come into his consulting room, dragging her steps, and she had looked around with a bored look, as if
to say, "Go on, then, show me." When her eyes did at last become
still, he had smiled into them, acknowledging her as a person who
commanded his full attention, but she had not returned the greeting. He recognized straightaway that, no matter how far she might
neglect herself (and it was very far, then), she appealed to his sense
of all that was superb in a young woman. Nothing could contain
such a spirit, once it began to soar. That was his task: to set her free.

She had borne with him listlessly while he went through the
opening formalities, name, address, age—she was twenty-three,
then—but after he fell silent, she offered nothing, waiting for him
to point the way.

"I want to talk about some myths," he had said. "Myths surrounding psychoanalysis and psychotherapy: what they are and
what they are not."

She said nothing, nor did she nod.

"You are not mad. I'm not a psychiatrist. It's important you
understand that. Your postnatal depression, however severe, means
only that you are functioning at less than your best."

He paused, but she continued to stare into space as if he were
not present.

"Our sessions together will occur at the same time each week
and will last exactly one hour. This is because the patient after you
wants me to be punctual and I must respect that wish, just as I
respect your wish that I should always be on time for you. It is one
way of saying that I can be relied upon."

"I see. Thank you."

He noted "relied = trigger" on his pad and continued, "It is
unlikely that you will still be in therapy six months from now. If,
after that, you haven't conquered the hostility you feel toward your
child, if you're not enjoying your life more, there will be little point
in our continuing."

He had said something that mattered. Her eyes were wide open
and she was looking at him properly. "I thought . . . I'm sorry, I
thought it would take years. Always took years."

"No. Myth number one."

"How will we know when it's over?"

"Therapist and patient know when the time has come to part.
Always. Next, myth number two: that therapy is pleasurable. Therapy is hard work. Unpalatable, unpleasant things will come out,

things you would rather not know. It is grinding, painful labor and I have no magic to change that."

"I didn't expect so much honesty." She hesitated. "Am I allowed to ask questions?"

"Anything."

"When it's over . . . after six months, or whenever . . . is there a rule that says we can't see each other again?"

He hesitated. He had been married for three years then: long enough to know that his relationship with Clara wasn't going to work. "No rule."

There followed a long silence, during which Anna's eyes roamed around the cluttered room. "Only I would like one day to ask you about yourself. Where you live."

He was startled. She struck him as a quick study, already initiating the games people used to delay him on his *via dolorosa* toward Truth, but more awesomely she had used the phrase "where you live" as if she understood the central place it occupied in his world. For that, ultimately, was all of his work: showing people where they lived, instead of where they imagined they were camping.

He had known in that instant that she was dangerous to him. There were well-established procedures for ridding oneself of patients who might be thought unsuitable. Gerhard ignored the signs.

"Gerhard?"

He came out of his reverie to find Anna in the garden below him with a towel around her shoulders, shivering. It was too early in the season for long bathes. He thought about encouraging her to change, then decided not to. A day's rest had restored most of the natural beauty to her face, and the plain black bikini did wonders for her lightly tanned body, still firm and devoid of stretch marks. Hard to believe she was thirty-nine.

"You seemed miles away," she said, as she climbed up the path to join him. "What were you thinking?"

"I was remembering something." He laughed and resumed his seat. "Unimportant."

She gave herself a few brisk rubs and sat down opposite him, keeping the towel in place for warmth. "Go on, tell me."

"Oh . . . there was a time when I used to dream about you. Often."

"I bet you say that to all the girls. But I'm willing to be flattered; don't stop."

"One night I woke up calling your name."

Gerhard had not meant to reveal himself, but Anna was always quick. "What did the woman with you say?"

He laughed again, although this time with none of his usual assurance.

Anna's smile was arch. "I bet she was cross. Did you try to seduce all your female patients?"

"I never slept with a patient. Never." That was true; it would have been perilous in the extreme. "I always waited until after the therapy was over."

"Ah, I remember. Friends, you said. Once the therapy's over, a therapist can be friends with his former patient. I loved the way you emphasized 'former'; you made me sound cured." Her face darkened, as if all of a sudden she had lost a battle with cancerous pain. "Was I ever cured?"

"You're a successful barrister, married, quite rich, I should imagine."

"Yes, but was I cured?"

He understood. She was testing him. Could he be trusted? No, it was worse than that: she needed to know if there had *ever* been a time when he was worthy of her trust. "What, in your book, is a cure, then?"

"Not being on the run. Not hearing voices in my head. Not doing bad things I can't remember doing."

"Such as?"

"Treason. Taking the file."

He felt a surge of guilty rage. "So it's back to betrayals, is it?"

"Your theme, not mine."

"You know perfectly well that at the root of all your problems lay a deep sense of betrayal: first by your mother, then by others. And you felt guilty about what you regarded as your own betrayals, particularly of Juliet."

"So you told me."

"I got rid of the guilt, that's all. I allowed you to see that having fun wasn't always so terrible."

"I'm sure." She waited, as if expecting him to speak again. When he remained silent she sighed, stood up and walked off the terrace.

Some ten minutes passed without her reappearing, but Gerhard only slowly mastered his anxiety. Today she seemed detached, in reasonable health . . . and fey. There was something missing. He wanted to analyze it, but his mind kept straying to London. *Would they do a deal? How much was Krysalis worth to them?*

How long before Barzel came?

He was startled out of these dark speculations by the discovery that she had again come to stand in front of him. She was fully clothed. Her suitcase sat on the terrace beside her.

"Gerhard, I'm going home."

No, no, *no!*

The sky seemed to darken. The sun disappeared. But there were no clouds. He waited until he could again be sure of his voice; then—"I think that's a very silly thing to say," he said smoothly, coming out of his chair.

"This isn't right. The sooner I go back and face whatever's coming to me, the better."

Don't panic, don't worry, just think, yes, that's right, control . . . "I really don't believe you're in a fit physical or mental state to—"

"Please, let's not argue. I appreciate what you've done, but I can face things by myself."

He swallowed. There was an impediment in his throat that refused to go away. "What's brought this on?"

But he knew. His grip on her had weakened. God knows, the signs had been obvious enough. He'd programed Anna to open the safe, bring him the file, wait while he copied it, take it back, then forget everything. But she could remember a lot of what had happened. She recalled hearing "voices." One voice in particular. And now this . . .

He had to bring her back under control. *But how?*

"David is going to be very surprised if you just turn up, after arranging for him to come out at the weekend."

"He's missing me, Gerhard, he's worried sick about me. Can't you see that?"

Despite her words, Kleist detected a hint of irresolution when he'd mentioned David. "He's already been through rather a lot on your account."

She said nothing.

"I don't think he's quite prepared for your arrest at Heathrow. The photographers. The TV cameras and so on. It will all come as rather a shock to him."

"Maybe that won't happen. Perhaps they'll hush it up. I just know that he needs me and I love him and that what I'm doing is right. I have to go."

He studied her face. Her eyes were never still. Sometimes they lighted on him, but for the most part they seemed hardly to focus at all.

"Anna. Are you sure?"

"Sure."

He examined her a moment longer while he sorted through the alternatives, which turned out to be few. "Very well," he said slowly.

These words seemed to take her by surprise. "You'll let me go?"

He laughed. "Why, do you think you're some kind of prisoner, or something?"

Now a longer pause. "I know I've got no right to ask you this, but . . . will you come with me?"

"All right. I didn't bring a suitcase so I've nothing to pack. Do you mind walking to the village? It isn't very far, and I'll have to persuade Yorgos to drive us down to the port."

"I'd love a walk."

"Good. There's only one ferry a day, it doesn't leave until five, but if we go early at least you'll be able to say you saw the sights of one Greek harbor. Now if you'll excuse me . . ."

Gerhard went to his room, shut the door behind him and leaned against it with his eyes closed. So this was how it felt between the devil and the deep blue sea; at last he knew.

He swayed slightly, not quite in command of himself. Anna was preparing, all unwittingly, to put him in danger of death. To exterminate him. His breathing quickened, his stomach felt queasy. *Death.* That, suddenly, had become the reality. *You're going to die . . .*

Pull yourself together! Everyone's going to die one day. But not you, *not yet!*

He opened his eyes again and strode over to pull the bed away from the wall. The Luger lay in its usual place. He checked the magazine, then stood up, kneeing the bed back into place. He was shaking; his hand had become so weak it could scarcely hold the gun. He had never yet resorted to violence. Physical brutality sickened him. But he'd implanted the idea that Anna should stay on the island, and that wasn't working, so he had no choice.

If London played, he would win a fortune and a one-way ticket out of a life that had become impossible, thanks to Anna.

If London played, HVA would want revenge, but they'd never find him in Peru or Paraguay: both places where Gerhard had friends and where life, for the rich, was congenial.

If London played, his sister Ilsa would be destroyed . . . *don't think about that!*

If, on the other hand, London did not want to buy back Krysalis, he would contact Barzel, "admit" to having panicked, and simply allow the machine to take over, wafting him to safety in Berlin, together with Anna and the file. But everything depended on Anna's not surfacing. Once she began to talk, he was finished.

He gazed at the gun, trying to imagine how it would feel to point it at Anna, pull the trigger, see her stagger backwards, wet scarlet splashing on the walls, the floor. . . . *no, no, no.* He couldn't. Couldn't even *contemplate* it.

Why?

He laughed aloud, a scornful sound. Why . . . ? Because after that first session of treatment, he and Anna had become lovers, his first adultery. He had never quite stopped loving her, even when HVA ordered him to end the affair because it was a threat to security and anyhow they wanted her to fall in love with David.

Gerhard sank down on the bed, tossed the gun aside. Face it, he told himself: you still love her. Krysalis can buy a new life for *both* of you. You'll persuade her to come away with you. Given time, she'll love you again. It's inevitable. By selling Krysalis, you'll compromise her: in London, they'll never believe she's innocent after that. She'll *have* to come with you. All you need is time to prepare her. *Time!*

He put on a jacket, picked up the Luger, and dropped it into his pocket. There was one chance left. When earlier he'd mentioned David's agony at her disgrace, her face had changed. Give her a few more moments . . .

———

Anna had begun to wander around, wishing she could explore this beautiful island, and the house in its perfect setting. The insidious thought made her angry, because a moment ago she had known only a fierce desire to go home.

Her headache was back with a vengeance; she felt nauseated. The attack had come on at about the time she'd made up her mind to leave. Don't fuss, she told herself. Find something to do.

Beside the fireplace stood a bookshelf. She leafed through the few quartos of sheet music lying on top, then her attention was snared by something on the next shelf down. It contained a dozen paperbacks. One of them looked unaccountably familiar. She picked it up and to her surprise realized that it belonged to her.

The first grown-up novel Anna could remember having read was O'Hara's *From the Terrace*. To that day she could close her eyes and visualize one scene, just one, and it came at the end of the book when Alfred Eaton, the principal character, had been very ill. While he convalesced he would sit in the California sun on the terrace of the title, and look back over a life that had promised at every turn to be successful, yet never quite delivered. And he did not know why.

Anna had once lent this book to Gerhard, who forgot to return it. And here it was, a little the worse for suntan oil and salt water, but still intact.

Gerhard showed no signs of emerging from his bedroom. Anna carried the book out to the terrace, her own terrace, and sat down facing the sea. The sun made the water look like freshly applied sapphire-blue paint, glossy and fierce. She closed her eyes, trying, like Alfred Eaton, to pinpoint the moment when she had known the promises would never be fulfilled.

Yes. That dinner party. Barristers. All talking law. Poor David.

Robyn, her best friend, had just gone back to the States, leaving her angry and desolate. Everyone at the table was talking, talking, talking, laughing, laughing, laughing, drinking, drinking, drinking, talking, drinking, laughing, and nobody in the room (apart from David) loved Anna at all.

The food was rotten.

She'd been busy, it wasn't her fault. She couldn't be everywhere at once. Only because she was a woman, that's exactly what she had to be: omnipresent, able to cope with everyone and everything. But her cook for the evening, recommended by a friend, turned out to be a disaster: the duck was dry and the mousse separated. Fortunately, David had chosen some marvelous wines, so while the others forced themselves to eat she'd planted both elbows on the table and held a glass close to her face, concealing the tears.

They were so sleek, so self-satisfied, all these guests. They talked easily and well, scarcely even aware of their power to enthrall. She had devoted a lifetime of mind-bending hard work to the task of joining their ranks, but as she looked along the lines of Hogarthian features, the sharp, pointed noses, fat bellies, pudgy hands, greasy foreheads, now she realized that they were parasites and she indeed was one of them. How David must have hated it all.

How she hated it, she suddenly realized.

Next day they had dropped by her room at work to thank her for the evening; which almost to a man they characterized as "wonderful." So mundane an adjective, she thought. Only Guy Samuelson, one of her roommates, smiled the rather secret smile that was his specialty, as if to say, "Yes, the food *did* taste ghastly, didn't it?"; and to him she felt she perhaps ought to apologize (her specialty?), but instead she heard herself say aggressively, "You should be bloody grateful for a meal your wife didn't have to cook and wash up for a change," enjoying the way Guy's smile slipped, as if he'd unexpectedly found himself dealing with someone quite *outrée.*

But she was going to need them when she got back. These were the people who would help her fight the massive negligence claim she so dreaded. They would defend her at the Old Bailey against a charge of treason.

One more day without them wouldn't make a scrap of difference.

Think of David.

And prison . . . think of that.

"Are you ready?"

Gerhard's voice brought her back to reality. She stood up, mechanically stuffing the book into her handbag.

"Yes."

He picked up her case and held the front door open for her. When she did not pass through it at once, he went ahead, striding down the white, dusty path, almost as if glad that he would shortly be rid of this tiresome house guest.

"Anna?"

Gerhard reached the gate. He laid a hand on the signboard, the one in the photograph of Robyn that Anna loathed so much, and turned. From the doorway she watched him, so tall and powerful and fine, so untypical of everything left behind in England.

Of everything waiting to devour her.

Suddenly she heard herself say, "I think I would like to stay a bit longer. Perhaps a day or two."

Gerhard fumbled over closing the gate; the latch seemed to be giving him trouble. When he started to walk back to the house, Anna noticed that his face was pale and running with sweat. She could not think why.

CHAPTER 14

As David walked through the Temple on his way to Anna's chambers the last of the sun provoked angry amber glints in numerous windows. They made him feel as though he were being watched; but then of course he was. Albert had known about his appointment with Broadway this Tuesday evening. How? There could be only one answer. They were tapping his phone. The knowledge made him angry. He also felt a little sick.

Never mind Albert, he told himself sourly. You've got a long list of questions to ask; concentrate on them.

Anna worked in a four-story Georgian building, strangely isolated from the other eighteenth- and nineteenth-century sets of chambers at this hub of London's legal universe. Yet the accouterments of a more modern age were not lacking. The first thing to meet his eyes as he entered the clerks' room was a fax machine humming away. There was a photocopier, one of the larger models that could collate as well as reproduce, a Telex terminal, a laser printer. If the hull was Dickensian, the engine room was twenty-first century.

David approached the clerk's desk. "Good evening, Roger."

"Hello, Mr. Lescombe." The young man called Roger deftly cleared his screen of outstanding fees and stood up.

"I've come to see Mr. Broadway."

"He's in con. Shouldn't be long."

The phrase "in con" was short for "in conference," or, more accessibly, "in a meeting"; it usually reminded David of "in labor," and made him want to laugh, although not today.

"I'll wait. Is my wife's room empty?"

"Should be."

Anna's office overlooked Temple embankment. It was cramped, part of what had once been one enormous room, now partitioned. She had to share it with two others, who tonight, mercifully, were absent.

Three reproduction desks, all the worse for wear, took up most of the space. Beneath the window was a table, covered with briefs wrapped in pink tape, some of them thick, some thin, some consisting of half a dozen box files with miscellaneous papers bundled on top. Nothing brief about them. The whole of one longer wall was taken up with bookcases filled with Law Reports. On the mantelpiece opposite stood a clock; next to it was the bottom half of a green wine bottle cramfull of dried-out ball point pens and pencil stubs.

Ranged along Anna's desk were several blue counsels' notebooks, a paper rack containing notepaper and envelopes, a shiny, perpetual-motion executive toy, and a telephone. Three textbooks stood on end, their spines facing Anna's seat: a typist's swivel chair, stark, simple, good for the back. David picked up one of the books: *Scrutton on Charterparties.* He grimaced, then quickly replaced it.

He sat down at her desk and began to open drawers.

At first, nothing. Old circulars, still sealed; fee notes; bills; a few handwritten envelopes marked "Personal"; the usual flotsam shed by a professional person too busy to keep up with daily life. Then he came to the bottom right-hand drawer, of double depth, and as he pulled something clinked inside.

A vodka bottle, nearly empty. David stared down at it. Hell, all kinds of people kept alcohol at their places of work; it meant nothing by itself. If you were going to query a quick, companionable drink at six o'clock, you'd end up pointing the finger at most of the cabinet and their outer offices.

But no sign of any mixers. Or of a glass, come to that.

Anna drank. Often a lot. So, admit it—she might have a drinking *problem.* Then, he had to go a step further and confess that he didn't really know her very well, perhaps hadn't wanted to, because confronting her predicaments or, worse, trying to resolve them, would have needed more time than he was prepared to give.

For the first time it occurred to him that his love might have been blind. . . .

It was the absence of a glass that bothered him most.

The top left-hand drawer would not open. The lock appeared flimsy. David, suddenly desperate to find an outlet for his unease, picked up a paper knife and used it to break in.

The drawer contained several bank books, check stubs and, right at the back, a small leather case: one of those folding albums with space for two photographs. As David picked it up the feel of the bright red leather, tooled with a gold strip, told him it was sumptuous: the sort of thing you wouldn't buy for yourself but might give a favored friend.

He opened it. One side was empty. The other contained a color snapshot, somewhat overexposed, of a woman standing in front of a white background. David looked closer: the whiteness belonged to the wall of a house, with a garish pine doorway just visible over the woman's shoulder. Italy, maybe. Or Spain. Continental, anyhow.

The woman was positioned slightly to the left of center, her narrow face tilted away from the camera. Her right hand lay on top of a rugged wooden board, bearing letters. David peered closer and saw they were Greek letters, which solved the location. The edge of the photo excised the bottoms of the words, but the first two looked like *"i oikia,"* the house. The last word was obscure. David took a stab at it: *mikra.* The Little House.

The woman had dark hair, cut in a bob. She was wearing a large, loose jacket over a plain shirt. The outfit struck David as somewhat formal in such a setting; maybe she'd been traveling and this snapshot had been taken to celebrate her arrival. He tried to examine her features, but the focusing wasn't perfect and too much light flooded the foreground. Attractive, in a cosmopolitan kind of way. She wasn't Greek, he decided.

David took the photograph out and stuck it in his pocket. Then he looked at his watch. Duncan Broadway was in no hurry to meet him. Damn them, a senior barrister had disappeared, and now the head of chambers couldn't even be bothered to see her husband on time.

When he went back to the clerk's room, Roger glanced up without evident sympathy. "He's still in con," he said, as if to forestall any protest.

David's face tightened. He began to pace about, nine steps up, nine steps down, every so often jerking his wrist from its sleeve to see how many seconds had ticked by since he'd last looked. As he completed one of these time checks his eyes met Roger's. "Don't do that," the clerk's expression said; "you're putting me off and I'm late for the wife and the telly as it is."

There were things David urgently had to find out: Broadway might hold the key. He needed to know: not tomorrow but *now!*

David did a smart left wheel, all but ran down a passage leading out of the front office, and threw open the door at the end.

Duncan Broadway stopped in mid-sentence. "Startled" seemed too mild a word to describe his face; he looked shocked. The world did not intrude into barristerial meetings. The world had no place there.

"I'm busy," he said frigidly. "Can't you see that?"

The room held a lot of people. Everyone was staring at him, this representative of the world that they wished would go away, enabling them to resume communion with the man behind the desk, the leader. *Their* leader.

"I can see you're holding forth," David said shortly. "Which may or may not amount to being busy."

A gasp went round the room. But Broadway only smiled and said, in a lower voice, "I'll see you in a moment, David." He followed this up with a nod of the chin and a narrowing of the eyes, a conspirator's look: You and I are professional men, we realize that *hoi polloi* must be humored, but as soon as I have finished with these distasteful people we can move onto our higher plane of consciousness.

"You'll see me now, Duncan."

Roger had silently materialized at David's shoulder. "Is everything all right, Mr. Broadway?"

David turned through a half-circle. "Shove it." He put his hand in the center of Roger's Marks and Spencer tie and pushed with all his might. The clerk went sprawling backward against the opposite wall of the corridor, hands splayed in an attempt to keep upright.

"This is a monstrous intrusion . . ."

Broadway was standing ramrod straight behind his desk. But perhaps this opening struck even him as likely to be ineffectual, for he tailed off, and when he spoke again his voice was its usual conversational self. "Well, we were just finishing, anyway."

David stood to one side while the acolytes filed out, careful to avoid looking at him. As tail-end Charlie shut the door, Broadway snapped: "What the *hell* do you think you're doing, bursting in here like that? What do you think those solicitors thought, have you any idea? Three of those men, *three* of them, are partners in the finest firm of commercial solicitors the City has to show, and you come thrusting yourself in here like some thug off the streets." He paused, and stuck both thumbs in his waistcoat pockets. "Sit down," he commanded.

But David ignored him, going instead to stand by the window. "You gave me an appointment, fixed the time," he said to the glass. "I came. You were late. When your lateness crossed the line into downright bad manners I decided to play the same game. What's wrong with that?"

"My God, you've got a nerve!" Broadway was swelling up like a frog, his rounded stomach pressed against the black cloth of his waistcoat in a desperate fight for freedom. "And your rudeness to me, your personal rudeness, it defied all bounds of decency . . . of . . ."

"Duncan." David turned away from the window. "My wife has run away and no one can tell me where she's gone. They think it's possible she may have taken an overdose of sleeping tablets before she went. People I don't know are trying to convince me of things concerning Anna that I utterly reject. If you found yourself in my place, don't you think you might behave badly too?"

Broadway lowered himself into his chair, continuing to survey David with coldness. His eyes were large, so large that they sometimes reminded people of a horse's eyes. The center of his head was bald, but two neat manes of black hair still clung to the sides of his skull where his barrister's wig did not prevent the air from circulating. His face was round, like the eyes, and he suffered from a surfeit of chins, but the feature that stayed with people meeting him for the first time was stubble. No matter what the time of day, the lower part of his face looked as if it had recently been dipped in soot.

David sat down opposite Broadway—the chair was still warm from one of the finest commercial bottoms the City had to show—and glared at the barrister.

"In the circumstances," Broadway said, "I suggest we leave the topic of your disgraceful entrance and move on."

David said nothing. I must keep up the pressure, he told himself. This man wears a suit but he's a street fighter. Don't yield.

"I'm glad you rang up asking to see me, David, because the

police have been here asking all kind of damn fool questions about Anna and I can't trace her."

David felt angry, afraid. The police . . .

"Do you know where she is?" Broadway asked.

"No."

"So you're as much in the dark as we are?"

David nodded.

"Have you any idea how risky it was for us when we took her on? We'd never had a woman in these chambers before. But she came in and she did wonderfully well: worked all hours, charmed the clients, charmed *me*, I may say, got on famously with the bench. She had this gift of making people want to do things for her. Then suddenly it begins to go to hell and I want to know why."

"Are you telling me that Anna hasn't been working normally?"

"On and off."

"But she was up for a judgeship, you told me so yourself, at that party."

"Yes, last Christmas. It was true, then."

"Then why—"

"Because she hasn't been concentrating, that's why!" Broadway's voice had turned snappy and shrill. "There were times when she couldn't keep her mind on the ball from one moment to the next. You're her husband, surely you must have seen that?"

David seemed to hear the clink of glass on wood again and his gaze slipped from the accusing face opposite. "I knew she . . . she could be a little absent-minded. It's a human enough trait, who isn't?"

"Generalizations are dangerous." Broadway had obviously decided to give his patronizing side an airing. "Particularly in the case of people close to one, where habitual assumptions frequently take the place of accurate observation."

"If you say so."

"I began to hear murmurings from other tenants of these chambers, from people who'd always liked her. Her behavior was so out of character."

"Just a minute. When are we talking about?"

"Different times, different tenants. Some of these complaints go back a good many years. Some are recent. Some people never had anything bad to say against her at all. She was moody. Unpredictable."

"How did you deal with these . . . murmurings?"

"I played them down. On the whole, they related to minor matters. Anna's always had her touchy side and I don't blame her for that."

"Anna? Touchy?"

"You have to be aggressive if you're a woman and you want to get on at the bar. You have no alternative."

"But—"

"Why, only a few months ago our best typist left because she couldn't stand Anna's complaints."

"Mrs. Mayhew?"

"That's right. I was surprised. Anna had seemed to be performing at her best, then suddenly—"

"Anna said . . ."

"What did Anna say?"

That Mrs. Mayhew had suffered a mental breakdown, they'd had to let her go.

"I . . . I can't exactly remember. I didn't get the impression that her leaving had to do with Anna."

"I see. Well, you mustn't think your wife didn't get any sympathy. She was popular, you know; people were prepared to give her masses of leeway. Everyone knew she was working under the most tremendous strain. She'd put in for the judgeship, she was probably going to get silk next time round, and then that writ landed on her desk. It's enough to make anyone—"

"Writ?"

"The damages claim." Broadway shunted some papers around, annoyed by the interruption. "Three million pounds is a pretty big claim in professional negligence terms. We carry insurance up to twenty-five million, but even so." He glanced at David and his face changed. "You didn't know?"

David shook his head. He felt winded. "Can you explain? Please?"

Broadway celebrated that "please" by making David wait. "Anna drafted an agreement, some years ago," he said at last. "It involved the sale of a thriving business, with a number of subsidiaries, to a rather well-known public conglomerate. She was asked to include warranties as to the state of the company's accounts, and so on. She appears to have . . ." He snapped his fingers, angry with himself. "It is *alleged* that she left out certain vital clauses. I won't burden you with the details."

"But . . . I mean, what's the position?"

"Position?"

"Well, will she win? Will they win? How much . . . ?"

"I think it's unlikely the plaintiff will recover. But there are . . . factors. About which I'm not happy. Evidential considerations."

"Explain that."

Broadway's face betrayed deep dissatisfaction. "It's irregular. But you are her husband. . . ." His voice hardened. "Dammit, you ought to know at least something about this."

"I agree. Please can you tell me what the problems are."

The barrister unlocked a desk drawer, using one of the keys on the end of his watch chain, and took out a tome; David saw "1987" embossed in gold on the back.

"Two years ago?" he inquired.

"Yes."

"Haven't they waited a long time to make a fuss about whatever it is?"

"The problems only surfaced recently." Broadway opened this office diary at one of many bookmarks and pushed it across the desk. "You see that entry, there?"

"Ten-thirty in court, a conference in the afternoon . . . something's been rubbed out."

"That's the point. She had a lunch engagement that day. The date's significant."

"Why?"

"Because that afternoon conference related to the mess she's got herself into, the one she's being sued for. The other side are going to say she arrived late and appeared . . . 'distraught' is how they tactfully put it, as if her mind wasn't on the case at all."

David stared at him. "That's the whole of their case?"

"Would that it were! *All* the pages I've flagged were days when Anna went out to lunch, stayed out a long time, and then erased the entries afterward."

David flicked through several pages. "These markers, they're from about May to . . . October?"

"Yes. Sometimes she juggled appointments to make those lunches; once she even asked another member of chambers to do a summons for her so that she could keep the date. Look at July 31st."

The summer of 1987; two years ago now, but David remembered it easily. He and Anna quarreled, then somehow failed to make it up. Ostensibly the fracas concerned Juliet, what they ought to do about her. The child was unhappy at school. Anna had been all for moving her; David stubbornly resisted, saying that life in the real world was often unaccommodating and the sooner Juliet learned that the better. But there had been something else, something that could not be explained.

He flipped through pages until he came to the end of July. "Someone's written a number . . . telephone?"

"The police seemed to think so."

"You mentioned them earlier . . . did they say what they thought might have happened to Anna?"

"No. Neither of them brought it up."

"Neither?"

"There were two. The older man just sat there, keeping mum. The other fellow asked all the questions but wasn't about to supply any answers."

Broadway's gaze no longer quite met David's. It was easy, even pleasurable, to imagine that scene: haughty Q.C. worked over by the the police. Broadway had a nice line in splutters.

"The talker, the young one in glasses, he was very interested in those entries. He took the diary away; we only got it back this afternoon, in fact."

"What kind of glasses did he wear?"

"Does it matter?"

"I wondered if . . . no, too much of a coincidence."

"Know him, do you? Tall, thin, sandy hair, very weak specs; I'm surprised he needed them at all, really. Those dreadful tinted things."

"What colour tint?"

"Pink." Broadway sniffed. "Bloody little pansy."

"Albert a pansy?"

"Albert?"

"Didn't he introduce himself?"

"No."

"Albert's cagey."

"He is that! They wanted to search Anna's room. I told them to come back with a search warrant." Broadway stared at David. "Do you mind telling me what's going on?"

David decided he had no option. "Anna's disappeared. It looks as though she took one of my files with her. It's a file a lot of people would like to get their hands on. I'm sorry if I'm not more specific, but at least you lawyers understand what confidentiality's all about."

"Good God." By now Broadway was almost whispering.

"No one knows where she's gone, who she's with, or anything. I can't get any cooperation."

"My dear chap." Broadway's voice sounded less than warm, but there was a change in it. "What an appalling thing."

"Yes. And I . . . Duncan, you know what they say, about not realizing what you've got until you've lost it. . . ." David laughed in an attempt to cover his discomfiture. "Well, it's true."

Broadway looked away, embarrassed.

"Is there anything, *anything* at all that might help me find her?" David's voice was beseeching. "Perhaps you think I'm being pathetic, but when a man loves his wife . . ."

He couldn't go on.

Broadway cleared his throat a couple of times, obviously wishing he could be somewhere else.

"Look, I'm sorry . . ." David made a great effort and recovered some of his composure. "Is there anyone in chambers she was close to, who might know where she is?"

"No. I've already asked." Broadway grunted. "I suppose Robyn might just conceivably know something."

"Who is Robyn?"

"An American lawyer."

"He's here? In England?"

"I shouldn't think so for one minute. It's a she, incidentally, not a he. A woman attorney from New York. She spent a year here, researching for some thesis she was doing, comparative law as I recall."

"Oh yes, that rings a sort of bell. Anna mentioned her. But why do you think she might know something?"

"Because they were like two peas in a pod. Robyn shared her room, you see. After she went back to the States, Anna was always getting letters from her. She used to read out bits to us at chambers' tea."

David gawked at him. "What was that again—letters?"

"Yes."

"Anna shared a room with this woman for one whole year, a friend, you say?"

"Yes. You find that astonishing?"

"It's just that I . . . I hadn't realized they were quite so close."

"She never told you about Robyn?"

"She mentioned her a couple of times. But as a professional acquaintance, not . . ."

A thought struck David, and he thanked God for Broadway's punctilious refusal to let Albert search Anna's room without a warrant.

"What does she look like . . . here, is this her?"

He pushed the photograph he had found in Anna's desk across to Broadway, who nodded confirmation. He went on to say more about Robyn's work in chambers, but David was no longer listening. His mind had leapt to the interview before the Krysalis vetting committee, with him airily confessing that Anna's circle of friends did not overlap with his. The words had meant nothing to him at the time; now they were starting to assume a frightful reality.

"Did you tell Albert about Robyn?" he asked Broadway. "And these letters, did you mention them?"

"No. I wasn't asked."

"Do you know if the clerks said anything about them?"

"I know they didn't."

"How?"

"The police questioned me with the clerks at the same time and I jolly well saw them off the premises as soon as the interview ended."

David felt that was good, without knowing why; but he had precious little else to comfort him. "I just don't understand any of this. The writ, this woman lawyer . . . why should Anna have personal post sent here, and not the house?"

He stared at Broadway, as if the Q.C. might have an answer, but it was so obviously his own department. If the husband didn't know . . .

What other things didn't the husband know?

"I shall tell chambers that Anna's ill." Broadway pursed his lips and looked up at the ceiling. "Hepatitis, say. Contaminated food. Been ordered to rest."

"Thanks," David mumbled.

Neither man spoke. David realized that he had come to the end of this road; and with the knowledge came a sense of shame. "Look, I'm . . . I'm sorry about barging in. I shouldn't have done that."

"Forgotten. Ah . . ." Broadway again seemed to be having trouble with his throat. He coughed, blew his nose, all the while looking everywhere but at David. "I really don't know how to say it, but . . . well, it's annoying, Anna going off like this. Downright annoying. But . . . I can't find words to tell you how much I hope you find her and that everything's all right."

"Thank you."

"Because . . . we had our little differences, but we were all immensely fond of her. Are immensely fond of her. She's a wonderful woman, a fine lawyer. And if anything bad were to happen . . ."

He trailed off, staring at the blotter on top of his desk.

"Thank you," David repeated quietly. "But . . . please don't say any more."

The two men shook hands. Then David was going down the corridor, passing through the clerks' room, making his way into the deserted Temple. A busy road. Cars hooting, the squeal of brakes, another world, nothing to do with him. He found himself sitting beside the river, staring at the Embankment wall, while he struggled to refocus his picture of Anna. He sat there for a long time, so long that dusk came quietly down on London, obliging Albert to move one bench closer in order to keep his quarry in view.

CHAPTER

15

Jürgen Barzel joined the HVA's Athens Watch just after eight o'clock on Tuesday evening.

"Who?" he rasped.

Erich Rehlinger pointed. "Over there. The one in white jeans and a green shirt, carrying a rucksack."

Barzel did not follow his gaze immediately, but concentrated on Rehlinger instead. He was within inches of an ignominious end to his career; he was tired, he was famished, and here he was, forced to depend on people he didn't know and had never worked with for his sole chance of salvation. Rehlinger seemed efficient, though. All Barzel could do was put his faith in him and beg for luck.

They were standing on the first level beneath Omonia Square, jostled by crowds heading for the railway station. Barzel reluctantly took his eyes off Rehlinger and followed the direction of his pointing finger. He could make out a Greek youth of about eighteen, loitering by a bank of phone booths some twenty meters away. He seemed uncertain whether he really wanted to make a call.

This was his last, his only hope. Barzel gazed at the boy like a wolf eying food.

"What have you found out?" he murmured.

"Nothing much. He's got a packet of money in his wallet. Station's working on it now."

"Name?"

"First name: Iannis. That's all Heinrich managed to pick up."

"*Shit!*" Heinrich was another unknown quantity. "Where's Heinrich got to?"

Rehlinger nodded. "Almost next to him."

"Will he be able to overhear if friend Iannis makes a call?"

"Should be."

"How's his Greek?"

"Five-five."

"Thank God!" That was the code for bilingual standard in speech and writing. The knowledge that a first-class interpreter had been placed at his disposal was the first bit of solid good news to come Barzel's way in quite a while.

"Where did you pick him up?" he asked.

"A Telex-and-fax bureau down an alley off Zinonos Street."

So, thought Barzel: Margaret did her stuff. That brought scant consolation, however. He lit a cigarette and rested his back against the wall in such a way that he could always keep tabs on this strangely hesitant lad called Iannis. This whole exercise was a very long shot. But his instincts weren't usually wrong.

Relax, he told himself. Be calm. Think it through. *Again.*

He had panicked HVA's Athens Station into having them shadow all known MI6 and CIA legmen to see if any of them seemed unduly interested in public fax offices, and got on a plane. By the time he reached Athens, there was a response. Rehlinger's target, an MI6 operative of minimal experience and careless methods, was tracking, none too subtly, a Greek boy who visited the same office every two hours, on the hour.

A movement caught Barzel's eye. "He's going to phone," he said quietly, stubbing out his cigarette. "Move in. But keep it *clean.*"

The boy at last seemed to have plucked up the courage to enter a vacant phone booth. He looked around several times, as if making sure that no one was watching. Suddenly Barzel stiffened. "What the—"

Iannis had produced a black bag from the rucksack he was carrying. He used it to cover his hand while he dialed, and Barzel swore under his breath.

"A pro," Rehlinger murmured in his ear.

"Or an obedient amateur," Barzel grated. "We've got him, Erich." He wanted so much to believe his words!

"Looks like it."

"Where are the boys?"

"In the square."

Barzel squeezed his arm. "Upstairs, now, give them a Go."

Rehlinger slipped away, leaving Barzel on watch. Iannis pressed money into the slot, said something rapidly, put down the phone and walked off, shouldering his rucksack. He took the moving stairway up to street level, where he crossed quickly over to Stadiou and began thrusting his way through the crowds. Heinrich caught up with Barzel at the intersection.

"What did Iannis say?" Barzel snapped.

"He said: 'I sent it; no reply yet.' "

"That's all?"

"Yes."

"Got him! Come on, we mustn't lose him now. You follow on foot; I'll pick up the others."

As Iannis came to Santaroza he bumped into a gang of students. There was a moment of confusion while the various parties sorted themselves out. The youth walked on, rubbing his arm; once or twice he looked behind him, as if something about the recent encounter troubled him. Suddenly he lurched against a shop front, clutching his stomach. He tried to cry out, but the words couldn't force their way past the blockage that had materialized in his throat. By the time an ambulance screeched to a halt beside him and two men were helping him into it, he was nearly unconscious.

Barzel slammed the ambulance's doors, ran around to the front, and climbed in beside the driver.

The journey to Piraeus took an hour and a half; Athens's evening traffic was heavy and Barzel had an aversion to direct routes. At last the ambulance pulled up on a dingy and darkened quay beside a cabin cruiser. The vessel's engines were already turning over. Iannis was swiftly carried aboard on a stretcher. Less than a minute after they'd arrived the boat had put to sea.

Barzel clattered down the companionway to the forward cabin, where Iannis was lying on a bunk. Leather straps held him fast around the chest and thighs. He was breathing quickly; his face looked clammy.

Barzel picked up the boy's rucksack and rifled quickly through it. A few clothes, toothbrush, razor, and a battered, dog-eared paperback book with the picture of a half-naked woman on the front. Barzel's expression set into a faraway look; then he grimaced.

"Wake him," he ordered.

The man called Heinrich produced a doctor's bag and administered an injection. The effect was almost immediate. Iannis opened his eyes, tried to sit up. Barzel tapped Heinrich's arm. "Get on with it."

The other man began to address Iannis in Greek. Barzel had no idea what he said, but he assumed Heinrich was trying to soothe his "patient." If so, he seemed to have little success; Iannis's eyes bulged and his face, so pale a moment before, turned scarlet. After a while he realized that the straps were unbreakable and gave up struggling.

Heinrich dug into his bag and produced a roll of cloth. While Barzel watched with interest, he spread it out on the boy's chest to reveal six syringes, each containing a different-colored liquid. His voice hardened; now Barzel knew he was explaining the effects of the various shots.

The boat began to pitch. That meant they had left the protection of the harbor, causing Barzel to breathe a little easier. He wanted a lot of water between him and Piraeus before what was going to happen next.

He looked down at the bunk. The boy had pure skin and an even purer look in his eyes. Good-looking, too.

Barzel felt a peculiar sweetness arise within him. There was something exquisite about having an untainted soul in your power. He cared nothing for physical torture, which gave him no pleasure, or the finer techniques of mind control. What delighted him was the *anticipation:* the waiting time, before the torturer went about his squalid, unartistic work.

Today his pleasure was destined to be short. Heinrich looked at him and said in German: "This boy will talk."

Barzel tossed the paperback aside. "Make it quick."

When Heinrich spoke to Iannis the boy answered at once, the words tripping over one another in his anxiety to spill everything he knew. Suddenly Barzel heard a word he thought he recognized.

"What did he say about Kleist?" he shouted.

Heinrich held up a hand to stanch the boy's flow and turned to Barzel. "He says he comes from Paxos, a small island to the south of Corfu, off the west coast of the mainland."

"I know where Corfu is, you fool, go *on!*"

"His father works for Kleist."

Barzel clapped his hands together, once, and nodded.

"Yesterday, Kleist came to the island, with a woman. Blonde. About forty. Iannis was sent to Athens, almost immediately. Kleist gave him plenty of money and a document, explaining how he wanted it transmitted to London by fax."

"A moment. Does Iannis speak any language other than Greek? Could he read the document?"

"No. Although he can recognize the Roman alphabet. He was worried at first that this might disqualify him for the job Kleist had in mind—"

"Whereas in fact it must have been a vital requirement."

"Of course, to maximize security."

"Shit! What else?"

"That's all, so far." Heinrich readdressed himself to Iannis. Another babble of Greek followed.

"He says he was told to visit the fax office every two hours and ask if they'd received an answer to the document they had transmitted for him this morning. If there was a response, his instructions were to contact Kleist by phone, always a different phone, and spell the document to him. If nothing, he still had to report every evening at the same time. He was to sleep in a different hotel each night, and keep moving around during the day, until Sunday. Then he could go home."

Before Barzel could speak, Iannis again broke out into a spirited monologue. Barzel looked at Heinrich, who shrugged.

"It seems Iannis doesn't want to go home. He spent part of today hunting for work. The season's just begun. Hotels and restaurants will soon need staff."

More voluble Greek. This time Heinrich smiled. "He's hoping to pick up an American woman. Then maybe he needn't ever go home."

Barzel grunted. "Ask him: what did he think was the point of all this? Did Kleist say?"

During the conversation that followed, he never once took his eyes off the young Greek's face.

"Nothing legal," Heinrich said at last. "He says no one pays that well for legitimate errands."

"Smart," Barzel commented. "Is that all? Ask him about the woman."

When Heinrich did so, Iannis's expression changed. His face lost some of its terror, the eyes softened.

"He says she was beautiful. He would like to marry a woman

like that one day. She looked tired, perhaps she was ill; but Iannis regretted being sent away."

"Name?"

"He was told once, but he couldn't remember. He was too busy giving her the eye."

"Forty, blonde. Gerhard, Gerhard . . ." Barzel slowly shook his head. "Come up," he said to Heinrich.

Once on deck, Barzel rested both hands on the rail and stared at the sea. He was holding Iannis's paperback again, turning it over and over as he spoke.

"Do you want us to take you to that island now?" Heinrich asked him.

Barzel knew a desperate moment of indecision. "Yes. No! There's something I have to do first, in England. But I can't afford the time. . . ." He tossed his head again, as if trying to shake the demons out of it. "Or can I . . . ?"

"The husband?"

"Yes. It was his file; he holds the key to this. I don't know what the hell's going on. Kleist's a mystery to me. Did he panic? Or is this part of a plan?"

Heinrich shrugged.

Barzel reached a decision. "I *must* speak to Lescombe. No choice. Take me back."

"What do you want done with the boy?"

"Keep him safe, keep him happy. Make sure he phones Kleist every evening, as planned. The same message as tonight: 'Nothing yet,' okay?"

"Right. For how long?"

"Until Sunday—he was told he could go home then, isn't that what you said?"

"Yes."

"Or earlier if I say so."

"And then?"

"Then?"

"The boy—what do you want us to do with him after Sunday?"

"Hm." Barzel's expression showed a touch of melancholy. For a long time he studied the crude picture of the front of the paperback, as if it held all of Kleist's secrets.

"You say he doesn't want to go home?" he said at last.

"That's right."

"I think he must have his wish," Barzel murmured to the

waters below. "Use plenty of anchor chain. And put him in a sack: I don't want him surfacing. Oh, and, Heinrich . . ."

"Yes?"

"Make sure he's well and truly asleep before you throw him over the side, hein?" Barzel hesitated, the memory of that innocent, bronzed face strong in his mind. He smoothed the cover of the book, once, twice. "None of this is his fault."

WEDNESDAY

CHAPTER 16

Wednesday began with one of those peerless Greek mornings that normally only find their season in May or June: a brilliant perspective of long horizons and lofty cloud, of crystalline water and warm breezes.

Anna awoke to find herself lying in her low whitewashed room, now suffused with the warm savor of a Mediterranean morning. Sleepily she yawned and stretched. This wasn't her bedroom . . . what was she doing here? Yes, of course: she had been ill. She had done these irrational things, for no apparent reason, her memory was failing, and Gerhard had agreed to look after her until David arrived at the weekend.

Thoughts of David sent her hands involuntarily roving across her breasts. How long to Saturday? Too long . . . but she might as well stay here until then.

Her bed stood opposite the only window. Someone had put a vase of fresh bluebells on the sill. She looked at the flowers, knew who had picked them, and sat up. Dear Gerhard. Such an old-style romantic. Flowers . . . how like him.

David gave her a bouquet every Friday evening; he bought them from the same little stall by the entrance to Westminster underground station. How that memory made her yearn for him! His

comforting voice, the feel of his strong arms holding her close . . .
"David," she whispered. "Why aren't we together?"

She must telephone him right away. Gerhard would take her
down to the harbor, where there was a phone. How wonderful that
he spoke Greek; he could help with the operator.

She jumped out of bed, hastily pulling on her clothes. As she
emerged into the hallway a few moments later, she became aware
of odd sounds coming from Gerhard's bedroom. Suddenly she felt
curious to know what he could be up to. Why not give him a shock?
Anna giggled. She slipped out of her sandals and padded across the
breakfast area, along the corridor leading to the front of the villa.
His door was ajar.

She sidled along the wall until she could look through the gap.
As she did so, Gerhard straightened up from kneeling by the bed.
He had his back to the door, unaware of her presence. He put
something into his pocket.

For a second, Anna refused to believe what she had seen. Her
first instinct was to challenge him. Then caution prevailed. She
retreated, not daring to stop until she had regained the relative
safety of the living room.

Gerhard had put a gun in his pocket.

"Good morning, Anna. How are you feeling today?"

Fortunately she was facing the sea, or he could not have failed
to detect her unease. She clenched her teeth until they hurt, widen-
ing her lips in the mockery of a smile, and turned.

"Much better, thank you, Gerhard. You?"

"Wonderful." He seemed not to notice anything amiss. "Look
at that . . . sunshine, blue sea."

Anna, grateful for the respite, turned her back and stared out
the window.

She must not let him think she knew. She must keep control.
Her life might depend on that. Anna examined this latest instinct
with wonder. Was she really in danger, from the man she'd trusted
for nigh onto sixteen years?

Why didn't she come straight out and ask him?

No. She knew somehow that everything depended on her not
doing anything until she was alone. For now, safety lay in blanking
out the recollection of that odious weapon in Gerhard's pocket. *It
hadn't happened.*

"I thought we might go for a picnic," he said.

"Good," she replied, keeping her back to him. "What a lovely idea."

"So you've definitely changed your mind about leaving?"

"Oh, yes." She managed a tense laugh. "I'd like to stay here forever, if I could."

Now it was his turn to laugh. Then he turned serious. "Is something the matter?"

Anna struggled to find a satisfying answer. "I'm worried, naturally."

"About what?"

"At home they'll be waiting to arrest me, won't they?"

"If you go back now, without waiting for the results of my preliminary overtures, then yes, I'm afraid they will."

"*Embarras des riches.*"

"How do you mean?"

"Not one court case but two. First the trial for treason, then, when I've got a moment, there's that claim for three million pounds to fight, the one I told you about, remember?"

"Yes."

The words were coming out naturally, and they were the right ones to persuade Gerhard that she was completely ignorant of the gun.

"Oh . . ." Anna heaved a deep sigh. "The thought of going back to chambers and facing them all . . ."

"*Out*facing them. You can do it."

"Mm. I didn't behave very well toward them. Not always." She produced another little laugh from somewhere. "I'm sure a few more hours' freedom won't change anything, will they? And perhaps your . . . overtures will come to something."

She drank a cup of coffee but could eat no breakfast. It was a silent meal.

Gerhard borrowed Yorgos's car and drove them across to the west coast, where he kept a boat moored in one of the coastal hamlets. Anna stared out the car window, concentrating her entire attention on the scenery. In happier circumstances she could have fallen in love with this isolated place. The peach trees were a mass of white flowers, irises and marguerites were everywhere in full bloom, orange and lemon trees stood laden with young fruit. It was to be an olive year, and already buds were blooming on their twigs as they strove up toward the spring sky. Everything she saw appealed to her: geraniums, poppies, roses in tubs, peeling walls in need of paint; terraced, overgrown gardens; cocks crowing . . . how swiftly these things beguiled!

They took his boat, the *Medina,* to a smaller, uninhabited islet that lay to the south. There they swam in a deep place where you could see the bottom three fathoms down. It reminded Anna of a cathedral, with broad shafts of light pouring through limpid water straight onto the sand. Gerhard was in a light-hearted mood: first he ducked her, then held her tightly around the waist. Anna fought until she had no breath left and he had to carry her ashore, thinking it was all in play.

By the time she had toweled herself dry, she was ready to think again. She knew what she had to do. She must find out about his real intentions. Then, if she had to, she would find a way to escape.

"Tell me what you're planning," she said.

"Lunch, followed by a siesta."

"Planning to do about me, I mean." She let him see she was in earnest. "It's all such a mess."

"I've already got in touch with London. We can't do anything until my people reply, so you might as well relax and forget about things for a while."

"I must ring David, make sure he's all right."

She waited in suspense. How would he deal with that?

"I've been thinking about David," he said. "Your Islington phone is almost certainly being monitored. If you try to make contact, you could put him on the spot in a very big way, you know."

"Mm-hm."

So. He didn't want her to contact David. Her heart produced a sickening thump. Anna felt the onset of rage. The fear was still there, yes; but more than anything now she was *angry.*

They lunched simply on fresh fruit, cheese, and luscious "black" wine before sunbathing awhile, scents of jasmine and resin deep in their nostrils and the drone of nearby bees soothing Gerhard to the verge of sleep.

Anna opened one eye. He seemed relaxed, unapprehensive. She had come up with a theory; now was the time to test it. "Holidays," she murmured drowsily. "When I was a child, I never liked them."

"Why do you say that?"

"It always seemed like water behind a dam, a holiday. You'd think about it for ages, savoring every minute before it happened. . . ." She carved out a ball of sand and squeezed it hard.

"Then on the first day there was a trickle of water through the dam, just a few drops that first day, because there were still thirteen more left, weren't there? And tomorrow was going to be the same as today . . . but the trickle became a flood . . . and suddenly all that was left of the water was tears on your face . . . and you'd lost it."

Anna raised her head, pretending to be struck by a thought. "Therapy's a grownup holiday, isn't it? You have sessions, life becomes perfect, but then it fades. Like our affair . . ."

She was conscious of him sitting up. "Any regrets?" he said lightly.

"No. And yes."

"What does that mean?"

"I love David. But the times with you were . . . were so outside normal human existence. So exhausting."

He chuckled. "Thanks."

"You know what I mean. Those days were heavenly. But they faded."

"I . . . hated losing you, you know?"

"I didn't want you to divorce Clara."

"I know. But love, real love, doesn't 'fade,' to use your word. It petrifies. Becomes a monument to something wonderful that was but can no longer be."

Anna squeezed her eyes tight shut. She was analyzing every note, each timbre of his voice, and she knew, she could have cheerfully sworn an oath, that he meant what he said. Somewhere inside he was conscious of personal grief, an emotional ulcer that refused to heal.

Her theory was right. He wanted her all to himself. Wanted her *back.*

After their siesta she swam again, investigating strange channels carved in the rock by the currents of a luminously turquoise sea. Gerhard fetched the boat and they ventured further out.

He sat in the stern, watching Anna alternately swim and dive. The current took her gently away from him, toward the shore. She drifted so far that he did not hear her first scream. Only when she yelled a second time did he jolt upright, his heart thumping. A scream filled with salt water and terror. It fired him to action. He gunned the Johnson 50 and put the *Medina* hard about.

Gerhard grasped everything in a second. Fifty yards of sea separated him from the beach. Anna was racing for the shore. Close behind and swiftly gaining was a long, sinuous shadow.

There were two empty wine bottles left over from lunch. As the

Medina sped off, Gerhard flung them one after the other, timing each to fall ahead of the shadow. Then he picked up an oar and began to beat the water with it.

The engine was howling. He dropped the oar, grabbed the spare petrol can and threw it at the shadow as hard as he could before again starting to thrash the sea. The world wrenched sideways; there was a sudden crack, and Gerhard was falling backward.

He pulled himself up with the aid of a thwart. Not ten feet away from him, the remains of his oar were floating in two pieces. Something had bitten through one and a half inches of seasoned wood as though it were a breadstick.

He scanned the water for yards around, but it was empty: the black shadow had gone. As the pounding in his ears died away he heard Anna start to sob. He saw her crouched on the sand. Thank God . . .

He waded inshore. She ran to him, knocking him over, so that they collapsed in a tangle of arms and legs on the sand.

"I was swimming out there, by the cave. . . ." Her voice sounded flat and low, her eyes looked straight through him. "I dived a couple of times. As I was coming up, I saw . . ." She gnawed her hand. "It was terrible . . . such teeth, such *jaws*. I could *feel* it catching up."

Gerhard chafed her hands, spoke meaningless things.

"What *was* that?"

"I think . . . I'm sure, it was a moray eel. They don't normally attack unless . . . A freak . . ."

She felt herself in a whirl of confusion. Gerhard had somehow become her enemy. But when compared with this terror of the sea, that scarcely seemed to matter any more. Almost without realizing what she was doing, she hugged him tightly. Gerhard laid her down on a towel and began to massage her shoulders with deep, firm strokes. His hands ranged to and fro along her back until he was tired.

You're a fool, she told herself. You shouldn't let him do this. It's wrong. But, oh! how wonderful, how soothing to feel those hands on my skin.

"It's been ages since I massaged you," he murmured. "Do you remember the first time?"

She said nothing, unsought sensual pleasure competing for superiority with a deep-seated fear. *You're such a fool. . . .*

"It was after one of your first dates with David."

In spite of herself she smiled. "The Beethoven concert."

"When you spent all evening wondering what this dry old civil servant would be like in bed."

She tried valiantly to suppress the memories, but they fought through. "And when I got home, and he'd said goodnight, I called you."

"I told Clara one of my patients had been admitted to emergency care. I came . . . and I grabbed you." He laughed softly. "I could sense that all evening you'd been making love to David, in your mind . . . his body, but with my face."

His voice was caressing, scarcely louder than her own. Her affair with Gerhard had all but run its course; it was autumn on the streets and in her life, too. . . . You loved this man once, she reminded herself. In those days he was real.

When Gerhard loosened the strap of her bikini top it felt like being jolted awake in the middle of a macabre dream. Anna tensed. "No."

He began to massage her inner thighs. She pulled herself away, and sat up.

"Really no?" His smile was teasing. *"Really?"*

"That was over, long ago. You know that."

A part of *her* still didn't know it. No man understood how to touch a woman as Gerhard did.

"It wouldn't be important if we made love. Bodies, that's all. Bodies." His voice was agonized, matching his expression.

"And the minds? The emotions, what about them?"

He looked away. He might almost have been ashamed.

"You don't believe people can change, do you?" she snapped. "You—a psychotherapist!"

"You've changed."

"Good."

"Changed enough to come and spend a few days here, on the island. Not many people are privileged to be invited."

"Really? What about the other women? What about . . . ?"

He completed the sentence for her in a whisper. "Robyn."

"My best friend!" Anna wailed. Then, almost immediately— "God! As if that mattered!"

"When you married David you made it clear that you didn't want our affair to continue. Friends, you said: let's just stay good friends. And Robyn was recent—1987."

"There were others in between, you mean?"

"Isn't that as presumptuous as my asking if you love David?" He embraced their idyllic surroundings with a long, slow look before once more facing her. "Do you, by the way?"

His question outraged her to the point where words ceased to flow. "Are you implying," she said at last, "that I set this up? This . . . crude little seaside seduction, you think it was my idea?"

His laugh had degenerated into an uncertain smile. "All I'm saying is that you've changed."

"Yes. I've grown. I've got some self-respect."

"And don't I get any credit for that?"

"You know what you did."

"Certainly, I showed you how to—"

"Make love." She dashed something from the corner of one eye with the back of her hand. *"Fuck."*

Anna snatched up her towel and marched off down the beach. She was angry, she was frightened, she felt utterly exhausted. But at the bottom of that violent, thundering waterfall of emotion, in a cool, protective lagoon of sanity, lay fragments of knowledge that might yet save her life.

The therapist she had put her faith in for sixteen years had no intention of either letting her contact David or releasing her. This marvelous island was nothing but a picture-postcard Alcatraz. If forced to it, he might even use the gun inside his pocket.

Anna could not understand why she felt so certain that the good doctor whom she trusted more than any other man, apart from David, had betrayed her, but her instincts would not be denied. It was as if Christ had invited the disciples to walk on water . . . and then laughed while they sank.

Yet Anna could see a gleam of hope, just one. Gerhard no longer loved her, because you didn't imprison someone you loved. But his hands had told her something important, as they worked along her back.

He still desired her with a passion that was terrible.

CHAPTER 17

Albert had an easy journey to Cornwall; it was a Wednesday, and too early in the year for holiday traffic jams. Once he'd passed Bodmin the roughly turfed, unfenced moor stretched out in every direction, and occasionally he caught sight of dirty sheep grazing by the side of the road, or sheltering in the lee of crude but strong stone walls. Ahead of him, a pale blue sky descended to meet the black moor in a hem of pink and yellow. Puffy clouds danced along, their fat fleeces thinned by the breeze, like balls of cotton being teased into strips. The sun often shone in his eyes, but he did not mind, for after the gloom of London, this was bliss by comparison.

David Lescombe obviously did not know that Albert was following him. The assignment looked as straightforward as could be. Albert's cassettes of *La Bohème* provided the only distraction from what would otherwise have been a boring journey.

He had found New Pendoggett Farm on his Ordnance Survey map and that clearly was David's destination, so he wasn't worried at the prospect of losing him. Now that the country lanes had grown narrow and cars were scarce, it would probably be best if he dropped out of sight for a while; in such a rural district, even Lescombe would eventually manage to figure out that someone was on his tail.

Albert looked at his watch. Lunchtime: what he needed now was a pub, a sandwich, and a pint of real ale. He would drive on to the coast. Perhaps he might even find a fish stall, where he could buy a nice slab of freshly caught cod for Montgomery's supper.

But as they were approaching a village called St. Breward Albert realized for the first time that someone else might be shadowing his quarry, and he swiftly had to revise his plans.

Parked down a side road on the outskirts of the village, near where the road forked, was a black Audi with tinted glass windows. It made little impression on Albert until the other car pulled out almost into him and he hooted angrily. The Audi accelerated, taking the same branch of the fork that David had followed a moment ago.

Albert had to make a split-second decision. He elected to leave them to it and drove on as far as the village post office, where he stopped the car and got out. He put a call through to Fox, quickly establishing that no western intelligence agency was on Lescombe's tail.

"Stay away," Fox warned him. "We don't want you figuring in the opposition's frame, not yet." When Albert said nothing, he went on, "I *said*—"

"I heard you. So long, then."

Albert left the post office, got back in his Morgan and roared away in pursuit of the black Audi.

———

New Pendoggett Farm proved easier to find than David had anticipated. He parked in the yard, got out, and stretched, tired after his long drive. The wind was blustery here; it smelled of the sea. Gulls hovered overhead, calling their penetrating, repetitive cries. A rich smell of horse dung arose from a pile of steaming straw in one corner of the yard, next to the entrance to a corrugated iron barn, piled high with straw.

David made his way over to the house and raised the front door's cast-iron knocker. The "bang" seemed to lose itself at once inside the gray stone walls. No one answered.

Directly opposite, across the yard, stood a low two-story building, which might once have been a generous-sized cow shed. A steady hammering was coming from inside. David advanced to the only visible entrance, a door split horizontally, and pushed on the top half. It swung open to reveal what looked like an old stable, the rusty manger still containing hay.

He stepped inside. A hole had been knocked in the wall.

Through that he could see a large room, barely lit by two windows overlooking fields at the back. A man in a leather apron was sitting astride a bench, still hammering away. He was young, with a faint ginger stubble coating cheeks and chin. Under his apron he wore a vest and a pair of old white jeans, and moccasins on his feet. David looked down to see he was mending a shoe, upended on a last.

"Hello?"

The man went right on working. When David's shadow fell across the shoe he looked up sharply, but without any sign of alarm.

"Hello," David repeated cautiously.

The cobbler's face was ugly. Acne had left its traces on a skin already disfigured by birthmarks. The pallor of his complexion was heightened by red eyelids and lips, the latter dotted with small blood scabs. His arms looked thick and muscular; and even though he wore a vest, David could see how his chest rippled whenever he moved.

"I'm sorry to disturb you. I just wondered if . . ."

But the man started to utter noises: groans and little clicking grunts that made no sense. He pointed inside his mouth, then, using both forefingers, at his ears; all this accompanied by an empty grin.

A deaf mute.

David forced his face into an inane smile and tried to work out what to do. But he was distracted by the thought that Juliet had to live here, with this handicapped man, and God knows who else. The cobbler went across to one of the windows, leaned out and made a succession of hoots. Shortly afterward, a quiet step fell on the threshold and a female voice said, "Who are you?"

David was not sure what to expect. She's living in a commune, Anna had said. They're doing arts and crafts. Someone's given them a grant. Her tone had sounded utterly despairing when she told him that, and he sympathized. Lesbian feminists smoking pot and chucking out the aspirins; or maybe not lesbian, maybe she'd get pregnant. . . .

Here, now, was the reality: a bright-eyed, attractive young woman, whose hair had evidently been washed in the recent past; who wore simple earrings and a wooden cross around her neck on a leather thong; whose Indian shawl came down over a tartan skirt nearly as far as soft leather boots; whose accent identified her at once, with ease and composure, as *all right.*

Her eyebrows struck the only discordant note. They were thick and slanted upward at a sharp angle. She had plucked them until they occupied only a short midsection above each eye. The effect was brutal.

David, relieved despite the eyebrows, said, "I'd like to speak to Juliet."

"Why?"

"I'm her stepfather."

"I asked for a reason, not an ancestry."

The feeling of relief was wearing off. "I have things I want to discuss with her."

"Two I's in one sentence."

"I asked for Juliet, not an English lesson."

"Everyone who lives here does so for a reason." Her voice turned aggressive. "We came to escape from people like you."

"And what am I like?" His voice had started to echo hers for harshness.

"One of those who make demands we're not prepared to meet. Not obliged to meet." She spoke the word "obliged" with her chin thrust forward to challenge him.

"I have news for Juliet."

"You can leave a note, if you want."

"Or I can come back with a policeman."

"Oh yes?" The girl leaned against the door jamb, letting her contempt show. "There's no crime in not wanting to see someone. Not yet."

"She's still under age."

"So buy a court order. Access. *Then* come back."

"To find her gone, I suppose."

"You're starting to get the idea."

David counted his options, found them remarkably few. "All right," he said. "I won't bother with a note. Just give her a message, will you?"

"I don't write blank checks. Tell me what you want to say. If it isn't racist, sexist, or abusive I'll probably pass it on."

"Say: Anna's disappeared, the police are looking for her, I'm worried about her. I'll go back to my car, now. I'll wait a quarter of an hour, then I'll leave, and I shan't come back. That's the message. The whole of it."

He walked toward the door and the girl made way for him. He did not look back until he was sitting in the Rover, quaking with anger and frustration.

"Hello."

He jerked his head around to the left. All he could see through the passenger window was a black-clad torso and an arm. The arm was attached to a hand that was trying to open the nearside door. David released the lock. "Hello, Juliet," he said. "How are you?"

"All right." The torso bent, acquired a head. "Would you like to come for a walk?"

David got out. "Where shall we go?"

"The sea."

She sounded anemic; her voice came trickling out of her skinny body without conviction. Despite the spring warmth around them she must have been cold, for she wore a black roll-neck sweater with a zip-up front and thick black woolen stockings. Around each leg was an eye-blinding turquoise muff: not a leg warmer, too short for that, but perhaps a knee warmer. Ankle-length boots with pointed toes heightened her resemblance to an undernourished elf.

"We'll go through the fields. The farmer doesn't mind."

She led the way down the side of the old cow shed to a stile. Half a dozen fence posts were stacked against it, and Juliet somehow managed to dislodge one of them. David, driven by his innate sense of tidiness, stood the post back up again before following her.

Once over the stile the wind came cold off the sea. Juliet folded her arms across her flattish chest, tucking the hands under her armpits in an effort to keep them from turning red. She stumbled awkwardly between the cow pats, as if her boots hurt her.

"I got your message," she said at last. Her flat, piping voice dissolved away any emotion she might have felt.

"Good. Who was that other girl I saw?"

"Fergie? Did she scare you? She's Sarah, really. But we call her Fergie. Or the duchess. Not to her face, though."

"She doesn't have much of a sense of humor."

"No." Juliet sighed. "You wouldn't, if you'd been through what she has. What's mum up to, then?"

"I don't know. You haven't seen her?"

"Not since Christmas."

They had reached the stone wall that bounded this field and the girl prepared to climb over another stile leading to the next. Once astride it she stopped and said, "Joe keeps a bull here. He's not supposed to, because there's a right of way. You bothered?"

"Are you?"

"No."

David followed her over. What seemed like a long way away,

a huge animal raised its head in his direction and treated him to a thoughtful stare.

"That's the bull?"

"Yes. He's all right. He keeps people away from our beach." But she was moving faster now, and he noticed how she carefully avoided looking in the bull's direction.

It looked as though they were making for the end of the world, like lemmings: ahead of him David could see only blue sky and a black line where the land stopped. At last they came to a wooden staircase, sturdy and painted.

"Watch out here, the rocks are sharp," Juliet said as they reached the bottom. David took off his shoes and socks.

Huge boulders, two or three times higher than a man, lay scattered over a long, narrow expanse of sand the color of wheat. Rollers creamed in to lose themselves in a mess of suds, leaving the beach washed and shining. David had forgotten how loud, how insistent an interrupter the sea could be.

Halfway down the sands lay a round, flat rock. Juliet sat down on it, facing the horizon, and waited until David had settled beside her before she spoke again.

"You made it, then." She kept her face to the front, but he was aware of her eying him surreptitiously. "Not very civil servant-ish."

"Oh, you'd be surprised."

"Would I?" Translation: No I wouldn't, not by you.

David knew better than to rush it. For five minutes he just sat staring out to sea, relishing the feel of salt drying on his face and the deep sough of the sea's constant movement, like the masses preparing for revolution. An angry, impatient sound. He thought of his Nicholson 38 and wondered when next he would sail. He could not imagine it without Anna, and she wasn't coming back. . . .

Why did he think that?

"I'm not what you wanted, am I?" Juliet continued to stare into space, her little-girl voice competing bravely with wind and sea. "Sorry."

He turned and looked at Juliet then, wondering what he did want and how she knew it wasn't her. The girl's red hair hung almost to her waist; it caught the late-afternoon sun in myriad tints, ranging from burnished copper to fine old gold. Her complexion remained pale, despite the healthy outdoor life she mentioned in her rare postcards. Her thin, nervous face still betrayed all the old sensitivity it had shown at five, which was when their destinies had first crossed.

"I thought we got on pretty well," he said lightly.

"You didn't chase me, when I left that bloody school."

"Did you want us to?"

Juliet merely shrugged.

"We discussed it for weeks on end." My God we did, he thought. The only thing Anna and I ever rowed about was you.

"I'll bet."

"Your mother wanted to come after you."

"And you talked her out of it, is that what you're going to say?"

"I talked us *both* out of it," David said firmly. "We thought you were making a mistake. But we decided to leave you to it for a bit."

"Hoping I'd grow up? Grow out of it?"

"Grow into whatever's right for you. How are things, anyway?"

"Oh . . . we live. It's okay in the summer, Sarah says. People buy our stuff. The weaving. Timmy's shoes. Pottery." She hesitated. "There's hardly any money."

David heard the note of apprehension in her voice and felt a twinge of sympathy. "Does that worry you, love?"

"I'm not your love. I don't love anyone." She jumped off the rock and trotted down to the sea's edge, but not before David had heard her say what sounded like "Nobody loves me."

He made himself sit there, watching her dodge the waves, until at last she tired of the lonely game and came back to stand a few yards away from his perch, not quite looking at him, not quite ignoring him either, just hovering, in case there was something to be said, after all.

"Anna hasn't visited you, then?" David had to raise his voice against the sea.

Juliet shook her head.

"Or phoned?"

"No. Why, d'you expect her to?"

"I just thought she might. Nobody knows where she is."

"Run away at last, has she?" There was satisfaction in Juliet's voice. Told you so . . .

"What do you mean, 'at last'?"

"Sorry. Can't help."

"Don't you care?"

Juliet must have heard the tightness in his voice, for she looked

at him for the first time since her spell down by the sea. "No more
than she cares about me."

"She cares about you a lot. She loves you."

"That's why she's run away, is it, without a word to me—
because she loves me? God, thanks!" She came back to the rock,
haughtily tossing her long hair. "Does she love you?"

The words "Of course" sprang to David's lips. But somehow he
ended up saying nothing.

"She doesn't love you." Another pause. "She wouldn't have
left you otherwise, would she?"

David bit his tongue, managed to stay silent.

"Who knows, with mum? She was always . . ."

"Say it."

Juliet shrugged. "I heard her talking to herself, once. At night.
After she met you."

"What did she say?"

"She was wondering what to do with the body, that kind of
crap."

"Body?"

"She had this thing about her body. She didn't want anyone
to find it. If she killed herself."

Silence. Stillness. No sea. No wind. No breathing. Nothing.

Slowly the world came back to him. First the insistent sound
of the waves crashing down to pulverize the sand, then a gull's
shriek, malevolent and dark against the sunny sky, finally the wind.

"Anna talked of killing herself?" he said slowly.

"Once."

"You're sure you didn't get muddled up with something else.
I mean, it is a long time ago."

"It's not the sort of thing you forget, is it? I'm sure, all right."

"Tell me." And when she looked at him, superciliously, without friendship, "Please."

"She just wanted to . . . disappear. She didn't rate herself, mum
didn't."

"No." He remembered. "Not when I first met her."

"You think you changed anything?"

"I think so. I loved her." He paused. Then he said, almost
humbly, "I love her."

"Maybe. I was never there. Perhaps she . . . I don't know. She
was always loopy." She eyed him as if struggling to work out a
complicated piece of mental arithmetic in which he figured some-

where as a cipher. "Have you seen her shrink?"

"Her what?"

"Shrink. Psycho-whatsit."

David swallowed. "Anna was seeing a psychiatrist? Before we met?"

"Yes."

"But . . . why?"

Juliet shrugged. "Don't know."

For the second time that afternoon wind and waves receded, to be replaced by the cotton-wool deadness of shock. When he came to himself, Juliet was saying, ". . . look through her diaries, in the holidays. She never knew. She always had these dates with G., always on a Thursday evening. I just thought it was a friend. But then it bugged me, not knowing. One day there was this phone number against the G.; I think he must have changed houses or something."

He waited, but Juliet seemed to think she had communicated everything of importance. "And?"

"I rang the number. This woman answered. 'Mr. Somebody's consulting rooms,' that's what she said."

"You don't remember the name?"

She shook her head. "The receptionist said it so fast. 'Who is this?' she asked. And I said, 'I want a consultation.' And she said, 'Who is your G.P. and do you have a referral?' And I said, 'Not yet.' And she said, 'To see a psycho-something you need a referral,' but I just heard 'psycho,' see, that was enough. I put the phone down. Mum's barmy, I thought." She sighed, a great long shudder that rose from the depths.

David slipped off the rock and marched down to the sea.

He rejected all that Juliet had said. His wife was a barrister, sane and successful in a mad world. Her grip on things was total. And they had no secrets from each other, none whatsoever; the openness of their shared existence was almost tedious. If Anna had consulted a psychiatrist before they met he would have known about it. Surely?

Yes, but it would explain a lot. Suppose Anna wasn't at fault? What if she was very sick . . . hence the vodka bottle in her desk, the writ alleging negligence that wasn't negligence at all, but illness . . .

But why had she never told him?

It seemed she had never confided in her daughter, either. Poor

Juliet. A somber thought entered his mind: how would it be for her if Anna never came back? He remembered reading harrowing stories of people who just disappeared, leaving their families not knowing whether they were alive or dead.

How would it be for him?

David swung around to find that the rock he and Juliet had occupied was now empty.

"Juliet!" he cried. The wind took his voice, nullifying it. Then he caught sight of her at the cliff stairway, and he began to run. But he had to detour in order to collect his shoes and socks, so that by the time he caught up with her she was already striding across the field.

The bull seemed closer this time.

"Juliet, listen to me. I need to talk to you. Oh, for Christ's sake, can't you slow down?"

She shook her head and ploughed on.

"Juliet, you have to hear what I've got to say. Your mother . . ." Suddenly his ankle turned awkwardly, making him stumble. "Your mother took something when she left. Something of mine. A file . . ."

Juliet was running. For an instant David did not understand her sudden urgency. Then he heard the beat of hooves and, ignoring the pain in his ankle, started to sprint.

The girl side-vaulted the stile, landed in a crouch and tumbled over, clutching her knee. David, still twenty or so yards from the wall, dared not look around. His throat was dry with terror. His chest hurt. He tried desperately to listen for hooves but the blood coursing through his eardrums blotted out all other sounds. Ten yards. Five. Then he was clutching the top bar of the stile, his stomach pressed against it. As he brought up the left foot to complete the crossing, his toe caught in a rung and he fell down beside Juliet, banging his forehead on the ground.

Only by screwing up every muscle in his face did he manage to keep himself from blubbing like a kid. He had wrenched a muscle in his right thigh and his arm rippled with fiery pains where he'd landed on it.

He sat up. Through the stile he could see nothing. There was no bull. Not without difficulty, David managed to haul himself back to the vertical. The bull had changed position, but now he was unconcernedly plucking at a patch of long grass. David realized that for most of his sprint he had been chased by a phantom.

He wheeled around to catch sight of Juliet's face contorted into a scowl. She backed away, fists clenching and unclenching by her sides.

"You say mum took a file. Stole it, you mean?"

"Look—"

"You're accusing her of being a thief, stealing government papers." Her eyes blinked, two tears jetted down her cheeks. "How can you do that, David? You . . . *shit*!"

She broke into a run, sobbing. When David tried to follow, another shaft of fire sprang up his leg, crippling him. Purple patches floated before his eyes. He swore, then limped after her in the direction of the farm.

By the time he got there the sun had mellowed to an orange disk, bathing the yard in flame. As he made his way around the gate he found himself confronted by a wrathful trio: Juliet, the girl called Fergie, and Timmy the deaf mute.

"Get in." Fergie jerked a thumb toward his car. "Don't stop till you hit the road." She was seething with rage. "If you come back, we'll call the police."

"I want to talk to my stepdaughter," he grated.

Sarah tapped Timmy on the arm, and when he looked at her she pointed toward David. The cobbler advanced slowly, still carrying his hammer.

"Are you threatening me?"

"We're exercising the right to have you off our premises."

"*Your* premises? Don't make me laugh!"

"We've had enough of you. And your German friends. Tell them to stay away, d'you hear?"

"David . . ." Juliet's voice sounded fearful. "Just . . . *go.*"

"Not until we've talked. Talked properly."

Timmy was within a foot of David now. He stopped and uttered a selection of horrid grunts, culminating in a drawn-out moan. His eyes were fishlike, cold. He looked brutish.

"I want to talk to Juliet," David said quietly, but with great force; and Timmy hit him.

He did not use the hammer, which was as well or David would have been killed. Instead, he dropped the tool on the cobbles and punched David's jaw. David saw the blow coming and ducked, but Timmy's fist landed on his forehead, setting off a fresh round of explosions in his already damaged skull. He swayed groggily, once more unable to see straight.

Timmy came at him again, butting into his stomach. David doubled up with an "ouf!" of pain and fell to his knees. While he fought to regain control he found himself looking up at Timmy, silhouetted against the sky. The deaf mute clasped his hands and raised them above his head.

Before the blow could connect, however, it was intercepted.

Another black figure had come to stand behind the first, with something long in his hands. This object swung through a horizontal plane into the small of Timmy's back. The shape dissolved, reorganized itself, and the shaft came down vertically to land on the cobbler's left shoulder. David heard a crack. Timmy collapsed to the ground, holding his neck while he rocked to and fro. Above him . . .

Above him, Albert was practicing off-drives with considerable *élan,* using for bat the fence post that had just broken Timmy's collarbone. "Evening," he said, catching David's eye. "Get in the car, will you, be a good chap."

As David staggered away he heard Albert ask engagingly, "Any more for any more? Come on, don't be shy." But the two girls backed off, numbed by the controlled, precisely directed violence radiating from this stranger. Albert threw away the stake and came around the front of the car to let himself in. "Right," he said as he slid into the passenger seat. "Off sharpish, yes, mm?"

David put the Rover into gear. The last thing he saw through the rear-view mirror was Juliet running forward to help Timmy up while Sarah continued to stand rooted to the spot.

"You do get yourself into some scrapes. Ouch! As indeed . . . do I. What on earth . . . ?" Albert felt underneath him. His hand emerged holding a white paper bag. "Chocolates?"

"Juliet's favorites." David sighed. "I didn't even get a chance . . ."

"Never mind."

Until this moment David had been driving on automatic pilot. Now he started to come to himself. "Er . . . thanks." He paused, embarrassed by the inadequacy of his reaction. "You may have saved my life back there."

It was true, he realized. If he was able to drive away from New Pendoggett Farm it was all due to Albert. This man was going out of his way to help. He felt gratitude flood through him without knowing how to express it. "Do you have a car?" he asked awkwardly.

"Yes, I left it at the gate. There it is, beside the postbox."

David pulled over next to Albert's Morgan and switched off the engine. "It was really lucky you arrived when you did."

"Coincidence, wasn't it?"

"You were sent to interview Juliet, I suppose?"

"Mm-hm. Doesn't seem much point now, does there?" Albert sighed. "David, David, David, what are we going to do with you?"

He was wearing cavalry twill trousers, a checked shirt, knitted tie and a riding jacket, while a tweed cap was pulled well forward over his eyes, its brim almost resting on the tops of his flattened spectacles. It occurred to David that it would be difficult for the communards to describe Albert's face to the police.

"Do with me? I don't understand. We agreed I ought to try and find out as much as I could."

"Yes, but not by using the third degree."

"*They* attacked *me!*"

He felt almost churlish, defending himself against his savior, but Albert seemed not to mind. "What did you manage to extract from Juliet, before the fracas?" he asked.

"Very little. She hasn't seen Anna, nor heard from her."

"Was she telling the truth, do you think?"

"Yes." David opened his mouth to tell Albert what Juliet had said about the mysterious doctor, but to his surprise heard himself say instead, "Why did that girl mention German friends?"

"I wondered if you'd taken that on board. Mean anything to you?"

"No." David knew he ought to tell Albert about the "psycho-whatsit," as Juliet had called him. It was important. But because it was so important he wanted to think about it first. To package it. Construct some way of passing on the information that wouldn't make him out a complete idiot for not having known. "I don't have any German friends."

But Anna did! Brewster, the chairman of the Krysalis vetting committee, had said so.

"Did Juliet say if anybody else had been snooping around asking questions?"

"No."

"German friends, now. Anna Lescombe, whatever are you up to?"

David wanted to ask what was going through Albert's mind but the other man forestalled him by abruptly getting out of the car. "Be seeing you, then," he said through the window.

As David watched him start the Morgan he suddenly resolved not to tell anyone about Anna's psychiatrist.

CHAPTER

18

Barzel drummed his fingers on the steering wheel while he stared through the windshield down the road that Lescombe must surely use. He looked at his watch. Dusk already; soon it would be dark. He desperately wanted the by-now-familiar Rover to appear within the next ten minutes. Once night fell, he could easily miss it.

A mistake, wasting today. For two pfennigs he'd give up, now, and catch the next plane to Corfu . . . only then he remembered what was at stake, and resolved to give David those extra few minutes. *He had to know if Lescombe was part of Kleist's plot.*

But things were going badly. If he had been a superstitious man he might have believed that some unseen power was on Kleist's side. He'd had to use an HVA charter jet to fly back to London from Athens the night before. First they had run into headwinds and then a thunderstorm. The pilot wanted to divert, until he saw Barzel's gun. Then he changed his mind, which was all right in one way but Barzel's stomach still heaved at the memory of their landing.

He'd driven down to Cornwall early, after snatching a couple of hours' sleep, on the strength of an update that told him David Lescombe was planning to visit his stepdaughter. Before getting entangled with David, Barzel wanted to put to rest an ugly hunch

that had occurred to him overnight: that the blonde woman with
Kleist wasn't Anna Lescombe at all, but a decoy, deliberately chosen
to lead him away from his real quarry. The Cornish farm where
Juliet lived was said to be out in the wilds. Suppose Anna was
shacked up there; what in hell would *that* signify?

He'd prowled around the farm boundary, keeping out of sight.
A lot of people seemed to live there; too many for Barzel's liking.
Anna wasn't among them, or if she was, she certainly didn't show
herself.

He was making his way back to the Audi when two people
stepped out into his path: a ferocious-looking dyke and a male
humanoid who communicated only in grunts.

"What do you want?" the woman snapped. When he didn't
answer immediately, she'd asked the same question in fluent German, catching Barzel on the raw. He prided himself on how well he
fitted into the landscape.

"You're trespassing," she went on. "Clear off or I'll call the
police.

"My dear young lady—"

"Shove that! Timmy . . ."

The humanoid had advanced threateningly. Barzel looked
down and noticed for the first time that he was carrying a wicked-
looking hammer. "Can I speak to Juliet?" he'd asked quickly.
"That's all I want to do. I've got a message from her mother."

"Have you indeed?" the girl sneered. "You can give it to me,
then."

"It's not written down."

"Tell me what you want to say."

"No. It's private."

"Timmy, junk this pig."

The humanoid grunted in what sounded like satisfaction. Barzel swiftly weighed up the situation. The only sure way out was to
draw his gun and he didn't feel like doing that—too risky; once he'd
gone they'd call the police for sure. Retreat.

Now, sitting in the Audi and waiting for David to drive around
the corner, Barzel regretted that hasty departure. If only he'd been
able to bring some muscle . . . but with Krysalis on the move, no
one knew where, HVA's London Station was stretched to its limit.

He looked at his watch. Something had to go right today. The
thought of having wasted twenty-four hours was too terrifying to
contemplate.

Where had Lescombe got to?

His question was answered almost immediately. A Rover came around the bend, accelerating past him. Barzel started the engine and pulled out of the side road where he'd been parked. Before long his Audi had settled down a hundred yards behind David's tailgate. Barzel tried to remember the geography. They would go through a village—St. Breward, wasn't it?—after which came a winding lane some half a mile long. That's where he'd take him, before he got to the next main road.

The light was fading quickly now. David had his headlights on, but for the moment Barzel contented himself with parking lights, not wanting to draw attention to himself.

Here was the village. . . . David picked up a little speed along the straight high street, then had to slow for an awkward turn beside a pub.

Now they were in the road that Barzel remembered. David's lights fashioned a dull yellow aurora, which preceded the silhouette of his car down a dark tunnel. He came to the start of a twisting, narrow hill and braked, careful to protect his paintwork from the sheer stone walls, thick with moss, bounding what here was little wider than a single-track lane.

By this point it was dark. Barzel glanced in his mirror. No lights visible. His gaze darted back to the front. *Now!*

As the Audi overtook, David was forced to jam on his brakes. His reactions were swift, but not quite good enough: he went slamming into the offside wall. Stone shrieked against metal. Barzel left him no time in which to worry about the cost of a respray. He slammed the Audi to a halt diagonally across the lane a few yards ahead of Lescombe and opened the door.

He began to walk back toward the Rover, hand already moving to his pocket.

David wound down his window. "What do you want?"

Barzel made no reply. The Rover's engine was still running. David suddenly engaged reverse and let off the handbrake. The car began to move backward. Barzel swore. He knew it wouldn't be easy maneuvering the car up that hill, but he also recognized that as long as Lescombe kept his speed low he might manage it.

Then Lescombe made the mistake of revving the engine and the car jumped against the wall with another expensive-sounding crunch. He slammed on his brakes. The engine complained, telling Barzel that he'd wrenched the shift too hard, putting the Rover into third instead of first. The car lurched forward, came within an ace of a stall.

David let out the clutch, letting his Rover slide forward out of contact with the wall. He still had his headlights on. Barzel stood in the center of their beam with his legs apart and arms outstretched, knowing Lescombe would be able to see how his arms culminated in a point. A black, stubby point, with a barrel and a sight . . .

The Rover's engine coughed and died. Barzel kept the gun leveled while he came alongside. "Get out."

"Who the hell are you to tell me to—?"

Barzel yanked open the door and reached in with both hands to haul David out by the lapels, keeping the pistol rammed against his jaw. He spun him around and hurled him against the side of the Rover.

"Do what I tell you," Barzel rasped. "If you do anything except what I tell you to do, you will be shot. Understand?"

David, still trying to catch his breath, nodded.

"You will stand upright—*wait!* I will tell you when to move. Stand upright, place your hands on top of your head, walk toward the Audi. Do not look at me. Look straight ahead until you reach the Audi. Then stop. Got it?"

"Yes."

"Move!"

David put his hands on top of his head and turned. "Do not look at me," Barzel cautioned him again; his voice had risen in pitch, revealing how edgy he was.

David began to walk toward the other car. He stumbled, and Barzel knew he was afraid. *Good!* He swiveled in such a way as to keep his target permanently within range. Ten yards to the Audi. Five yards . . .

"Stop. Place your hands on the lid of the trunk. Keep them well apart."

David complied.

Barzel was about to speak again when he heard something. He swung around, looking back past the Rover. Surely his ears hadn't deceived him? Nothing mechanical, no engine: it wasn't a car. Yet there was something. . . .

He hesitated. While he was still trying to work out what to do, somewhere behind the Rover a horn hooted and lights came on. Barzel, looking straight at them through the windshield of David's car, flinched. In the next split second he thought he saw a human figure rolling to one side of the road. Then—"David!" a voice yelled. "Get down!"

Three shots shattered the night peace in quick succession. Barzel flung himself to the ground and fired at random beneath the Rover.

Hopeless! No target, into the lights . . . out, out, *out!*

Next second Barzel had rolled to one side and was diving into his Audi. Mercifully he'd left the engine running. As his tires screeched and he disappeared around the next tight corner, his brain was already supplying him with a series of sickening truths.

Someone was "minding" Lescombe. That someone had switched off both engine and lights while still short of the Rover, coasting down to take up position in total silence. It was prescient, it was well executed, and it betrayed a degree of professional daring when pitted against an armed assailant that Barzel found very frightening.

He struggled to keep the Audi on the road, but all the while his mind kept active. He didn't like failure. The more people tried to stop him, the more determined to succeed he became. One thing was clear. David Lescombe couldn't be the mere innocent cipher they'd taken him for up to now, not if MI5 went to such lengths to protect him. He was a key player.

Lescombe would have to be fixed.

THURSDAY

CHAPTER

19

Albert knew a great deal about butchery. He had been studying it, on and off, for years.

Knives, they were the important thing: buy a good one and keep it sharp. His knife had saved him and the squadron more than once, on ops. Such delightful games their masters loved to play: drop a handful of bods into Libya, single ticket, find your own ways home, last one in's a sissy. . . . "Fortnight of sun and sand, gentlemen, there's them as would give their right hands . . ." Oh yes, it was a man's life in the army. As long as you had a tempered steel blade, however, you need not starve. Albert's Sabatier had lived with him since Oxford days, although it was much thinner than of yore. Now it resembled a bodkin rather than a kitchen knife. He kept the blade keen enough to kill, skin and chop a snake, but today *ossi buchi* were on the menu and veal required less of an edge. Albert had cultivated the same butcher for years, until he could be assured of getting meat from a calf under three months old. Later he would use the same knife to chop parsley for the *gremolata*, which strictly speaking was against the rules, but a well-honed knife would always forgive.

He had just poured the remains of a bottle of Soave around the browned meat and was turning his attention to chicken broth for the *risotto alla Milanese* when the entry phone buzzed. He glanced up at the clock. Fox was early, no doubt a ploy designed to throw Albert off balance. Why did even the best MI5 staffers suffer from simple-mindedness?

"Visitors, Montgomery," he murmured. "And get your filthy nose out of that carcass. . . ."

As he went to the front door his mind was busily reviewing the pitch. This interview would be critical, he knew, and he experienced an unusual tingling in his stomach. A lot had come to ride on the Lescombe case. This morning there was an axe to grind as well as a kitchen knife.

Today Fox managed to look more than ever like an operator of risqué nightclubs. He raised his eyebrows at the sight of Albert wearing a plastic apron. "Do Lea & Perrins pay people to advertise their sauce like that?"

"You live in a fantasy world. I can see you've never bought an apron."

"Never worn one, either. Did I interrupt anything?" Fox sounded arch, as if he suspected Albert might be wearing lacy underwear beneath the laminate.

"No. Come in. Wait . . ." Albert went back into the kitchen, where he put a lid over the dish and stuck it in the fridge.

"Entertain a lot, do you?" Fox had followed him and was watching with scarcely disguised admiration.

"No." Albert took off his apron. "But I like food and I don't have the necessary physical coordination to cope with a tin opener."

They went back to the living room. "Nice place," Fox said as he sat down. "Watercolors . . . nice. What's that one?"

"It's a Callow. John, unfortunately; not William. Nineteenth-century seascape."

"And the one next to it? *Very* striking."

"I did that. Hobby. I see you're allergic to cats."

Montgomery had entered the room, sniffed and made a beeline for Fox, who now was viewing him without enthusiasm.

"Well . . ."

Albert made no attempt to remove Montgomery, who had put his front paw on Fox's trouser leg in preparation for a leap onto his unwelcoming lap. "Have you read my Cornish notes?"

Fox was wearing a two-piece suit today, but habit still sent his hands to nonexistent waistcoat points. Albert monitored the nervous tic with interest. A man who could not change his ways was a marked man. Never mind that; Fox has the power to change your life, he reminded himself. Watch your manners, Albert.

"We've all read them."

"The Yanks as well, I trust?"

"Oh yes. There's a daily copy command out." Fox hesitated. "They're not best pleased with our failure to recover the file," he admitted at last.

Good, thought Albert. Progress . . .

"What do you make of this man Lescombe?"

"He's well-meaning."

"Well-meaning . . ." Fox gave the word some consideration. "I gather you trust him, from that. Do I? Look, would you mind if I put this cat . . . ?"

Montgomery curled his claws into Fox's trousers and began to purr contentedly. Dots of fat, products of the recent frying, had settled on Albert's spectacles. Now he tore a square of wafer-thin lens tissue from a booklet on the dresser and cleaned them, in no hurry to answer. "It's unlikely that Lescombe's a traitor, or involved with his wife in this," he said at last. "She's rotten to the core, of course. But the problem with him's different: he can't be trusted not to get in the way. Do put Montgomery down, if you're worried about your suit."

Fox lifted the cat as if he feared it might be radioactive and lowered him to the carpet. "Do you want us to clear you a path?" he asked.

"Not necessary. Yet. Anyway, it looks as though the opposition may save us the trouble."

"Mm? Oh, the man in the Audi, you mean?"

Now we're coming to it, Albert thought. Softly, softly.

"You made a mistake there," Fox said, with some satisfaction. "You're *not* in favor. I warned you: keep a low profile."

"What was I supposed to do—let that bandit highjack Lescombe?"

"No, but shooting—"

"I fired in the air, to avoid hitting our man. The guy returned fire, then he took off. Where's the risk?"

"The risk is that by drawing attention to Lescombe you'll succeed in turning him into a target. We don't want that. We want him to run and keep on running."

"So? He's still on two legs this morning, isn't he?"

"All right, you were lucky. You may not be lucky a second

time. We're providing him with discreet cover from now on. Just in case. *Down,* puss."

"Good idea. I approve. Listen, this is getting out of hand."

"Yes, I'm sorry, I don't really like cats. . . ."

"The *case* is getting out of hand. I don't have a role. A function. Use me or lose me."

"You're still on hold."

"Then it's time I came off it." When Fox looked away, Albert pressed home his advantage. "Give me a commitment. Anna Lescombe has to be neutralized, you know it, I know it. So do you want me or not? If yes, let's agree on a price."

Fox was silent. Albert interpreted this favorably and felt another twinge of excitement. "What about it?" he said.

"Not everybody's keen on the idea of making use of your services for this one."

"Don't kid me! The Americans are *bursting* to see some action."

"Then let them arrange it."

"On your turf? I don't think so."

"Mm."

"Well, it's up to you." Albert affected not to care, although he knew he was being undervalued. No SAS officer was obliged to accept a nonterrorist contract to kill. Few would do so. Albert was by far and away the best of the few.

"They'd like to see me back down in Hereford," he said smoothly. "I was talking to the adjutant only this morning."

"Don't . . . go back just yet."

"Price?"

Fox's hands strayed to the imaginary waistcoat, withdrew. "I'm authorized to agree on your price, but on a purely theoretical basis."

Albert fought to keep his face expressionless. "Meaning?"

"Meaning that you're not authorized to act independently and we don't want you playing Cowboys and Indians in country lanes. Any more of that and the deal's off. Got it?"

Albert nodded. Fox, seeing his host on the point of speaking again, continued quickly: "I had a session with the lady's G.P. yesterday, while you were shooting up Cornwall."

Despite his disappointment, Albert was interested. "And?"

"He prescribed the pills in the bottle. He said she'd only asked for sleeping tablets once, more than a year ago."

"Before that?"

"Nothing. Anna Lescombe's been his patient for approximately nine years, since moving to the Islington address. She changed doctors when she married."

"But this new doctor must have her previous records?"

"He doesn't. He filled in the forms, but somehow they never turned up. Happens all the time, apparently. At least, that's his version." Fox sniffed. "Did you know doctors come high on the list of alcoholics?"

"That kind of doctor?"

Fox nodded. "You don't look surprised."

"I'm not." Albert's voice was cold; Fox had touched on one of his bugbears. "We used to be able to trust professionals in this country. Now they're like everyone else."

"The 'going to the dogs' syndrome? Funny, I thought you took a more positive view of things."

"What are you doing about this sot of a doctor?"

"We'll catch up with the records eventually." Fox heaved a sigh. "But it won't be tomorrow or the next day. Matchups with national insurance numbers, that kind of thing."

"Seems to me I can stand down, then?" Albert could not keep the sulkiness out of his voice. Agreeing on a price was one thing, but if they weren't going to let him get on with the job that didn't amount to a row of beans.

"No. You're working well. Apparently Mr. Hayes likes your literary style." Fox's expression was withering. "On the ball, that's how he described you."

Albert felt a fresh glimmer of hope, but this was no time to let Fox see that. "On *what* ball? Lescombe screwed up any prospect we might ever have had of learning something from his stepdaughter; the lady pulled the wool over the eyes of her lawyerly colleagues . . . this case is crying out for someone to get after that bloody woman."

"Even if Five and Six both agreed, where would you look for her?"

"Why don't you let me go to Athens, sniff around?"

"Because there are already plenty of people working on the Greek lead."

"What brief has Six sent to Athens station?"

"Find out who's going in to ask about faxes every day, follow him, get us a name. Oh, of course—you haven't heard."

"Heard what?"

"Athens-Six came up with something. There *was* someone who fitted the description. Young Greek chap, very interested in this fax office."

Albert leaned forward. "Well?"

"They lost him. But they'll find him again."

"I'll bet! What a waste of time."

"So how fortunate it is that we have something much more important for you to do."

"Which is?"

"Lunch." Fox stood up, evidently glad to have an excuse for moving down range of Montgomery's haughty stare. "Sorry to spoil your culinary arrangements"—he nodded in the direction of the kitchen—"but the department would like you to eat lunch today. It being Thursday. Oh, and whatever you may have heard, there is such a thing as a free one."

CHAPTER

20

Anna knew she had to escape.

She set her wrist-watch alarm to wake her very early on Thursday morning, when she felt sure that Gerhard would still be asleep. The previous evening she had made herself be agreeable, pretending that she forgave him for his insulting behavior on the beach, and they had caroused together until late. Her head still ached from all the *retsina* they had drunk: those artful glass containers, like beer bottles, with no need for a corkscrew . . .

Cautiously she peered into the passage. No sign of Gerhard. She tiptoed to the front door, silently turned the handle, and eased her way out. If he caught her now, she could pretend she was just going for a walk. Down the path . . . careful with the gate . . .

She was on the track, running. Left at the road, through the village. Don't look back.

Although the sun shone down from a cloudless sky Anna scarcely felt it. What she did feel was the first stirrings of nausea, a sickness far beyond any alcoholic hangover. She only fell ill when she resolved to go away from Gerhard; the same thing had happened the day before yesterday. Something evil implanted inside her brain . . .

She wiped her face. The back of her hand came away wet, sweat or tears, she could not tell. She was her own last resource: beyond help.

The walk was a long one. When she had been on the move for over an hour, the sound of a car distracted her. She looked back hopefully. But soon she realized that the engine noise came from a section of road above and parallel to the one she was on. Anna caught a glimpse of red paintwork. The Fiat belonging to Yorgos was that color. Gerhard, on his way in search of her . . .

She ran down the bank and hid behind a tree, gulping in deep breaths. She heard a noisy gear change; then the car was on the strip of road she had just left, passing over her head before disappearing toward the harbor. Anna slid further down the slope to rejoin the road. She continued to descend through the olive groves, traversing the road twice more before it became straight and ran through the outskirts of the port. She could see the quay; beyond that, a thin line of choppy cobalt-blue water and, in the distance, a green and mauve hill.

But Gerhard was ahead of her.

Anna sank down at the side of the road, afraid she might faint. What would he do when he failed to find her?

The answer to her question came almost at once. She heard a car's engine start. Anna ran off the road, hugging a boundary wall, to conceal herself behind someone's house. She peered around the wall in time to catch sight of the Fiat as it roared along the road and disappeared up the hill. She waited for the silence to resume sway before emerging from her hiding place.

Dimly she began to perceive the beginnings of a strategy. The ferry left at five, Gerhard had told her that. Wait under cover until ten to, then make a dash for it.

You can meet the ferry, but so will he.

He can't use his gun in front of other people.

Thoughts of Gerhard served only to confuse her. Who *was* he? What did he intend to do with her? Why had he brought her to this place—to seduce her, as he had tried to do the day before? To rape her; was that the purpose of the gun? Gerhard the psychotherapist, suddenly transformed into the rapist . . .

No. All that could have been stage-managed in London. She was on the wrong track. But *why . . . ?*

Anna wanted to get well away from the road. As she looked around anxiously, three old Greek women came down the hill. They wore what Anna had come to think of as "the uniform": two all in black, right down to their stockings, the other in dark blue. They did not walk so much as hump, or limp; each had her own distinctive way of moving, but there was nothing fluid about any of them.

These women carried plastic shopping bags; from the tops of one of them peeped a towel. They were going for a swim! One of the trio treated Anna to a sharp-eyed, inquisitive glance from gleaming black eyes, and nodded. *"Kalimera!"* she rasped in a throaty voice.

"Kalimera."

The other two women sang out the word, but not in unison, each treating it differently, *"Kal-ee-mai-rah! . . . Kalim'ra."* Then the first woman beckoned her. "Swim," she declared throatily. "You! Come!" She beckoned again, this time with a smile, but as imperiously as ever. Anna took a step forward. "Thank you," she said. *"Ef haristo."*

The Greek women cackled and walked on. They knew of a side road that skirted the main square. Before long, to Anna's unspeakable relief, she found herself following a winding footpath up the side of the hill opposite the port, protected from curious eyes by the olive trees that seemed to cover every square inch of this island. After a while the path petered out, so that by herself she would not have had the faintest idea which direction to take, although her guides seemed unperturbed. The going was rough, but just when she thought she couldn't manage another step, they breasted the hill and started to slip and slide their way down the seaward slope. The port had been left well behind them. For the first time since leaving the villa, Anna almost felt safe.

At the bottom of the hill they came upon a shingly beach. The old ladies found a patch of shade for their things, then disappeared, each behind a separate olive tree, only to emerge a moment later clad in surprisingly garish bathing suits and sunhats. One by one they ploughed into the sea, still wearing their floral bonnets. The eldest waved vigorously at Anna, who shook her head, indicating with the help of sign language that she had no swim things. She sat under a tree and watched them wallow: three genteel Greek hippos.

Despite her anxiety, Anna found herself fantasizing about what it was like to be old on this island, without ever having known an alternative world: born here, courted, married, and one day buried, all within the same enclosed society. Maybe their husbands had given them fine, lusty sons to look after them when they were old; they looked like mothers.

Somewhere, perhaps, her own mother still walked the earth. Now, as she watched the three old ladies, Anna felt stir within her the familiar longing: to seek her out, take her by the hands, ask her: Why? Why did you abandon me, you whose task it was to love me most? What had I done?

The law would help her do it. But there was something the law could not do: provide the necessary courage, and that was lacking.

The ladies floated inshore, where finally they beached. They offered Anna fruit, which she declined, accepting only a drink of water. There was much banter directed at her, which she bore in good part, not understanding a word of it. After a while, however, the trio fell silent and, as if at a prearranged signal, dropped off to sleep.

Anna stayed awake, too frightened to relax. Sometimes the day seemed to pass slowly, sometimes fast. *Why didn't the ferry come?* She had to escape; but Gerhard would be waiting. . . .

Suddenly one of the women stretched, yawned, and rolled up into a sitting position. She murmured a few words, looking out to sea. Anna scanned the horizon. A dark smudge had appeared far out on the strait, a smudge trailing smoke.

She looked at her watch. Four-fifteen.

The ladies were packing up, thank God! That meant she would be able to stay with them until the last moment. Anna followed them homeward. At the brow of the hill she paused, surveying the port that lay spread out below like a model village. No sign of the red Fiat.

She walked quickly, soon outstripping her companions, who clucked and muttered pleasant-sounding goodbyes as she passed. Anna arrived back in the port to find it coming to life after the siesta. Two noisy motor bikes, driven by youthful, unshaven Zorbas, dusted the quay. The owner of the one small boutique was setting out her wares. Earlier that day Anna had noticed a travel agent's located in the same building that housed this boutique; on a blackboard outside were chalked fares to the mainland and other tidbits of information designed to appeal to seemingly nonexistent tourists.

Anna slowly made her way around the boutique's scarf rack and past a revolving stand for paperbacks, until she was on the threshold of the travel agent's office. The agent himself, one of those middle-aged men who like to keep themselves fit, pulled in his gut at the sight of her and smiled.

"Do you speak English?"

"Off coss."

"I have to get back to England. Today. Can you help?"

"Cer-tin-lee. Yiss." He stood aside, extending his right arm in what was meant to be a gesture of welcome, but he overdid it and succeeded only in looking like a policeman on traffic duty. He started to say something about ferries and flights, how they didn't connect. Anna tried hard to make sense of his fractured English. "So what I want is a . . . a boat ticket to Corfu, then a taxi to the airport, right?"

"Yiss. Plin tick-ay you muss' buy at airpore."

"Do you take plastic? American Express?"

When he shook his head, Anna gazed at him in terror. She had no local currency. Panic came flooding back. *She could not get off the island.*

Seeing the look on her face, the Greek smiled. "You haff poun'? Ingliss poun'?"

"Yes!" She burrowed in her purse. "Here, take them! Is it enough?"

He counted the notes, pursed his lips, and sold her a ferry voucher with enough reluctance to suggest that he was doing her a favor, instead of awarding himself a three hundred percent mark-up. Anna almost ran out into the square, now alive with many voices. Where to go?

The concrete pier was merely an extension of the road, which itself shaded into being the square. At the end nearest the sea was a wedge-shaped hump, used for loading and unloading vehicles when the ferry docked. Several other passengers were already sitting on it, ready to embark as soon as the boat arrived. Now the motor bikes she had seen earlier zoomed back and the Zorbas began preparing them for embarkation, *good!* People, machines, there was a three-wheel cart stacked high with cardboard boxes, the more cover the merrier . . .

Anna looked at her watch. A quarter of an hour still to go. Ah, the boutique! She would stay in the shop until the ferry had actually tied up, wait until they were ready to lift the gangplank, then make a dash for it. She swiveled and saw the ship's bow, its white paintwork flecked with rust, clear the cape. *Wonderful!*

As she reached the boutique's doorway, however, she heard a

car and out of the corner of her eye caught sight of a red flash. Gerhard was here! She began to pick her way along the center table, nervously turning over keyrings and shells. After a moment she became aware of someone watching her.

Anna jerked her head up. The owner of the shop, a woman in her mid-thirties, wore large round spectacles, lending her an owly look. She continued to stare at Anna in dignified silence, occasionally moving her head as if to give her great round lenses a better shot at their target.

A car door slammed. Anna jumped. The lenses shifted slightly, taking note. By maneuvering herself through the narrow gap between the Greek woman and the far end of the table, Anna was able to look through the window without seeming to. What she saw made her legs tremble. The ferry was reversing up to the pier. But between her and salvation Gerhard stood with arms folded across the car's roof while he surveyed the crowd.

Anna heard the woman stir and thought, Christ, she knows Gerhard.

The woman eased past her, obviously intending to go outside. "Excuse me . . ."

Anna had spoken in such a servile whisper that the boutique's owner did not hear. "Excuse me!" This time her voice was a shout. The shopkeeper turned back, the glasses magnifying her eyes as they widened in surprise until the owlish effect was almost comical.

"Excuse me, this smock, do you call it a smock only I've never seen one before . . . ?"

Anna held the garment up between her and the window, lest Gerhard chose to turn around. She could not stop grinning like a manic guide in pursuit of a tip. The owner hesitated, then reluctantly came back.

A movement on the other side of the window tore at Anna's gaze. Gerhard stood upright before striding off to the left, in the direction of the biggest taverna. She dropped the smock and rushed for the exit, stepping on the shopkeeper's foot. She didn't stop until she was safely behind the concrete hump. There she squatted down, trying to locate Gerhard through the forest of legs that sprouted above her head. No sign of him.

The ferry's back plate banged open. The forest swayed as if in a gale. Anna rose to the crouch, ready to run. There was a delay while two cars reversed out of the hold. She fretted that such a patently *simple* maneuver could be made to take so long by stupid men; then she was thrusting her way to the front of the crowd.

The inside of the hold stank alarmingly of diesel oil and car exhaust fumes. People aimed for the left-hand side, where a metal ladder led upward to the light. She set foot on the bottom step. The strap of her handbag caught in the rail. She tugged it. Behind her, passengers were starting to become impatient. She gave her bag a final wrench and clutched it to her chest.

The stairs were almost vertical; the only way to negotiate them safely was to keep staring straight ahead, which is why when she bumped into someone coming down all she could see was first his two-tone brogues with little holes in them, white and brown, then his cream flannels; and inconsequently she thought, How funny, cricket, nobody wears shoes like that these days, why is he wearing cricket flannels over them . . . ? Then her eyes were hard up against his shirt, more creamy flannel, how hot, he should give way . . . one hand held a new hardback book, *Women in a River Landscape,* Böll . . . then his other hand was closing over her wrist, brown, like the shoes, thin fingers with bony knuckles . . .

"Sprechen Sie Deutsch?"

The sibilant whisper came from somewhere over her head. She looked up and found its source in a fat-lipped mouth. Her eyes ranged over a pointed Adam's apple; a mustache of brown and black hairs matching those that splayed out from each wide nostril; and, crowning all, a faded Panama hat, its black band besmirched with what looked like talcum powder.

She could feel nothing around her, there was no longer a world, a context. She knew only the frenzy of despair.

"Anna!" Gerhard, it must be. But it was not Gerhard's voice. "How wonderful to see you! What a coincidence, ya?"

She shook her head, wanting to deny him with words, but her tongue was caught up in the general revolt.

"We'll go, have a beer." Now he was pushing Anna down the stairs, the Böll pressed against her chest, using her body as a ram to batter the disconsolate passengers below. The newcomer, she perceived, was extremely tall, well over six feet, and thin enough to raise doubts whether his torso could possibly hold all his vital organs. He dominated the ship's hold and Anna, forced to look into his eyes across her handbag, understood that this power derived not from the clothes, with their overtones of merchant marine uniform, but from the depths of his pale gray eyes.

"No," she managed to get out, "I have to go! I have a plane to catch. I don't know you."

When the stranger continued to force her back down the stairway, Anna saw that the time for observing conventions was past. She opened her mouth to shout "Rape!" meaning it to be heard in Athens. But even as she was drawing breath, another hand tapped her on the shoulder and a familiar voice said, "Anna, my dear, where do you think you're going?"

"Let *go* of me! Help! *Won't someone help me?*"

Gerhard was standing there, a policeman at his elbow, and for an absurd moment her heart soared while she pretended to herself that the officer had come to arrest him. But then Gerhard spoke some words of Greek, and the policeman translated as if for her benefit: "You are ill, your doctor says."

"No I'm not! I'm fine. I have to get to Corfu, *let go!*"

"Your doctor—"

"He's not my doctor, he's a killer, he's got a gun, oh, won't anyone help?"

At that the policeman's face turned sour. He seized her by the wrists.

"David!" she sobbed. *"David!"*

"You are a danger to yourself," the policeman barked.

"And to others," Kleist added with a commiserating smile.

CHAPTER

21

Fox had identified the restaurant by reference to the transcript of David's interview before the Krysalis vetting committee. Situated on the boundary between financial and legal Londons, it nevertheless managed to attract its share of media folk; and the conservatory-style décor had good associations for Albert. As he sat down, preparing to study the large, but not inconveniently large, *carte,* he wondered who you had to be to rate one of the three best tables, each spaced a generous distance from its fellows and located up some steps inside a semicircular recess overlooking a garden. The restaurant was well patronized, but that alcove stayed empty. One of the tables it contained was laid for two; and whichever couple sat there would be able to observe all the other lunchers while at the same time preserving their own privacy.

He settled down to the menu with feelings of unalloyed pleasure. He loved food and he was open-minded enough to believe that an intending hotelier could always learn something worthwhile from eating in a competently run restaurant. This, he knew instinctively, was a dead end as far as the Lescombe case went. No skeins led out of such enjoyable ambience into the heart of darkness.

He ordered a smoked fish pâté to start with and went on to plainly grilled steak, that Becher's Brook of a test for any restaurant.

The man who came over carrying the wine list wore a red tie, which clashed with his gray suit. That, coupled with his polite yet unservile manner, persuaded Albert that he must be the owner.

"Do you by any chance have an '85 Barolo?"

"I'm afraid not. We do have some of the 1986."

"Even despite the hail?"

"Ah! I'll tell you what . . . it's not on the list yet, because I've yet to try it myself, but out back I do have some other Piedmont. A Carema DOC. The last shipment was really rather exciting."

"Luigi Ferrando?"

"Indeed, yes." The man's preoccupied expression had mellowed into one of enthusiasm.

"I'll take a chance, then."

Albert's eyes kept straying to the alcove, where the table for two remained untaken. There was a "Reserved" plaque on the cloth, half hidden behind a vase of spring flowers, but even when one-thirty came and went, no one removed it. Some well-respected patron, who could be relied on to be late . . .

Who never came at all, in the event. By two-twenty-five he was the last remaining customer and, as he had hoped, the proprietor came around to pass the time with him.

"Did you enjoy your meal?"

"Excellent. You were spot on about the Carema."

"This is your first visit?"

"Though I hope it won't be my last. Have you been open long?"

"Thirteen years."

"Ah. I'm obviously not as in touch with London as I like to imagine."

"We changed our name awhile back. That often confuses people."

Albert toyed with the idea of abandoning further inquiries, but then remembered that, contrary to Fox's assertion, this lunch was not entirely free. "Would you care for a *digestif?*"

The man glanced around to see what still needed doing. "You're very kind. Perhaps a malt . . . ?"

He served himself from the bar and came back, pulling a chair from one of the other tables to sit down opposite Albert. "My name's Seppy Lamont. Not too many people around called Septimus these days."

"Mother had a sense of humor, like mine?"

"Father, actually. What's your millstone?"

"Albert."

"Not so bad. At least Victoria loves you."

Albert chuckled. "Army?"

"Guessed, did you? Scots Guards. Got damned bored, actually. Then my wife's father died, left us a bit. She's a fantastic cook, though I say it myself." He treated Albert to a long, cool stare. "Which is your outfit?"

"Shows, does it?"

"Um-hm."

"Paras."

"Still?"

"No." Albert took out his wallet and Seppy Lamont, misunderstanding, said, "I'll get your bill."

"In a minute. Have a look at this, first, would you?"

Seppy glanced at the plastic-protected card, matched up its photograph with the man opposite and said, "Pull the other one, old chap. Special Branch you ain't. Look, let's go into the office. I'd like you to meet my wife."

Albert rose and followed him through a door at the back of the bar to find himself inside an unaccommodating office; it was long, but scarcely wider than a single bed, and if you wanted to get to the desk at the far end you had to squeeze around a filing cabinet.

Seated at the desk was a woman, in her mid-forties. She had her legs crossed, giving Albert a good view of fish-net nylons and patent-leather shoes, very French. But then she swiveled around from the accounts she'd been working on and he saw that above the waist she became something else: red lips the same lurid color as Seppy's tie, masses of mascara, medium-length hair that was obviously dark by nature but had been dyed blond, unskillfully and a long time ago. Hungarian, perhaps. Something Eastern Bloc.

"This is Albert, darling. One of the firm. Albert, meet my wife, Racine."

"Charmed to know you." Racine uncoiled herself from the chair in which she'd been sitting. She held out a hand with the same studied slowness that characterized everything she did, including the way she spoke: her voice was soft and she chose her words only after deliberation.

"Thanks for a splendid meal. Do you do the cooking yourself?"

"I do. I have help, of course, but one must have a hand in everything. I cook. I shop. I lay the tables. I choose the flowers."

He could not place the accent, but by now he was moving slowly west. Austria, maybe . . .

"Where did you train?"

She threw back her head and laughed, too theatrically for Albert's taste. "I did not train. I had a father, who liked to eat only the best." Her head came back to horizontal. "And a mother who died when I was young. Before we got out, my father owned an establishment in Brno. He taught me . . . *everything!*"

"You're Czechoslovakian?"

"I am."

"Your name faced me. Racine."

"I changed it when I came here. I disliked the one my father gave me. It is something I have in common with Septimus. But fathers are . . . You've been to Czechoslovakia, perhaps?"

"Passing through."

Seppy grunted. He meant it to be a laugh, but it turned into something less funny. Albert was starting to dislike this man, who understood rather more than was convenient.

"Albert wants some help, darling."

"And how may we help you, Mr. Albert?"

"Do you recognize this woman?" Albert handed over a photograph of Anna, one they had taken from her album; and then, acting on an impulse, he asked, "Did she have a reservation for today? For two, by any chance?"

Racine shrieked, "Oh my God!" and burst out laughing, a hand held to her throat. Her fingernails, Albert noticed, were painted an unattractive shade of green. "I thought she must be dead, at least."

Albert briefly wondered what was more than death, in this context, but he had no time for whimsy. "Do you know her name?"

Seppy took a good look at the photo before settling back against the filing cabinet, hands in pockets. "That's Mrs. Lescombe." Suddenly he seemed less assured, a man apprehensively waiting to see whether the squib will be damp or dry.

"She used to come here often?"

"At one time." The Lamonts exchanged faintly mocking glances that excluded Albert. "It's been more than two years now."

"That empty table, it wasn't for her?"

"No," Racine said. "It wasn't for her."

"But you're close. You see, that reservation was made—"

"Septimus, excuse me, but . . . who is Mr. Albert?"

"Ah, sorry. Would you mind . . . ?" Seppy raised his eyebrows and this time the mockery excluded Racine. Albert showed his identification card.

"Police?" She sounded afraid. Albert remembered where she had grown up. He knew he would have to ask the Czecho desk about Racine, which bothered him, because the Czecho desk would then get all excited and start opening files where there was nothing to be filed.

"Sort of police."

Husband and wife looked at each other for a few moments, sending messages back and forth. When Seppy at last said, "Of course, we'll do whatever we can," Albert mentally tipped his hat to Fox, who had counseled the approach oblique, rather than the attack direct. Aggression would not have dented these people. They put on their clothes each morning, but their armor they never took off.

"Tell me all you know about this customer of yours, please. About Anna."

"I never understood what he saw in her," Racine said. "She was so dull. All those black clothes, black stockings."

"She's a barrister," Albert explained.

"I guessed she was a lawyer of some kind," Seppy said. "Very precise. Lovely manners, though."

"And from the way you talk, she had a companion. A regular companion?"

"Yes."

"His name?"

Septimus did not answer at once. Albert knew he was missing something and it irked him. Something so obvious it would stand up and bite him in a moment . . . "His name?" he repeated curtly.

Racine answered. "Gerhard Kleist."

"Kleist." Albert, remembering one further detail picked out of Lescombe's vetting file by Fox, was startled. "German?"

"Yes."

"And he used to eat here with Anna?"

The atmosphere was icing its way toward absolute zero. *Why?* thought Albert.

"Look, Septimus, darling, I really ought to be seeing Vanessa about those cloths, perhaps you could deal with Mr. Albert."

"I'd rather you stayed." Albert's smile only produced itself after a pause. "Mr. Kleist, he's a lawyer?"

"No," said Seppy. "He's a psychotherapist."

Albert stood very still. Butterflies had started to flutter inside him: beautiful, multicolored, richly textured Lepidoptera. . . . "Say again?"

"A psychotherapist. He became a regular customer of ours. Then he turned into a friend."

The last vestiges of Albert's boredom finally dissolved into intense elation. *Someone had gained access to Anna Lescombe's mind.* Perhaps he had manipulated that mind; perhaps she was mentally ill. And if that was right, the discovery could supply him with the lever he so desperately craved: there was only one thing to be done with a mad dog. . . .

He thought of the empty table, its prize location. "This man Kleist was supposed to be lunching here today?"

"Yes."

"But he didn't keep the reservation. . . . Did he telephone?"

"No."

"Is that usual?"

"Sometimes he gets held up with a patient." Racine was whispering now. "He doesn't always . . ."

"He doesn't always bother to let us know." Seppy finished his wife's sentence.

"He used to eat here with other women, would I be right in thinking that?"

"Very infrequently. He was rather a solitary sort of chap."

"I suppose you don't, by any chance, have an address for Mr. Kleist?"

Septimus stared at the floor. At last Racine said, "I'll look it up for you." She opened a drawer. "My diary . . . an old one. Here we are. . . ."

Albert wrote down the address.

"Is there anything else you need?"

"I'd like to look at your bookings over the past five years. No, that's unreasonable, isn't it? Over a period going back as far as you can and ending with the last time Mrs. Lescombe ate here."

The diaries were produced, after a search. Albert skimmed through them, looking to see if Kleist's reservations married up with the dates in Anna's chambers diary, and was not surprised to find that they did.

She had been seeing a psychotherapist. He could think of only one reason for that. It was because she needed help. *What kind of help?*

"Is it all right if I take these away for a while?"

Seppy nodded. "Of course."

"We'll have to analyze them in detail, but perhaps you could help me . . . Was there a pattern?"

"Pattern?"

"What I mean is, did they lunch here twice a year, something like that? Or three times a week for six months, followed by a break . . . know the sort of thing I mean?"

Seppy thought. "At the beginning, years ago, they were a couple. Then it changed. There was a long break, as I recall."

"A row of some kind?"

"I wouldn't know. After two or three years, suddenly there she was again. But by then it had become more like you said earlier: lunch twice a year. Birthday, perhaps. Catching up on the news."

Damn, thought Albert. Twice and thrice damn. But there's no need to harp on inconvenient details when I make my report. "It went on like that, until . . ."

"Two years ago. Or so."

"And then it stopped. But Kleist continued to be a regular customer?"

"On and off. His wife died of cancer, we didn't see him for a while. Look, this is all a bit . . . Is there anything else?"

Albert thought hard. "Only my bill, please."

Seppy produced it very quickly. Albert paid in cash, Fox's cash, adding a reasonable but not lavish tip.

"I'll show you out," said Seppy. At the door he said, "If you do have to get in touch again, perhaps you'd make a point of coming through me?"

"Understood."

"You see, my wife . . . she was a patient of Kleist's. When her father died." Seppy made a face. "Cost us an absolute bloody bomb."

"I'm sorry." Albert knocked his forehead with a knuckle. "I was being thick."

"Anna Lescombe wasn't the only one, you know. Kleist had a few, how should I say, favorites. After his wife died."

"Lovers, you mean?"

"I would think so. One in particular. An American. Don't know her surname, but he used to call her Robyn."

"Did Anna and Kleist . . . ?"

"Screw? I was never there, so I can't say. But I'd guess yes, at the start. You get a nose for what people are up to in this business."

"And later?"

Seppy shrugged.

"Did you ever hear them talk about . . . about anything, really?"

"Nope. Inflexible rule: no eavesdropping. It's their business and none of yours."

"Racine, would she have heard them discussing anything?"

Seppy guffawed, then subjected Albert to a look of pity not unmixed with scorn. "Understood," he said quietly, putting obvious quotation marks around the word. "That's what you said, old bean. 'Understood' . . ."

Then, yes, it did dawn, and Albert realized what he had been missing earlier, that obvious "something." "He became a friend," those were Seppy's words, what kind of friend, thought Albert, how close, on a scale of one to a million, just how *intimate*, would you say?

The sudden vision was disturbingly real: Racine Lamont standing in the doorway of her long, narrow office, watching the table overlooking the garden, week in, week out, one face sometimes different but the other ever the same, monotonously the same, with eyes for *l'amie du jour*, not for her. Never again for her. . . .

"Correction," Albert said lightly. "Under orders. Sorry."

CHAPTER

22

Anna tried to struggle, but they bundled her into the car, Gerhard and the stranger off the ferry, yes and the policeman, too. For her own good. For the sake of her health. When she cried out, at first the onlookers frowned; then they noticed the police uniform and their indignation gave way to smiles. She found herself sitting in the back of the Fiat. Someone had bandaged her wrists together; she was helpless. A prisoner of the man she had once trusted more than any other, apart from her husband, David.

"So, Kleist, it's good to find you still alive."

The last English words she heard for a long time. She remembered nothing of the journey back to the house except lengthy exchanges in an ugly, guttural language she didn't understand but assumed must be German. Then she was sitting at the kitchen table, while Gerhard took beers from the fridge.

"Untie me," she demanded.

"Will you promise to be quiet?"

"Go to hell."

Gerhard shrugged and moved away. "Suit yourself."

Anna fought the bandages but they were expertly knotted; all she succeeded in doing was chafe her wrists.

"I'll be quiet," she said in a low voice. "Just untie me, will you?"

Gerhard cut the knots with a kitchen knife. He sat down opposite her, next to the stranger, and for a time the two of them drank their Hellas without speaking. The man in cream had a habit of sucking both lips after he'd taken a swig, first the lower one, then the upper, his tongue always careful to milk the ends of his mustache of their last vestiges of sustenance.

"Aren't you going to introduce me?" she asked Gerhard defiantly.

He looked at the other man first, as if seeking permission; only when the newcomer nodded did he say, "This is Jürgen Barzel."

"You know him?"

"I know him."

"Who is he? What's he doing here?"

Gerhard stared at her. It was as if a sheep had miraculously asked its shepherd what butchers did for a living.

"He's a kind of . . . troubleshooter."

"Why do you say it like that? As if you were enemies."

Why? thought Gerhard. Because HVA has found out about this villa and I don't know how. I don't know what *they* know, don't know anything except that I'm terrified. That's why my throat constricts and my saliva dries up, Anna.

"Mrs. Lescombe . . . have I pronounced it rightly?" Anna found herself being drawn into Barzel's eyes as they inflated to fill her own vision.

"Yes."

"It's a pleasure meeting you. You have stimulated us! We have been working late nights on your account, Anna . . . I wish to call you Anna. Do I have permission?"

"I suppose so."

"And I am Jürgen. Tell me about yourself, Anna."

She obviously didn't understand what he required. Barzel must have sensed what was in her mind, for he smiled and said, "Don't be nervous, I pray you. I am your friend. That is why I'm here—to help you and Gerhard."

Not so, thought Gerhard.

"What should I tell you, then?"

"About yourself. David. And your daughter, Juliet."

"You . . . know a lot about me."

As Anna began to speak, Gerhard mentally begged her to be

careful. If HVA had discovered the fax he'd sent to London, they would kill him. Execution, that's what they'd call it, because that's what you did with traitors; no good planning a new life in South America, too late for that. . . . And since Anna would be a witness, then she too must die.

When did things start to go wrong? The plan he'd put together looked so foolproof. For a long time now he had wanted out; some grand finale on which to bring down the curtain of his nerve-shredding career as psychotherapist-cum-spymaster. He'd been cultivating his contacts in Lima and Asunción, old friends of Clara, knowing he must flee. Even if it meant the end of his own sister and her family, he could do that. He could do it because each new job for HVA had come to represent a fresh episode in a serial nightmare that would one day destroy him, and when the chips were down it looked simple enough: he was more important than Ilsa.

Fear of detection, of prison, had all but disabled Gerhard Kleist. The Krysalis débacle was the last straw; he knew he would never forget that moment of dread when he had made himself enter the Lescombes' house, only to discover that David might return at any moment. Even a cultured life in England could not compensate for such horrors.

Things had been all right when he was younger, and the tension affected him less. In those days he could lose himself in work. But then, too suddenly, and although not yet fifty, he was a widower and growing old. The slack skin at the jowls. Face no longer quite smooth, more the texture of an orange. Waking at three, most mornings and not only after a night out, to urinate; then unable to sleep again before dawn. Then sleeping like unto death until the alarm clock slugged him with its dreadful, heavy burden of consciousness.

He'd never stopped dreaming about the woman sitting opposite. In those dreams her face was bright, alive with intelligence, ever youthful. After marrying David she had forgotten Gerhard Kleist; or so he'd believed until the day before, when as she lay on the beach her body had told his massaging hands an altogether different story. Yesterday the fantasy had taken on a new tangibility. He knew she could be persuaded to go with him, forget the past, live only for the present. . . .

But first it was necessary to concoct some way of dealing with Barzel. He must find an excuse to go to the bedroom. Once he had the gun . . .

Gerhard came back to reality to hear Barzel say, "So now tell me—" he smiled, a beau soliciting some naughty confidence—"I am a convert. Having talked to you, I understand everything. But why must everyone else in Europe fall in love with you at the same time as me? Mm? Tell me!"

Anna's nervous laugh alarmed Gerhard. Be careful, Anna. Keep it bottled up, as always; don't choose this of all moments to change. As long as you have a secret, no matter how trivial, your life is safe.

You must get the gun, he told himself. *Now.*

"Everywhere I go, I find my dear colleagues ahead of me. At the station. At the airport. Everywhere it's the same. The English. The French. The *other* Germans. The—dear God help us all!—Italians."

Anna's eyes flickered, but she could not look away.

"Even at Corfu airport there were old-time spies standing around, trying to look like touts. You'd think they could afford at least one bottle of fake suntan lotion between them. Fortunately they didn't see me, or I would have been obliged to nod my head, at least. One cannot be rude to colleagues. But Anna . . . in *Corfu!*"

By now Anna was shrinking, or so it seemed to Gerhard.

"What have we here? I will tell you. A major security alert in NATO. You are 'hot,' Anna, that is how we say it. Scalding. I could cook a nice steak on you, and it would be overdone. Why? Perhaps you have something these people want very badly, *ja?*"

Anna swallowed. There was a long silence, which Barzel broke by saying, "Do you have the Krysalis file here, perhaps?"

"No," Anna said. Then, incredulously, "You *know* about that?"

Barzel nodded. "I know." Gerhard noted with relief that he was smiling. "Where is it?"

Gerhard rapidly listed the possibilities. Lie, pretend the file was still in London? Hopeless. Either Barzel would tear the place apart and find Krysalis, in which case he would kill them; or he would use the HVA machine to run checks in London that must come up with the truth eventually. In which case also he would kill them. Tell the truth now, and have done with it? Once Barzel had Krysalis, there was no incentive for him to leave either Kleist or Anna alive. . . .

"The file's in my bedroom," he said. "I'll get it."

"*What?*" Anna was on her feet, her face white. "But you said . . . you told me you'd leave it."

Then Gerhard's expression completed the tale and her legs gave way beneath her. At first she covered her face with her hands, but suddenly she seemed to lose all strength, for her head drooped forward onto the table, where she cradled it in her arms, defeated.

Gerhard stood up, telling Barzel with a look that he should guard her; only when the other man nodded his assent did he leave the room.

He closed the bedroom door behind him and ran to the bed. Seconds later, he was retrieving his Luger. He wiped the sweat from his forehead with the back of a hand that shook, only to find that the beads of moisture broke through again at once. This was no time for cowardice. You have a weapon, he told himself. *Use it!*

As he rose from beside the bed, the phone rang. Gerhard stared at it. Who on earth . . . ?

Then he remembered. Iannis.

While in the very act of reaching out for the receiver, he heard footsteps in the passage. Torn between the needs to silence the phone and to conceal the gun, Gerhard gritted his teeth, powerless to act. Next second he had thrust the Luger under the bed and was clamping the phone to his ear so hard that it hurt.

"Ne?" he snapped, as Barzel entered the bedroom.

"I went again today," the boy said. "Nothing." Then Gerhard heard only the purr of a severed contact.

"Who was that?" Barzel asked.

"No one. Where's Anna, you shouldn't have—"

"What the hell do you mean 'no one'? *Who?"*

"Wrong number. Happens all the time, the phones here are crap."

Barzel stared at him in silence, as if weighing the truth of his words. "Where's this file?" he said at last.

Gerhard once more pushed the bed aside and rummaged in the hole. "Here . . ."

The two men returned to the kitchen. Gerhard poured himself another beer, knowing he'd lost more than a golden opportunity to dispose of his unwelcome visitor; he'd lost vital ground. Whatever Barzel thought when he arrived, he definitely mistrusted him now. Damn Iannis . . .

The boy had sounded odd. As if he wasn't alone, someone was listening in. A girl? Gerhard hoped not; the last thing he wanted was Iannis messing around with strangers.

Strangers. What if Barzel had somehow managed to trace Iannis and . . . no, it was impossible. In that event, Barzel would have come to the island with reinforcements and enough hardware to fight a war. Keep your head, he told himself firmly; don't panic now.

Barzel breezed through the file before beginning to study it more carefully. After he had finished he sat for a long time staring into space. At last he turned to Gerhard and said, in English, "I think, if Anna will excuse us, we must talk quite seriously. . . ."

"Will she run away?" he asked, as they reached the terrace.

"I doubt it. Even if she does, she won't get far."

"Unlike you. You, Kleist, appear to have got very far, without telling us. Surprised to see me here, *was?* You thought we didn't know about your little love nest?"

"How the devil did you—"

"Oh, a little bird, you know? Many, many years ago. People used to have a good laugh about it. 'The look on his face!' that's what we used to say. 'When Kleist finds out that we know!' "

"What made you think I'd be here?"

"Berlin put out an alert when you and the woman were missing. Different people are searching for you in different places: I drew Greece." Barzel glanced back toward the house. "Does she understand German?"

"No."

"All right, we speak German then." Barzel looked at his watch: a busy man with a plane to catch who had allowed himself to be sidetracked by a snake-oil salesman. "You're an idiot."

Gerhard had been expecting an accusation of rank treason. Barzel's mildness took him off guard. *Think,* he told himself savagely. You're not dead yet.

"Why?" he said, falling into the sofa-swing. "I bring you the biggest prize you've—"

"Point one, you brought us *nothing!* You have sat here quietly, keeping us guessing. We shall discuss that, I promise you. Point two: the file is *too* big! Files like that don't come our way, Kleist."

"But—"

"Suppose you were the President of the United States. Imagine someone approached you, just before a major superpower summit, and told you that he had papers, a microfiche, setting out the entire Warsaw Pact military dispositions and strategy. Would you believe him? Of course not. Why? First, because one of the ways you defeat spies is by keeping information in tiny gobbets; second, because in the run-up to a conference you don't believe anything you're told anyway."

"England doesn't work like that."

"*Everybody* works like that, comrade! This is a plant. We're meant to read this rubbish, shuffle a dozen divisions in and out of Poland and I don't know what else. It's a trick; you've fallen for it. I'm telling you, Kleist, you're a dead man. Dead."

"But *you* told me to do this! 'Anna's your patient, she's married to a top civil servant who's interesting to us, get the file!' "

"Exactly." Barzel swung around to face Gerhard. "That's the point. Someone in MI5 discovered what was going on. This is pre-summit counter-intelligence. It means your cover's gone; mine too." He paused. Then, amazingly, he smiled. "Ah . . . if only I could believe what I'm saying."

Gerhard stared at him, incomprehension written all over his face, and Barzel chuckled. "Either the British are being very clever, or . . ." He came to sit beside Gerhard on the swing, one arm stretched along the back of the cushion. "Some prizes are so valuable they lure with such power. . . . The wolf won't ignore this lamb, not with Vancouver mere weeks away."

"The wolf . . ."

"Oh yes. It's being run from Normannenstrasse."

Gerhard felt a seed of hope sprout inside him. HVA's commander did not take a personal interest in silly tricks. If he could only manage to persuade HVA to see this as a coup, rather than a betrayal. . . . But then Barzel asked, "What about the woman? Whose side is she on?"

"No one's. She hasn't a clue what's happening."

"Maybe that's so, maybe it isn't. We've been rooting around, but so far without success. We can't make a clear picture of your Mrs. Anna Lescombe. She's hazy. We need focus. Does she realize you were responsible for introducing her to her husband?"

"No. As far as she's concerned, we went sailing together, Lescombe happened to be in the next berth."

"Coincidence?"

"Yes."

"Then she must be very naïve." Barzel shook his head, laughing. "How come people never seem to see through you, Kleist? Why have you dragged her here, anyway?"

"Because she screwed up."

"Explain."

"I knew her husband was away for the weekend, so I programed her to open the safe, bring me the file, wait while I copied it, take it back, put it in the safe, and forget everything."

"So what happened?"

"She had a kind of breakdown. She'd built up inner resistance to my suggestions."

"Didn't you realize that at the time?"

"No, she seemed normal enough."

"Aach, I don't understand." Barzel stood up and began to pace the terrace. "You were attempting the impossible. Everyone knows you can't force a person to do things they don't want to do under hypnosis."

"*Do* they?" Gerhard scoffed. "Then 'everyone,' comrade, is about twenty years out of date."

"Are you telling me that if you put that woman into a trance and ordered her to sleep with me, she would?"

"No, not like that. But there are other ways."

"Such as?"

"Given time, and a deep enough trance, I could persuade her that you were a doctor, and that it was necessary for you to examine her intimately. I could arouse her sexually by feeding erotica into her mind."

"That would work?" Barzel sounded incredulous.

"How do you think I got the combination out of her in the first place?"

Barzel rejoined him on the swing. "Tell me."

"I persuaded her that her husband's career was in danger, because he couldn't open the safe and needed help remembering the combination."

"And she accepted that?"

"Of course." Seeing the skepticism on his colleague's face, Gerhard continued, "Remember, that woman has been my patient, with gaps, for sixteen years. She trusts me. She loved me, once."

Barzel thought this over. "Why did she have that breakdown, then?" he snapped. "How come she failed?"

"I'm not sure." Gerhard looked away. "I went too far too fast. We hadn't seen each other for two years, my . . . my influence, if you like, must have faded."

"You were lucky to get out of England."

"Yes. What do you intend doing with her?"

"What do you think?"

For the first time Gerhard turned to look directly at Barzel. "You'll kill her." He could not keep the anguish out of his voice.

The other man's hand strayed along the cushion to grasp Gerhard's shoulder. Suddenly he smiled. "Of course."

"You'd be making the biggest mistake of your whole career. Huper would never forgive you."

"What?"

"Without the woman, you can't begin to assess Krysalis's importance. That file is like a beautiful painting: perhaps it's an old master, perhaps it is by a gifted pupil, maybe it's a fake, after all." Gerhard sat forward, eager to impress Barzel with the sense of what he was urging. "You need to know its *provenance*. You must interview the *dealer*. Besides, by holding on to her, how can you lose?"

Barzel frowned. "I don't follow."

"Well, isn't it obvious? Either she's the source of disinformation, like you say, stealing a hoax file at my behest, or she's the possessor of the real thing. You've got to take her back to Berlin. There she can be interrogated properly and at length. If she's a phoney, you'll learn a lot about British methods. If she's real, you'll discover whatever it is that she knows about her husband's affairs; not just this file but perhaps many other files as well. Now do you see?"

Gerhard could scarcely control the wild beating of his heart while he waited for Barzel's reaction. When he'd first clapped eyes on his control coming off the ferry he'd turned numb. Yet HVA did not know about the fax he had sent to London, that much was obvious. If he once got them to accept that Anna should be brought to Berlin, he'd undoubtedly be called upon to play a role in her interrogation there. The power he had acquired over her as hypnotist and therapist was beyond any coherent form of valuation. And when they had finished with her . . .

She will stay with me, Gerhard thought. She already loves me, deep down. I can make her forget David. I am growing old; there is a woman in this world for me to love.

You're jumping ahead, he reminded himself. First you have to make Barzel swallow it. And that won't be easy. But—

"Perhaps you have a point," the other man said slowly, making Gerhard's heart miss another beat. "It would be difficult to move her, though. So many observers, on the lookout . . . There could be no question of doing it openly. A boat, maybe. Submarine, even . . ."

Gerhard studied his colleague's face and read indecision. He's frightened. *Why?* Ah yes, of course, a basic human reaction: *he's frightened of making a mistake.*

In that instant he knew that, whatever might happen in the future, Barzel did not carry orders to execute either of them immediately; and his spirits soared.

"I need to report back," Barzel said at last. "Then we'll see."

Gerhard scarcely dared to believe what he heard. *It was going to work!* "What do you want me to do in the meanwhile?" he asked quickly.

"Stay put, protect your 'art dealer' in there. Above all, maintain control."

"I can do that."

"Good. I'll live here, in this house. Back-up will come from Berlin as soon as I can arrange it. From now on, you'll be watched, all the time. Don't try to be clever again. Before, I told you you were dead. Maybe I was a little too pessimistic. But there'll be no second chance. Do you understand?"

The light was behind Barzel, rendering his expression a dark mask. Only when Gerhard stood up could he read his eyes. They were not cruel, they were not even particularly cold, just *uninterested;* and Gerhard the psychologist knew this man could do any necessary killing.

"Don't get carried away," Barzel warned, as he too rose. "The risks of transferring Anna Lescombe to Berlin may yet outweigh the advantages. Got that?"

Gerhard nodded, afraid to betray his emotion by speaking.

Barzel said, "I'm still worried about the woman. What if she tries to escape again?"

"I intend to hypnotize her. I'll use drugs, too."

"What kind of drugs?"

"A mixture of sodium pentothal and Desoxyn. That will totally eliminate any remaining resistance to hypnosis."

"Inject her now."

"If you insist. But I warn you: she's much more likely to put up a fight with you around."

"Don't worry about that, Kleist." A dreamy smile played about the corners of Barzel's mouth. "I believe I'm big enough to take care of Mrs. Lescombe. Just about, *ja?*"

CHAPTER 23

The front door opened and there it was, that smell, that overpowering, all-pervasive scented air bottled up like incense inside an Eastern temple only David knew it wasn't incense because Anna's parents would not have countenanced such a thing. Old cooking . . . and something more than that. Old age.

"So nice to see you again, David." Anna's mother took him into the living room. "Would you like a cup of coffee, to refresh you after your journey?"

In her mouth the drive to the south coast became a Himalayan trek.

"Yes, thank you."

When Mrs. Elwell went out to the kitchen he looked around him, reabsorbing the stage set upon which the Elwells lived out their lives. The house was substantial and detached, too large to be kept up by a couple in their seventies, but there was such a thing as pride. As long as you had your own property, you were not old. David understood that without quite being able to admire it.

Mr. Elwell had made a little money out of supplying the needs of amateur painters and decorators at a time when the breed had begun to sprout, but not yet proliferate. On his fiftieth birthday he received, out of the blue, an offer that looked too good to be true.

It was. The newly formed chain that took over his four shops employed him as a regional manager; that came with the deal. But before long Mr. Elwell, "Chappy" Elwell people called him, David couldn't remember why, realized he had been shunted into one of life's duller backwaters. He found out what it was like to live on a salary, the whole salary and nothing but the salary; no longer were there "good" months from which to finance a holiday, and "bad" months, rainy days against which you saved. Now there were just months. The months began to pile up. In the end they buried Mr. Elwell under a mountain of dead time.

His wife survived.

"Do you take it black?"

"Mm?" David, lost in a mixture of memories and contemplation of the shiny, renovated horseshoes that flanked the brick fireplace, was nonplused. "Uh, a little milk, please."

As usual, he did not know what was expected of him. Where he came from, where he worked, you did not have coffee served from a silver pot into bone china, accompanied by an ivory-handled spoon for brown sugar that was free of congealed, crunchy lumps.

He remembered Anna's face as she told him of the summer evenings when she had been forced to lie upstairs in her room, watching the light through the shade, because it was after seven and seven was bedtime for little girls. . . .

He had never liked Mrs. Elwell, but today he needed her help. He was not relishing the prospect.

"Is Chappy well?"

Mrs. Elwell picked up her knitting and for a moment did not reply. She had a Madame Defarge style with the needles, shoving them through the wool with the same vigorous determination that she had used to shove Anna through life.

"*Very* well, thank you, David. He's sorry to have missed you. Thursday is his bowls morning."

"Not to worry."

"He's become a little set in his ways, I'm afraid."

"Do give him my best."

"I will." Mrs. Elwell paused in her knitting for long enough to push her spectacles onto the bridge of her nose. She puffed a sharp sigh out through her nostrils and said, "We only ever see you here when there's trouble, I was saying to Chappy over breakfast."

We, I . . . Chappy drifted in and out of the house like old smoke from one of his Player's, intangible but somehow real.

"Yes. I'm sorry. We just don't seem to have a lot of time for visits and entertaining."

"I'm sure. Two busy professional people." She resumed knitting, flashing him a receptionist's smile. "Time for a straight talk, isn't it?"

"That's what I hoped."

"Anna never used to be like this."

"Like . . . ?"

"Secretive. She used to confide in Chappy and me. Particularly me, I don't think she and her father ever quite shared the same wavelength."

Straight talking? Should he tell her, then, that Anna had of necessity been lying about things to her parents since she was old enough to understand that she had a secret, inner self? Or remind Mrs. Elwell of how she had always criticized Anna for *not* confiding, when she was a teenager, long before he, David "Wrecker" Lescombe, had come on the scene? Or Anna's confessing to Juliet's imminent birth only when she became too "fat" for Lydia to go on ignoring her daughter's condition any longer. . . . Shall we have some "straight talking" about these and other matters that your daughter revealed to me quite early in our marriage, madam?

No. He repressed the anger seething inside him and molded his face into the expression of polite deference that represented his only hope of obtaining results.

"Lydia, look, I am really awfully sorry about what's happened, but . . . Anna's vanished into thin air, taking one of my files with her." He paused. "You'd better know that there are some very unpleasant accusations flying around."

"I'm sure. When a file is missing . . ."

"The accusations are utterly without foundation. Baseless as well as base. Anna's not a traitor and no one's ever going to convince me of the contrary."

"Well, at least we can agree on that. Have you heard nothing from her since she disappeared?"

"Not a word. You?"

Lydia Elwell shook her immaculately permed head. "We find we don't have as much contact as we used to."

"Before she married me, you mean."

"I suppose you could say that. She was such a lovely child, so obedient . . ." The woman's eyes lighted on a framed photograph of Anna that adorned the mantelpiece. It showed a tense, bespectacled face, with black gown just visible and mortarboard held self-consciously where the studio photographer had instructed her to hold it. "So obedient . . . and so *fresh.* Her eyes used to light up whenever you did something for her. Childlike. Innocent . . ."

"You did a lot for her, didn't you?"

"Only what any parents would have done for their daughter. It was a drain, I don't mind admitting. When Juliet was still a baby and Anna kept on working . . . everything was spend, spend, spend, in those days. Nannies. Train fares up to London for Chappy and me. We didn't begrudge any of it, although when I *think* of what we had to go without . . ."

"Where do you think she is?" David asked.

"I haven't the faintest idea."

"What do you think she's up to?"

"How would I know?"

"Well, she lived with you all those years, you might have some idea what goes on inside. . . . Sorry. I'm extremely sorry, that was unforgivable."

Click, click, click went the needles. David looked at her, realizing that this was a crisis for Anna's mother, too; and he envied Mrs. Elwell her composure.

"It's just that I'm under strain."

"If your nerves are bad, David, perhaps you ought to visit the doctor."

It was clear from the way she spoke that "nerves" and "doctors" alike were due to be relegated to one of Dante's less-pleasant outer circles."

"Did Anna ever see a doctor when she was young?"

"She had the usual coughs and colds."

"No, I mean a mind doctor. A psychiatrist."

Lydia Elwell's hands fell into her lap again, still clutching the needles, and she stared at him speechlessly, as if he had just said something obscene.

"She didn't?" he prompted.

"Anna had a brilliant career at school and after that at Oxford. She is a very successful barrister. People like that don't require the services of a psychiatrist."

David realized that she had avoided giving him a direct answer. "Juliet said her mother did see one," he persisted.

"Juliet is artistic. Children like that frequently have overheated imaginations. I shouldn't pay *too* much attention to that quarter."

"You certainly had no reason to suspect she was seeing a psychiatrist, anyway?"

"Anna was happy and well adjusted and lacked for nothing. As an only child she had all the love Chappy and I had to give." She colored a little, the broken veins in the dry skin of her cheeks becoming raw. "You know we couldn't . . ."

Conceive, is what she meant to say; but David, who had met Chappy Elwell any number of times and still had trouble remembering his face, wondered if there was a hint of some deeper, darker meaning.

"We gave her a model childhood. Except for that business at St. Mary's, which I still believe Anna brought on herself, there was never the slightest need for her to be counseled, or consoled, or whatever it is people call it."

Somehow David knew she was lying. But Lydia Elwell's evasions weren't in the forefront of his mind. *That business at St. Mary's . . .* Although he had no idea what she was referring to, he couldn't bring himself to tell Lydia that. "Oh, the St. Mary's thing," he said casually. "She got over it, didn't she?"

"Yes, but we had to move her. The *expense* . . ."

"Ah, that's right, she changed schools. . . ." David, in the dark, was running out of improvisations. "Let me see, she'd have been . . . how old?"

"Seven."

"I thought it was eight . . . no, silly of me, seven, of course it was. I never quite knew what to make of all that."

"Really? Isn't it notorious that convent schools can be difficult? Anna didn't know she'd been adopted, of course, so when those dreadful Catholic girls started to call her illegitimate . . ." She raised her needles and let them fall again, staring at David with something approaching appeal in her eyes. "How could she have borne that for a year without telling us, her own parents?"

David avoided meeting her gaze. "Perhaps she was . . . afraid."

"Afraid? *Of us?*"

"How did you find out what had been going on?"

"Anna never told you?"

"Not that particular detail, actually, no."

"She started crying in games one day and couldn't stop. She cried for four hours. The doctor had to give her an injection. At the hospital . . . they called us to the hospital. That's when we first found out. . . ." Lydia suddenly covered her eyes. "I'm sorry," she said after a pause. "Children can be such vicious animals."

"Yes."

"Before that day, we never knew, Chappy and I. She didn't tell us. She thought she was being brave."

"I see."

"They expelled three girls. The ringleaders, the mother superior called them."

"Did Anna know that they were expelled?"

"Oh, yes." Mrs. Elwell drew in a deep breath. "We received these foul letters, from the parents of one of the girls who had to go. If that's what religion . . . Anna found the letters."

"She read them?"

Mrs. Elwell nodded. "It was naughty of her, but . . . But it's nonsense to talk of psychiatrists, there was never any question of that. Our G.P. gave her a good talking-to, that's all. Psychiatrists, indeed!"

This was the first time David had heard the story. He could see, however, that Mrs. Elwell knew it all too well, *and that in some way she was lying.* She was not the sort of woman who lied easily. What secret seemed so terrible to her that it had to be covered up at all costs, even if that meant deceiving Anna's own husband?

He must not resent her. This was too important to let petty dislikes get in the way.

"She got over the change of school," he said uneasily; and was it not true? for Anna had never mentioned the episode to him. . . .

"Of course she did."

"But perhaps it affected her . . . changed her in some way, do you think?"

"It was marriage to you that changed her, if anything did."

The watery eyes remained glued to her needles, determined to avoid David's gaze.

"Changed? In what way?"

"Made her less communicative. Except right at the start. She used to phone us a lot then." Mrs. Elwell resumed her knitting. Click, click, click. "When you were away. Or late back from the office." Click. "When Anna was unhappy."

He stared at her; she could not see the intensity of his look but she must have felt it, for she went on. "Her attitudes and yours were very different. She needed pushing, if she was to get anywhere. I told her not to be so silly. I pointed out that when young people are recently married they often want to give in."

"*Give in?*"

"She used to say she couldn't stand it. Life with you."

"She actually said that?"

"She implied it, let's say."

For a long time he was aware only of the clack-clack-clack of her knitting needles as they created some seemly garment in a delicate shade of green.

"What was wrong with me?" It sounded so lame!

"A lot of things, I imagine."

"Like what?"

"She wanted a child. Desperately."

"She told you that?"

"A mother always knows."

"I wanted one too."

"Not at the beginning, I believe."

"Well . . . we both had our careers."

"Didn't you understand how much it meant to her? With her background? She'd been adopted, although of course she got over that, but . . . anyway. She'd been adopted. Juliet was always a problem child. Anna wanted to make everything right. Didn't you *see* that?"

She continued to gaze at her son-in-law, until it became obvious he wasn't going to answer. "Having a child of her own, by you, born into a secure home, that would have made such a . . . well, you won't take it from me, I'm sure."

"She never said anything. Never."

"Anna found it hard to talk to you, about certain things. I could see that easily enough. You didn't know?"

David shook his head. But then his mind jumped back to the meeting with Duncan Broadway, and even beyond that, to the summer of 1987, the year of the quarrel. Their disagreement had simmered, with neither of them able to find an honorable compromise. Ostensibly they had been fighting over Juliet's future. Now he allowed himself to admit, for the first time, that they had fallen out over something quite different.

It would have been ridiculous for Anna to have another child at her age. And her career! She could kiss goodbye to the silk gown, the judgeship. . . . Yet in his bones David knew that this was no lie. Anna wanted another chance at motherhood, to compensate for her failure with Juliet. Not just wanted. *Needed.*

"Your backgrounds were so different," Mrs. Elwell said. "Not at all the same outlooks on life. Quite a shock for her, I should imagine."

"I'm common, is that what you mean? The wrong accent?"

She smiled and raised her eyes for a second, as if to say: "You see?"

"Sorry, didn't mean to shout. I know you think I went to a rotten university. I know you think civil servants are beneath contempt. But I fell in love with your daughter and she happened to love me."

"What do young girls know about love?"

"When Anna married me she was almost *thirty!*"

"Shared attitudes. Common assumptions. They're more important to a marriage than any amount of love, as you call it."

"Why, what would you call it?" He stared at her, unable to cross the divide, until it occurred to him that this was becoming too absurd for words. Mrs. Elwell, faced with an uncommunicative daughter who'd betrayed her by marrying not once but twice, had constructed this ridiculous figment of the imagination as a means of covering up the hurt. He felt sorry for her.

"So." He sat back in his chair. "She's left me because she's unhappy, is that what you're saying?"

Click-clack-click.

"Yet I notice she hasn't come running home to mother."

"You sound very pleased about that."

"Ecstatic."

"You're a bitter person, David. Chappy was saying so only last night."

"Is that why she left me? She's got her share of bitterness too, you know."

"She had nothing to be bitter about. She was a sweet child."

"A sweet child who unfortunately got herself pregnant and had to marry Eddy—"

"That's an appalling—"

"On *your say-so.*"

Mrs. Elwell laid aside the knitting and sat with hands clasped in her lap. She might have been fighting for self-control or she might have been silently praying. "What a monstrous thing to say." Her voice was hardly a whisper.

"She never felt loved. Never. That was her trouble. You gave her things, you forked out, pushed her, but somehow in all of that love got over the wall."

"Strange she never complained."

"How could she, when you managed every waking thought?" Now his dormant anger was rising to the surface, leaving him powerless to prevent it. "And even if she did assert herself, on those rare occasions, you moved the goal posts, pretending that that was what you wanted all along."

When Mrs. Elwell spoke again her voice contained a hardly audible demisemiquaver of doubt. "You make it sound as though everything's our fault."

"She came out of this house, into the world . . . feeling she was bad."

"She told you that?"

"Often. I didn't realize why, but now I'm beginning to. She felt it was her fault those girls were expelled, didn't she? If she'd been stronger, kept her mouth shut, there wouldn't have been any problem. All her fault, for being a bastard."

Another lengthy silence followed. Mrs. Elwell broke it by picking up her needles and getting back to work. Now, however, she knitted less stridently. "I'm glad you came," she said.

David heard how the demisemiquaver had ceased to taint her voice and felt his heart sink. "Why?"

"I understand things better now." She sounded satisfied with her judgment of men and affairs. "Things between the two of you, I mean. If you spoke to her . . . as you've spoken to me . . ."

David considered this in silence. The momentary flash of sympathy he had felt earlier scarcely survived its birth. So he rose and walked out of the room, without saying goodbye, and he closed the front door behind him with all the respectful, lower-class deference that his despicable, lower-class soul could command.

This was a tidy neighborhood, where people owned garages and used them for their intended purpose. Apart from David's Rover, only one car stood in the roadway. He heard its engine start the moment he left the house, and remembered that MI5, like the poor, were always with him.

FRIDAY

CHAPTER

24

Albert knew things were getting really tiresome as soon as he clapped eyes on the ait.

"Ait" was just a fancy word for island, and in his world it did not necessarily mean anything to do with the sea. It signified a position surrounded by space with good lines of sight in every direction and adequate defense mechanisms; they called it "ait" rather than plain old island because the former encoded comfortably as "8" and the latter did not; one of those things.

Never mind, he thought. You need to see Anna's first husband, because he'll be hard on her. He will give you clues to her instability. He can help build a case against her, leaving room for only one conclusion: that she is too dangerous to live. Like all the other vicious, Communist rats that lurk inside this sewer of a twentieth-century world. . . .

The "ait" comprised a Victorian house, standing all alone off Manchester Road in London's East End, with a view across the Thames to Delta Wharf and a gas holder, its silhouette like a huge confectioner's basket of spun sugar. Beyond the gates lay a brief stretch of lawn, giving way to gravel. Crunchy gravel, Albert thought to himself, you could market breakfast cereal under that name, people would buy it, there's one born every minute . . . up to the front door comes a visitor, crunch, crunch, crunch. An ait. A bloody ait.

He had a bet as to what he would find around the side of the house: an alley with a Porsche 944 parked half on and half off the pavement, the driver's door conveniently placed opposite a steel shutter capped with a closed-circuit TV camera. A camera not unlike the one that would be mounted in the front porch.

Albert got out of the car. As he drew near he glanced up to see that a camera was indeed regarding him with apparent unconcern. He arranged his body between the lens and the bank of buttons. An American Express card materialized in his right hand. The front door was on an ordinary night latch; it yielded within seconds.

Somewhere close by a typewriter clacked intermittently, and, as Albert listened, a phone began to chirrup. The stairs were at the back of the house. He climbed three floors in swift silence, noting how anonymously the tenants kept themselves to themselves, and paused on the last landing.

His instincts had suddenly started to become very edgy. He went up the next flight on tiptoe, craning his head to see the corridor now coming into view on his left on the other side of the banister.

He stopped while still five steps short of the top. Three doors: one to the right of the stairwell, one opposite him, another down at the far end, toward the front of the building. Albert completed the climb and stood still, head on one side, listening. Here there were no typewriters, no phones rang. On the door opposite the stairs was fixed a minute ebony plaque bearing the words ASIATICA LIMITED.

Albert's fingers brushed the door handle, dithered an inch or so above it, withdrew. Because he was concentrating on the ebony plaque he was almost too late.

As the right-hand door swiftly opened, he felt the draft of air and turned, one hand already groping for an inside pocket. A blur of browns and blacks. Something long coming down fast. Human, male, beard, tall, tough. Without thinking, Albert jabbed his left hand up to intercept whatever might be about to land on his skull. A shock ran the length of his arm, nothing smashed, tendons okay, back off, *mind the bloody stairs!*

His assailant looked Arabic. As Albert retreated a couple of steps he saw that the man was holding a blackjack; no wonder his arm hurt like hell.

The Arab went into a crouch, jumped upright, feinted left.

Albert read the series of movements correctly and spun around to put his back against the wall, minimizing the target. His attacker's rush brought him opposite Albert instead of sending him headlong into him, as he'd intended. Albert stuck out his foot. The Arab saw it, tried to jump aside but succeeded only in entangling one hand in the rails of the banister. He cried out at the pain, then had the sense to follow through, swinging his whole body around in a semicircle so that he was facing Albert, who still had his back against the wall.

This time, however, there was a difference. The Arab was starting forward, off the banister, when he caught sight of the gun in Albert's hand and froze.

The door bearing the plaque opened first a fraction, then some more. Another Middle Eastern type, fatter than his colleague, cautiously emerged, nodding his head to right and left like a bird searching out worms. He, too, saw Albert, registered the gun, and did a comical double-take.

"Oh, God!" drawled an English voice from inside the room just vacated by the fat man. "Not *again.*"

Albert waved the gun, indicating that the Arabs should lead the way. He was careful to keep a distance between him and his attacker, who had taken a silk handkerchief from his breast pocket and was dabbing at the knuckles of one hand, scraped raw on the banisters.

The room they entered was about fifteen feet wide and twice as long. Stark, cushionless chairs on either side of the glass conference table were offset, slightly, by semi-stuffed leather sacks dotted around, presumably for sitting on. A single white lily arched out of a long-stemmed black vase on the blackwood desk opposite the door, behind which sat a man wearing a dark suit, almost fluorescently white shirt, and burgundy silk tie.

"Oh . . . *God,*" he said again, as if weary of life's incessant demands upon his patience. "Not the Browning version."

Albert knew a second's surprise. His gun was, in fact, a Browning.

"I suppose you're going to tell me you've come to read the meter." The man's voice essayed Oxbridge arrogance, although Albert already knew he wasn't out of the top drawer. Now he sighed, a long, stagy job, and said, "You are trespassing, you do know that."

The harder he tried, the more his voice turned into a queeny bleat. He sat with his hands folded in his lap, where Albert couldn't see them. Albert didn't like that. "Hands on the desk, please."

Another theatrical sigh. First fingers appeared over the lip of the desk, then two hands scurried along the surface to rest, palms down, a couple of feet apart.

Albert gestured the two Arabs over to the far end of the room while he focused on the face behind the desk. It was pale, clean-shaven, with a thin mouth too long for the narrow cheeks above. His hair was brushed straight back from the forehead in furrows. Age, about forty, which would be right.

"Mr. Eddy Clapham? Or is it some other name now?"

Sigh, sigh, sigh. "Edward Clapham, at your service. What *can* we do for you, Mr. . . . ?"

"Albert."

"*Really?*" Eddy seemed to have trouble accepting it. A black phone tremolo'd. He picked it up, said, "Fuck off," and replaced it. Then he picked it up again for long enough to say, "That's an entire morning's fuck-off, you understand."

Silence fell. There was a general air of resignation in the room that this kind of incident was to be expected in their line of business, whatever that might happen to be.

"I'd like to ask you a few questions," Albert said.

Sigh. "Look . . ." *Sigh.* "If it's about income tax . . . no, they don't carry guns, you must be an excise man. If it's about the warehousing . . ."

"It's about Anna Elwell. Your wife."

"Oh." For the first time, Eddy looked less than sure of himself. "You what?"

Albert, hearing that sudden coarse slang, noted the descent from Oxbridge to Redbrick. "You're rather elusive. No one answers the phone and we don't have the facilities to interview you in . . ." he raised his eyes to the ceiling . . . "Teheran, Damascus, Baghdad—"

"Yes, all right, I'm on the computer, I get the message."

"And Tel Aviv. How ever do you manage the visas?"

The fat Arab giggled. Eddy must suddenly have found the two bodyguards as distasteful as Albert did, for he said, "Oh, do shut up. Get out, both of you, go on, get out."

The attacker led the way, haughty and lithe, while the fat Arab waddled in his wake, struggling to keep up like a tug they'd forgotten to unhitch from the cruiser.

Albert, watching their departure, was struck by a sudden, recent memory. "Do you own a Porsche 944?"

"Now look, I paid for that. . . . What's wrong with Anna?"

"She's disappeared."

The ensuing silence was a long one. "Who are you, exactly?"
Eddy asked.

Albert put away his Browning and produced a card. Eddy held
it up to the light, as if suspecting a forgery, before handing it back
with the comment "You're not Special Branch." He was neither
disturbed nor angry; just certain, in the same way that Seppy Lamont had been certain. "Let's go over to the window. I don't like
a desk between me and my guests. It's a real no-no, where I operate."

Eddy pulled one of the austere high-backed black chairs away
from the conference table and sat sideways on it. Albert stood in his
favorite position, right elbow on left palm and the back of his free
hand covering his mouth.

"What do you want to know about Anna, then?"

"When did you last see her?"

"Light years back. Clean break. Not *au revoir,* strictly *adieu.*"

"What about Juliet?"

Eddy's face softened a fraction. "I still see her sometimes. She's
in Cornwall, rotten setup if you ask me."

"You last saw her when?"

"Couple of months ago. I can check the diary. . . ."

"Not necessary. Why did you leave Anna?"

"How's that relevant?"

"We want to know where she is, what she might be doing, who
she might be meeting." Albert rounded on Eddy. "What she's . . .
capable of."

"Nothing bad, if that's what you're implying. Anna's strictly
one of the good girls."

Another long silence.

"Why did we break up?" Eddy said suddenly. "Oh, all kinds
of reasons. Blonde kinds. Brunette kinds. Redheads."

"You were a womanizer and she was jealous."

"You could say that. It wasn't my fault she was frigid, now was
it? You can blame that on her bloody mother. That and a whole lot
of other things."

Good, Albert thought to himself. Frigid . . . maybe even neurotic? Yes, he could tell Fox that Anna was neurotic.

"Her mother . . . I've met Mrs. Elwell."

"Then you're halfway to understanding Anna," Eddy commented. "The wonder is how she survived. It puzzled me, the way she could be so strong."

"Why is that puzzling? Isn't a loving home supposed to be the best preparation for life?"

"Don't you believe it. The best preparation for anything is hardship. Opposition. Everything else is just padding."

"Why did you marry her in the first place?"

"Why did you marry your wife?"

Albert ignored the question. "Anna was pregnant."

"So?"

"She was pregnant, you'd both just come down from Oxford, she with a first in Law, you with a third in PPE. You got her knocked up, her mother brought pressure to bear."

"Pressure! Good God, more like the Spanish Inquisition."

"How long did it last?"

"What, the marriage? A year, say."

"A year that wasn't all bad." Albert stood staring out the window at the river. Sometimes it was possible to see for extraordinary distances, even on a day as gray as this one. "And you didn't marry her just because she was pregnant, did you, you married her because she was a good woman, and fun to be with, and she had prospects, am I right, mm?"

Sigh, sigh, *sigh!*

"So now tell me . . . that year you spent together. What was she like"—Albert turned away from the window—"then?"

Eddy rested one elbow on the table and the other on the arm of his chair, interlacing his hands in front of him. "Like?" he said after a long pause. "She was like . . ."

Albert idly filled in the gap with possible descriptions. She was fun. Cold. Jolly. A real bitch.

"She was like a goddess, then," Eddy said; and Albert, hearing his voice, hearing what lurked behind it, was catapulted out of his speculative reverie into an immediacy for which he had not bargained.

"Explain, if you will, what you mean by that."

"When we were at Oxford, I thought of her as beyond my reach. I was nothing, came from nowhere. She . . ."

"Go on."

"She . . . gave off light. Always a little joke, soothing away your troubles. I've seen people stand up when Anna came in. As if she was royalty, you know? And they wanted to get a better view, get close to her. She excited people. Was interested in them. She brought out the best in you, by listening."

Albert remembered the photograph of Anna that he'd seen in the Lescombes' drawing room. "I see."

He was having to adjust his mental picture of Eddy Clapham. Until now he'd assumed that the man's sole motivation was financial, which by itself caused no problems because Albert, too, had a healthy respect for money. What differentiated him from Clapham was his idealism, the principles that made life worth living: whereas the only convictions a man like Clapham had were criminal ones. Or so Albert had thought. Now he wasn't so sure. He began to listen for the things that weren't being said.

"When she said she'd sleep with me, I thought this was it, y'know, let's do it and die, there isn't any more to be had, not here, not in this life." Eddy grunted. "Talk about a let down."

"And on her side . . . what was it about you that Anna found attractive, I wonder?"

Eddy laughed, an artificially elegant sound. "That's easy."

"So enlighten me."

"It was such a fabulous time to be at Oxford. Suddenly there was pot, and women, and no need to work if you didn't feel like it. I used to play the hard man; I grew a beard. Anna was just . . . goggle-eyed. She'd never had any contact with someone like me before. Never been *allowed* any, in case she caught fleas, you know?"

"She was infatuated by someone radically different?"

"And dangerous. Somebody *alive.* Someone who cared about things—you'll never believe this, but I had a social conscience then. Demos. Love-ins, I was into all that."

"And was she?" Albert sneered.

"Only for my sake. Not that she didn't have a conscience; hers was even better developed than mine. She didn't care for the, how shall I put it, the stagecraft."

"But in the end she found you . . . irresistible?"

Eddy shrugged. "We were both young, the genes with a G were singing and the jeans with a J were too tight, y'know the kind of thing."

Albert didn't. "You *wanted* her to get pregnant?"

Eddy laughed self-consciously. "I've even asked myself that. Maybe I did, yes."

"You were happy enough to get married, anyway?"

"Yeah. Except . . ."

"Except for what?"

When Eddy shook his head and continued to stare at the floor, Albert prompted him. "She was working too hard because she wanted to get to the bar . . ."

"The exams were tough."

"And then there was the kid. . . . What were you doing at that time?"

"Nothing much. I thought I might qualify as an accountant, but—"

"Those exams also were tough."

When Eddy shrugged, Albert reminded himself that first impressions were often the most reliable. Here was one of life's losers. Albert could not envisage his funeral. Who on earth would give up an afternoon to mourn Eddy Clapham?

"And then someone told you about the gold," he said. 'A world where every so often, just two or three times a year, people need to buy the physical stuff, in bars. And because there's so little about, and because hardly anybody knows where to find it, there's this exclusive club, isn't there, which can fix that, mm? Everything from chartering the plane to bribing customs to working out how many Heckler and Koch sub-machineguns the guards will need when they land in Benin. Or Belize."

"It's a dicey world, friend."

"I don't doubt it. But profitable, very."

"If you get it right."

Albert suppressed irritation. Clapham's milieu resembled his own in enough ways to make him wonder whether there might not be other, distinctly off-putting similarities between them.

"And did you get it right," he rasped, "you with your contacts and your drinking in nightclubs, while Anna was feeding the baby before staying up half the night to study, mm, did you?"

"What's with all this moralizing? Have you got something going with Anna, or what?"

Albert smiled, although he didn't feel particularly jolly. The picture that Eddy was painting of Anna left much to be desired, from his point of view. Perhaps if they moved forward in time . . . "Anna passed her exams, didn't she?"

"Yes."

"And wanted support, someone to look after the child while she practiced."

"That kid always was a pain. She's not much better now."

"Ah. The devoted father."

"Look—"

"I'm looking."

"It wasn't my fault Anna got frightened she might kill herself. I didn't give her PND, now did I?"

Albert slipped into overdrive, don't think, don't pause, act your heart out, make him think you knew that, "PND meaning postnatal depression?"

"Yeah," Eddy said; and—*"Miracle!"* Albert thought to himself. A copper-bottomed miracle . . .

"By the time Juliet was born I wasn't having much to do with Anna. She was way over the edge before I came along. She'd got ripped up over finding out about the adoption, changing schools and that. Then after the brat was born, she got this, you know, this terrible downer some women get. Kept on saying, 'I'm going to kill Juliet, I'm going to kill myself, if somebody doesn't help me.'"

Way over the edge . . . all ripped up . . . "I'm going to kill myself" . . .

"Would she have done it, d'you think?" Albert asked.

"No. Definitely not. She had too much guts for that. But she wasn't responsible, according to the doctor."

"What happened to Anna after that?"

Eddy was looking at Albert now, really looking at him, making assessments. "Liking this, are you?"

"What happened?"

"I heard she was seeing a shrink."

"Who did you hear that from?"

"Mrs. Elwell told me. Meant to rub it in. Blame me." He slipped into a silly voice: " 'Edward, I felt you had a right to know, Chappy didn't want me to say anything, but . . .' Christ all-bleeding-mighty." *Sigh!*

"Do you know which psychiatrist Anna saw at that time?" Albert asked.

"No. I mean, Lydia Elwell may have mentioned the name, but I can't remember now, offhand."

"Was his name Kleist, by any chance?"

Eddy pursed his lips. "Doesn't ring a bell."

No matter, Albert thought. I've got more than enough. "If you should remember, give me a ring." He started searching through his pockets for a piece of paper but Eddy forestalled him.

"Here, use this. Appropriate."

"This" was a photograph extracted from Eddy's wallet. Albert flipped it over to see a color print of Anna's upper half. She was holding a baby, smiling away from the camera at the child. The snapshot had faded a kind of rusty color and there was a crack across its top left-hand corner.

Albert scribbled a number and handed the photo back to Eddy. "The only other thing I need to know is how I get out of here without your sidekicks taking their revenge on the way."

"I'll call 'em in."

Eddy picked up the phone and spoke soft words of Arabic. The door opened to admit the bodyguards. Albert put his hand on the Browning in his pocket, but the newcomers concentrated on their master, two dogs awaiting a command or a biscuit, there was no way of telling which.

As Albert reached the door Eddy said, "If you find her . . ." He uttered a high-pitched laugh, mocking himself. ". . . You might . . . give her my love. Or something like that, yeah."

CHAPTER

25

nna awoke late on Friday with a blinding headache, doubtless caused by the foul stuff Gerhard had injected her with the night before. The house seemed unnaturally quiet. As soon as she had dressed she went to the kitchen. Barzel was there, reading the book he'd carried off the ferry the previous day. When he put the book down her eyes followed it, to be ensnared by another object lying on the table.

Anna gazed at it, fascinated. The weapon's surface bore a faint sheen, as if greasy. It was so obviously *metal*, serious. On television, at the cinema, the guns might as well be bits of wood, for all the sense of realism they conveyed. This was different. This had a function.

She looked away to find Barzel examining her with detachment, rather like an attendant in the better class of ladies' room, standing ready to hand you a towel: aware of what you'd been doing behind the locked door but wholly impassive.

Anna marched across to the sink, meaning to fill the kettle, and in doing so somehow managed to dislodge Barzel's book. It fell to the floor with a crash. She ignored it. But then suddenly his cruel face was inches away from hers, he had both her hands in an unyielding grip, and she was paralyzed.

He stared at her for a long time, as if she were some particularly repulsive insect. Then he said, in a soft voice she hadn't heard him use before: "Pick it up."

He released her. For a second Anna could not think what to do: his stance, his whole manner were so threatening that they deprived her of the power of movement. Then, almost unconsciously, she knelt and picked up his copy of Böll's novel, handing it to him without a word.

Barzel peered at the jacket until he was sure it had suffered no lasting damage. Anna was about to pass on her way to the sink when he again restrained her.

"Where you come from," he grated, "it's just a book." He paused, as if seeking the words of a magic spell, the only thing that could possibly influence such an alien being. "I know that."

Anna swallowed, said nothing.

"Don't . . . *ever* . . . touch any book of mine again."

She wanted to protest that it had all been an accident, but the expression in his eyes prevented her. He was, she saw, on the brink of violence. She stood quite still, waiting for the storm to break or pass, one or the other.

Barzel let go of her and went to sit down at the table, not taking his smoldering eyes off her face. Fortunately, at that point Gerhard entered the kitchen.

"Good morning."

He spoke in English, so presumably this salutation was directed at her. Anna nodded curtly. "I need some air," she said.

"How about the terrace? I'd like to talk to you."

"We'll go for a walk." She nodded at Barzel. "And I think we'll leave the dog at home."

When Gerhard sought Barzel's assent with a silent expression of interrogation, that really shook Anna. In their world, the one she'd shared with Gerhard up until now, he doled out the permissions. He'd given his consent to her practicing as a barrister, sleeping with him, marrying David. She remembered the day her father sold his shops to the chain and invited the buyers home to dinner; that night, for the first time, she had realized he now no longer was the boss, he had a boss.

"Don't do that," Gerhard whispered warningly as they left the house. "You can't play games with him, Anna."

"I know. He's proved it."

"What?"

"Forget it. Take me to the church on the other side of the bay, the one you can see from my room. I want to explore."

"That's too far."

"So what are you going to do?" She stopped dead, causing Gerhard to bump into her, and swung around. "Shoot me?"

He stared at her. "No," he said at last. "I wouldn't do that. I couldn't. But . . ."

"But Barzel could, yes, I know. Don't worry, I can guess the rules. We'll walk to the church. If we meet anyone, I won't try to speak to them. I won't try to escape. I give you my word. There! Does that satisfy you?"

It satisfied *her*, she discovered, to make a promise she had no intention of keeping, because by doing that she entered his world on his terms and thereby secured her only chance of escape. When Gerhard reluctantly nodded, she walked away from him without a backward glance.

The approach to the church lay along one of those paths with myriad branches always splitting off and then coming together again to make islands. The church itself stood in a cypress grove. Two or three goats were tearing at the thin grass that sprouted between its damp walls and the surrounding earth; at first Anna wasn't sure how to deal with them, fearing from their impatient expressions that they might trample her; but after standing still for a while they went back to their lunch.

Between the church and the side of the hill she found a grave-yard sheltered by cypresses and one large, shady birch. Anna could see only five graves. Two of them were old, mere grass-covered mounds, but the others looked recent. The biggest had a marble surround. Stone chips of a lurid and, Anna thought, singularly inappropriate shiny green color overlaid it. The stele, surmounted by an Orthodox cross, bore a faded photograph of the deceased: an old woman whose gray hair was drawn back tightly enough to be painful. Her cheeks were not so much sunken as collapsed, making her appear already dead, but the eyes were wide open and unmistakably quick. They contained a hint of challenge, not unmixed with humor. Her own mother's mother had looked just like that, sometimes.

She sat down on the marble tomb, suddenly overcome by memories. When Gerhard finally caught up with her she glared at

him, resentful of the intrusion. "Do you remember Nan?" she asked
him.

"Of course."

"I was thinking how she helped me. After that awful business
at school."

"Yes."

"Only she died soon afterward."

"Oh, Anna . . ."

"Leave me alone. I want to think."

But that was hard, when memories of her grandmother would
insist on forcing their way through.

Nan had taken some of the sting out of being an Elwell only
child. She always resolutely sided with Anna, infuriating Anna's
mother. Then one day Lydia had come to the new school, the one
Anna had been sent to after the débacle at the convent. It was
lunchtime; Anna found herself dragged from the table, into the
headmistress's study, wondering what fresh misdemeanor was to be
laid at her door. There was no crime, however, only punishment.
Nan had died in the early hours of the morning, of a heart attack.
Anna could go home now.

From her seat in the shade of the cypresses, a cool sea breeze
ruffling her hair, she could not quite recapture the flavor of that day,
no matter how hard she tried. She had been dreading afternoon
school, because it was netball and she hated netball. As she ate her
lunch she was thinking she would do anything to get out of it.
Anything . . . but not kill Nan. She felt confused now, as she had
done then. She knew in her brain, because Gerhard had shown her,
that Nan's death preceded her desire to be let off netball, knew also
that she must have realized it at the time, but something more
powerful than any brain would insist on muddying the waters. If it
had not been for her desire to escape the day's sport at any cost, Nan
would still be alive.

The man standing with his back to her, hands in pockets, had
patiently explained, many times, that this was a normal reaction.
But also he had, she felt, ever so gently derided her feelings about
the incident, breaking his pattern of treating what she said with
serious concern.

She had only one aim now: to escape from this island and its
infernal Prospero. Nothing else mattered a damn.

"We're going to straighten a few things out," Anna said
abruptly; and Gerhard turned toward her.

"Of course," he said. "That's what I'm here—"

"No. You're here to do the opposite. That's been your plan all along."

"I don't—"

"When I first met you, I was suffering from postnatal depression, right? A bad case."

"Yes."

"And you said all my problems went back to guilt, and you were going to cleanse me of guilt. I felt guilty because I'd been given away at birth and I saw it as my fault."

"Yes," he agreed again. "You felt, quite literally, guilty for having been born. Born substandard."

"And guilt, for me, had become a habit. I was screwed up because I saw myself as responsible for having had those girls expelled, and for killing Nan, do you remember that?"

"Certainly. You may recall I told you so, at the time."

He had told her so many things, at different times. She would have to examine them all again, sorting out those that were valid from the lies that formed part of the web of deception with which he'd ensnared her. But that could wait. A specific memory was struggling for mastery in her head.

After Nan's death there had been a funeral at which she was present without being present. She had been kept outside the crematorium chapel, in the car, with her father, unable to say goodbye properly, stuck for life with an overweening impression of death as something sinful from which children ought to be protected. She was nine: old enough, she felt, to mourn. Perhaps being made to stay outside was part of the punishment for having murdered Nan.

She'd never cried for her grandmother's death. Even now, she could not cry.

The cold marble hurt the undersides of her calves. As she shifted physically, so her perspective changed also, enabling her to see a hitherto concealed link between Nan's passing and one of Gerhard Kleist's more poignant insights.

"I want to ask you something," she said. "To check something, if you like."

"Yes?"

"Do you remember telling me about the most difficult problem a therapist has to face?"

"Not offhand. Remind me."

"Death without a corpse."

"Oh. *That.*"

"Someone disappears, for good. Is he dead? Suffering from amnesia? Or has he just abandoned his family, crushed by pressures they couldn't understand. Yes?"

"Yes. There's nothing for the therapist to seize on, you see."

"The survivors always feel *guilty,* don't they? They think they're to blame, they drove the missing person away, by not measuring up."

"What's prompted all this?" He was genuinely at sea.

It was the not knowing that brought these hapless souls to Gerhard: ignorance compounded by feelings of wholly unjustified guilt. Anna was beginning to perceive something until now kept at bay: just as Nan had gone with no goodbyes on either side, so, by giving her up for adoption, her real mother too had "died," without affording her daughter an opportunity to mourn. And both women had thus caused her to feel guilty, for different but related reasons.

She'd always felt she had failed them in some mysterious way. But how, Anna wondered, could she have failed her mother while still a child too young to know evil, let alone do it . . . ?

There was only one possible answer. She hadn't failed at all. *The adoption was not her fault.* And—another blinding flash of light—*it might not have been her mother's fault, either!*

She studied this revelation for a long time. "You didn't even try to erase my guilt over Nan's death, did you?" she said suddenly. "You *nurtured* it."

"You really mustn't let things distress you to the point where—"

"You wrecked me."

"*Wrecked* you?"

Gerhard had come to stand in front of her and was reaching out to grasp her shoulders, but on hearing these words his body became as immobile as if she were the Gorgon reincarnate.

"You knew I felt guilty because I'd been adopted, knew I blamed myself for not being good enough for my real mother. But you took my guilt and stood it on its head, until it wasn't *my* guilt any more, it was my mother's."

"And why not? Wouldn't most people see that as a natural way of regarding it, of trying to come to terms with it?"

" 'Most people' haven't got the first idea of what my real mother went through before she decided to give me up, any more than I have. The agony. The fear. Suppose she was poor, rejected by her parents . . . my God, I don't even know *why* she had me adopted, and if I don't, you certainly don't. You just pretended to."

"You're rambling."

"No, I'm learning. Waking up at last. My mother gave me away when I was born, and that was her betrayal of me, you said: not *my* fault but *hers.* And all my life's been dedicated to believing that, and ensuring the betrayal never happened again."

"For God's—"

"Be a better traitor than your mother, that's what you said." Anna smiled a brittle smile. "Quote: 'If you're worried about being betrayed, do it yourself. Do it fast, do it first.' End . . . of . . . *quote.* Oh, what a fool I've been! Because I was so infatuated with you, I let you do it. I'd have believed anything. I made it *easy* for you!"

"Anna!"

But she had jumped off the tombstone and was striding toward the house. She knew in her heart that he was her enemy. If she was to have any chance of saving herself, she must fight him as he had fought her: deceitfully, with evil intent, to the last gasp of breath in her body.

She could afford to take no prisoners in her war with Gerhard Kleist.

CHAPTER

26

NATO's chief negotiators assembled at a pleasant house near Crowborough that overlooked two thousand acres of Sussex farmland owned by the Ministry of Defence.

Albert waylaid Fox and Shorrocks in the paddock while they were on their way from the helicopter up to the house. As they approached he squared his shoulders, swallowing a couple of times in an effort to summon saliva into his dry mouth. This would be a make-or-break meeting for him. He knew it wasn't going to be easy.

"Progress." He had to shout to make himself heard above the noise of the Bell Jet Ranger's rotors.

"You'll have to be quick," Shorrocks brayed. "Half Europe's waiting for us in there and they're dancing up and down."

"Hold the chopper; I'm due back soonest."

Fox showed the pilot two downturned thumbs and the engine died. "Let's try the stables," he said.

The farm had once housed a livery; there was plenty of space for a crash conference.

"Why have our glorious allies been assembled here tonight?" Albert asked, plonking himself down on a bale of straw.

It was Fox who answered. "They're hopping mad. Word's leaked out about what Krysalis might contain. We asked them to trace a woman, but we didn't tell them the file enabled the Warsaw Pact to switch off its tactical computers and save electricity."

"So you're soothing?"

"Trying to. There's a new deadline."

"What?"

"Redman was forced to bring in the State Department. State is giving the company another four days to sort out the mess, failing which, they intend to call off the Vancouver summit. That leaked out, but the rest of NATO don't know the reasoning behind it, and *we* aren't allowed to tell them the whole story."

"I see." Albert looked down at the straw. "Rats." He sighed, apropos of nothing in particular. Then he raised his head. "Give me a contract," he said tersely.

Shorrocks looked at Fox. No one spoke for a long time. Then Fox said: "It's still too early."

"Look—"

"No, you look." Shorrocks impatiently glanced at his watch. "Tell us your news, and if there's time we'll discuss your position later."

"I need to know—"

"You don't *need* anything." Shorrocks sounded bleak. "Report."

Albert stifled his anger. He knew he wouldn't get anywhere unless he gave them something solid in exchange. He cautiously began to put his cards on the table. From his vantage point, the hand looked incredibly thin.

"It shapes up like this," he said. "There's a psychology guy called Kleist. Anna Lescombe was seeing him for ages. They had an affair."

Albert outlined most of what he had learned at the Lamonts' restaurant, omitting the inconvenient detail that Kleist and Anna hadn't lunched there for the past two years. He paused. Now came the hardest bit.

"Ex-husband told me this morning that she's always had problems," he went on, trying to sound matter-of-fact. "Acute depression, wanting to kill herself, maybe harm the baby. That kind of thing."

Fox and Shorrocks exchanged glances. "Interesting," said the latter.

"This woman is *very* disturbed," Albert resumed. "She's a traitor, she's mental, and unless something's done about her—"

"Yes, but wait a minute," Fox said. "That all happened a long time ago. Juliet's a teenager now. Anna Lescombe's long since cured of whatever it was, presumably."

"Besides," Shorrocks put in, "you've only got the ex-husband's word for it. Hardly the most reliable of witnesses, I'd have thought."

"No, you're wrong." Albert knew he could defeat that ploy, at least. "Her old medical records turned up after lunch. And sure enough, she had been referred to one Gerhard Kleist, on the basis that she was a potential suicide. She went into therapy and it looks as though she never came out of it again."

"How long ago?"

"Nineteen seventy-three."

"God!" Shorrocks made a face. "Sixteen years. In therapy all that time? I don't believe it."

"But they've undoubtedly been seeing each other ever since! The Lamonts said so. How long are you going to keep on farting about, playing games with NATO's security?"

The stables were lit by a single low-power bulb, making it hard for Albert to read the other two men's expressions. He wanted that contract: *needed* it with a deeply rooted intensity that was no longer exclusively concerned with money. Anna Lescombe was a traitor. A Communist, clearly. She had gone the same way as England was going, down the drain, and, like the other rats in this stable, she had to be eliminated, "negotiated," in the SAS regiment's detached-sounding phrase. So obvious. *But why couldn't the others see it?*

"How come none of that showed up on her husband's vet?" asked Shorrocks.

"It *did* show up. Indirectly."

"Explain."

Albert again fought to master his impatience. "Remember that note in the file about Anna Lescombe having lunch with a German? Same restaurant. Kleist was the German."

"Why the *hell* didn't Five cotton onto that?"

Shorrocks had put the question to Fox, but it was Albert who burst in with an answer. "Either it was too long ago to be caught in the net, or her earlier medical records were already missing by that time, or I don't know what. It happens often enough. My guess is that Kleist got his hooks into her, they became lovers, something much more than doctor-patient."

"Control–agent, for example?"

"I'm sure of it," Albert said confidently. "Think what a golden opportunity it was: therapist gains access to the wife of a top civil servant . . . magic! So next we need to see Kleist's case notes on the lady."

"Can you arrange it?" Shorrocks asked; and Albert heaved an inaudible sigh of relief. They were nibbling the bait. *At last!*

"Easy," he said. "Kleist's vanished. He was supposed to have lunch at their usual restaurant yesterday, when I was there. No show. Can you check the computers, see where he's gone? Anna Lescombe's with Kleist, I'd bet my life on it."

"She's somewhere in Greece," Shorrocks said.

Albert looked at him. "Tell."

"Greek immigration came up with the goods. Private plane, chartered in France, landed at a flying club outside Igouminitsa. That's on the west of the Greek mainland, opposite Corfu. Pilot and two passengers, one male, one female. The flight plan showed them on their way to Athens, but the pilot reported engine trouble and requested an emergency landing. Then it turned out that the female passenger was sick, so they got special permission to clear immigration then and there."

"Anna Lescombe being the sick party?"

"Right," Shorrocks confirmed. "The other passenger was traveling on confetti: passport issued in the name of a dead man."

"That's Kleist."

"Could well be. He claimed he was a doctor and he had the lingo off pat."

"He said he was taking her to a hospital, I suppose?"

"Got it in one," Shorrocks agreed. "But we know he didn't, because the Greeks have checked. One lead, though: someone *may* have seen them boarding a speedboat and haring off west."

"Where would that take them?"

"Corfu, or any one of half a dozen smaller islands. Of course, they could have doubled back. The Greeks are combing the place now, but . . ." Shorrocks shrugged.

Islands, Albert thought savagely. That meant crossing the sea. Perhaps a confrontation on water. . . . His skin crawled, settled itself again. *You've done it before.* No problem. Absolutely not.

"If that's all you've got for us . . ." Fox had been fidgeting with his watch for the past few minutes. His eyes were hooded with tired folds of flesh that Albert hadn't noticed before.

"One more thing," Albert said. *Forget the island, forget the bloody sea. Concentrate!* "David Lescombe."

"Ah." Shorrocks folded his arms and leaned back against a beam. "The Americans now reckon he was in this from the start. They want him, as they chillingly put it, neutralized." He jerked his head toward the house. "Some of that lot are bound to take the same line."

"Neutralized . . ." Albert was startled. The word opened up a whole new ball game, rich with fascinating possibilities. Louis Redman's thinking had obviously moved on since they'd last spoken. Suppose he ended up having not one contract, but two. . . .

He had yet to land *one* contract, he reminded himself bitterly.

"You don't think the CIA was behind that attack on Lescombe in Cornwall, do you?" he asked.

"No," said Fox.

Thank God, Albert thought. Rein the Yanks in; foreign operatives we definitely do not need. But Fox was speaking again.

"That was probably HVA. We'd better go in . . ."

Albert stood up, recalling the day at the Cornish farm. German friends, the girl had said to David: "Tell your *German* friends . . ." "Why pick on HVA?" he asked.

They were outside now, and nearing the house.

"Ah," Shorrocks said. "You're not up to date. . . . Did Fox tell you about the lead picked up by Athens-Six: the young Greek who was interested in faxes?"

"Yes."

"They put tabs on him, then they lost him."

"I know."

"But do you know what happened next? They dug around and discovered that he's been snatched off the street. Word is, HVA ran the op."

The three men had almost reached the front door; but now Albert stopped dead. "Are you *seriously* telling me," he began slowly, "that East Berlin actually does now know where Anna Lescombe is and who she's with?"

"If the Greek boy talked, yes, it looks like it," Shorrocks confirmed. "We have to proceed on the assumption that he received his orders directly from Kleist, face to face, and that he knows how to get in touch with him to report back. So unless HVA has lost its notoriously heavy touch—"

"The boy will have talked."

"You can bet on it. It follows that the East Germans will know all about that bloody fax, too, of course."

Albert's mind raced ahead. "And that means HVA could want to talk to *David* Lescombe, find out what *he* knows, whether he has some connection with Kleist, for example—so that's why you think the man in Cornwall—"

"Could have been HVA, yes. Your very brief description might fit a number of candidates, although our money's on a character called Barzel."

"Why?"

"Because he's disappeared and none of HVA's other London people have."

Albert thought with the speed of light. "David Lescombe," he said urgently. "You *must* let him run."

"We've only got four days," Fox said doubtfully.

"Doesn't matter. If he's guilty and makes a break for it, we've got him cold. If not, he may, just may, lead us to *la femme* whom we are so busily *cherch*-ing. How can we lose?"

"I'll tell you how," Fox said, again looking at his watch. "We can bloody well lose *him* when he runs, that's how."

"Not," said Albert, "if you give me a contract."

"I don't follow that," Shorrocks snapped. "Why should—"

"Because if you give me a direct, personal stake in finding the woman, and Lescombe's heading straight for her, I'll stick to him like glue." Albert drew a deep breath. "I guarantee it."

"What, no kill, no fee?"

"Right."

When Shorrocks still hesitated, Albert played his last card.

"I've put a lot into this," he said. "Solid legwork, with plenty of results. I've demonstrated my good faith, up to the hilt. But I won't be used indefinitely. Let me loose, or I quit."

"You can't."

"I can if the regiment needs me. And it will need me *soon*, I promise you that."

Shorrocks looked at Fox. "A private word . . . ?"

Albert paced about while they moved a few yards away and talked in low voices. His heart was beating fast enough to surprise him; until this moment he hadn't realized how much this operation had come to mean to him.

Anna Lescombe was part of a conspiracy, directed against England. A dreary, uniform England, admittedly; a place in many ways hardly worth saving . . . but still England, his country. And she was laughing at the people sent after her, kissing her lovely fingers at them. . . .

If he couldn't persuade them now, the game was lost.

They were coming back. Albert drew a deep breath and held it.

"All right," Shorrocks said. "We'll make you a one-time offer."

Albert released his pent-up breath, but his heart still pounded. "Go on."

"Forget tracking Lescombe; leave that to the pros. Get Kleist's case notes on Anna, *quietly.* No traces, mind."

Albert nodded.

"Then you're cleared for Greece."

Done it!

"At liberty to act with full discretion?"

Shorrocks hesitated. "Yes."

"At the price agreed?"

"As agreed. *But . . .* there is one very important but."

Albert swallowed his elation. "Which is?"

"You're to make it look like an accident. If you can't guarantee that . . ." Shorrocks made a chopping movement with his hands.

"When have I ever failed?" Albert murmured.

A military policeman was holding the front door open. The last, gritty words Albert heard Shorrocks say as he passed through it were: "There's always a first time, colonel."

THE SECOND WEEKEND

CHAPTER 27

obyn Melkiovicz. Strange name: the kind that existed only in the fantasy land of films, among those credits at the end, the ones that strained your eyesight: best boys, gaffers, they were the Melkioviczes of this world. They, and New York lady lawyers . . .

For the hundredth time David looked at the photograph he had taken from Anna's desk in chambers, willing its subject to assume life enough to talk. Anna's head of chambers had supplied Robyn's missing surname, along with her New York address. David wanted to talk to her. But . . . ever the same nagging question. Would they let him go?

His phone was tapped. He was being followed. He had given up trying to trace Anna through their shared network of friends, afraid he might contaminate them. For the Lescombes, it seemed, had begun to stink. The security services suspected he was in league with Anna, that here was a plot to betray the Western alliance in which both of them were participants. This knowledge generated a knot of hard, bilious rage just below David's stomach. For the first time he understood the true meaning of the word "depressed." You were pushed down, hard, against a rock. Crushed.

He had to do something or go under. But if he tried to see Robyn, *would they let him?*

He had a plan. Once he was in the States he could make it work. But leaving England, that was the problem. At Heathrow and all the other U.K. airports, the authorities kept a list of those who weren't allowed out. Was his name on it? If so, he could not flee the country, for, like most people, he possessed only one passport. Perhaps they would arrest him at the gate, with hundreds of curious travelers looking on and a press photographer ready to immortalize his downfall. Or perhaps the man in the black Audi would get to him first. . . .

He wanted to telephone, or even visit, his mother, but that might mean trouble for her, and David couldn't risk it. She was not a well woman, emphysema . . . father had died some years before, he could have taken this to him. Or Natalie, but she was in Australia, with Bob; she hadn't done so badly for herself, not with that latest photo of the pool, and the kids, the eldest was nine now . . .

David realized he'd allowed his thoughts to stray as a means of putting off what had to be done. His bag was packed, one of those foldover suit carriers you took away for a weekend: nothing elaborate that might signal long-term absence to the watchers. He had spent the best part of a day in the local library's reference section, mapping his route. Then a single purchase at an electrical hardware shop and he was ready.

He looked at his watch. Time to go.

He was locking the front door when a voice behind him said, "David Lescombe?"

He made himself straighten slowly, so they wouldn't think he had anything to hide. So the man from the Audi would have no excuse to open fire. Did Special Branch need a warrant, or could they—

"We haven't met. I'm Eddy. Anna's ex. How d'ye do."

For a moment David stared at him while his brain caught up. "I'm in a hurry," was all he could think of to say.

"Going somewhere? Give you a lift?"

Over his shoulder David could see a black Porsche double-parked. "This isn't really—"

"A quiet word in your ear and you might, as they say, learn something to your advantage."

"We've got nothing to say to each other."

"We've got Albert."

David had been pushing past, on his way down the steps to the pavement, but Eddy's words brought him up short. "Who?"

"In his thirties. Glasses he doesn't really need. Intent type. Taut."

"You've met him?"

"Oh, yes. Not from choice. Give you a lift, can I?"

David hesitated. "I'm catching a plane, I—"

"Thiefrow?"

David nodded.

"Come on, then."

He drove the car in much the same way, David suspected, that he powered through life: at great speed, with reckless disregard for the safety and interests of other people. "Look," Eddy said. "I know this isn't the greatest introduction in the world."

"It isn't," David agreed bitterly.

"But she's in trouble, and I mean a lot of trouble. You don't have to talk to me. But it would help."

"Help who?"

"Anna." Eddy took his eyes off the road and gazed at David for what seemed like a perilously long time. "We got divorced. But we're still married here." He tapped first his forehead, then his chest.

"You think she feels the same way, is that it?"

"No. Oh no."

"Then I don't—"

"Albert's visit set me thinking. I want to help. I told him a few things." Again that unroadworthy glance at David, supercilious and a trifle mocking. "But not all the things he needs to know if he's to function."

"Did he tell you what his job was?" David hadn't meant to sound so eager, but the words were out.

"No. He didn't have to."

"What is it?"

Eddy drove in silence for a long way. When he spoke again he did not address himself to David's question at all.

"Juliet and I meet up, now and again."

"I know. What—"

"It was she who told me about Kleist."

"Who?" Then David guessed: "The psychoanalyst?"

"Psycho-whatever, yeah. Him. She had his address and phone number."

Juliet had said she did not know the name of Anna's analyst, and that was a lie. She did not trust her stepfather but she trusted Eddy, a depressing thought.

"Did you tell Albert about Anna seeing a shrink?" Eddy asked.

"No."

"Great. Don't."

"Why shouldn't I?"

When Eddy did not answer, David's resentment boiled over. *"Why?"*

"Because he's not all there. Not quite out to lunch, but not exactly eating his sandwiches at the desk either, know what I mean?"

"What's wrong with him?"

"Which terminal do you want?"

"I'm asking you a question!"

"So am I. Do you want to fly today or not? Which bloody terminal?"

David spat out air through his teeth. "Four."

"Right. No need to get ratty. You mustn't tell Albert any more about Anna, understand?"

"I'm damned if I'm taking orders from you."

"Your privilege, David. But I'm assuming you care about Anna." He hesitated, suddenly less sure of himself. "Care more than I ever did."

"I love her, yes." David looked down at his hands. His eyes prickled, he felt a bit of a fool . . . but then the momentary embarrassment passed and he said in a firm voice, meaning it: "I love her more than I ever realized."

"I understand that. If things had been different . . ." Eddy shrugged. "All I gave a toss for in those days was bed. I never had any truck with frigid women, until Anna came along. I'm more tolerant now. I'd have given her more time. . . ."

"Now *look.* If all you've got for me is maudlin sentimentality about your failure as a lover—"

"All right, keep your hair on."

"Just tell me what Albert's job is. Just that."

"You really don't know? Here we are . . . which entrance?"

Eddy was slowing for the last turn, David felt desperate, *he had no time.* "What does Albert do?"

"If you don't already know . . ." Eddy squealed to a halt . . . "I'm in no position to tell you, old man. Too scared. Sorry."

"Scared?"

While David was still struggling to find words, Eddy leaned across him to open the door. David looked at his watch: he could stay and argue or he could miss his plane. He hesitated a second longer, then raced into the terminal.

He drew a lot of money out of a cash dispenser before buying himself a stand-by ticket to Washington, grateful that the department had obliged him to keep his American visa up to date. They let him through into the departures area, although that didn't even amount to the first hurdle; it was what happened next that mattered. Pick a line, the shortest, get it over with, know the worst. His passport officer was a middle-aged woman wearing thick glasses. Did she know this passenger had deliberately chosen her? Was it part of their training to detect such things?

Three steps. His heart was beating at a furious rate, his breath came and went, his stomach tied itself in that familiar knot. "Good morning." The woman nodded unconcernedly. *Great!* She glanced at something beneath the lip of her desk. Then she closed his passport with a snap and handed it back, her near-sighted eyes already focusing on the person behind him. David Lescombe did not interest her.

He made himself walk on, don't look back, bag onto the rollers, pass through the arch, *beep!*, "Turn out your pockets, would you, sir? . . . Thank you . . ." Then he was in the neon-lit hangar of Terminal Four airside. By now his legs were wobbling so that he half walked, half ran to the nearest bank of seats and flopped just before his knees gave way, and he was still in England; this was the easy bit.

On the plane he felt a great desire to drink. The harder he fought the worse it became, but he managed to content himself with two scotches. If they did little to raise his spirits, at least they took away some of the anger he felt toward Juliet. In the end he convinced himself of the truth: by not revealing Kleist's name she had been trying to protect Anna.

Something else that Eddy had said worried him a lot more. "A frigid woman"—were those the words he'd used? David could not come up with a less-appropriate adjective to describe Anna. So what had changed between the divorce and her meeting David? *Who had brought about the change?*

Kleist?

What sort of therapist was he?

David turned to look out the window. It was a sunny day;

he could see the polar snows, only another couple of hours to go . . .

Entering the States proved as easy as leaving England. David told the cab driver to take him to a hotel on Dupont Circle in the northwest of the city. He knew nothing about this place except that, according to the street map, it was right by a subway station. As the cab pulled in to the curb David caught sight of the brown four-sided pylon with an *M* for Metro on top, and he felt a tickle of excitement. He could make this work.

The moment the door closed behind him he placed an order with room service, then opened his bag and scattered its contents over one of the two double beds. The waiter arrived with hamburger and french fries to see a guest who plainly intended to stay a while; he was on the phone, inquiring about a tour of the Hillwood Museum in two days' time. The waiter, who had received certain instructions unconnected with room service, did not think this looked like someone with a deep-seated interest in Russian art; but maybe, as he told the two CIA agents who were waiting for him downstairs, the guy just wanted to take in the gardens.

David counted to fifty after the man had taken his tip and left. He went to his bag, pulled out the tape recorder he had bought at Dixon's and switched it on. Then he grabbed a pale green cagoule very different from the gray suit in which he'd arrived, before silently letting himself out.

As he ran down the fire-exit stairs two at a time he went over the calculations again, persuading himself that it would work. Contrary to popular belief, fueled by contemporary fiction, the CIA and FBI do not have limitless resources or manpower; they had no idea where he intended to stay in Washington, because he didn't make an advance reservation; it would take time to put men in place; he had been in this hotel for less than twenty minutes; *run!*

At the bottom of the flight he paused for long enough to throw the cagoule across his shoulders and put on a pair of sunglasses. He raced through the shopping area to Connecticut Avenue; then he was in the Circle and pounding down the subway steps.

He bought a farecard and boarded the first Red Line train to come along. He played all the tricks he'd absorbed in cinemas over the years: waiting for the last moment before the doors closed, then jumping in; retracing steps; crossing from one set of tracks to another. At the interchange station on 12 and G streets he took the

Blue Line out to Arlington Cemetery. There he let several cabs go by before hailing one.

"Are you available for a long trip?"

A pair of suspicious eyes materialized in the driver's mirror. "How long is long?"

"Baltimore?"

"*Balt*-imore? Shit, man, d'you know how far that is?"

"No. How far is it?"

"Two hunnud dollars from here."

"A hundred, says my map."

"Well, I dunno . . . you got the cash?"

"Yes."

"Lemme see it."

David held up a clutch of bills.

"Yeah, yeah. Okay."

The driver became taciturn after that, much to David's relief. He was hungry, he wanted to sleep, but he dared not relax until he was in Baltimore, on the Amtrak train, heading for New York. Then he could rest.

Is this how Anna did it when she fled, he wondered, as the landscape unwound across his tired vision? Was she alone then? Now? Or was she with Kleist?

How did he measure up against his wife's, his apparently *frigid* (God, how he hated Eddy!) wife's performance, when it came to deception? To flight?

No, she hadn't fled. She would not have gone willingly. Unless perhaps . . .

He realized he didn't know what he believed any more. He simply didn't know anything . . . except that he loved her and had to find her.

Nothing else mattered a damn.

CHAPTER

28

On Saturday afternoon Anna visited the church again, only this time she went alone. She passed through the kitchen, where Barzel and Gerhard were still at lunch. "I'm going for a walk," she said offhandedly. After she had gone about a hundred yards she looked back and to her surprise found that no one was following her. Anna frowned. What did that mean?

This time she did not pause at the tombs, but straightaway entered the church. Dried leaves, stirred by the breeze, drifted around the floor with a desiccated scratching sound. At the far end stood the altar, a simple cross, and two candlesticks; above them she could just make out traces of once-colorful paintings of Jesus and his apostles, done directly onto the wall. The only face she felt confident about identifying was John, reasoning that as Jesus loved him and he was seated next to the central figure in the main fresco, he must be John.

There was a box of votary candles, and a brass stand to receive them. But the faithful stayed away, so no flame enlivened the interior, apart from a red spark in the lantern suspended from the ceiling, which, she supposed, was God.

Anna placed a candle in the holder before realizing she had no means of lighting it. To one side hung a curtain, which half concealed a hole in the wall leading to the vestry. Inside this cubicle she found a rickety cupboard containing nothing save, oh miracle of miracles, a box of matches.

She sat cross-legged on the floor, watching her candle dissolve into the firmament, with only the red, red eye of God for company. Be vigilant, she warned herself. Use the time to think, before *he* comes. . . .

———

Barzel replaced the phone on its rest and turned to Gerhard, who was watching him anxiously. "Well?" the latter said at last. "What does Huper say?"

Barzel kept him in suspense a moment longer. "He says yes."

"We're going to Berlin—the three of us?"

"That's right. Your orders are to keep her under control until Monday night, when the submarine will come."

"A submarine . . ." Gerhard was taken aback. "It'll be a terrible strain for her."

"That's your problem." Barzel stood up. "We haven't got anything in these waters, but the Soviets have agreed to help."

He was worried about that. What if the Russian commander had orders to take them to a Black Sea port and then forward them not to Berlin but to Moscow? Barzel had a backup now, a man called Stange, but the two of them couldn't hope to overpower an entire crew and—he eyed his companion contemptuously—it was no use looking to *him* for help.

Kleist had turned traitor, that much Barzel knew; but he couldn't afford to let on, not yet. The woman still responded to her former therapist, making life easy for the HVA men whose job it was to take her to Berlin, sane and in one piece. Kleist had been a wonderful agent, once. He still might be capable of engineering an escape if he discovered that he'd been rumbled. So, for the moment, Kleist was safe. But that didn't mean he could be trusted.

"The woman . . ." Barzel said casually.

"Mm?" Gerhard made an attempt to focus. "What about her?"

"She felt something for you?"

"Once."

"And you fell in love with her."

"That's past history."

No, Barzel thought to himself, it isn't. And this will require very careful handling. "Berlin said something else. Anna's husband is starting to make a nuisance of himself."

"What? Even after you threatened him that day in Cornwall?"

"He doesn't scare easily. Now he's on his way to America. Can you guess why?"

Gerhard's face twitched. "No," he snapped. "And you worry too much. He'll never trace me here."

Barzel thought it over. Kleist was plainly scared out of his wits by the reference to America. HVA files showed that he'd had a brief affair with a United States citizen called Melkiovicz, in 1987, and that Melkiovicz was a close friend of Anna Lescombe's. Which meant . . . what?

"No," he said thoughtfully. "He won't trace us. It can be taken care of."

"What does that mean?"

"We have an excellent organization across the Atlantic. Whatever Lescombe's after, our people will ensure he doesn't find it. And if by some chance he *does* . . ."

Gerhard swallowed. "Yes?"

"He won't be allowed to use it." Barzel studied him from under lowered eyelids. "You're losing control of the Lescombe woman. This isn't a secure place. I'm worried."

"No one ever comes here."

"So *you* say."

Barzel went across to the bedroom window, first collecting a pair of binoculars from the top of the chest of drawers. Suddenly he paused in midsweep and cursed under his breath. "So no one ever comes, eh?" he grated. "Look at *that!*"

Gerhard came to stare over his shoulder and Barzel handed him the glasses. A small sailboat had anchored on the far side of the bay. People were lounging on the sundeck, the sound of happy voices drifted faintly across the water.

"They come and go," Gerhard said with a shrug, lowering the binoculars. "In the holiday season. They're early, it's still only April; there won't be any more between now and Monday night."

"What if Anna were to see them?" Barzel suddenly remembered how she'd left the house. "She might try to escape! For God's sake, go and see where she's got to."

Gerhard looked at his watch, chewing his lip. Barzel understood. It was late in the afternoon, Iannis should be making his call soon, and how embarrassing it might be if he, Barzel, were to answer the phone. . . .

"Go!" he commanded urgently.

After Gerhard had left the room, Barzel padded across to the door to make sure it was shut before again sitting down on the bed. He'd visited Moscow once and hadn't liked it. The time had come to run up Kleist's phone bill a little, talk to friends in Berlin, make sure that this damned Soviet sub didn't turn left when it ought to turn right.

Barzel also needed the reassurance of a chat with Colonel Huper concerning his collection of books. He trusted Huper to keep his word, but there were other colonels in the HVA, illiterate men . . .

Before Barzel could pick up the phone, however, his mind again diverted to David Lescombe. Anna's husband was playing a game too deep to fathom. An amateur, said the HVA official line; someone blundering about in a daze. But he seemed to be a remarkably gifted amateur.

Time Lescombe was *stopped* . . .

Barzel arranged himself on the bed in such a way that he could continue to keep an eye on the boat. Berlin would have to wait. He picked up the phone and asked for a New York number.

————

In the church, Anna, like Barzel, was busily devising a plan of campaign. She needed to uncover Gerhard's weaknesses. Unfortunately, the only one she could remember was sex.

Her feelings of bittersweetness comprised memories of their love-making and resentment at being unable to shake those memories off. When his hands touched her, that day on the beach, it was as if someone had turned on a long-dormant switch, flooding her with power. He still lusted after Anna, the old Anna; and she couldn't pretend to be indifferent.

During the golden time, they had consumed each other's bodies like starving ship-wrecked mariners, gorging themselves to fulfillment and beyond. Their appetite grew by what it fed on: the more they made love, the deeper their desire intensified. He could open a moist channel down to the neck of her womb with a single look, making her forget to breathe.

Sitting here in the empty church, she told herself that the affair was all over long ago. Anna the lawyer yearned to believe this rational voice testifying inside her head . . . and was skeptical.

Somehow she had to find a weakness in him that did not overlap with hers.

When the door crashed open she spun around to find Gerhard

framed against the hot brightness outside.

"I'm sorry if I startled you."

She nodded token remission. But when he tried to touch her, she stood up, pushing his hands away, and went to close the door. As she reached it, something made her raise her eyes above the level of the path. A man she had never seen before stood a dozen or so paces up the hill, one hand resting on the bole of a eucalyptus tree, the other in his pocket. Now she understood why they had let her leave the house: a guard was already in position, waiting. She slammed the door shut and leaned against it.

"Another Barzel?" she inquired.

"Anna." Ignoring the two or three rickety chairs scattered around, he sat on the floor, inviting her with a gesture to do the same. "We have to talk."

"I'm listening." But she did not sit down.

"It's time you heard the truth. About me."

"I think so," she agreed.

"You've had the bad luck to fall in with someone who isn't what he appears to be." He paused. "Anna, this is very difficult to say."

"Go on."

"I work for an organization called Hauptverwaltung Aufklärung. HVA. It is the East German secret service."

"They ordered you to steal David's file. Using me."

"Anna, listen—"

"Just tell me one thing," she said, ignoring him; and the resolution in her voice surprised her. "Why did you do it, Gerhard?"

"Why?"

"Is that such a difficult question? Sixteen years we've known each other, we've been lovers, and now suddenly you're a spy."

He hesitated. "I have a sister. Her name is Ilsa."

Whatever Anna had been expecting, it wasn't this. First a spy, now a spy with a hitherto unsuspected sister. "You never mentioned that. Not once."

"There are lots of things I never mentioned."

People were shut off. Anna thought she knew Gerhard, just as she thought she knew David and Juliet; she had lived her life in a certain way on the strength of such assumed knowledge. But she did not know them.

"For instance," Gerhard went on, "I told you I was born in Germany, and you believed I meant West Germany, but it wasn't so. My father was a high-up in the Communist party. He got me out, to the West."

"Why should he want to do that?"

"I was his . . . favorite. I could do no wrong in his eyes. Ilsa, you see . . . our mother died in labor, when she was born. Father couldn't forgive Ilsa. He spoiled me." Gerhard laughed, without humor. "I longed to study in the West, have a good time as well. And although I didn't know it then, that suited some important people who wanted a tame therapist in London, or maybe Paris or New York."

"These HVA people?"

"Yes. But when they stitch together such deals, there's always an insurance. Someone has to stay behind, to act as magnet. A guarantee that you will come home, and a security for good behavior while you are away."

"And Ilsa was your magnet?"

He nodded again. "She's younger than I am. We were always as close as blood to the vein. When father died, it left just the two of us. She's a pediatrician. A good doctor. Dedicated."

He spoke the last word with a mixture of resentment and admiration.

"Before you and I met, HVA came to me one day. One of my patients was a secretary in the cabinet office. She was terrified of her employers' finding out she was in therapy. HVA told me to go to work on her, play on her fears." He laughed, a hateful sound. "Make her fall in love with you, why don't you?—that's what they said."

"And you said yes."

"I said no."

"But—"

"I was . . . encouraged to think again. If I wanted Ilsa and her family to go on working. Eating. Walking about the streets. Don't you see the irony, Anna? If I bought this deal, I'd be prostituting everything I'd trained for. Whereas if I refused, the only effect would be to destroy my sister's career, and she's no prostitute."

"What happened?" Anna asked coldly.

"This wretched girl, this secretary, told me a few odds and ends that I passed on. Enough to satisfy HVA."

"And when I married David, they came to you again."

"In a way . . ."

She looked at him expectantly. His face told her that whatever came next she would find difficult.

"Anna, I have to tell you this. They . . . they knew about David before you did. HVA asked me to find a way of introducing the two of you. And I did."

It mattered to him more than to her, she realized. "The sailing weekend?"

"Yes."

"It worked." She sighed. She knew he felt bad about it, presumably because that had spelled the end of his hopes of one day divorcing Clara and marrying Anna, but she couldn't share his regrets. By bringing her and David together, Gerhard had done her the biggest favor in his life.

"So HVA wanted to get at David, through me," she said. "Is that it?"

"Yes."

A long pause followed. "And you agreed," she said at last. "Even though we'd been lovers, friends . . ."

Gerhard was eager to justify himself. "You see, Ilsa and I, we . . . we had a sort of conspiracy. Against my father. Even before I opened my first textbook I knew how wrong he was to blame Ilsa for our mother's death. It made us even closer, somehow. Once she was married, had children, she became even more vulnerable. Anna, can't you find it in yourself to understand how I felt?"

"What do you want?" She was genuinely curious. "Sympathy? Forgiveness?" She could have told him: You get used to the guilt, after a while. After a lifetime. But somehow that would have sounded cheap, and would have brought her down to his level. So instead, "I understand," was all she said.

His expression told her that he found this hard to accept; but Anna found it equally difficult to elaborate. She imagined the HVA holding Juliet, or David; "Behave or else," that's what they would say, and she would behave, oh yes. . . .

Gerhard started to apologize, but she cut him off. "Is there anything else?"

For a long time he continued to gaze down at the floor as if the secrets of his motivation lay concealed beneath the flagstones. Anna sensed he was casting about for an explanation of why he had, after all, decided to sacrifice Ilsa; why in the end she had proved as expendable as anyone else. Anna knew the answer: when it came down to a straight choice between Gerhard and Ilsa, it had seemed the right thing to do at the time. Now . . .

"They are sending a submarine to take us off the island," he said at last. "That's what I came here to tell you. A Russian submarine."

She fixed him with one of her level stares, the kind she knew he most abhorred because she could use it to veil herself from him. "Of course."

"Why do you say 'of course'?"

"They'll want to interrogate me, won't they? See what else I know about David's work. You'd better hypnotize me again, remove whatever it was you put in my head to stop me from leaving."

"You knew about that?"

"Oh, I've worked out a lot of things. When does this happen?"

He did not answer immediately. Anna felt like a condemned prisoner who hears that her appeal for clemency has been rejected, that it remains only to pencil a date in the diary. *When?*

"Monday."

"But that's the day after tomorrow!"

"Anna, what you said was right: I did implant a suggestion that you shouldn't try to leave here. So now we really must try to prepare you for the journey, sort you out."

"Get lost."

"Unless you make an effort—"

"You'll *what?* Go on, tell me, you bastard! Twist me and bend me and make suggestions in the hope I'll believe I thought of them first . . . Come on, you can do it! After all, you made me into a *traitor!*"

She raised her hands to her eyes, wanting more than anything to sleep, perhaps faint; it didn't matter what form oblivion took as long as it came. But then she remembered: if she did not save herself, nobody else could.

She had one solid, useful piece of information: she knew how he had broken her. She understood his methods. If only she could find a way of turning them against him, discover the weakness that *must* be there. . . .

"Gerhard," she said, wiping her eyes.

"Yes?"

"I'm all right now." She lowered herself down beside him, in such a way that he could not easily see her face.

"I'm glad."

"But there's something else I'd like to ask you."

"What is it?"

"When they've finished with me in Berlin, or wherever it is, assuming I cooperate . . ."

He became unexpectedly animated. "Yes, I wanted to talk to you about that. When it's over—"

"Can I go home then? To David?"

Gerhard's gaze dropped. He said nothing.

"That's the one success you did have. He's all I ever prayed for, dreamed of, and I love him." She looked down at her hands, folded in her lap. "I love him," she repeated, "and he must be feeling desolate beyond belief."

"He's a sensible man." Gerhard's voice was indifferent. "He'll come to terms with it."

"But he can't, you see. Don't you realize what he must be *feeling?* He thinks that I've abandoned him, that I don't love him." She paused, seeking some way to reach Gerhard. "Another death without a corpse. You remember, we were talking yesterday: the worst thing in the world?"

When he remained silent she raised her head and looked at him beseechingly. "If you promise me I can go back to David, I'll do anything you want. I won't try to escape."

He was almost convinced. "You promise?"

"Yes." *Now she was on the brink. Suppose he put her under, then tried to make love to her, no, don't think that. . . .* "You can hypnotize me, if you like." *It was done!* "If that will make you feel more . . . more secure. Only please don't use the drugs again, they're so dreadful. Just put me into a trance. Relax me." Anna breathed in deeply, closing her eyes. "Do it now," she said in a rush.

"Here?"

"Yes. It's peaceful here."

"Anna, listen to me." He took her hands between his own. A spasm of treacherous delight ran down her spine; with an effort she repressed a gasp. "There was a time when we had something, wasn't there? Something . . . perfect."

She stared at him.

"If you came to Berlin and . . . and they decided they couldn't afford to let you go . . ."

She snatched her hands away, but he caught them again and held them fast. "If that's what happened . . . could you . . . bring yourself to forget the past, forget David—?"

She jumped to her feet, where he could no longer use that insidious touch to play upon her innermost vulnerability. *You fool,* she cried to herself. *How could you fail to realize . . . ?*

"Anna, please say you'll consider it." He was imploring her now. "Please!"

"No!" she cried, running to the door. "I love David." The words acted on her like a magic charm: she felt an upsurge of energy as she seemed to grow in stature, and it was true! "I love David," she shouted again, this time with triumph in her voice.

"And what if something were to happen to him?" he said harshly. "What then?"

She wheeled around to stare at him. "What could happen to—"

"Who do you think these people are, these HVA men we've been talking about so gaily? Kindergarten nurses? Eh?"

Her exultation drained away, she became frightened. "Tell me," she whimpered. "I know you're hiding something. *Tell me!*"

He was on his feet now, his face twisted into an expression of hatred. "He's going to New York. They'll—"

"How can you know where he's—"

"Unless he backs off soon, they'll stop him." He strode forward, catching her unawares, and grabbed her arm. "Anna, don't you understand? *They're going to kill your husband!*"

CHAPTER

29

I t was night, the streets of New York were jammed with cars and pedestrians. David made his initial pass quickly, first examining the façade of Robyn's apartment building from the opposite side of Park Avenue, then walking by close enough to get a good look at the doorman, wearing his peaked hat, with a pair of white gloves tucked into the left epaulette of his overcoat. David turned off the avenue and ducked into the first bar he found. He ordered a scotch, straight up, found the last empty table, and wrote a note. Then he went straight back onto Park, walking fast, and accosted the door-man, who had just escorted a mink-clad lady from her Mercedes to the door.

"For Robyn Melkiovicz," he said, handing the note to the man. "You might be good enough to inform her that it's somewhat ur-gent." David did not know he had such reserves of true-grit Brit accent to call upon. "And I hope you will have a drink on me later this evening. Good day." Wrapped around the envelope was a twenty-dollar bill.

David walked away without looking back, turned right at the next intersection, and broke into a jog. He loped all the way around the block, glad to be jostled by passers-by, because they afforded him what he most needed: cover.

The FBI would be closing in now. Perhaps they had already intercepted the note. David pushed through the door of the same bar he'd visited earlier and ordered another scotch.

Fifteen minutes, he had written in his note. Such and such a bar in fifteen minutes' time; don't phone anyone, don't tell a neighbor, you're being watched, your phone is tapped, you may be in great danger. He had signed himself "Anna Lescombe's husband, David" and he had included the photograph found in Anna's desk, not knowing if that would work, but praying, praying . . .

He looked at his watch. The CIA and FBI might be finite organizations, but their capacities were great. He had been on the run now for six hours. People would be looking for him, a lot of people. She was late. She wasn't coming. She had not received his note, she was out of town. He should have called, *no, you couldn't call, her phone may be tapped.*

From where he was sitting he had a view of the door. Every so often it swung open to admit a wave of cold air from the street into the bar's overheated fug, and David tensed, sure it would be the police. Feeling another blast, he raised his head in time to see a boisterous trio of men come in. The door swung shut.

He half rose in his seat. A second before the door closed he had caught sight of a figure outside. Female. Hands thrust deep into the pockets of a short jacket, spoiling its shape. Not walking, not talking to anyone, just standing there.

It was she, he knew it had to be she. Suppose she had called the police, "Officer, there's a man trying to molest me. . . ." What if she had shown his note to someone? "Go to the bar," they might have told her. "Persuade him to come outside in the street where we can overpower him. . . ."

What should he do?

A man was sitting at the bar alongside a woman who looked considerably younger than her companion. Now they stood up and bade noisy goodbyes to the bartender. They seemed to be in the middle of a good-natured argument.

"Look," the man was saying. "Look, on Monday, you just . . . you just *tell* them, right?"

"Oh, you know, you can't just tell those guys. . . ."

"No. Listen. Wait. You just, you know, you go in, and you say, 'Look, fellahs . . .' "

They had reached the door. As the man opened it, David caught another glimpse of the person on the pavement. She hadn't moved. He stood up, quickly paid for his drink, and maneuvered himself behind the couple who were leaving, did it in such a way that to anyone outside he must look like a member of their party. *Don't scare her. Do not, whatever happens, scare this woman. . . .*

As the three of them went out David peeled away from the couple, who had not noticed his existence, and stopped while still a few feet short of the lone figure.

"Don't come any closer," she cried warningly, holding up both hands. "Stay where you are."

David froze. His world began to fall apart. She'd tricked him! Now passers-by would rescue her, maybe somebody had a gun. To come so close and now this!

"Look, I'm telling you . . ."

"You know, look, will you please listen . . . ?"

The sound of the departing couple's discussion died away. David realized that none of the pedestrians on the street had stopped, or so much as looked in his direction. People went right on hurrying by.

"Robyn Melkiovicz?"

"Stay away from me!"

"I wrote you a note."

This time the woman said nothing. David took a step forward and she at once retreated, but silently.

"I'm David Lescombe." He spoke fast, knowing he had seconds left. "Anna's husband. She's in danger. I don't know where she is. I'm trying to help her." He stopped, awaiting a reaction, any reaction, from the woman in front of him. "You're my last chance."

"Oh my God," he heard her say softly. Did her voice have an impediment . . . ? "Oh my God," she repeated and suddenly he knew what was wrong with her, she was crying, at the end of her rope. . . .

"Come and have a drink," he said gently. "Please."

Robyn held her fists to her eyes. "Give me a minute." At last she lowered her hands and whispered, "Let's get off the sidewalk. I feel . . ." A violent shake of the head completed the sentence.

He took her inside. There were fewer customers now; it was getting late. They found a place flanked by two other empty tables, right at the back. David ordered a third scotch for himself and turned to Robyn.

"Perrier . . . no, Canadian Club. On the rocks."

She sat with both hands cupped around the glass, staring at him across the table. He tried to form an impression of her but she was such a mixture of things. Medium height, slim, with no bust to speak of. She wore a baggy black jacket over dark pants and looked as if she might be going out for an evening date, except that her auburn hair had been coiled on top of her head in braids: a tight, decorous style more appropriate to women lawyers at work than at play. Her features were small, delicate, with shadows around the deep eye sockets. Her nose had an upturned tilt, which would have given her an appealing childlike quality, were it not offset by the mouth, which was hard to start with and made harder by dark lipstick applied in a thick layer. Her face was oval-shaped, the eyes beautiful, having a misty quality of intuition.

She was the woman in the photograph. She was lovely. She was also very frightened.

"I've been warned not to have anything to do with you," Robyn said. "With anybody."

He stared, trying to make sense of what she'd said. How could they think he posed a threat? "Warned? Who by?"

"They said they were CIA."

"So why are you meeting me now?"

"Because . . ." Her voice shook, as did her hands when she tried to drink; David heard the click of glass against her teeth. "Because I'm just worried to death about Anna."

The last word was swallowed up in a marsh of unshed tears.

"That makes two of us."

"These men who came to see me . . ." Robyn swallowed a couple of times and went on, "They didn't . . . smell American. I have a friend who works for the FBI. I asked him to find out if they were leveling with me."

"When?"

"This afternoon. Not long before I got your note. He's going to check it out and stop by for a drink later, at my apartment."

David sat back. He mustn't be around when the FBI man came. By now his would be the hottest name on the entire Atlantic seaboard.

"I want to come to sit next to you," he said softly. "I'm unhappy not being able to see the door. Okay?"

She hesitated, searching his face. "All right."

He changed seats. "Those men you described," he said, "may be dangerous to me." Albert lurched into his mind. "Was one of them young, with pink-tinted glasses?"

"No. Nothing like that. Middle-aged. Slav faces. Or German, maybe. Russian. Kind of rough, anyway."

German. Russian.

"Did they mention me by name?"

"No. Just . . . if anyone came around asking questions about Anna Lescombe, say nothing. I'm scared."

"Me too."

That was the truth. If Anna had gone over to the other side, "they," the mysterious hunters-and-watchers who lived on the borders of his imagination, could consist of more than just Albert and his cohorts. "They" could have been sent to guard and protect their latest acquisition. "They," these new ones, intended to keep Anna. "They" did not intend to let a mere husband devalue their investment.

He remembered the man from the Audi, in that narrow Cornish lane. He, too, had seemed "kind of rough."

"Anna's in trouble," Robyn said. "I just *know*, that's all. David, we were that *close!* If something happens to her I feel it, here, inside, like somebody is playing a musical instrument in my chest."

"I had no idea," he said, sounding foolish in his own ears. "I mean . . . no idea."

The bar was hot and stuffy, but David felt cold right through to the marrow of his bones. He was shivering.

"Are you okay?" Robyn was regarding him strangely.

"No. I'm not."

He examined the other tables, one by one. Those yuppie types over by the bar, were they CIA? KGB? The two women sitting in a window alcove, talking with their hands, did they have pistols in their bags?

Robyn jumped when David brought his fists down on the tabletop. He was breathing quickly. His eyes were clenched shut.

"What's the matter?"

He shook his head.

"Are you in some kind of trouble?"

David nodded three emphatic times.

"Is it to do with Anna? It is."

Again the three forceful nods.

"You have to tell me! She's my best friend."

"This is going to sound crazy."

"Try me."

"Anna's gone away. It looks as though she may have taken some papers of mine; they're missing, anyhow. Important papers. The sort of papers that men with German or maybe Russian faces would like to read."

"Oh God." It was hardly even a whisper.

"I've been looking for her. But if I look too hard, maybe, just maybe, they'll try to stop me from looking any harder." He burst into a cackle, making Robyn start. "God, I told you it was crazy!"

"It's not. David, do you understand? I want to help."

He told her about the last few days: the visits to Anna's chambers, her daughter and mother, Albert, Eddy, the flight to America, the simple tricks that had allowed him to stay one step ahead of "them."

"And now I don't know what to believe," he concluded. "Broadway said she was being sued for this huge amount of money, her career was in the rough; did you know she drank?"

"She could handle it."

"Oh, yes! She could handle keeping it from me, anyway. Then Juliet told me Anna had been seeing some kind of shrink. Eddy would have me believe my wife was frigid."

"Take it easy."

"You say that, but I didn't know *any* of those things! Can you imagine what it's like, realizing you've been married for nine years to someone you can't recognize, not even *from her own family's description* of her?"

Robyn shook her head.

"Can you tell me anything at all that might help me find Anna?" David asked her.

"It's not easy. Oh, Jesus, I don't know. I have to go back to the start. . . . When I came to London, Anna was so . . . so damn *kind* to me. We shared an office."

"What beats me is why she never brought you home."

She took a deep breath and sighed it out with great force. "This is where it gets tacky. We had something in common. I'd been going through a hard time here in New York. I was in therapy. That's the connection."

"I don't get it."

"That's how I met Gerhard. But then she told me you didn't know about him. And . . . well, she thought you and I wouldn't relate, anyway. She saw us as two very different kinds of people, and she was afraid I might blurt out something about Gerhard without thinking—I tend to do that. So we figured we had to kind of make a choice, you know? I could be part of Anna's home scene, or part of Gerhard. And—"

David wanted to shout with frustration. "I don't follow anything you're saying. Who's Gerhard?"

"Gerhard Kleist. Anna's therapist."

"Kleist . . . Eddy talked about a Kleist."

"She'd been seeing him on and off for nearly thirteen years, when I first met her. That was 1986."

"Thirteen. Years."

Robyn nodded. When she put a hand over his, David scarcely noticed. "She wanted to protect you. She didn't think she deserved you. She believed that if you knew she'd ever needed therapy, you'd abandon her, maybe. She couldn't take that chance."

He pulled his hand away.

"But it made life hard for her. There was no one she could discuss her treatment with. Not even you, especially not you. So when I came into her life, it was like springtime for Anna. Suddenly she could talk about experiences with someone who'd been there too."

"I want you to tell me something straight. Why did Anna need therapy in the first place? What brought her to Kleist?"

"I can't tell you that."

"You've got to."

"No. It was her secret. She dreaded it ever coming out. She knew it could ruin her career and break up her marriage: her words, not mine."

"You've told me all this, and now we get to the really important part you're refusing to help me."

Robyn shrugged. Her hard mouth had set in a straight line; he could detect no sign of give in her. "This man Kleist," he said at last. "Have you any idea where—"

"Yes. I know where he might be."

"You do! But that's wonderful."

"No, it's not. David, there's more you have to know. Anna and I had a fight. I don't know if the fight is ended yet."

His mouth was dry. There must be some limit to this woman's revelations, *surely?*

"I didn't realize how . . . how she felt about Gerhard. So I became friends with him. We got along fine. He's very attractive to women."

Now David's heart was pumping blood too fast for his system to cope with. A lot of things seemed to be going on inside his body, none of them pleasant.

"We had an affair," Robyn said. "He took me to his villa, in the Mediterranean. On an island. Anna was . . . mad."

David gazed at her, at first refusing to follow where she led. "You mean . . . it's possible that she and Gerhard are . . ."

"Together. Yes."

"She . . . felt something for this man?"

Robyn said nothing.

"She loved him? Was crazy about him?" His voice rose. "Had the hots for him?"

"David, please!"

"Well, *which?*"

Robyn drew a deep breath. "Years ago, long before she met you, Anna had an affair with Kleist. And although the affair stopped, she remained fixated with him."

David had been expecting it, but the hard reality still knocked him cold. Long minutes passed before he spoke again.

"The affair stopped?" he managed to say at last.

"Yes. Anna told me that, so did Gerhard, and I believed them. David, she loves you very much. You're the best thing that ever happened to her."

"But you think she may have run to him?"

"It's possible."

"Why?" he said, and his voice was savage. "Why would she do that, if the affair was over?"

"Because whenever she found herself in anything deep, any bad time, she would go back to him for therapy. I think she may be having some kind of breakdown. If so, Gerhard's the one she'll go to."

He was silent for a while, trying to come to terms with the knowledge that Anna could not take her problems to her husband, only to another man whom he had never met. A man who had been to bed with her. Who while in bed had taught her . . .

"You told me that you quarreled," he said at last. "What was that about?"

"Gerhard and Anna managed to find a way through their affair to a kind of equilibrium. But when she found out that he and I had . . . she was wild. She knew she was being irrational, she admitted that. Still, if I'd foreseen the trouble it would cause, I'd never have gone with Gerhard."

"But you did go. To the island." Suddenly his brain completed the circuit. "That's where the photograph was taken!"

"Yes. The photograph is what started the fight. It was the first she knew that I'd gone away with Gerhard."

"Have you heard from Kleist lately—is that how you know where he is?"

"I don't *know*. A hunch, that's all. And no, I haven't heard from him."

While speaking she had brought the photograph out of her handbag, David's note still wrapped around it. Now he took it from her and said, "Would you know how to get there again?"

"Yes."

"Can you tell me?"

"I don't know, David." She was facing him now, her gaze coolly analytical. "I'm worried what you might do, frankly."

His eyes could not meet hers. There was no answer to her doubts.

"David, listen to me. Please. I feel that Anna and I are . . . well, hewn from the same stone. She's still my dearest friend in all the world. We quarreled, yes, but we went some way to making up, and you know something? Every day I curse myself for my mistake in angering her. If anything bad happened to her because of something I did, or said . . ."

"I understand. But *you* must understand this: I love Anna. I'm her husband. I'm learning things about her that shock me, and, yes, anger me as well. But I know she's in trouble and she needs help. That's all I want to do: help her."

He gazed at Robyn, putting every ounce of feeling he possessed into it, until she wavered.

"You promise me you'll be patient with her?"

"I promise you I'll help her all I can. And if when I've talked to her I'm convinced she's doing this because she genuinely wants to, if she'd rather be with Kleist than with me, then . . ." he drew a deep breath ". . . I'll let her go."

He had been putting off the moment for too long; but as soon as he spoke the words aloud he knew that this decision was the right one.

"You mean that? You love her that much?"

"I do."

For a long moment she sat motionless. Then she reached for her bag and took out a pen. "Do you have paper?"

"I don't want anything written down, in case I'm stopped. Just tell me; I'll remember."

Falteringly she began to recite directions. "You start by going to Corfu. Then you have to get to the other island. There's a man with a speedboat; it's quicker than the ferry. His name's Amos, I think. Yes—Konstantine Amos, with a *K*. . . . He'll take you to the west coast of the island, this really small place called Avlaki, just a landing pier. . . ."

When at last she had finished, and David had repeated each leg of the journey several times to impress it on his memory, they knew it was time for them to part. "There's one more thing," he said as he stood up. "Your FBI contact. What will you tell him—about me, I mean? This talk . . . and about Gerhard?"

"Tell him . . . ?"

"I need a start. Maybe I won't make it as far as the airport, but I want at least to *try* and get to Anna before anyone else does. Please don't say anything about the villa."

"I don't know how long I can hold out. I'll do my best."

"Thank you."

The door opened, admitting a breath of air from the street, along with a middle-aged man. For a moment this newcomer looked around the bar, as if seeking someone particular; then he caught sight of Robyn and his eyes narrowed.

While David watched in mounting fear, the stranger made his way to their table, pulled up a chair and sat down. "Larry couldn't come," he said to Robyn. "Sends his apologies, and will I do instead?"

David stared at Robyn. "Who is this?"

"David. Oh, David . . ." He saw with amazement that tears were coursing down her cheeks. "I am so . . . so very sorry."

Still he did not understand.

"I didn't level with you. I told my FBI friend I was coming to meet you, and where. I was so scared. You have no idea. I was so scared."

The man raised ironical eyebrows in David's direction. "Tom Burroughs," he said. "FBI. Glad to know you, Mr. Lescombe."

CHAPTER 30

Shorrocks leaned back to rest his elbows on the arms of his chair, hands steepled in front of him. "Run that past me again," he said softly.

Hayes coughed; the kind of cough, Albert thought, a person uses when he's nervous and wants to conceal it, not realizing that he only gives the game away. "Lescombe, ah, checked into a Washington hotel on Saturday afternoon around three o'clock and left a tape recorder in his room. It made noises like a guy eating, knives and forks, you know, and then taking a long shower. Fancy editing, acoustics."

"Fancy my arse," Albert said. "Anyone could do it. How long before you registered?"

"Say one hour."

"An *hour?*"

"Tape lasted forty-five minutes. Then there was nothing for a while and our guys got suspicious."

"And then," Shorrocks said, "you lost him. This civil servant, this . . . amateur."

Hayes said nothing.

It was just after dawn on Sunday morning, six days since Anna Lescombe had disappeared. Hayes, Redman, Shorrocks, and Albert occupied a barely decorated cubbyhole without a window on the top floor of the American Embassy in London. Redman's offices were not deemed sufficiently secure for this meeting. A background hum was supposedly guaranteed to frustrate would-be eavesdroppers, but Albert mistrusted modern technology. He had seen it fall apart too often.

He could scarcely conceal his frustration. The precious contract was slipping away with him, along with the Lescombes, and Krysalis and every other goddamn thing. Even if he got clearance now, this minute, whom should he go after—David or Anna? And all because these stupid, so-called "experts" couldn't stake out a hotel room.

He didn't know what he wanted from this meeting. Suppose Redman had changed his mind, was now prepared to sanction Anna Lescombe's death. Why should he assign the job to Albert, rather than his own side? Albert didn't like the thought of competition.

On the other hand, if Redman was still wimpish and wielded his not inconsiderable influence, his attitude might yet discourage Shorrocks from sending Albert to Greece in pursuit of his prey. There was never anything in writing on these touchy occasions: the legendary "contracts" were purely gentlemen's agreements. Albert wouldn't be truly free to act at will until he'd left England.

He ground his teeth, and kept silent.

Redman and his two English guests sat in easy chairs placed around a coffee table. Each held a copy of Hayes's report; they might have been actors at a read-in. Hayes alone occupied a stark metal and plastic chair. He was sitting higher than the others and this should have given him an edge but did not. Perched up there he looked more like a schoolboy on trial before his betters, Albert thought with barren satisfaction; monitors conducting an informal inquiry into misdemeanors among the lowest grade.

"I am sorry, Jeremy." Redman's voice was rich with melancholy. "No one's infallible."

"Funny." Shorrocks, at least, was enjoying this; Albert could see. "Funny, I thought that was the point of your people, Louis. Infallibility. Or so we were given to believe."

"Where is he now?" Albert did not expect a concrete answer, but he wanted the question written into the record. He knew he should have insisted on tracking Lescombe.

"We'll pick him up, sure thing." Hayes looked straight ahead as he spoke, not meeting anyone's eye. "Just a matter of time. He must know people in the U.S.; we can trace them."

"Then you'll have better luck than we did," Shorrocks said in a tone that undercut his polite smile.

"At least we know where we stand," said Redman. "By running away, Lescombe proves he was in it from the start." His face brightened. "As we did suggest to you earlier, I seem to remember."

"You did," Shorrocks acknowledged. "Although if someone attacked me in a Cornish backwater, I might be tempted to run, too."

"Well, at least you'd agree it's unlikely Lescombe wouldn't have known his wife was consulting a psychiatrist over a long period?"

"He's not a psychiatrist," Albert put in, with tendentious appeal to accuracy. "He's a psychotherapist and hypnotherapist, as well as being a qualified psychologist."

"Thank you, colonel." Louis Redman's most ambassadorial smile was Albert's sole reward. "To resume, however: what we have to concentrate on now is, who's he going to meet and where? His wife?"

"Don't *think* so, Louis," Shorrocks ventured. "She went east, he's gone west. Ne'er the twain shall meet, I fear. Kipling, and so on. Looks like a marital double-cross, after all."

"Well, okay, Jeremy." Redman dusted an invisible piece of fluff from his right knee. He did it several times, peering closer with each sweep of the palm, but the fluff was evidently a resistant strain. "Do you have any suggestions, maybe?"

Shorrocks and Albert exchanged glances before simultaneously focusing on Hayes's hunched figure. It was obvious that they could think of at least one.

"Kleist," Shorrocks said, "appears to be the key. Albert, you're a little more up on him . . . ?"

"I went back to that restaurant with a photograph we dug out of his permanent-residence application: old, but they recognized him at once. So there's a long-standing connection between him and Anna Lescombe. He's disappeared, too. We're wiring our photo to Athens, so that they can show it to the airfield people at that place, what was it called?"

"Igouminitsa."

"Igouminitsa, right. We've also got our consul working on it, but we don't expect much from him."

"Why not?" Redman asked.

"First, because our consulate on Corfu isn't geared to this kind of thing; second, because the holiday season's just starting to build and the place is filling up with tourists. Greek organization isn't the greatest, of course. Trying to interest the KYP in tracing what looks like an unhappily married woman running away with her lover requires more ingenuity than we possess. Sorry."

"Even if the woman in question has a NATO file stashed away in her luggage?"

"A joint English and *American* file, Louis." Albert paused to let the message sink in. "I'm sure it won't come as any surprise to learn that you're not terribly popular in Athens at the best of times. In any event, you don't want us to be too specific, remember? Keep the lid on, and all that?"

"Okay, okay." Redman sighed. "Didn't this guy Kleist leave a forwarding address? Contact phone number?"

"We have a problem there. We don't want to ask too many questions up front."

"Why?"

Shorrocks cleared his throat and Albert looked across at him, grateful to have the heat taken off. "Policy, Louis. We don't know what we're dealing with. Kleist could be heading up a cell. If, for the sake of example, his housekeeper—he has a housekeeper, by the way—is in cahoots with him, it would be bad tactics to march up to the front door with a warrant."

Redman essayed another of his famous diplomatic smiles. Somebody, perhaps a CIA charm expert, had schooled him in the need to reveal all the teeth back as far as the molars when you smiled. Albert wondered if he realized that, since his teeth were big and he suffered from receding gums, the effect could be disturbingly sharklike, the opposite of what he intended. Presumably not.

"Therefore?" Redman inquired.

"Therefore, we intend to enter by the, ah, back door. Which takes a little time to organize. As you know."

Or should by now, Albert mentally added. Except that you CIA people all seem to possess the two-second memories associated with particularly slow-witted goldfish. My God, but if only I'd had the sense to stick with Lescombe . . .

"Time is something we do not have."

"I know, Louis, but—"

"Excuse me, Jeremy, but I'd like to give you the one piece of good news. As far as our detectors on the ground can tell, the Soviets haven't yet taken a single step that might be consistent with their knowing about Krysalis. State now accepts that the risk of their obtaining the file outweighs any short-term inconvenience factor in Europe from disclosing the Krysalis directives and options to our allies. If it will help obtain their cooperation, tell them what the file contains. As of now nothing, repeat nothing, is barred."

"Thank you, Louis."

Albert toyed briefly with the idea of telling Redman that this permission had already been anticipated, which would have given him great satisfaction. But then he caught sight of Shorrocks's angelic expression and thought better of it. "Albert," said Redman, "I'd like you to liaise—"

An electric bell set just below the ceiling in one corner of the airless little room suddenly sprang to life. Redman grunted in annoyance and jerked his thumb at Hayes, who went to open the door and returned carrying a sheet of paper.

While he was doing that, Albert's mind busied itself trying to complete Redman's sentence for him. Liaise with whom? About what? His eyes narrowed as he studied the American's face. *What did that man want?*

What might he be persuaded to want?

Redman looked at the sheet of paper, then handed it back to Hayes with a lift of the eyebrows, but the other man shook his head.

"Jeremy, does this name mean anything to you?"

Shorrocks took the paper and shared it with Albert. "Russian?" queried the latter. "Polish, perhaps?"

"I mean, for Christ's sake . . ." Hayes sounded relieved to have at last been presented with an outlet for his feelings, "what kind of a name is Melkiovicz?"

CHAPTER

31

The minute they arrived at JFK Robyn excused herself, saying she wanted to visit the women's room. David shot her a quick glance, aware of what was really in her mind: to get to the nearest phone.

"Come," Tom Burroughs said, taking his arm. "Let's go bankrupt ourselves."

Tom bought his own ticket first, careful not to look at David, before rejoining Robyn at their prearranged rendezvous in the cafeteria. When David gave the British Airways clerk his American Express card and her phone call verified his creditworthiness as meriting a ticket for the morning *Concorde* to London, he wondered if life would ever again revert to a semblance of normality.

Tom saw him coming a long way off and was on his feet by the time David arrived back at their table. "Take it easy," he said softly, guiding him into a chair.

"I'm broke now, I suppose. More than broke."

"Me too." Tom glumly waved his own boarding pass. "But look at it this way. Do you want to find your wife or not? If so, how much is she worth to you?"

David made the effort to smile. "I really can't thank you enough for offering to come with me. It makes me feel a whole lot safer."

He glanced at Robyn. She shook her head and shrugged, minuscule movements scarcely visible to anyone who wasn't looking for them.

"Something bothering you, Robyn?" Tom asked.

Robyn fidgeted smiled wanly. "No."

"Good," Tom said. "Now drink some orange juice and relax."

David couldn't do that. He knew that Robyn had something to tell him, but not in front of Tom. Something important.

As he looked from Robyn's concerned face to the genial countenance of her FBI contact, he felt only the tension of the past few hours. The gray-and-white boarding pass in his top pocket, evidence of a freedom that for the moment was being allowed to continue, merely heightened his sense of foreboding.

Last night, Tom Burroughs had shepherded him and Robyn to a Pontiac Sunbird parked near the bar where they'd been drinking. David, supposing this was the end of the line, got into the back without a protest. The first hint that he might still have a chance came when Tom parked the car under one of the approaches to the Brooklyn Bridge and switched license plates, a tactic he was to repeat twice more before dawn.

"What's happening?" David asked Robyn. A little to his surprise, he found he did not resent the way she'd turned him in. If their roles had been reversed, he might well have done the same.

"I don't know." She was sitting in front. Now she turned sideways toward him and clutched the headrest of the driver's seat, her fingers gripping it with nervous spasms. "I've met this guy, once, briefly. He's something to do with Lawrence Pattmore, the friend I told you about. But I . . . he's coming back."

She released her hold on the headrest and turned away.

"Shouldn't really be doing this," Tom confided as he got back into the driver's seat. "Though it seems like Robyn okays you . . . is that right, Robyn . . . ?" She nodded. "And I don't want anyone to know where you are for the time being. David—I'm going to call you David, if I may?"

"Yes."

"We have some serious things to discuss." He shifted into first gear and pulled away from the curb. "Depending on how it goes, I may make a report, I don't know yet. The thing is, I feel we in the bureau ought to have some instructions concerning you, and yet we don't. It bugs me. I tingle right down my backbone—you ever have that sensation?"

"Sometimes."

"Okay. You listen to your tingling?"

"Sometimes."

Tom laughed: a relaxed, country-club sound that David found reassuring. "For the record, you are officially clean as far as my office is concerned. We have no interest in you. Now you tell me: should I be interested in you?"

David hesitated. He felt drawn to this man: a handsome, middle-aged, just the right side of fat American, with a pleasing manner and homely voice that reminded him of the actor James Stewart. But the thought of confiding in a stranger, even a friend of a friend of Robyn's, gave him pause.

Robyn, sensing his doubts, turned around and said, "You'd better tell him. The harder you make it for the FBI, the harder they'll have to be on you."

David, still unsure, had replied lightly, "He can be hard?"

"Don't be fooled. They're all hard." She paused. "Even Lawrence."

They'd driven around New York while David, haltingly at first, and then with greater fluency, explained the situation. At one point Tom stopped in Chinatown to stock up on spare ribs and Coke, but mostly he just drove without speaking. When David at last had finished he kept his thoughts to himself for a good few miles.

"One thing occurs to me," he said at last, "and it's this. We aren't stopping off anyplace until we get to the airport tomorrow morning." He checked his watch. "Correction: this morning."

"You're letting me go back to England?"

"I've no reason to hold you. But I sure as hell know one thing, my English friend: I *ought* to have a reason. If all you say is true, and I don't doubt a word of it, the CIA should be breaking every back in Langley to finger you. There's a procedure for that: well-worn and true. It involves briefing the FBI for what we call cooperative action. Yet you don't show up in that frame."

"You've made inquiries about me?"

"Sure. Where the FBI and the CIA interface, there are gray areas. Give and take, you know? We hack their computer, they hack ours, nobody sweats. But sometimes the gray area turns into a *big* black hole. So much nothingness you can't believe."

"What does that tell you?"

Tom shrugged. "God knows. I plug in my computer and tap a few keys, and what my screen notifies me is that David Lescombe exists and is of relevance to the United States of America, but that at the same time he does not exist and is of no relevance to the United States of America. With me?"

"Enough to feel pretty sick."

"Yeah. I need gas; you guys watch out for someplace open, will you?"

The found an all-night gas station. While Tom went inside to pay, David leaned forward across the front seat and said, "Do you trust him?"

She did not answer at once. When she did find words, they were not entirely reassuring. "I . . . think so."

"What's that meant to mean? He's not who he says he is?"

"Oh, yes. But . . ."

"But what?"

"Remember what he said about . . . tingling sensations?"

David sat back slowly. "It seems odd that he should help me," he admitted. "Isn't he double-crossing his own side?"

"I just . . . don't . . . know. Look, David, when we get to the airport, I'll make some excuse to leave you and I'll phone Lawrence. Ssh, he's coming over."

David waited until Tom had again settled himself in his seat. Then he said: "Why are you doing this?"

"Helping you, you mean?" Tom eased his Sunbird into the scant, small-hours traffic before he replied. "Robyn's a part of it," he said at last. "That's a big plus. But the real answer to your question is that the CIA has been trashing us for too long. I think you're a straight guy and the company's using you. I've seen it before and it makes me want to puke. Call it idealism, if you like." He gave one of his relaxed laughs. "In fact, I really wouldn't mind if you accused me of being an idealist: no one ever has before."

"That's it? The reason, I mean."

"I could tell you a lot of things about the politics of interagency infighting, David, but they wouldn't help you. Just accept that you're kind of useful to me and a few of my friends, right now. You . . . well, let's say you represent an interesting opportunity to do good in the world."

"I'm grateful. But I can't make it up to you."

"Yes, you can."

"How?"

"By pretending we've never met." When David laughed, Tom's voice sharpened into hostility. "I'm serious. If this goes wrong, and someone asks you how you spent tonight—lie." He glanced over his shoulder. "You too, Robyn."

David heard the tension in his voice and knew he wasn't faking it.

"Now," Tom said. "I've been doing some thinking. Seems to me your worst problem is with the goons who called on Robyn."

"The Eastern Bloc?"

"The whatever, yes. I'm guessing they're from the same outfit that attacked you in Cornwall. They've tried to speak to your daughter; no joy—we know that from your conversation with Albert. They've tried to neutralize Robyn; even less joy. But what's clear from all of this is that they want to break off any line of inquiry that might lead you to Anna."

David swallowed. "Break . . . ?"

"Oh, let's not get overdramatic. Nobody's died yet, and if they wanted to kill you, believe me, they could. Something else to remember: there are other, very powerful agencies that don't want you stopped at all. Your people: MI6 and the rest. If I read the signs right, they're praying you'll find your wife, and anyway they think you know where she is. So they'll help you run wherever, no problem there; not until you either find her or give up the hunt. Then they'll move in on you."

"Which leaves?"

"The good old company. The CIA: US of A Unlimited, incorporated in the state of nowhere, without liability or responsibility. And I'll tell you: after the Eastern Bloc, as you call it, that's what's worrying me most."

"So what am I to do?"

"Keep running. Run fast. If you can beg or steal enough money for *Concorde,* do it. And count cents."

"What?"

"It's a saying we use in the department. It means, oh . . . be suspicious of your own mother, heck, *especially* your own mother. Don't take anything at face value. Don't trust anyone; assume everything put in front of you is rotten through and through. Check the small change. Count cents."

"I will."

"You know what? The more I think about this, the more I wish we were in England right now. There's people there who'd talk to me."

"About what?"

"The CIA's true motivation in all this. You see, David—" even though they were in the car and isolated from the street, he lowered his voice "—an increasingly important task of my department is to monitor the law-breaking activities of other U.S. intelligence agencies. Unfortunately, there's more to monitor all the time."

He turned sideways to Robyn. "I'm almost tempted to go with him; what d'you think?"

"I can't ask that." David meant his voice to sound final, but yearning showed through. The prospect of an FBI agent riding beside him gave infinite reassurance; nothing, no one, could touch him then. "You can't just leave your job and spend a fortune on air fares."

"The bureau would pay my fare."

"David has to face this alone," Robyn said fiercely. The two men reacted in different ways: Tom with a chuckle and a shake of the head, David by slumping back in his seat. He knew that Tom was eying him in the mirror and tried not to let disappointment show.

"It's tempting," Tom said. "Very."

"You've done enough already," David put in reluctantly. "I don't need any more help."

"Right!" Robyn seemed almost desperate. "Why won't you see how impractical you're being? Tom, please!"

David felt confused. How come Robyn was so adamant that he should go back to England alone, when this man was ready to accompany him? He worked for the FBI, she'd admitted that herself; what greater protection could he hope for?

He unwillingly began to wonder if she had told him everything back there in the bar.

"It would mean my slipping away without a word to anyone," Tom said after a long pause. "Or there'd be no point. And I have to be careful—the FBI's strictly speaking an in-country organization, although . . ."

When he tailed off, Robyn said quickly, "I could phone Lawrence, tell him where you are, if you want."

David at once understood the test she was setting Tom. In the nerve-racking seconds of silence that followed, he wondered with mounting uncertainty what Burroughs would say.

"Great idea, Robyn. You do that, once we've taken off." Tom laughed. "Don't want Larry canceling the trip, now that I've decided."

David's heart soared. "You've made up your mind to—"

"Hell, yes: I'm coming with you."

Now, sitting in the cafeteria of the British Airways terminal at Kennedy, David felt mortally relieved that he would not be going back to England alone. Seeing Tom in the light for the first time, he discovered a face dark with stubble and lines, blue eyes remarkable for their absence of movement, a heavy-framed torso on which to hang so many cares of state. If anyone could help him, this man could.

"They're calling BA 002," Tom said. "That's us."

David stood up to shake hands with Robyn. Suddenly she held him close in a hug, enabling her to whisper in his ear unobserved.

"Couldn't raise Lawrence. Got the answering machine at his apartment. Nobody at the office knows where he is."

David's heart gave a jolt. Somehow he managed to hold her at arm's length, raise a smile. "I won't forget you. Thank you."

"Remember . . ." she pleaded. "Count cents."

CHAPTER

32

On Sunday, Anna awoke at the crack of dawn. Her head felt muzzy, which was strange, because she had drunk no alcohol the night before. Was Kleist putting sedatives in her food now? Still half asleep she went to the kitchen, where she found Barzel sitting at the table, a new book, a paperback this time, propped up in front of him.

He was reading voraciously, as if consuming words was a substitute for eating. He scarcely seemed aware of Anna's presence. She ignored him, as usual.

A cup of coffee revived her. As soon as she'd drunk it she set off for the church. Sunrise had begun to enrich the landscape, but the air stayed cool and she thrust her hands into the pockets of her jeans. She'd brought Juliet's corn dolly with her. Miss Cuppidge seemed to be the only link she had with the world outside, with normality. Although nothing about her relationship with Juliet was normal, she reflected sadly as she picked her way along the path. It made no sense to say she was losing Juliet, when her daughter had never really been there.

In the old days, Kleist would ask: "Why on earth do you want David's child so much? After all you've gone through with Juliet . . . ?" "That's why," Anna used to say. "Because of Juliet."

Now she found herself wishing she'd replied: "Because I'm brave." That would have been nearer the truth.

But she didn't feel so brave today. David's life was under threat. Anna couldn't eradicate the fear that extended through every crevice of her brain whenever she thought of his peril, which she did constantly. And the worst of it was, she lacked the power to help him.

Once at the church she looked behind her, expecting to see either Barzel or the other guard, whose name she now knew was Stange; but the path remained empty. Should she make a run for it? No. Even if she could not see them, they were there, waiting for her to do just that; and her only hope, however faint, lay in building up their trust.

Anna entered the church to find the remnants of yesterday's candle burned away to a sozzled heap. She cleaned out the holder and was about to light a fresh one, when she remembered having seen huge altar candles standing in a corner of the vestry the day before. She carried one into the church and, not without difficulty, mounted it on a brass candlestick to the right of the altar, before sitting down with her back against the wall and her legs folded, a hand on each knee. The red eye of God continued to watch her, malevolently, benevolently, Anna didn't know. She found herself wondering who tended the lamp and kept it burning through the dark ages which had come again. Yorgos, perhaps.

Although she lacked all religious belief, was faithless in a most fundamental sense, the red eye in the Greek church seemed to vibrate something inside her, like a glass that is struck. She dropped to her knees and prayed. Her petition was very simple: save David, she repeated over and over again. Save him, God . . .

A quarter of an hour ticked away while Anna alternately prayed and listened with half an ear for the sound of Kleist's footsteps on the path. She did not doubt he would come. He wanted to hypnotize her, as a way of consolidating his control. Since she had deliberately implanted that very idea in his mind the day before, the prospect didn't daunt her. For the first time, hypnosis would become not a therapy but a weapon. A two-edged weapon.

Long ago, Kleist had told her of a famous doctor who once said something profound about hypnotherapy: "When a physician employs hypnosis with a patient it is wise always to be aware of who may be hypnotizing whom."

At last the footsteps came. "Good morning," he said, radiating confidence. He spoke as if he had some inkling of what lay before them.

Anna put Miss Cuppidge down on the floor beside her. "I hope you slept well?" Her voice was as formal as the sentiment it expressed. Her feelings toward him had undergone a subtle change since the previous day. The knowledge of danger overshadowing David's life had wiped out that treacherous brush of sympathy mixed with lust. Kleist was an uncomplicated enemy, now.

"Very well, thank you," he said. "You?"

She nodded.

"Yesterday you said something about wanting a trance. Do you still feel that way?"

No preliminaries. She had him hooked. "What do you think?"

"It can do no harm. As you pointed out, I need to erase the instructions I gave you to prevent your leaving."

"Up to you," Anna said, with a shrug; but at the same time she was arranging herself on the floor as comfortably as she could. She closed her eyes. Her heart was beating fast enough to make her afraid for her own well-being.

"It is peaceful here in the church," he began, "very quiet, very safe . . ."

She thought he must realize that it wasn't right. He used to be susceptible to all her vibrations. But when he said nothing to indicate awareness, she remained silent. She knew what she had to do: persuade him of her total submission, so that he would cease to guard her and tell Barzel that she no longer posed a threat.

"I want you to relax every muscle in your body. . . ."

This morning he took his time over the introduction. Anna knew he was preparing her for something special and made a supreme effort not to tense. Part of her wanted to run away: how dare she enter the lions' den, fight him on his own territory? But she knew the answer. Only by doing this could she escape; and besides, it would prevent him from injecting those terrible drugs. Use the lesser evil to ward off the greater. . . .

At last he was counting her down to extinction of self with his customary slick skill. But she closed her mind against him and did not go under. It was a sort of under, without ever becoming the real thing. Although she knew the euphoria, the lightness of soul and of body, which accompanied a true trance state, she was conscious of all that she did and said. So she lay quietly, not daring to open her eyes, no longer irked by the hardness of the stone floor but afloat on an ocean thousands of fathoms deep. Her business was to stay there, on the surface; his was to drag her down.

"I'd like us to go back in time," Kleist murmured. "You are growing younger now, further and further back, year by year. To the moment when you first met David."

"Yes. I remember." She was struggling to articulate her thoughts; but they came easier today, because the trance seemed light and she still had control.

"You were tiring of me. You realized that you could be happy with him."

Anna laughed. It was easy to laugh in a trance, even in a half-trance, surrounded by all that light and lightness of being. "Yes. I was ready to accept happiness again. At last."

"You married him. And were happy. Until quite recently." He paused. "Why do you think you regressed?"

The fringes of the light canopy shivered, just for an instant. Anna struggled to act in character, not knowing how she usually behaved when in a deep trance. Should she deny that she had regressed? No, he was testing her; and anyway, she knew very well what he meant. *Say something!*

"I . . . I felt so . . . afraid."

"Afraid of what?"

"Losing . . . David."

"Why would that be so terrible?"

"He . . . made me worthy. In my own eyes."

"Why?"

Why, why why? she wanted to scream; don't you know any other words? "David . . . he . . . made everything all right."

"How?"

"How?"

"What did he do to make everything all right?"

"He . . . liked me."

"Why?"

Anna swallowed her resentment and said, "I suppose . . . he liked me because I'd put up a front, as usual. And he couldn't see through it."

"Front?"

"Successful, calm, no hangups."

"Ah, yes." Kleist allowed a long pause to develop. Anna would have given anything to be able to open her eyes, find out what he was doing. Had she fooled him? *Had she?*

She could smell danger, without being able to identify the source; knew how witnesses felt in court when she was still two questions away from springing her trap.

After what seemed an interminable time, Kleist spoke again. "But of course this man David, this nice man, liked and respected you for the image you tried to project, not the reality beneath, which would have shocked him?"

A long silence.

"It would have shocked him," Kleist repeated, with studied emphasis. "Wouldn't it?"

Anna's chest was heaving. Her head rocked from side to side. The waves of that fathomless ocean were sucking at her now, drawing her into its depths.

"Even today, after all those years of marriage, it would still shock him, if he found out."

She felt despair brush her consciousness. Tears were very near.

"I'm going to tell you the time now, Anna. I need to look at my watch. It's my best watch, the gold one. The Omega . . ."

A lead shutter came down between her eyelids and her brain, bang! Suddenly she was no longer afloat on the surface of an ocean, she was in a fog without metes or bounds. She did not know who she was or where she might be, not even the dimension of time and space she occupied. Everything was nothing. And yet part of her brain still registered that this was familiar, although she had never consciously experienced any of it before.

Somewhere in the distance a child was calling her.

There were other voices in the grayness, several of them, all speaking at once, and something had gone wrong with her ears, as when she had a cold and woke at night with aural catarrh soldering her into a landlocked world.

Wake up, cried the child.

Kleist's voice asserted itself over the rest, but even so it echoed inside her head as if from a whispering gallery.

"There were mitigating circumstances," she heard him say. "Adoption and a repressed childhood had conspired to damage your personality, long ago. You were exhausted, without money, husband, or hope. On the day of the crime, life held nothing for you."

"Nothing."

Had she said that? It sounded like her. And it was true. That day, she had nothing. . . .

Wake up. Wake up. Wake up.

No, that wasn't so: she had a daughter. A bundle of joy. A screaming, sleepless, vomit-and-shit-dispensing, smelly, ugly, bad-tempered . . .

Kleist again: "You had no one . . . except Juliet. Your own child. And here we have the nub of the problem, don't we, mm?"

Anna wanted to speak. Alive inside her was this vast, all-comprehensive explanation that would make everything right if only she could manage to articulate it. But the words remained trapped inside her, like a still-born infant.

"Because if there are points to be raised in your defense, there are aggravating factors as well."

Anna opened her mouth and discovered she could speak; but the words that came out were different from those she intended to utter. "I don't understand."

"Well, let me help you, then." Kleist no longer whispered; his voice sounded in her left ear as if he were lying down next to her.

"Your life at that time was, when viewed objectively, good. People envied you for your education, your looks, your comfortable, secure, middle-class home. You had been blessed with a healthy child. Your first husband, Eddy, was a mistake, you were well shut of him. You had no *excuse* to be unhappy, there was no reason for it. Yet you despaired."

Anna's head felt as though it would explode. She wanted to scream: *"That's what I always told you! And you said I was wrong, wrong, wrong! You said I was suffering from postnatal depression!"* But no words came out. When two tears trickled down her cheeks she was powerless to wipe them away.

"So now we will go back, together, to that day, just before you and I first met."

"No. I don't want . . ."

"It is evening. You are at your parents' house."

She was dimly aware of a sensation in her hands. As they clenched and unclenched, the nails were grinding into her palms. "Don't . . ."

"Yes? What did you say, Anna?"

"Don't . . . do . . . this . . . *please!*"

"But we must. You are there, at the house in Ferring. Your parents have gone to bed. You are in your room, with Juliet. Just the two of you. Alone."

"Don't . . ."

"You can see what you saw then. Feel what you felt then. Hear what happened then."

"No."

"*Yes*, Anna."

Her heart was beating uncontrollably. Tears flowed down her cheeks, a poisonous migraine throbbed inside her skull.

"Juliet is lying in the bed, beside you. She is helpless, utterly dependent on you. She has been crying; you have been nursing her."

"Nursing her . . ."

"Tell me what you feel, Anna."

"Nursing her . . ."

"Tell me what you feel."

"I . . . can't reject her."

"No, you can't." His voice had a new note in it now, telling her he'd scented victory. "But you want to, don't you?"

"Can't do what my mother did to me. Can't . . . give her away."

"So what *do* you do?"

"No!"

"What do you do?"

"You *promised!* Gerhard! Never again, you needn't go back to it ever again. . . ."

"What do you do?"

"I . . ."

"Yes?"

"Put my hands . . . desperate . . . oh Christ, I'm so unhappy, so depressed. She won't take my milk . . . won't feed."

"What . . . do . . . you . . . *do?"*

"I put my hands . . ."

"Where do you put your hands?"

Anna cried out, but Kleist was remorseless. *"Where?"*

"Around . . . Juliet's . . . throat."

She began to keen, beating her clenched fists against the floor, but still unable either to rise or to open her eyes.

"And then your mother came in, didn't she? *Didn't she?"*

"Yes."

"And your baby was saved. Your innocent, beautiful child, who'd never done anything wrong, was saved. So that David need never know who you really were, what kind of woman you were."

She saw him then, quite suddenly, even though her eyes stayed closed. She could see every lineament of his twisted face, each of the hundred tiny details that betrayed his need to destroy her before she did the same to him.

He wanted to render her harmless. He was prepared to do anything, and he had chosen the weapons with which he was most familiar.

No. There was more to it. He wanted *her.* He had to eradicate David. Once he'd done that he could take her to Berlin and hold her there, his creature, for the rest of time.

Anna's hands pounded the floor as if she were having a fit. Suddenly one of them made contact with the roughness of the corn-stock doll and—*Wake up,* the child's voice screamed. Juliet. Her daughter.

"Anna? Anna, why don't you answer?"

Silence.

"Anna." Gerhard's voice was low, coaxing. "Anna, can you still hear me? If you can, raise the middle finger of your right hand."

But she did nothing of the kind. Instead, she slowly opened her eyes. She emerged into the light.

"You can't do that to me." Her voice, astonishingly, was perfectly calm. "You can't say it. I love David. And he loves me. In spite of what you've done."

Kleist looked at her, his face expressionless. Anna understood what he could see: not a tired, frightened woman on the edge of forty, but a threat to all his hopes, of everything he'd worked for: the Krysalis file, the protection of his masters, and the hope of the good life to come. Anna saw these things through his eyes and braced herself.

He pounced with a clumsiness born of his own awkward leap from the floor, wrenching her shoulder muscles. At first, all she could think about was the pain: she closed her eyes against it and tried to raise a hand to protect the spot from further damage. But Kleist, intent on achieving his twin goals of revenge and punishment, dashed her hand aside, twisting two of the fingers until she screamed.

She fought back. "Gerhard," she cried, "don't . . ."

But the next thing she knew he was rolling her over, using his body weight to keep her pinned down. Her right hand thrashed wildly, sending Juliet's corn dolly scudding across the floor into the vestry. She clenched her fist and swung it against the side of his head. He howled with surprise and pain; it did her good to hear that. But when he continued to pummel her with his head, his torso, his legs, she knew she had to change if she wanted to survive.

Anna extended all her fingers. Go for his eyes.

He saw it coming and arched upward. His body was off hers, she was free. Anna tried to rise, slipped, and found herself face down on the floor. She began to wriggle away from him. The altar: some muddled, atavistic instinct made her turn east for sanctuary. But then her strength deserted her and she lay spreadeagled with her head toward the red eye of God, waiting.

A blessed silence filled the church. Slowly she raised her head. Through a mist of tears it seemed to her that now the red eye beside the altar glistened like freshly spilled blood.

"Anna," she heard him say. "Oh, God, I am so sorry . . ." Then he made a strangulated sound, one she had never heard before. It took her a few moments to adjust to this new awareness: Gerhard was crying.

"Forgive me," he said. "Forgive me, forgive me . . ."

She dragged herself upright. Gerhard sat hunched against one wall of the church, hugging his knees to his chest. She could not see his face. He was shaking: palpitating with grief.

She approached cautiously, still not sure if this was a trap. Would he lunge again? But he remained where he was, defeated.

Anna sat down, legs folded beneath her, and studied him. He was, she realized with amazement, broken. The violence represented a pitiful outburst against the fates that seemed determined to rob him of everything, even his last shreds of self-esteem.

"Gerhard," she said, and her voice was tired. "Don't cry."

She could not tell if he had heard. "Gerhard," she said again. "In all these years, I've never once thought of you as pathetic. No time to change."

At that he raised his head and she saw that, yes, he really had been crying. Water still glistened on his cheeks. "Sorry," he muttered.

Anna sighed. "It's all right."

Sometimes Juliet raged against her, calling her all manner of filthy names, but she always ended by telling her child that it was all right, it didn't matter, because that's what mothers did for children. Part of their naturally assigned function.

Gerhard wiped his eyes with his sleeve. "Pathetic," she heard him say. "Good word."

Anna, feeling an impulsive need to reach out and touch him,

cursed the trick of fate that had brought her into the world a female.
"Don't say that."

"Such a fool . . . I thought I could make you forget David, fall
in love with me again. But you were stronger." Now he looked at
her squarely, for the first time since the attack. "How long have you
been pretending?"

"Only today. I planned to trick you. Find out what you meant
to do with me." She shrugged. "Maybe detect a weakness."

The smile with which he greeted those words reassured her. It
was as if Gerhard's soul had temporarily departed, giving way to a
demon; only now the soul had come back, reasserting pride of place.

"I'm sorry," she said wearily. "But I can't ever forget David and
come to live with you. Not . . . ever."

"I know. I thought you might, once. That's why I took the file
and offered to sell it. One reason, anyway. I believed I could make
you come away with me, to South America maybe."

She stared at him. "Offered to . . . you offered to *sell* Krysalis?"

"Yes." He looked directly into Anna's eyes, letting her see the
courage his confession took. "I thought if I did that you'd be compromised. MI6 would take you for a traitor. So would David. When
you saw that everyone was against you, you'd come to me."

"Because there wasn't anybody else. I see."

But she didn't, not really. All that mattered now, however, was
building bridges. For in a sense his plan had worked. There *was* no
one who could help. "What are you going to do?" she asked.

"The only thing I can do," he said, with a half laugh.

Anna understood. He'd try to protect her from Barzel and his
stooge. Avoid the worst excesses of violence, or physical restraint.
Hold her hand when they went on board the submarine. Talk to her
nicely. Bow to the inevitable.

Gerhard said: "I'm going to help you escape."

CHAPTER 33

lbert locked up his apartment, scarcely able to contain his excitement. A few hours earlier, at Grosvenor Square, Redman had been on the point of saying something he desperately wanted to hear. But Albert didn't resent the interruption, not even when it was the fault of someone with a name as outlandish as Melkiovicz. When he finally made a deal with Redman, the last thing he needed was witnesses.

Redman's Granada pulled in to the curb alongside him. "Thanks for coming so fast," Albert said as he jumped in. He looked over his shoulder, not caring that it gave away how anxious he was. "Drive, please; I don't want this on the record."

"Anywhere special?"

"I was thinking of taking a walk in the park."

"Okay." Redman drove off. "How much time do we have?"

"An hour, no more. I'm due in Hampstead later on."

"Hampstead . . . ah, to take a look at Anna Lescombe's case notes, right?"

"Time to prepare the ground, anyhow."

Redman swung the car left out of Queensway. "Do you mind telling me what all this is about?"

"Business proposal," Albert said. "First of all, let me pick your brains. What's happening Stateside?"

Redman made a face. "Someone called me from Washington this morning and . . . well, the situation has definitely not improved."

"Can you tell me?"

"I guess so. We managed to locate Lescombe in New York only because his contact, this Melkiovicz person, called a friend in the FBI. His name is Lawrence Pattmore. She told him about some foreign hoodlums who'd come to lean on her."

"And?"

"Pattmore's secretary is sympathetic to us. She made a phone call to Langley; we ran a watch on Melkiovicz . . . and Lescombe showed up in the frame."

"Do I gather that the CIA's monitoring this Pattmore character?"

"Damn right. Pattmore was *not* a friend of ours."

"Was . . . past tense?"

"Uh-uh. He's dead. Found in his apartment a couple of hours ago, with a wire around his neck."

"Who the hell did that? Not Lescombe?"

Redman shook his head. "They're working on it right now, but no suspects yet. Maybe there's not even a connection. Anyway, looks like David Lescombe has an alibi: he spent last night driving around New York with this Melkiovicz woman and an FBI buddy of Pattmore's called Burroughs."

"You make it sound as if that's bad."

"It complicates things if Lescombe's changed sides, yes. Burroughs has a big, wide-open mouth: a Freedom of Information man at heart."

"In the FBI?"

"Unbelievable, isn't it? Anyway, Pattmore and Burroughs were pretty damn close, and if Lescombe's going to defect to the Communists, the thought of him taking anything from either of them causes us deep concern."

"This does rather presuppose that Lescombe will defect."

"We're convinced of it."

"So am I. But I can't get my people to see it."

Redman grunted. "I will be very frank with you: the loss of Krysalis represented some kind of low point in Anglo-U.S. relations. What's made things even worse is the way you Brits are handling it."

Although Albert kept quiet, he'd begun to breathe unevenly, a sure sign of jubilation. He'd anticipated having to lead the American, even prod him. But now it looked as though events might take their own course. Redman was saying all the right things.

"The call I took this morning originated from the Executive Building," Redman said. "My caller was taking a break from what I think you call a full and frank exchange of views, have I got that right?"

"If you mean he was getting his ass—have *I* got *that* right?—kicked, then yes."

"When the Chief of Staff demands to see the Director of the CIA at eight o'clock Sunday morning, you can assume that more than one ass is going to be kicked." Redman shook his head, patently angry. "Unless we can manage to save Vancouver, and plug these Whitehall leaks at the same time, seems I'll be going back to live in the States."

"And you'd like to prevent that?"

Redman laughed. "Is what you've just said meant to stand as an example of ironical British understatement?"

"No. I want to suggest a means of ensuring that you stay right where you are."

"I'm listening." Redman's voice had lost its relaxed tone; he was paying close attention now and Albert secretly exulted.

"How would you feel about briefing me to undertake a one-off assignment for the United States government?"

Redman shrugged. "Why? We have plenty of our own skilled labor."

"But none of them in place, or easily put in place. The reason I'm talking to you is that I'm exactly where you need someone to be if he's to do the job I sense we've both got in mind."

"Tell me something quickly," Redman said, "tell me now: does anyone else know about this contact?"

"Absolutely not."

"This, what we're doing, is principal to principal?"

"Correct. It would be part of any deal that you kept it that way on your side, as I would on mine."

"Go on."

"David Lescombe is likely to lead us to his wife within the next forty-eight hours."

Redman stopped for a red light and swiveled so that he could look squarely at Albert. "What you're getting at, if I follow you, is that an opportunity will shortly open up for you to do your job. Your *English*-sponsored job."

"Correct."

The lights changed; Redman drove into Hyde Park and sped along the Ring, down to the Serpentine. "Let's walk now," Albert said.

"Fine with me."

They got out and began to saunter along beside the water. There were crowds of people about doing Sundayish things; it would be hard, Albert reflected, to beat this location for what they had to negotiate.

"Let's take it a stage further," he said. "Sometime within the next two days, I will be presented with the opportunity I've been seeking. In the heat of such moments, mistakes sometimes get made. Two people have been known to die instead of one."

"You would like to sell us a mistake?"

Albert nodded. "More or less."

"Why have you waited until now to make this proposal?"

"No one on my side rated Lescombe highly, not even me. Until he managed to shake surveillance in Washington, I didn't realize that he was a pro. But now I'm convinced he didn't lose that file, he was part of a plot to steal it. He's going to get to Anna and he's going to manage to go over the wall with her. A lot of people *ought* to want to prevent that. But they still won't see the danger. People like Fox and Shorrocks have somehow persuaded themselves that he doesn't represent a danger, and they can't be shifted."

"Mistakes," Redman said after a pause, "can be costly."

"You have funds available. Something left over from the Contras. Or you could always sell another missile to Iran."

"Now, Albert, that's not funny." Redman smiled, nevertheless. "What kind of figure are we talking about here?"

Albert drew a deep breath. Fifty thousand pounds was enough to buy him release from the army, a rundown hotel and all the fish Montgomery could eat. Fox and Shorrocks had promised him twenty thousand. Which left . . .

"Thirty thousand pounds."

Redman whistled. "That's quite a piece of change."

"Care to give me an initial reaction?" Albert asked.

"Difficult."

Albert stopped for long enough to pick up a discarded can and drop it in the nearest litter bin. "Is that another word for impossible?" he said moodily.

"Well . . . Langley would demand total, watertight, absolute deniability."

"No problem."

"After all, and forgive me for doubting what you said earlier, colonel, the task you have in mind *could* be done by an American."

"Except that you must be particularly keen to avoid the fall-out that any American involvement would bring. I mean, shooting one of your best ally's top civil servants and his wife, in cold blood . . . hardly friendly, now is it? Try selling that to a congressional committee, mm?"

They walked in silence for a long way after that. "What makes you think we'd be interested?" Redman said at last.

"I'm in place, as I say. But also . . . because I believe that the powers-that-be in Langley share my view of what is wrong with the world. That they hold to their convictions every bit as passionately as I do to mine. That they want to make a severe example. But above all, that they are *angry.*"

"Not a word about my own personal convictions, I notice." Redman's smile was wry. "In fact, ideologically I'm not so far away from the man who called me this morning. We are lurching to the left, we lack control; the talk is all of rights and none of obligations, duties."

"The center cannot hold," Albert murmured. "Yet I hear a but somewhere, do I?"

"It's the methods I quarrel with."

"Ah. My methods, in other words."

"Right."

Damn, thought Albert. *He's not buying.*

They walked on. To Albert's irritation the cafeteria was shut; he would dearly have liked a hot drink. But this was an English Sunday in April and the sign outside said OWING TO STAFF SHORTAGES . . . ; they must not expect too much. Work, for example. Service.

"Do you think Langley would be interested in the proposition?" he asked, this time with a hint of urgency.

"Perhaps," Redman said.

Albert brightened. "Despite your personal reservations?"

"They couldn't be allowed to enter into this." Redman scowled at the Serpentine. "As of this morning, I've been left in no doubt that, to pick up on something you said earlier, an example has to be made. A very dramatic example that can be broadcast to our allies as a warning they can't ignore."

"Shape up or ship out?"

"Exactly." He paused. "But thirty grand . . . you know, don't you, that we don't operate the same system as you Brits? When your people want somebody blown away, they pay you to do it. But the CIA could always have a staffer kill Lescombe for free."

"You're conveniently overlooking one thing: the law doesn't allow you to have a staffer do that. But if my finger's on the trigger, there's no way either Congress or your European allies can nail you for unauthorized covert action. Your hands would be clean, I'd see to that."

Redman pursed his lips. "If we choose the right man from the list at our disposal, he won't get caught."

"Why even risk it?" Albert knew that time was running out; he had to ram the message home. "I'm available, I'm disclaimable—"

"You're pretty damned expensive!"

"Louis, come *on!* You wouldn't even miss thirty thousand out of the petty cash. And I'm worth it. You know my track record."

The other man stopped walking and stared at the ground. "I'll tell you what," he said at last. "Someone has to waste Lescombe. If, *if* you get to him first . . . well, we know your terms."

"You mean, you won't give me exclusivity?" Albert was incredulous.

"I can't afford to. In several senses."

Somehow Albert managed to control his features. "Suppose I get to do the job," he said sulkily. "What then?"

"Like I say, we know the terms you're operating on." Redman smiled briefly. "I guess we'd have to sell that missile, after all."

Not far from where they stood, a brace of magpies were pecking ferociously at some morsel of food, flung down, Albert supposed, by one of the oicks who populated England nowadays. Now Redman nodded his head at them and said, "English is such a rich language. I love the old sayings. Do you know that saw 'one for sorrow, two for joy'?"

Albert had to think about that. "Right," he said at last, relief sounding in his voice. "Two for joy. Right."

Redman stared at him, his face expressionless, and Albert wondered what he was thinking.

"Don't know about you, colonel," the American said at last. "But I could really murder a large scotch."

CHAPTER

34

Davids Lescombe knew he was eight miles high over the Atlantic, but beyond that he could perceive only the dazzle enveloping the British Airways *Concorde.* Supersonic flight, he'd soon discovered, held no allure for him. Everything aboard appeared to be the same drear gray color, even down to the menus and the headsets—the latter being useless, in David's case, because he was sitting so far back that the noise of the engines drowned out everything else. The famed curvature of the earth lay concealed behind a yellow-white glow, and anyway he found it impossible to see out the portholes that passed for windows. The cabin felt stiflingly hot. He took little pleasure in traveling at—he glanced up at the green fluorescent screen—twice the speed of sound, in the high-tech equivalent of a wood-burning stove.

David and Tom sat close but apart, wanting to avoid giving the impression that they knew each other. Awareness of his companion behind him brought David great comfort.

This morning, a Sunday, the plane was nearly empty: the dozen or so passengers had scattered themselves around the two double banks of leather-covered seats. For the most part they sat quietly, except a couple in the row across the aisle and immediately behind David, opposite Tom: young, American, and, it would seem, on their honeymoon. They had spent the entire flight so far swilling champagne, cuddling, kissing, and exchanging some of the most ridiculous dialogue David had ever endured. He felt that if he heard the word "Smoochums" again, once this flight was over, he would throw something at the speaker. But when he tried to change seats the chief purser demurred, making unctuous noises about payload distribution that made no sense to the uninitiated.

David was half aware that Tom kept looking at this ridiculous couple. Did that mean he suspected them? Surely not . . . but then why did the FBI agent spend so much time keeping them under surveillance?

David pushed his feeling of unease to the back of his mind and tried to plan. He loved just one thing about *Concorde:* its speed. His only complaint on that score was that it couldn't fly fast enough.

He didn't want to eat. He tried to sleep and could not. He realized that somewhere aboard, perhaps in the cockpit, it was a certain time; this plane, supersonic or not, could no more divorce itself from the world of which it formed part than it could travel back through the centuries. But in his seat there was no time. They were chasing the day's end. So far it had eluded them.

David sought truth. It was as elusive as the sunset.

He tried to remember why he had gone to New York in the first place, to understand the nature of his pursuit.

He'd wanted to find his wife, knowing in his heart that she would not be there, which seemed in retrospect an odd thing to do. Perhaps he had merely gone to find out about her. So what had he learned?

She'd once had an affair with her analyst. She might be with Kleist now. He couldn't avoid it any longer: she might have betrayed both him and her country. A lot of evidence suggested that this conclusion was the right one.

But David's recent experiences had affected him strangely: he was more in love with Anna than on the day he'd married her. He did not believe that she was a traitor. He wanted to save her from whatever peril threatened her, and then, because he loved this woman so much, he would help her to become whole again. Become what she once had been.

Which was what?

A businessman in the row of seats opposite stood up, adjusted his shirt cuffs and walked back along the aisle in search of the lavatory. David eyed him warily, sensing that Tom Burroughs was doing the same. But the man passed by without so much as a glance in their direction. Moments later he returned. As he drew level, the plane gave a lurch and he fell awkwardly against David's seat, putting out a hand to steady himself. David flinched as if the man had tried to stab him.

"Sorry, old boy. Sorry about that . . . can be a bit rough, the last hour. Do this often, do you?"

"No." David heard Tom's restless movements in the seat behind him and resolved to be extra careful.

"Wish I didn't have to. Ninth time this year and it's still only April. What line are you in?"

Fortunately, at that moment the plane gave another leap across the sky, flinging his tormentor back into his seat. The FASTEN SEAT-BELT sign came on, once again enabling David to pursue his thoughts.

Why had Anna sought therapy in the first place? That was the one question Robyn had ducked. What had been her last straw? *Why had she never discussed any of it with him?*

David raised the blind and stared into a seamlessly domed sky. Beneath him, a little to one side, he could make out the beginnings of a white blade, and he shook his head. A wing but no prayer . . .

Did he still love her? *Of course.* Even though she may be with Kleist, may be in love with him . . . ?

It was not too late. He could get back to London, seek out Fox, say, "Look, I realize I've been pig-headed about this one. Anna's a bitch, I see that now. How can I help? Let me tell you what I've managed to discover about her so far. She's a lush. She's been in therapy for years—bet there's a few red faces about that with you MI5 chaps, eh?—and she had an affair with the therapist, and by the way, can I have my career back, still not too late to hitch a ride to Vancouver, is it . . . ?"

The businessman across the aisle looked up in surprise to see what had made his fellow-traveler laugh out loud; but David was sitting bolt upright with both hands clenched, staring at the seat in front of him.

David glanced over his shoulder to find Tom still intent on the honeymooners, lips slightly parted. The FBI man's forehead creased in a frown; he seemed tense, edgy.

David tried to ignore the implications of his companion's behavior, but felt his heartbeat quicken nonetheless. Surely the sozzled couple couldn't represent genuine danger? *Surely?*

Everyone was dangerous. Everyone. No, don't think about that, plan ahead, use the time. . . .

When he'd gone down to Yarmouth, that first day of life with Anna, he had been in search of a bracing weekend and had found love instead. It came late, unlooked for, and was rich. He could choose, if he wanted, to put it all behind him. It would require a supreme act of will, but he could do that. He could turn his back on love, preferring not to know.

Perhaps that blindness was genetic; for there was, he realized, a precedent.

His grandfather had been a mean, cold-spirited man, a hospital porter who hoarded money in tobacco tins and stuck them under the mattress of the bed he shared with Gran. They possessed only a thin mattress, Gran was bony; she did not have to be the princess in the fairytale about the pea to suffer from those tins. She was a gifted woman, artistic before the lower classes had been allowed to think of themselves in such terms, so the neighbors were reduced to calling her "clever with her needle," or someone "who's got a real way with painting a room, you should see it."

She died on that bed, with the tins grinding her wasted body into eternity, one February, the bedroom hearth without a fire because Gramps didn't believe in throwing money away needlessly. She died insane.

After her death, grandfather had changed. In addition to being cold and mean, he began to suffer from a profound, cancer-of-the-bone–style remorse. He missed his dead wife. For the first time he realized that she had been a treasure, a woman beyond all price, who had loved him fiercely. The pangs of this horror began to wear him down, just as his tins with their rounded, hard edges and corners had ground her into nothing. In the end it killed him. The doctors called his disease cancer too, but David knew that for a lie. Remorse had killed his grandfather, as surely and as slowly as arsenic self-administered over a long period. David felt glad when he died. Mentally he consigned him to a hell of his own mind, for the sin of choosing not to know.

Later today he would be in London and, all being well, in Corfu by the following afternoon. Then, with Tom's help, he could go to the island, following Robyn's directions. By the time the sun went down on Monday, he could know.

If he wanted to.

David dozed for a while. He was wakened by the chief purser

walking down the center aisle, checking seat belts and chair positions for landing. Almost before David knew what was happening they had hit the runway and begun to hurtle along it without any sign of slowing. The engines reversed thrust, the brakes went on, he was thrown violently against his belt. The noise level inside the stuffy cabin became intolerable. Behind him, female Smoochums was uttering whoops of delight.

As the plane turned off the runway, David saw that the pilot had only ten yards to spare, and he wiped the sweat from his face with a handkerchief that came away soaked.

The honeymoon couple were keen to disembark. David sat in his seat gathering his wits while they and the boorish businessman who had pestered him earlier busied themselves with hand luggage. Male Smoochums escaped first, leaving the female of the species to wrestle with her Gucci bag. She could not stop giggling. "I can't get the strap right," David heard her say. "I can't fix it . . . you go on ahead."

"I won't leave you," the man said, throwing his arms around her.

"Lissenname . . . we wanna cart, right?"

"Righ . . ."

"Go get one, then. Go on." She shoved his shoulder. "Go on!"

Her husband reeled away toward the front of the plane. David rose to a half-crouch and slid sideways, ready to step into the aisle, when he felt a discreet tap on the shoulder. He looked back to find Tom on his feet, lips tightly compressed as he tried to keep both members of the young pair firmly in view. David hesitated, unsure what Tom wanted. There were very few passengers left now: just him, Tom, the businessman opposite, and the vile couple.

Something about their configuration spelt danger. David, feeling the onset of panic, took a pace backward.

When Mr. Smoochums was already some yards away, his wife managed to disentangle her bag. She tripped, still giggling. As she did so, Tom came smoothly out of his seat to take her by the arm, maneuvering himself between the woman and David. His jacket sleeve brushed David's own. In his right hand he held what looked like a leather wallet.

The boorish businessman chose that moment to stand up, reaching for the overhead locker. Because he had been sitting in an aisle seat, the effect was to bring him into the line of the drunken woman's awkward stumble, throwing Tom Burroughs off balance.

David saw the look on the FBI agent's face and for a second could not understand his rage. Then Tom's own words came back to him, *count cents!* and he knew why he was angry, just as he knew why the businessman's face had turned blue and he was now staggering back into his seat, fighting for breath. . . . So David grabbed the businessman's briefcase and, holding it in front of him like a shield, yelled at the top of his voice, *"Steward! Emergency! There's a dead man back here! He's been murdered. Help! . . ."*

Disjointed realizations flooded through his mind. Burroughs had been working for the enemy all along. He'd somehow managed to dispose of Pattmore and then come to the bar, intending to go to London right from the start. But before David could analyze the knowledge, he remembered, just in time, that he was still hemmed into the row of seats. Now he retreated as far as he could, until his back came up against the hull. *"Murder, murder!"* he shouted again. Tom Burroughs turned on the balls of his feet and lunged at him, holding out his wallet. After a second of disbelief, David's brain alerted him to the truth: somewhere in the leather there had to be a poisoned pin, maybe a blade; his only chance was to stay out of range.

"Stop!" he heard a voice shout from the front of the plane, but he dared not be distracted from his assailant. "Security!" the same voice shouted. "Stop or I shoot."

David parried Burroughs's next thrust with the briefcase, pushing him aside. Burroughs lowered his right hand; David caught a flash of something metal as the American prepared to lunge up, beneath his guard; but as he did so, from somewhere near the front of the cabin came a loud "plop!" The woman screamed in pain and fell across Burroughs, bearing him down, and he sank to the floor, where he stayed, pinned by her weight, until stewards dragged him away, leaving David with a drunk and a corpse for company in the world's most prestigious aircraft.

David could not move. He felt full of toxins and aches and pains. There was this voice, but he couldn't focus on it. At last he hauled himself into the aisle, to be met by a man he vaguely recognized as a fellow passenger who'd been sitting up front throughout the flight; he was in the act of holstering his pistol. "You've killed her," David muttered. Even as he spoke he was angered by the knowledge of how feeble he must sound.

"I doubt it. The bullet's just a bag full of sand, you see. Safe to fire even while we're flying." The speaker bent down to check.

"Yes, she's only stunned." He stood up again. "What was all that about, anyway?"

David, still too shocked to speak, merely shook his head.

"From where I stood, it looked as if someone was trying to kill you."

Yes, that was right. They meant to stop him, and Burroughs had been part of it. *Who was he working for, really?*

The security guard turned his attention to the businessman, who now sat white-faced with his eyes closed. "Got the wrong chap, by the look of it. Now he *is* dead, if you like. Can I have your name and address, please, sir?"

David complied. *They'll do anything to stop you. Anything at all. Your faith, against their force.*

"Occupation?"

"Uh . . . civil servant. Actually . . ."

Faith? Do you have faith in Anna?

The security guard had been writing details in a notebook. Now, hearing hesitation in David's voice, he paused. "Yes?"

They will do whatever they have to, to prevent you from reaching the woman you love.

David realized why he felt so uncomfortable: he had been holding his breath. "I'm about to resign," he said.

CHAPTER

35

Albert cut up steak for *boeuf bourgignon* while he
planned his assault on Kleist's Hampstead house.

He liked dealing with raw meat: its sogginess, its
moisture, above all, the smell, which lingered on the skin long
afterward. These views Montgomery shared. The stout tortoiseshell
sat on the drainboard, eyeballing his master in the hope of a tidbit.
Albert grinned at him. "Hypnotic puss," he murmured. "You'd be
a match for our Gerhard any day, wouldn't you? Stop looking at me
like that."

But he tossed Montgomery a piece of prime steak anyway. He
could afford such extravagant generosity now; or at least he would
soon be able to.

He'd just begun to mix the steak with seasoned flour, taking his
time over it, relishing the way the blood supped up gluten to make
his fingers sticky, when the phone rang. He gave his hands a cursory
wipe with a piece of paper towel and glared at Montgomery: "Don't
you *dare!*"

Albert lifted the receiver from its wall-mounted rest.

"Go now, right this minute."

Fox, in a phone booth, urgent, panicking.

"What's—?"

"M Center's gone berserk. Their cipher traffic's splitting our machines apart. Redland's on the warpath."

A long breath escaped Albert's lips. "When?"

"Eight o'clock. There's a connection. Tell you what it is later. And for the love of God, *be careful.*"

"Don't forget to warn off the police."

"Sorry, can't. Security overload."

"*Shit!*"

Fortunately he had dressed for the occasion earlier, so he did not even have to think; just lights off, car keys, out.

He drove carefully but fast, avoiding the main arteries and making every effort to keep his anger reined in, but that was hard. When they sent a man to do this kind of job, they always tipped off the police first. Routine. High on the "To Do" checklist. But this time Albert was on his own.

The phrase Fox had used, "Security overload," meant they had reason to be afraid of leaks. Albert was disclaimable.

Hampstead coming up . . . he forced himself to review his reconnaissance of the area.

After the meeting with Redman he'd spent the afternoon idling his way around Hampstead, guidebook in hand, to all intents and purposes an ordinary tourist. Kleist's house was halfway up a short hill. Trees, grass, big imposing houses set well back. Tiresome about the red boxes: each residence (he had somehow stopped thinking of these sprawling properties as mere houses) had a burglar alarm prominently displayed.

Trees in the street. Trees in the small front garden. More of them visible over a first-floor gable, around back. Great cover. An Edwardian pile, all bricks and red tiles, with fresh-looking white paint; privet hedge, a mixture of healthy yellows and greens, to the left; close-boarded fence to the right, no gravel to worry about, unlike Eddy Clapham's ait.

Plenty of other things to worry about, though. Burglar alarms . . .

While still some yards short of his destination Albert switched off the engine along with the lights, allowing his car to roll until at last he was parked in the spot he had marked down earlier. No more planning, no hesitations, just get in, target, penetrate.

He slipped through the darkness, a liquid, elemental part of it, flowing in silence around to the front of Kleist's house. The front garden was long: no other part of London offered such priceless facilities to nocturnal intruders, and that of course was why he now had to deal with a professionally installed alarm system.

He did not pause for breath until he had skirted the side of the house and reached an area of shadow at the back. Albert looked up. No lights. Perhaps the housekeeper had gone out for the evening, it wasn't yet ten o'clock. Check it out.

He found a terrace, onto which opened a pair of French windows. Albert risked a burst of light from his torch and made a face: metal shutter gates on the inside. But almost certainly there weren't any pressure pads. Another flash showed him only black rectangles, unmarred by the telltale white rubber circles. Risk it. No choice, anyway. Risk it.

He had passed the SAS regiment's Advanced Lock Neutralization course and he came better equipped than most burglars, but this part of the job was child's play. Mushroom-shaped blob of putty on the outside of the pane, a glazier's blade for the circle, one smart intake of breath, a tap . . . and there was a hole large enough to admit his hand.

No alarm went off. Albert smiled. People always thought they had done enough. They did not know it, but they had never done enough. It was only a matter of time before someone finally got away with the Mona Lisa.

Instinct made him turn his head. Behind him, the back garden—dark and peaceful. Beyond that, another house framed against the dim lighting in the street where he had parked. Upstairs, a single window was lit. Albert knew himself to be horribly exposed. What if the night owl behind the window chanced to look out? . . . don't think about that. *No time.*

The hole he had made was above the lock of the metal shutter gates but he couldn't see a keyhole on the outside. Fortunately Albert's hands were small; he managed to insert two fingers through one of the diamond-shaped gaps between the struts. The shutter lock yielded at his third attempt with the skeleton key and the fastening of the French doors themselves was a cinch.

He had started to sweat and he did not know why. He looked over his shoulder. Nothing. Only the house beyond the wall, where that light still burned. That ominous light.

Albert stepped back, wiping beads of perspiration from his face. What kind of alarm was this? He increased the odds in his favor by removing one entire pane of glass from the right-hand door, enabling him to pass through easily when the time came. That left the metal gates, unlocked but still shut, to circumvent.

Now he was tingling all over. He jerked his head around. Every-thing seemed the same. No it didn't. Someone stood at the il-luminated first-floor window in the house behind. Seconds ticked by, but the silhouette remained motionless. Was the person looking out, or did he have his back to the window?

Ignore him.

Since when have you ever ignored your instincts? The police don't know about this. Yet! Stay alive!

He had hunches but no choices, and Albert found himself cursing Fox. He lacked an alibi, resources, time . . . A minute passed. Too long. Use the shadows, just *penetrate!*

He made himself get on with the job. There were the wires! At the top of the gates, two of them, one at each side, which meant more glaziery and the removal of the other pane of glass. Albert took a closer look. The wires ended in square metal contacts, one male, one female, which linked when the gates were closed. Break the contact, and . . .

The wires extended right and left along the gates at the height of a man's mouth. They were attached to the struts by metal brack-ets. Screwdriver, some fancy double-jointedness on the part of Al-bert, who caught each bracket as he prized it loose, and the wires, still joined, hung in loops. Now, when he slid the shutters open, the struts moved independently of the wires, leaving the electric con-tact solid.

Behind him he heard a window open and a voice called "Who's there?"

Albert immobilized himself.

"Who is that? I can see you."

Long pause. The voice belonged to a man but it was high-pitched and quavery. Old? No, not old, but . . . something weird about it.

Albert ground his teeth, eyes flickering between the French doors and the window of the house behind. Now it was open, a shadow leaned out, probing the gloom. Albert did calculations with the speed of light. No alternative.

One last potential obstacle remained: contact pads under the rug beyond the windows.

Acrobatics. *Crash dive!*

He retreated a dozen paces, took a deep breath, and launched himself forward. As he reached the hole where the glass had been he was traveling horizontally, diving beneath the coiled wires, over the rug, to land on his stomach halfway down Gerhard Kleist's living room.

He was into the trap. And now he had bare seconds in which to work his way out of it.

Albert knew all the places where people keep burglar-alarm control boxes. They have to be near an entrance, so that when the owner comes back to an empty house he can shut down the system within forty-five seconds of entry. Most householders, worried by the thought of arousing neighbors and police unnecessarily, keep them mounted by the front door. Albert sprinted along the hallway and discovered that Kleist was the norm. Another skeleton key, into the control box, *twist,* safe.

He had been in the house for thirteen seconds.

Cut the phone. Junction box on the skirting board, one kick, two kicks, done.

Den, kitchen, dining room, study: each room got two seconds and a burst of light, nothing, *up!*

Waiting room, consulting room, *yes.* What was happening outside? Had the watcher called the police? Was he wasting time trying to phone Kleist's housekeeper?

Filing cabinets. Two seconds, burst the locks. Suppose the late-night watcher was making his way around to the front of the house right this instant, don't think about that, don't meet trouble before it comes, ten seconds, Lescombe, under L . . . no. *Shit!* Five seconds, E for Elwell . . . two thick, dog-eared cardboard folders, one orange, one a faded green. He opened the orange one, glanced through the first half dozen pages, yes, yes, *yes!*

Penetration exactly one minute old, time to go.

He pulled his black polo-neck shirt from out of his waistband and stuck one file up the back, the other up the front, before once again tucking the shirt back in. Not comfortable, not wholly secure, but it left his hands free.

The voice had been pounding inside his head almost ever since his entry. Now it suddenly became a roar, a chorus. Get out. Don't stop to think, don't wait, don't plan. *Out, out, out!*

He was leaving the consulting room when he heard the start of a furious knocking on the front door, accompanied by the bark of a dog, dogs, more than one. Then another sound caught his attention. Above. Second floor. Steps, coming downstairs.

Albert retreated into the consulting room while the fracas below steadily increased in volume. Two voices. Female, shrill, frightened. And a man who seemed to be mad, spitting a mixture of strangely accented English and a sibilant language suddenly identifiable as Japanese.

Albert opened the door a crack. " . . . working late, I see this man, he break, he smash, *ka-cha, ka-cha!* I watching, let's go, *pow-eeee!*" He recognized the voice that had challenged him in the garden. Now it was the woman's turn to speak in querulous tones too low for Albert to catch.

"Yes, yes, po'liss, po'liss, you cor, I rook."

Again the woman; this time Albert got the word "dangerous."

"No dangel, we have dogs. Hai, *hai!*"

But the woman must have instilled some caution into him, for next the man shouted, "Oh yes, then I ret the dogs go, dey fine him okay."

Albert heard the click of claws on polished wood and his throat tightened. He'd known Kleist didn't own a dog; he had come without gas or poison; who would have predicted a mad Oriental neighbor?

The dogs wasted no time on the downstairs rooms, but bounded straight up the stairs, lured inexorably by the intruder's scent. Albert closed the door; no key, *damn!* Then came a heavy thud, and claws began to work against the panels.

Find a weapon, anything. He flashed his torch around. A wood carving table . . . There must be a knife, a bradawl, something with a point to it. Steel files, they'd do.

But there were two dogs. Even if he managed to neutralize one, the other would get him. Keep the door shut. Which left . . . out the window, jump, run for it.

As Albert tugged the curtains aside, however, he looked down and saw a figure march around the side of the house: human, carrying what looked like a club.

The clawing at the door rose to a crescendo. Albert prepared to open the window, regretting the operational necessity that awaited him beneath. As he did so, however, the door gave under the weight of the dogs and sprang open.

Two black shapes bounded into the room. Albert shone his torch. Alsatians: big, bouncy dogs. Animals with body weight and teeth. Christ Almighty, how could he have failed to close the door properly . . . ?

He held out the brace of steel files, waiting for the brutes to home in. It took them less than a second. All the while his brain continued to function, as it had been trained to do in any crisis, analyzing data, forecasting possible outcomes, percentages, worst scenarios. Whatever happened, this was going to leave marks. If Kleist's housekeeper was in league with him, he would certainly know he'd been rumbled after this night's work. Catastrophe, disaster, *obliterate!*

Negotiate the dogs, negotiate the people downstairs, seal the house, run, buy maximum time, *execute!*

All this was processed in the instant it took the leading dog to stop, turn, and leap for the motionless person by the window.

He knew what to expect. They would have been trained to go for the throat. He forced himself to stand perfectly still until the first dog was within feet of him and already launched into its spring. Albert, both hands full and without light, judged his thrust as best he could, going low, underneath the beast's belly. He lunged upward, hoping for the stomach, but the point of the file glanced against bone and slipped sideways instead. The dog shrieked. Albert kept pushing, twisting, gouging, until his hand was suddenly showered with invisible wetness and a dead weight bore down on his hand, carrying him with it.

He expected the second dog to jump, so he kept his free arm up to cover his throat. He could sacrifice his forearm. As long as he kept the use of his hands and his legs, he could sacrifice any part of himself.

Things didn't work out like that. Instead, he felt long hard needles drive through his left hand: the agony was a mixture of having his skin doused in scalding oil and the electric shock of a deep cut from a razor. Albert dropped the second steel file. His jaws locked. Grenades were going off inside his head, he couldn't hear, think, move, but he *must not cry out.*

He knew what had happened. This dog could smell meat, best-quality steak. Albert had the blood of recent butchery on his hands and the dog wanted it.

He fought to separate himself from the corpse of the first Alsatian, but it was heavy and lay on his forearm. The second animal was tearing at Albert's left hand. He felt something give inside, a tendon; pain took him to the borders of unconsciousness and he knew he had to end this now or go under. Somehow he managed to yank his right hand free, still holding the file. The other dog growled rabidly; if he hadn't been starving, desperate for the blood left on Albert's hands, he would have torn out the intruder's throat long before. As it was, Albert had mere seconds' respite. He raised his one good hand and drove the steel file down into the back of the dog's neck with all his remaining strength.

Go, go, go!

Albert came upright, still holding the second metal file, and slid over to the window. The French doors through which he had entered were open, allowing light to stream onto the lawn. Through the flashes that tore across his vision he could see a middle-aged woman, her hair in curlers, hugging a lumpy pink dressing gown around her body. She was saying something, but her words were smothered by the noisy antics of a second person.

This man stood not more than five feet two in his white socks and sneakers, wearing a tee-shirt and blue shorts that extended down past his knees. On his head, pushed far enough back to reveal an almost bald pate, was a fluorescent orange sunhat that produced a tiny trail of light whenever he moved, which he did frequently. In other circumstances he might have come across as an eccentric, mildly amusing phenomenon, but he was holding a baseball bat in both hands and, as Albert looked down, he executed a series of Samurai-type sword exercises that were anything but funny. "Oh, God," Albert muttered. "Oh, God."

The Japanese lifted his head. He must have possessed remarkable night vision, for he caught sight of Albert's face at the window and cried: "Rook!" Next moment he was running into the house.

Albert, too, was running.

He took the corridor in three strides, vaulted onto the banister and slid all the way to the bottom. The front door was still open. Before he could reach it, however, the frantic figure of the Japanese sped along the parquet floor to land in the opening, baseball bat raised ready to strike.

Albert came to a dead stop. He lifted his hands in the traditional attitude of surrender, and the Japanese grunted with satisfaction.

Albert lowered his hands. As he did so, he allowed the steel file, which he had kept concealed inside his sleeve, to drop into his palm. The Japanese waved the bat warningly, but Albert made a break for the open door.

His opponent, surprised by the sudden onrush, backed up a pace and found himself against the wall. He brought the bat down, aiming for Albert's head as he skated past him. In the split second before it could land, Albert leapt into the air and spun around through a semicircle. The Japanese, impelled by the force of his own blow, floundered forward and fell. Suddenly he found himself rammed up hard against the banister, with Albert's face inches from his own. Then a wet, sticky hand inserted itself under his chin and began to push his head backward, until Albert had a clean shot at the underside of his jaw. The steel point rose inexorably up, through the man's tongue, through the roof of his mouth, into the brain, where Albert left it.

As he sped through the front door he caught the first blue flash from a police car's roof light turning into the street. By now he was opposite the entrance of the house next to Kleist's. He vaulted the wall and hid behind it, flat on his stomach. The car cruised up the street and came to a halt. Albert listened. Doors slamming. Two voices. Footsteps, swiftly entering Kleist's front garden. Any more in the car? Pray God not. He risked one look. All clear.

His sprint might have won him a place on the Olympic hundred meters team. He ran so fast that he was back in his car and rolling before he remembered that he had not stolen some precious object to give himself cover, and in a rage smashed his good hand down on the steering wheel, wishing with his entire soul that it could have been the Japanese man's bald, fluorescent but now dead head.

CHAPTER

36

When Anna and Gerhard returned to the house on Sunday, it was to find that Barzel had reached a decision. He was no longer prepared to allow Anna to slink away as she pleased.

"Stay in the house," he ordered her curtly.

"Tell me something."

"Did you hear what I—"

"I heard. What have you done to my husband? Where is he?"

Barzel looked into her eyes. They were level, wide open, and glowing with independent spirit. He was afraid of the strength that gave this woman her iron spine, so straight and true, because it jeopardized his chances of returning to Berlin as did nothing else.

"How would I know?" he said, with a smile that was meant to be reassuring.

"He's been trying to find me, hasn't he?"

Barzel looked accusingly at Gerhard. When he did not reply at once, Anna shouted: *"Hasn't he?"*

"Don't lose your temper."

"The hell with you! Tell me this one thing: *where's David?"*

When he still did not reply, she swung her arm back, meaning to hit him, but Barzel was quicker on the uptake than Gerhard. He

caught her wrists, first one then the other, and clasped them together, bringing his face to within inches of her own.

"Your husband," he hissed, "didn't know when to stop. So *we*
stopped him."

Anna held his gaze. Then, with a turn of speed that not even
Barzel could anticipate, she kicked his right calf.

"You *bitch!*" He squeezed her wrists more tightly, taking evil
pleasure from the sight of her teeth clenched in pain. "David's dead,
you hear me?"

Anna's eyes widened still further. "No," she whispered.

"*Yes.* And if you don't take more care over how you behave
from now on, you'll join him."

She stopped struggling. He felt the power drain out of her, she
went limp in his grasp, and after a few moments he let her go. She
fell into the nearest chair, where she sat staring at Barzel through
eyes that no longer glowed.

"Why did you have to do that?" Gerhard demanded.

"Shut up."

"You don't understand. She's sick. You think that was any way
to handle her?"

"Handling her is your problem."

Gerhard shook his head and sighed. "Jürgen," he said quietly,
"I need to talk to you." He used German, not wanting Anna to
understand. "We have to find some way of getting through the next
few hours. Come next door; let's talk."

Barzel hesitated. Anna seemed to have lost the will to fight, but
he distrusted her silence. There was something ominous about it.
He called for Stange and told him to keep an eye on their prisoner
while he talked with Kleist.

The two men went out onto the terrace, where Gerhard rested
his back against the balustrade and folded his arms. "Listen," he
said. "I want to get some things into the open."

Barzel regarded him coldly, saying nothing.

"When we arrive in Berlin, *if* we do, there'll be questions for
me to answer. I panicked, ran away with the woman, took the file.
All things I shouldn't have done. I'm going to have a hard time of
it, we both know that."

Barzel had begun to study him curiously. Kleist appeared perfectly in control of himself. He was talking sense and he made no
attempt to defend Anna or promote her interests. Here was the old
Gerhard, the one Barzel had recruited and trained.

It was a dangerously seductive moment for him. He needed another ally.

Notwithstanding his outward command of himself, Barzel found himself in the grip of a disabling terror. Colonel Huper's orders were to bring Anna to Berlin, with the file, in one piece and ready to talk *if possible.*

Barzel was desperate to save his own neck, along with his books and comfortable lifestyle. He knew that his chances would be vastly enhanced by getting Anna back to base. But he'd been given the option of killing her, once that turned out to be the only way of ensuring the safety of the Krysalis file. If it came to a choice between Anna and the file, the file won every time.

She was unstable.

Barzel had to make a decision about Anna. His inclination was to kill her now, before she could cause any more trouble. But oh! what a prize it would be if he could thrust her in front of Colonel Huper and say, "Here, look: I fought and I won."

Then there was Kleist.

Barzel didn't know what was going on inside that clever mind of his. He couldn't be trusted . . . yet he played a central role, *the* role, in the management of Anna Lescombe.

Gerhard was speaking again.

"Her mental state is poor, Jürgen. Telling her about her husband like that, so brutally, was the worst thing you could have done. It'll set her back years."

"Does it affect our journey?" Barzel rubbed his neck in an effort to ease the tension. He knew this would tell Gerhard how worried he was, but that no longer seemed important. He had to seek a way through the maze of decisions, great and small, that shrouded his only hope of salvation.

"It certainly could," Gerhard replied. "You're concerned about the submarine?"

"Concerned," Barzel thought savagely, is not the word. Suppose it doesn't come? Or if conditions were rough that night, they might miss the rendezvous anyway. And NATO was bound to be on the prowl by then; what if the Soviet commander decided not to risk his craft for a bunch of East German subhumans? Why did it have to be a *Russian* submarine?

"It's hardly my idea of fun," he admitted sourly. "And with a mad woman to control as well . . ."

"She's not mad. But if you continue to persecute her, she may go over the edge. Have you any idea what it would be like, in a confined space, locked in for days on end, trying to keep her sedated? I don't know what drugs a typical naval medic carries, but I doubt if they'd do her any good."

Naval medics . . . Barzel's mind kept looping back to the submarine. They wouldn't know until the last minute if the Soviet commander was prepared to honor the rendezvous. They'd be on the small island to the south, exposed, without any protection other than small arms, with nowhere to run if the sub didn't surface. And if at that point they couldn't control Anna, be absolutely confident of keeping her quiet . . .

"So what are you suggesting?" he asked, his voice harsh.

"I'm asking you to trust me."

Barzel smiled glacially. "Of course I trust you, Gerhard, what nonsense."

"That's a lie. But somehow we have to make our way home. I can help you do that. It will stand me in good stead when we reach Berlin: I did my duty when help was needed most. Do you see what's going through my mind?"

No, Barzel thought savagely. And I'd give anything, *anything in the world*, to know what you're really thinking, my friend.

"Controlling the woman . . ." he said casually. "Do you have a gun here, Gerhard?"

"No, I don't."

Barzel nodded, pretending to accept the answer, but inwardly he wasn't sure. He'd told Kleist always to keep a gun handy. He had to concede, however, that there were difficulties about bringing a firearm to a place like this: customs might open his bags, the police could search Gerhard before he got on the plane, any one of a dozen nightmares might become reality. It wasn't as if HVA had been given the job of arming Kleist on this island: their couriers' methods were relatively foolproof. But Paxos had been kept secret from HVA. Despite what he'd said on the day of his arrival, the first Barzel had known of Gerhard's hideaway was when Iannis talked.

If Kleist did have a gun here, it altered the picture, radically and for the worse. That was assuming he'd fallen in love with Anna again. Of course, if he hadn't . . . Barzel stole a glance at Gerhard. His face was impassive, concerned. But he must have realized the point of the question about the gun.

He'd always been a convincing liar: one of the qualities that had attracted HVA to him in the first place. He possessed, in greater measure than any other spy Barzel had known, the magical gift of knowing when to depart from reality and when to keep the story firmly anchored in the actual world.

What am I to do? he asked himself. How can I save my beautiful apartment, with its irreplaceable collection of books? Save myself, everything I've earned, worked for. . . .

"What do you want me to do?" he said wearily.

"Accept that in medical matters I know what I'm talking about. When I tell you to go easy on Anna, it's for a practical reason. Think in terms of crisis management, that's all I'm asking. The rest—recriminations, interrogations—can wait."

"All right."

"Keep off the subject of David."

Barzel nodded.

"Try to avoid her as much as possible. That goes for Stange, too."

"I'm not letting her out of my sight again."

"Then don't make it obvious."

Barzel stared at Gerhard. Either he meant what he said, or he was putting on the performance of a lifetime. "Tell me something," he said.

"Well?"

"Do you love her?"

Gerhard laughed, ever so gently. "Yes. You know that."

And for a second, Barzel actually trusted Kleist.

"So . . . you want her to escape?"

"No," Gerhard replied. "I want her to come with us. Very much."

"And you'll help me keep control of her?" Barzel asked anxiously.

"Yes."

Barzel stared down at the terrace. Perhaps he should change his mind about killing Anna? If Kleist was genuine . . . if the submarine came . . .

But before he could find his way through the next stretch of maze, they were interrupted by a scream from inside the house.

They ran back to find Anna howling, rocking back and forth, banging her fists down on the table, while Stange looked on in amazement. Barzel needed only a moment to appraise the situation.

"She's hysterical," he snapped. "Sedate her."

Gerhard went quickly to his bedroom and came back carrying

the black leather case in which he kept his syringe and ampules. Barzel and Stange held Anna down. She tried to bite Barzel but he was savage, rendering her semiconscious almost before the needle entered the vein. Only when her eyes were shut and she lay still did he release her. "Make sure she stays that way," he said.

"You think I have a factory for this stuff?" Gerhard's voice was a mixture of anger and fear. "Look!" He held out the case for Barzel to see. "One left!"

"How long will that hold her for?"

"God knows. So much depends on her general health, her resistance." He remained lost in thought for a moment. "Now's Sunday . . . tomorrow lunchtime, I think. When are we leaving?"

"Eleven o'clock Monday night. Have you got any rope?"

"Rope?"

"To tie her up if she wakes, idiot!"

"There should be some in the kitchen."

"Well, *find it!* Is this your idea of keeping control?"

"It's the best I can do," Gerhard hurled back defiantly.

Barzel wagged a forefinger under his nose. "You've got one more chance," he muttered. "One. Screw up again, and she's *dead.*"

The three men alternated periodic watches after that, never leaving Anna alone. She first showed signs of life on Sunday night, during Barzel's shift. When she was fully conscious but still unable to move, he summoned Gerhard and ordered him to put her into hypnosis. It didn't work. So Gerhard reluctantly administered the second and final shot of sedative instead, praying he had guessed right.

For despite what he had told Barzel earlier, if he had calculated correctly, Anna would surface not at midday but at dawn.

THE LAST DAY

CHAPTER

37

Albert had endured an eventful night since fleeing Hampstead: first the MI5 clinic, anesthesia, stitches; then, since the crack of dawn, he'd frantically been trying to find someone prepared to care-take Montgomery while he was away. The old lady in the downstairs flat, who usually attended to the job, had chosen this of all times to visit her daughter. As a last resort born of desperation he'd managed to saddle a deeply reluctant Fox, his chauffeur to the airport, with responsibility; and that, thought Albert, was only just, bearing in mind how he let me down yesterday evening.

What with one thing and another, he was feeling at a low ebb. His reaction on boarding the plane to find Bill Hayes in the next seat was therefore one of profound irritation. "Babysitting?" he inquired sarcastically.

"My role is designated a PAE one."

"A *what?*"

" 'Provide advice and encouragement.' But me, I'm way too old to play word games. I like babysitting just fine."

Albert stared at him. "Why should I need advice and encouragement from you?"

"Because last night Bonn issued an ultimatum." Hayes lowered his voice to a whisper. "Find Krysalis or we'll blow the whole thing. Tell the world that in the event of nuclear war the United States intends to sacrifice a West German corridor five hundred miles across, total civilian population three and a—"

"You can't be serious!"

"Better believe it. The West Germans say you British lost the fucking file, which you did, and allies like that they don't need. And the Pentagon doesn't exactly esteem your efforts up until now to find it again. I'm deleting some expletives in there, incidentally. What happened to your hand?"

Albert grimaced. "I caught it in a door."

"Yeah?" Hayes treated the bandage to critical inspection. "My sympathy's with the door," he concluded.

Their plane reached the end of the runway and accelerated to take-off speed. Albert gazed out the window, seeing only a bleak prospect that owed nothing to Heathrow Airport. If West Germany carried out its threat, it could put an end to NATO; simple as that. Yet he understood the logic of their position; for Krysalis's principal message was that if war came, they would be expendable; in which case NATO ceased to have relevance for them anyway.

Reluctantly he went back to his study of Anna's casenotes, now typed.

"You got the lady there?"

Albert nodded.

"I couldn't understand a quarter of that shit."

"It gives us a fairly comprehensive picture of who we're dealing with, I'd have thought."

I know what you're going to do, madam. I know the way you think, feel, love. Now I am Anna Lescombe, née Elwell, oh yes . . .

"Does it by any chance tell us where she is?"

"We should know that when her husband arrives in Corfu."

"I thought your police were holding him for questioning."

"That *Concorde* business, you mean? Lescombe's not a suspect, although he may have been the intended victim. Either way, we arranged for him to be processed very quickly. The last thing we want is to see him put out of the game."

"That's the very thing *we* do want! Did the other guy die?"

"Which other guy?"

"The man Burroughs stabbed, or whatever."

"Yes, he died very quickly. I thought you might mean Burroughs. He's dead, too."

"*What?*"

"Hanged himself in his cell last night."

"Jeesus!" Hayes shook his head. "Who do you reckon he was working for?"

Albert eyed him suspiciously. "Not you?"

"Oh, come *on!*"

"Kleist, maybe. HVA."

"Damn right. It's got HVA scrawled all over it. When does Lescombe get to Corfu?"

"If Olympic Airways' reservations computer is to be believed, in about five hours' time."

They were over the Channel by now. Albert gazed stonily at the seat in front of him, not wanting to see the placid stretch of blue water below. Funny: when he was flying, the prospect of crashing on mountain or tundra never troubled him. But he could not contemplate ditching without a clench of the guts.

"Do you believe in this submarine thing?" Hayes asked.

The submarine. In the course of his panic-stricken telephone call to Albert on Sunday evening, Fox had let slip that there was some unspecified "connection" between Moscow's sudden burst of activity and the need for early penetration of Kleist's house; but . . . "I'm worried by the coincidence," said Albert.

"So tell me."

"One. H.M.S. *Danae* is on her way to maneuvers off Crete when her sonar picks up a sub. Engine signature and wave configurations tell her officer of the watch it's a Russian Tango patrol class—old, noisy, identifiable. Pure chance?"

Hayes shrugged. "Okay, *Danae* was lucky. So?"

"So second, Russian submarines do cruise the Med, and they normally manage to do it without causing the Admiralty's officer of the day to have hysterics."

"Not while Krysalis is off and running, they don't," Hayes said." The course the sub was on would have taken it straight toward Kithira, ready for a turn into the Ionian."

"*If* it did not change course. And since we've lost contact with her—"

"Yeah, I get the picture. But it's all we've got, isn't it? Eastern Europe's one big yawnsville. Everyone's gone for the summer, *except* the crew of that submarine. Now if she is heading for an r.d.

near Corfu, she'll be there tonight. And that gives us maybe twelve hours, maybe less. So what do you plan to do?"

"The Greek navy has agreed—"

Hayes rolled his eyes. "Oh, Jesus, tell me you're kidding."

"No joke. I am to be the guest of the Greek navy, which is cooperating on the orders of its government. I imagine you're in the same . . . boat." Albert raised an eyebrow, awaiting a reaction, but none came. "It would help, of course, if this woman lawyer, this Robyn with the unpronounceable surname, would come clean about Kleist and his villa."

"We tried everything. She genuinely does not know the name of that house."

"Surely she must remember how to get to it?"

"She says not. Can't even remember the island's name, there are so many around those parts."

No, that was wrong. There were very few, as Hayes would have realized if he'd taken the trouble to scan a map. Albert could imagine himself falling in love with a lady psychotherapist and spending an idyllic month or so at her villa on a Greek island. He could not imagine failing to find out the island's name. But the woman whose grandfather had walked off the boat from Poland and run slap into one of the few immigration officers able to spell, she wasn't talking.

David knew where Anna had gone, Albert felt sure. His eyes strayed to the briefcase under the seat in front of him. He had the measure of Anna Lescombe, now; but her husband could yet prove tiresome. . . .

Albert liked Corfu on sight: dry sunshine that was truly hot, whiteness that without exaggeration could be called brilliant, scents that he nearly knew, not quite. He had only two items of luggage, the briefcase and a long metal box, but his left hand still stung, his body was full of antibiotics, and he was pleased when somebody came to smooth a path through customs.

Their host was waiting for them in the car park. The vehicle looked like a typical camping trailer, slightly larger than the norm; but as Albert approached he noticed an aerial on the roof and saw that the windows of the back cabin had been screened with newspaper; although the occupants might have been trying to protect themselves from the heat while they took a siesta, he doubted whether that was really so.

Inside the trailer there seemed to be hordes of people and only one electric fan, which was troublesome, especially since the phalanx of wall-to-wall radio equipment gave out a lot of heat and everybody smoked; but as Albert and Hayes entered, a number of men went out to make room for them. In the end, only one was left. He half rose from his folding seat behind a table cluttered with maps, and extended his hand.

"How are you? Vassili. Deputy Director KYP Implementation Group, Department Two."

When he offered no surname, Albert began to feel comfortable. As he introduced Hayes he managed to take a good look at the Greek, liking what he saw.

Vassili was in his fifties, with more thick black hair than a man of that age had a right to, and a chubby, smiling face. He wore a short-sleeved khaki shirt and lightweight trousers of the same material, ringed with a gold-buckled belt. The resulting military air was slightly spoiled by the wide-holed vest visible at his open collar. He wore a diver's Rolex on a metal strap, which puzzled Albert, because he knew how irritating that would be for someone with so much hair on his arms. Perhaps Vassili had scant regard for life's niggles.

"There's not a lot I can do," he said in excellent English. "But you are welcome to what I have. I spoke to Jeremy Shorrocks as you were leaving London, so I am, you might say, 'in the picture.' Not a pretty one. Smoke?"

Albert and Hayes shook their heads. Vassili took out a black cigarette holder, inserted a Papastratos and lit up. "We cannot find your Russian submarine," he went on. "And we cannot find your Mr. Kleist."

"Well, shit," said Hayes. "He's resident here. Surely the police—"

"Greek law," Albert broke in, "prohibits the ownership of land in frontier territories by foreigners. Am I right, Vassili?"

The Greek responded with a massive shrug, lifting his shoulders and hands together. His smile revealed a lot of gold and a lot more nicotine. "It's so. Many foreigners get around it by using Greek friends, Greek companies, on their certificates of title. Down in Athens, they are hunting. But . . ." Again the theatrical shrug.

The fan siphoned smoke from his cigarette, wreathing it around their heads. Occasionally one of the radios would squawk a babble of Greek, which Vassili consistently ignored.

"But what about the police? They must know him. I mean, the guy has to register or something . . . ?"

"Most foreigners never bother. Certainly no one called Kleist ever did."

"But some cop has to have seen him; he's been coming here for years."

"Mr. Hayes . . ." Vassili stubbed out his cigarette in a tin lid and removed the filter tip from his holder, "there is a great film I once saw. In English, perhaps I should say in American. Its name is *Witness*. You saw it too, perhaps? A man loses himself inside the Amish community. The local police can't find him, because it would mean searching maybe thousands of small farms and they don't have the resources, a thing that the city police could not understand. But *I* understood, because the Greek islands are like that. Each summer, thousands of foreigners come and go. Policemen too come and go. Your inquiry was made very late. No doubt you had your reasons for that. And I can assure you we are looking."

A long speech; really, his shrug said it all.

"I need to ask you a question," Vassili went on. "Lescombe will soon apply to enter Greece. What do you want to do about that?"

"Let him in." Albert spoke decisively; and Vassili nodded.

"I assumed that would be the case," he said. "You want to tail him, see which of the ferries he catches."

"Why a ferry?" Hayes asked. "Why shouldn't his wife be right here, on Corfu?"

Vassili waved a hand, dismissing the proposition. "Our resources are limited, yes, but Corfu is a cosmopolitan place and the police are efficient. We can assure you, neither Kleist nor Anna Lescombe is on Corfu."

"I'd rather you didn't tail him," Albert said. "I don't want him scared. You needn't worry, I'll be looking after him. I want to talk to Lescombe."

"You *what?*" Hayes was half out of his seat. "Now you just listen to me—"

"No," Albert said. "You listen. I've made contact with this man. He trusts me—or at least, he did. I think he'll talk to me. If I'm right, we can short-circuit this thing."

"But the guy isn't stupid! Once he sees you, he'll know there's bound to be others, that he's being followed. Hell, look what happened in Washington!"

"Yes." Albert flicked something off his knee. "Oh yes indeed."

"What do you mean by that?"

"That you fluffed it, it's our turn, and we're prepared to back our judgment against yours."

Hayes found himself looking through the palely tinted spectacles into a perfectly still pair of eyes.

"You're wrong. You are as far out of line as it's possible to be and stay in the ball park. Lescombe is going to lead us straight to his wife, Kleist, and Krysalis in one neat bundle. And you—"

"Lescombe gave Washington's finest the slip. So it's time to add another string to the bow." Seeing Hayes about to speak, Albert raised a hand. "Sorry."

Vassili lowered the emotional temperature a few degrees by saying, "You still have an hour or so. Let's go into town, get some lunch."

"Thanks," Albert said, "but I'd like to catch up on my reading." He tapped the briefcase with Anna's case notes inside. "You go," he said to Hayes.

He was surprised when the American accepted the invitation. And then, as he watched him get into the front seat of Vassili's car, he was suddenly overwhelmed by a conviction that letting Hayes out of his sight would turn out to be a crucial mistake. He waved, broke into a run . . . but the car was already at the car-park exit, heading for town.

Suddenly Albert knew in his gut why Hayes had come to Corfu. Redman didn't intend to part with thirty thousand pounds, so he'd ordered his own hatchet man to kill David Lescombe. And maybe— Albert swore out loud—Anna as well.

CHAPTER 38

Anna was still asleep when Gerhard again began his shift just before dawn on Monday morning. Barzel, who'd kept the previous watch, stayed with him, obviously mistrustful of his former colleague. But Barzel's face was haggard; he could scarcely keep his eyes open after so many hours of vigilance. Before long he had nodded off in a chair beside Anna's bed.

Gerhard gave him twenty minutes to sink into deep slumber before tiptoeing out, to find Stange snoring away in the kitchen.

Anna awoke as the room started to turn gray. Someone was shaking her. "No," she moaned, and a hand settled across her mouth. She opened her eyes to see Gerhard standing over her, his gun half-raised. After a second of immobility she began to struggle.

"Hush!" he hissed in her ear. "I'm going to *help* you. *Please* be quiet . . . please." He pointed at the chair. Anna looked, saw Barzel, and understood.

She lay still while she analyzed the messages her brain was sending out. Her limbs were stiff and useless; a headache tortured the backs of her eyes, blurring vision. She tried counting up to ten, then simple multiplication sums. She functioned; not brilliantly, but well enough.

Then she remembered: David was dead.

345

"Don't give up hope," Gerhard whispered, as if reading her thoughts. "You can't believe anything Barzel tells you. *Trust me.*"

Her mind was flashing a message, on and off, on and off, like a neon sign. Trust him . . . don't trust him . . . trust him . . . If this really did represent a chance to escape, it would be her last. So she could not afford to make any mistakes. What should she do?

"Will you promise to be quiet?" he breathed in her ear; and Anna nodded.

"Get up," he commanded in the same low voice.

Very cautiously, so as to avoid making the slightest sound, she tried to bend one knee. But her body, out of action for so long, did not find it easy to come back to life. Agonizing pins and needles shot through her leg from ankle to groin. It took her three attempts before the knee was straight. She looked at Gerhard. He nodded encouragement.

Now the other knee. This time it came easier, because she was expecting the pain before it could shock her. Both knees bent. *Good!* If she could only get them horizontal again. . . .

When she was once again lying flat she slowly drew her hands up the bed until they would go no further. The circulation was restoring itself, every move she made seemed less of an effort than the previous one. Using her right hand she stuffed the sheet into her mouth, to stifle any cry she might make. Then she pushed down on the mattress and tried to sit up.

The room spun around her, nausea swamped her stomach, she bit on the sheet for all she was worth. Blood throbbed through her temples at a frightening rate; she felt the arteries must surely burst. But no: she was sitting up, both arms at full stretch, while Gerhard smiled enthusiastic encouragement.

Anna massaged her legs beneath the sheet until she felt she could move without falling over. Then she slipped her feet sideways onto the floor and, resting her weight on her hands, struggled to the vertical. For several minutes she stood still, waiting for her body to adjust. She took a tentative step forward, quickly followed by another. She could walk!

What next . . . ? She looked at Gerhard, silently beseeching him to tell her what to do. He pointed at her dress, flung on the floor the previous day, and Anna picked it up.

"Can't go out by the terrace," he whispered, pointing to the windows. "Locked. The kitchen . . ."

Once in the passage she pulled on her dress. Gerhard took her by the hand. "Stange is in there," he said softly. "Don't worry, he's asleep."

"Gerhard," she whispered, holding him back. "You have a gun. Can't you shoot them? Or at least cosh them unconscious, so they won't wake up for a long time?"

He stared at her. "Could *you?*"

Anna realized that she couldn't. "Sorry."

"But I can use the gun to hold them here, if they wake up before you've escaped."

The kitchen door stood ajar. They glided through it. Stange sat at the table with his back to them. His head rested on his folded arms. He was fast asleep. Two enormous, battered suitcases were stashed either side of him. Anna had never seen them before; she wondered what they contained. But then everything else was drowned in the knowledge that if she kept her head and moved fast, she could get out.

She slipped through the kitchen door and was heading for the path to the front gate when Gerhard tugged her sleeve. "Not that way," he cautioned her quietly. "No use going to the port; that's the first place they'll look."

She gazed at him in confusion. "Where, then?"

"Come with me."

He led her around to the back of the house. All the while it had steadily been growing lighter. When Gerhard halted at the top of the steps and pointed, at first her brain did not register what she saw as anything other than an illusion, a product of the drugged sleep from which she had woken. But the longer she stared, the more convinced she became that this was no mere dream.

A small yacht, one of those flotilla cruisers built for amateurs, had anchored opposite the house on the other side of the cove, beneath the church. Holiday makers who—God bless them!—had chosen this of all bays in which to rest up for the night . . .

The sight dazzled her. She swayed a little, then held on to Gerhard for support. Less than a quarter of a mile separated her from freedom and safety. *All she had to do was reach the yacht.*

How? Did she have enough strength to swim? Gerhard was a strong swimmer; he could help her.

"You must hurry," Gerhard murmured.

He was right. The sun had risen halfway above the horizon. With every second that passed she stood to lose her chance: either her guards would awake, or the yacht would put to sea.

"Let's go," she said, taking his hand.

"No."

She wheeled around, stunned. *"What?"*

"I'm not coming."

"But—"

"Listen, Anna." He took both her hands and held them fast. "There's nowhere left for me to run, now. They've caught Iannis, I'm sure of it."

"No!"

"I try to speak to him whenever he phones, but somebody cuts us off. Poor kid . . . Anyway, I'm done for. After this, HVA will always find me."

She continued to stare into his eyes, knowing in her heart if not yet in her brain that this was the first moment of disengagement. The first moment of a life without Gerhard.

"I'll stay here, cover your escape," he said.

"I won't leave you!"

"Yes. You will. You *must!*"

"No!"

"Anna . . . get back to England as fast as you can, tell them everything. Tell them I'm sorry I couldn't return the file. Barzel has it now." He released her hands and stepped back, a smile creasing his haggard face. "Go." His voice cracked. "I won't . . . *ever* . . . forget you."

Her gaze fell. "David. He's . . ."

"Don't despair. Barzel was in a rage when he said that. He doesn't know anything, not really."

"Gerhard . . ."

He held a finger to his lips. "No more words. *Go!*"

She stared at him for a moment longer, grief-stricken, impotent. He had used her, betrayed her . . . but somehow, deep down, he was still Gerhard. Her Gerhard.

"Go," he repeated.

Instead she drew him to her and kissed him full on the lips, knowing it would be the last time. Her mind blanked out. "I—"

"Yes," he interrupted quietly. "For me the same."

Gently he held her away from him. She clutched both hands to her face in a vain attempt to stanch the tears, and ran down the path, through the garden. Once past the gate she followed the track until it petered out in the sand, and flopped down by the edge of the sea, sobbing out her anguish to the unresponsive morning.

She knew the one thing she must not do was think, especially about David or Gerhard. She had to reach the yacht. Nothing else mattered. After that there would be time to remember, and to grieve.

Somehow, she never afterward knew how, she managed to stagger to her feet. David perhaps dead, Gerhard above her, mere yards away, *no, don't think.*

A stretch of tranquil water, clad in *diamanté* by the early sunshine, still separated her from refuge. She could not detect any sign of life aboard the boat opposite. So near yet so far; surely she hadn't come this close only to be defeated?

She might swim. But she felt so weak. What if her strength deserted her halfway across? She would cry out, and no one would hear. The thought of drowning when on the very brink of salvation was too awful to contemplate. David, who loved the sea, Gerhard such a strong swimmer, *no, don't think.*

If she shouted from the beach, without attempting to swim, perhaps the owners of the yacht would come to her rescue? No, long before then her cries would have roused Barzel and Stange.

She wanted to sob. The sight of that small, rather grubby, indescribably beautiful boat lying at anchor almost within hands' reach was too much to be borne.

"Er . . . excuse me. Hello?"

Anna raised her head and looked around. No one was visible. Yet surely she hadn't imagined that voice—male, educated, *English!* "Who's there?" she called.

"Over here . . . behind the rocks."

She swung around, jerking her head in all directions. At first she could see nothing, but then she noticed a tousled head and a pair of red, blistered shoulders emerging above some boulders to her right. "Ah . . ." said the head. "This is a bit embarrassing actually. I'm off that boat over there, see, and I thought I'd go for a skinny dip. . . ."

"You're *English!*"

"Yes. Tony Roberts. I'm a doctor, actually. You look upset."

"Oh my God," she cried. "Oh my God, help me! *Help me!*"

"What's the trouble? I mean, I heard you coming so I . . ."

Anna stood up and stumbled toward Dr. Roberts as if to the savior of her soul. The head eyed her apprehensively. "Sorry," it muttered. "You don't have a towel or something—"

"Oh God, just shut up, please shut up. I'm desperate. My

name's Anna Lescombe, I'm being held a prisoner by the East Germans, they're going to kill me, I know they will, they've killed my husband, you have to help me. Take me on your boat. Please!"

The Englishman came out from behind his rock, no longer embarrassed. His eyes, now not quite so friendly, viewed her with professional detachment. Anna realized he was quite young and a little unsure of himself. "You're ill," he said. "What's the trouble?"

Anna grasped his arms. "I'll tell you everything, *everything!* Only please, please just call your friends on the yacht and take me away from here, get me to Corfu, to the British consul."

"All right, all right." His face had grown pink to match his shoulders. "Now calm down, do. Where have you just come from?"

"Up there." She pointed. "They're still asleep, but they'll wake up soon and then they'll come for me." Part of her acknowledged that he must think her mad, perhaps she was mad, but she must make him see, make him believe her enough to take her away from Gerhard, *no, don't think.*

"Okay. Okay, now, try to relax." He disengaged himself and put two fingers to his lips. A long, loud whistle echoed out over the water. "Pete," he shouted. "Show a leg!"

"Not so *loud!* They'll hear you!"

"Got to get things moving somehow. Ah, good . . . Pete's an early riser, like me." He waved a hand, beckoning to someone aboard the yacht. Anna heard an engine cough into life. She swiveled around to look up at the house, then gazed across the cove. The boat was moving, but slowly, so slowly! "Hurry up," she breathed. "Hurry up, for God's sake . . ."

Footsteps on the path. Barzel's voice: "Anna! Where are you?"

She froze. Terror held her immobile. *Why hadn't Gerhard stopped Barzel? Was he dead?* She forced herself to act, racing behind the boulder that until a minute ago had concealed Tony Roberts. "Help me!" she cried. "Don't let them take me!"

The yacht was about halfway across the strait. "What's up, Tone?" she heard a woman's voice shout.

"Got a bit of a problem. Gloria, chuck me a towel, for Christ's sake."

Anna peered around the rock to see something that for a moment she literally did not believe. She *refused* to believe it. Gerhard had come down to the beach, with Barzel a step behind him.

Something crunched against stones as the yacht went aground. Anna turned her head. A bikini-clad blonde girl was standing up to her knees in water, towel at the ready; two other people, one man, one woman, were on deck, assessing the situation.

Anna watched what happened next as if through a haze. It was happening, yes; but it could not be. Some things were so impossible that the mind automatically rejected them. Gerhard advanced toward Roberts, hand outstretched.

"Morning," he said. "Gerhard Kleist. I'm so glad you were able to come to our patient's rescue." He glanced back. "This is Dr. Barzel, of the Endemann Clinic in Hamburg. The other gentleman—" he pointed at Stange, now rapidly descending the steps to join the party on the beach—"is a psychiatric nurse on Dr. Barzel's staff."

"Did you say *Dr.* Barzel?"

"Yes. I'm a doctor also." He laughed. Anna, hearing the high-strung sound, lifted her head. Something was wrong. . . . "Sorry I don't have my cards with me," Gerhard continued. "I'm a consultant psychologist. You are . . . ?"

"Doctor Tony Roberts."

Gerhard's eyebrows rose. "A professional colleague! We don't expect to have such treats in our hideaway."

"We're all from the London Hospital, actually."

"Whitechapel?"

"Yes."

"Then you must know Rayner Acheson, your head of clinical psychology."

"I've never met him. I know *of* him, of course."

Anna could not believe her ears. A medical convention had got under way. "Don't listen to them," she blurted from behind her rock. "They're not doctors, they're spies!"

Barzel coughed and turned away, evidently to conceal a smile. Gerhard's face, however, remained serious. "Perhaps if your friends would like to come down from the boat we could discuss this more sensibly on dry land. I make a point of never concealing anything from my patients; there's been too much hole-and-corner psychology. Rayner did a paper on that very topic last year, funnily enough." He raised his voice. "Anna, come here, please. I want you to be a part of this. Don't be shy. You've nothing to be afraid of."

He had betrayed her. Again. The odd thing was that she felt nothing at all. This went beyond any possibility of emotional reaction. This was death.

"Dr. Kleist . . ." Roberts's voice had taken on a hard edge but

Anna had done with hope. "Can we be clear about one thing, please: is this lady free to come and go as she wants?"

"Most certainly." Gerhard cleared his throat. "Has she suggested otherwise?"

"Somewhat forcefully."

"Well, we can deal with that straightaway. It's a splendid boat you have there. If you feel you wouldn't be inconvenienced, I can't think of anything more therapeutic than for you to take Mrs. Lescombe on a tour of the island."

Anna caught sight of Barzel and Stange staring at Gerhard. The four young sailors eyed each other uncertainly. Anna realized that the two HVA agents shared their ignorance. Gerhard had been given a script. But he was departing from it. *He hadn't betrayed her after all.*

"You wouldn't have any objections?" Roberts's voice had lost some of its former harshness.

"None," Gerhard said firmly.

In the ensuing silence Anna said, "I'd like to come. Thank you."

"Tone . . ."

It was clear that the blonde in the bikini and Dr. Roberts made up a pair. She was looking at him bleakly, as though she suspected his sexual motives.

"Hold on, Gloria. Dr. Kleist, would you mind giving us a quick rundown on what exactly is wrong with Mrs. . . . . Lescombe?"

"Lescombe, yes. Not in the slightest. She's a successful barrister, married to a senior civil servant. She's been undergoing therapy with me, on and off, for several years. Recently she suffered a series of blackouts, culminating in a serious fugue, personality dissociation and resultant acute depression, necessitating rest and absence of excitement. I invited her to stay with me here, with her husband's permission. He'll be joining us at the weekend, incidentally."

"Mrs. Lescombe said her husband had been . . . said she'd been widowed."

"Certainly not. A delusion."

Roberts turned to Anna. "Mrs. Lescombe, do you suffer from delusions? How much of what Dr. Kleist has just said do you agree with?"

She couldn't think how to answer. Some of it was true, yes,

but . . . She scrutinized Gerhard, trying to fathom his mind. *What did he really want her to do?*

"Most of it's right," a voice said. Only seconds later did she realize that it must have been hers.

As Roberts turned back to Gerhard the smile on his face became friendly, less formal. "And Dr. Barzel—what role does he play in all this?"

"He is a professional colleague of many years' standing, who some months ago arranged to spend his summer vacation at my villa. By a fortunate coincidence he happens to be the world's foremost expert on fugue states. The circumstances are from our point of view ideal, as you can appreciate." Gerhard spread his hands. "None of which need impede a day's cruising in your company, should you be kind enough to agree." He laughed nervously, with an oblique glance at Barzel. "I might even be tempted to come with you."

He had them; they were his. For the first time Anna noticed the second girl: a brunette in a black one-piece bathing costume that looked as if it had been sprayed from a can onto her hourglass figure. She was staring at Gerhard with a star-struck kind of gaze that Anna recognized. She had contended with it in restaurants across London; in theater foyers, opera boxes, concert halls; while walking, while talking, in the act of raising a glass to her lips. Certain kinds of women always adored Gerhard Kleist: particularly the kind that saw how he could wrap them around his little finger, and wanted it.

Anna's attention suddenly divided. Barzel, keeping both hands in his pockets, had begun to saunter along the beach, kicking stones, peering closely at lichens where they sprouted from rocks. He had drawn almost level with Roberts; another few steps would bring him to her side. At the same time, she heard the dark girl say, "Dr. Kleist, I know Rayner Acheson."

"You do?"

"Mm-hm." The brunette nodded vigorously, eager, nay desperate, to please. "He lectures us nurses. I want to get into psychology. It's terribly hard, though."

"But *so* rewarding." Gerhard had become animated. He started to draw pictures in the air with his hands, bewitching the girl with his love of the job, his dedication.

"Anna," she heard a low voice say, and she jumped, for now Barzel was standing close by with his back to her and she had not seen him make his final approach. She waited for him to speak again, but he remained silent. Then she lowered her gaze to see that he had removed both hands from his pockets and was holding them clasped loosely behind his back. To the others, it must have looked a natural enough posture: relaxed, unthreatening. Only she was in a position to see that the right hand held his gun.

Then she dragged her eyes away and noticed, for the first time, how Stange stood to the rear of Gerhard. He, too, had his hands behind his back. It did not require genius to deduce that he also had a gun. Gerhard was risking his life to save her.

But Barzel had left no room for misunderstanding. If she persisted in trying to escape, she would oblige him and Stange to liquidate every trace of these people, perhaps Gerhard as well. On the other hand, she could save them. Her choice.

"Mrs. Lescombe . . ."

Roberts had to say it twice more before she realized he was talking to her, that everyone was looking expectantly at her.

"Yes." Her voice was scarcely audible.

"Would you like to come for a sail with us? We'd be only too pleased to give you a spin around the bay, as it were."

Anna managed to snatch her eyes away from the gun. For a moment she gazed sightlessly into the distance; then she refocused, looking as she did so from face to face: Roberts, amiable, concerned. His girlfriend, Gloria, still lowering, her mouth halfway between a sulky smile and a pout. The other man, Pete . . . no, she could not look at his face for he was stretched out on the deck of the yacht, catching the early-morning rays, fashionable sunglasses circling his head in a black band. And the brunette: the one person Anna might, just conceivably, have been able to order into extinction if it had been a clear-cut choice, her or me . . .

And finally, Stange. Smiling an unperturbed smile. Indifferent.

"Mrs. Lescombe. We really would be ever so pleased if you wanted to spend a day with us. Really." Roberts waited a moment. When still she did not speak, he said again, "Mrs. Lescombe . . ."

A tear rolled down Anna's cheek. Rescue had come from nowhere, had dangled tantalizingly before her anguished gaze . . . and departed. Human beings, mere people, were not designed to cope with such anguish. Such despair.

"I'm sorry," she heard herself say. "I'm so sorry to have made such a fool of myself. I think I'll go and lie down. I'm so very, very sorry."

CHAPTER

39

David's plane was five minutes late. Albert stood on the terrace, enjoying a breeze that might have come out of a blow heater, and watched the passengers disembark. The third man down the steps raised his hand as he reached the tarmac, evidently greeting someone who was waiting for him, as indeed Albert was. The signal meant: Our man's right behind me.

Albert drifted downstairs to take up position behind the glass screen facing the customs hall, working out what to say. David knew where Anna was. Somehow Albert had to extract the information from him. He didn't kid himself that this would be easy.

He watched David pass Immigration and pause, evidently unsure whether to join the crowd of holiday makers around the baggage carousel or walk straight out.

Then came a hitch.

A pay phone was mounted on the wall behind the nearest Immigration desk. David went across to it, lifted the handset and dialed. Albert swore. It was almost inconceivable that Vassili would have bugged that line. Who was Lescombe phoning? Did he speak Greek? Yes! He had studied classics at his minor public school, could almost certainly make himself understood. One minute into stress time, and already a gigantic hole was opening up before Albert's very eyes. . . .

The man who had got off the plane just ahead of David now stood behind him, tossing coins from hand to hand, but David kept his body positioned to conceal what he was doing. He made two calls, one short, one long, staying on the phone for about five minutes altogether. Then he came through customs without waiting for bags. Albert caught the other watcher's eye. The man mouthed the one word "Greek" and shrugged.

Albert scowled at the memory of the Washington hotel room, with possessions scattered around it and a tape recorder playing in the bathroom. No luggage, an empty pair of hands . . . expert, oh yes. Who had taught him these tricks?

He caught up with David as he was turning away from the money-changing kiosk with a wad of *drachmas* in his hands. "Hello," Albert said quietly, and David seemed to shudder.

"What are you doing here?" he asked. No fear, just righteous indignation.

"Waiting for you."

"Am I going to be arrested?"

"Haven't you had enough of the police for a while? Incidentally, I admire your grit. Not many men would have boarded a plane so soon after what you went through yesterday. Didn't it occur to you that they might try again?"

"Since Cornwall I've had to learn how to look after myself."

"Indeed." Albert smiled faintly. Ingratiation, his chosen method of attack, wasn't working. "Let's go and get ourselves a drink."

David stared at his bandage. "You've hurt yourself."

"An accident. Nothing serious."

"I see. Look, I'm late. My travel agent's sending someone to meet me at the harbor. I suppose I can't stop you from riding with me, if you want."

"That was a nice trick you pulled in Washington," Albert said as he settled back in the taxi. "Grosvenor Square had its share of red faces, but your score of brownie points with us increased dramatically."

"Is that why you've been letting me run?"

"Why shouldn't you be free to go anywhere you want?"

"Then tell me the reason you're here. Two weeks' holiday in the sun? Or is the regiment practicing beach landings?"

"I've come for one specific purpose: to talk to you about your wife." Albert unfastened his briefcase. "These papers are a transcript of notes maintained on Anna by a man called Gerhard Kleist . . . you've heard of him."

He had been intending to frame it as a question, but David's facial reaction to the name rendered that unnecessary.

"Kleist has been treating your wife, on and off, for almost sixteen years now; first for postnatal depression, then, at intervals, for other depressions usually triggered by crises at work. After the first treatment, the two of them became . . ."

"Lovers."

Albert nodded. "It's clear from the notes, however, that it didn't last."

"Three years! You call that not lasting?"

"They stayed friends. On and off. Until the final break."

"*What* break?"

"After Robyn Melkiovicz went back to the States, in 1987. There's no record of Anna and Kleist having been together after that. You must *study* these notes. They may help you to help us find out where your wife is."

"Don't you know?"

"I wouldn't be talking to you if I did."

There was a long pause. "Let me see those notes."

Albert handed them over and sat back to enjoy the scenery. They were descending a street of attractively color-washed houses, with balconies, and plants in huge amphora, and an occasional garden where yellow grass bunched thickly. A wonderful place. His hand was feeling better already. . . .

"How did you get hold of these? Make them up, did you?"

Albert regretfully turned away from the street to see that David's face had become white and drawn. Softly, he warned himself: Don't get angry, don't lose your head. . . .

"Judging by these notes, Anna's insane," David said. "Good God, how in hell could she have been a barrister all those years with this . . . this muck churning about inside her?"

"We haven't had time to take professional advice about that, but she's emphatically not insane. Not yet, anyway."

"What does that mean, not yet?"

"One theory current in London, on the basis of what I've shown you, is that Anna has been skillfully manipulated by a rogue therapist. He's been molding her, if you like."

"I've never heard anything so crazy in all my life."

"It's not crazy, David, it's simple fact. The techniques for treating depression are well known. The notes show that he applied them to Anna, but half-heartedly, not following through."

"Why should he do such a thing?"

"Because each time she left him, 'cured' as it were, he planted a hook to draw her back with later. Perhaps he wanted to get their affair back on the rails; maybe he was acting under orders from East Berlin, we just don't know. But he abused Anna, professionally; his own notes prove that much." Albert paused. Thus far, he had stuck more or less to the truth. The time had come for him to improvise a little.

"She's in great danger from this man," he said. "It's possible that when she fled she was suffering from something called a 'fugue.' "

"A what?"

"It's a state of personality dissociation characterized by amnesia and actual physical flight."

"But why on earth should—"

"Because she is very disturbed." Albert spoke quietly, willing David to believe. "She's in danger of doing something irreparable or, more probably, being *made* to do something irreparable."

"She'll go . . . disappear?"

"Yes."

The taxi drew up on the quay beside an sign that said PARGA, IGOUMINITSA, followed by an arrow. As they got out, the sea flashed white fire into Albert's eyes. He breathed deeply, relishing the feel of heat on his skin.

The sign apparently held some deep source of fascination for David. "I'll have that drink after all," he said slowly, but without taking his eyes off the sign.

"Good." Albert looked around the chock-a-block scene and his expression was wry. "Two things this place isn't short of are people and places to drink. Over there, look, we can sit outside. . . ."

They ordered beer. While they waited, David turned the pages of notes faster and faster until Albert knew he was not really reading, he was hunting for the end in the faint hope it might be a happy one.

"Cheers," said Albert.

David took a handkerchief from his pocket and used it to wipe his face. Beads of sweat broke out again at once. "She's a split personality," he said hoarsely.

"No. She is not. Multiple personality, which is what you are thinking of, is a class of psychoneurosis. Specifically: *grande hys-térie.* Anna couldn't have operated under those circumstances, and we know she led an outwardly normal life all the time she was under Kleist's care."

"Then how—"

"I want you to understand something. It's important. Your wife is an immensely brave woman."

David's face showed how taken aback he was.

"She had an oppressive childhood—she was an only child, remember—following on the trauma of adoption. A lot of people can handle that; she couldn't. Then came an unhappy marriage, which ended in desertion, at a time when she was still suffering from postnatal depression." He paused. "She may have tried to kill her child."

"Oh, rubbish!"

"You've read the notes."

"Compiled by someone you described as a rogue therapist."

"Not at the start. He had no motive to mistreat her, then. And you might be surprised to learn how many women come within an ace of damaging either themselves or their babies, in the postnatal state."

"But she's a barrister, damnit!"

"Isn't the real point that she's a strong, courageous woman?" Albert lowered his voice and curbed his delivery, radiating total conviction. "Against all the odds, she made it. Every single day of her life was a grueling, uphill battle with guilt, and feelings of rejection, and the fear of losing you, which is why she never told you about the stew she'd been in. A battle that she won, until right at the end. Until now. And now . . ." He leaned forward, resting on his elbows, until David could no longer avoid his gaze. "We've got to save her."

Albert modestly felt that it would have been difficult to improve on his performance. But—inwardly he trembled—that didn't mean Lescombe had swallowed it.

David broke the long silence that followed by saying, "How do you know all these things? You talk like a—"

"I was trained to know them. It's part of my job."

"Which is *what,* for Christ's sake?"

"Cleaning up messes."

"You see only a security 'mess.' I'm looking at my wife. I love Anna. She's my whole life, all I've got." David seemed on the verge of panic. "I don't know your real name, I don't know who you are, what you do. . . . You say you're an army officer but you talk like a psychiatrist. . . ."

"If you comb the army thoroughly enough you'll always find someone with certain skills." Albert grimaced. " 'In my father's house are many mansions.' Do you know anything about the vampire legend?"

"What kind of a question is that?"

"According to the myth, once the vampire has tasted your blood, you die. But it takes a long time. You exist in a twilight world, and with each passing day you slip further from the light, while the vampire continues to prey on you. That's how it is with Anna. Kleist's her vampire."

"Ridiculous."

"David, there's a possibility, a real possibility, that they're sending a submarine to take her off tonight. That'll be the end of it. No more twilight world. Anna will have gone." He grasped the other man's wrist. "Is that what you want?"

When David made no reply Albert sat back, releasing his grip, and waited. There was nothing more he could do, he realized dully. Either Lescombe took the bait, or . . .

"Can you help her?" David's voice was low. "She'll go to prison, won't she?"

"Not in the light of these case notes. I doubt if it would even get as far as a prosecution."

What, Albert wondered, was the nature of the struggle going on behind those flickering eyes, that moist forehead?

"Vampires . . . they drove stakes through their hearts, didn't they? Superstitious peasants hounding the village wise woman . . . stakes and silver bullets. All right. All right. I'll trust you, God knows why."

Albert's sigh of relief seeped through his lips without a sound. It took him a moment to recover his powers of speech. "You said you were going to see a travel agent. . . ."

"I lied. There's no one."

"Who did you phone at the airport?"

David's head jerked up; his stare had become dangerous. "I see. One-way traffic, is that it? I have to trust you but tails I lose, my God, what kind of man are you?"

"The airport?" Albert said gently.

"I was phoning first the operator, then directory inquiries. I wanted to find out if they had a number for Kleist in Parga. It's a port on the mainland. Kleist's villa is five miles inland and it doesn't seem to have a telephone. That's where I'm going. Where we're going, I guess."

Albert remembered something about David's calls that had struck him as odd at the time: he didn't appear to have the first number written down anywhere. That tallied. He'd kept his body close to the telephone, so there was no way of knowing how many digits he had dialed. And it sounded like the truth. Or would have, but for one thing.

"Robyn Melkiovicz told the Americans that Kleist's house was on an island," he said.

"She lied."

"Why should she do that?"

"Because I asked her to. I wanted a head start."

It could be true; Hayes had remarked earlier on how uncooperative Melkiovicz was. "All right," Albert said. "But we're going there together."

As they got up David pointed to the low, white roll-on roll-off car ferries waiting beside the jetty. "We get to the mainland that way. I don't know which one; we'll have to ask."

Albert, keeping a few steps behind David, noticed how as the Englishman scanned the busy harbor some object caught his eye. He glanced in the same direction, but nothing stood out: fishing smacks, a tug, several motorboats, including one fearsome red-and-white monster with its engine whisking the waters of the harbor into froth.

They were halfway along the pier. David stopped a passing Greek and spoke to him. The man pointed to the furthest ferry. David turned to Albert. "That one."

David's face looked terrible; all the muscles were working as if any minute he might have a convulsion.

"Are you okay? You look green."

"Been traveling too much. Jet lag. Feel a bit sick."

Suddenly he reeled to the side of the pier, holding his stomach. After a second's hesitation, Albert, who abhorred being close to water, reluctantly went to help. But the hands clutched to David's stomach turned out to form one big fist. As Albert came alongside him, he stood upright and the fist swung into Albert's abdomen; before the officer could regain his balance one hand took his collar, another landed in the small of his back, there was water rushing up to meet him. . . .

Albert shrieked. His skin turned icy cold. Water. The sea. Where lived whatever was worse than *death.*

Something black, cruel, terrible assembled itself from the slime in his subconscious and rose up to overshadow him, up and up it went, towering, blotting out first the sun, then the sky. . . . Then the steel grip he normally kept on his phobia reasserted itself. He switched off thought, concentrated only on the physical activity needed to get himself back to land, fast. He struck out for the nearest wooden pillar as if pursued by sharks.

Albert climbed up the ladder that was nailed to the pillar, rolled over on his stomach and was violently sick.

The unbearable trauma of entry, salt in his eyes, forks of agony sparking through his injured hand and stomach, all conspired to lose him valuable minutes. By the time he had finished vomiting and cleared his vision, there was nothing for him to see but the red-and-white speedboat creaming out of the harbor with David at its stern.

CHAPTER

40

Tony Roberts and his companions waited until lunchtime on Monday before putting to sea. They sailed clumsily, with self-mocking laughter that echoed dully across the narrow stretch of water between them and the house on the hillside. Barzel stood at Gerhard's bedroom window, watching through binoculars. Only when they rounded the cape did he lower the glasses.

"They've gone," he said in a conversational voice that held no warning of what was to happen next. He approached Gerhard, standing by the door, and, using all his strength, punched him in the solar plexus.

The blow was strong enough to send its victim reeling against the opposite wall of the passage. He slid to the floor, breath escaping from his lips in an odd, high-pitched whistle. Stange looked at Barzel as if for orders, read confirmation in his eyes, and kicked Gerhard below the rib cage.

They worked on him for five minutes. When they finally left him alone, his eyes were closed and a trickle of blood was oozing from his mouth to stain the pine floor.

Barzel went to Anna's room. The first thing he and Stange had done on returning to the villa was truss her up, with rags stuffed into her mouth and thick adhesive tape sealing her lips. She lay on the bed, staring at them through terrified, reddened eyes.

Barzel closed the door and turned to Stange. "What now?" he asked wearily.

Stange shook his head.

"Any problems with the radio?"

"None."

"It's going to be tough on you tomorrow."

"Not so bad. Once you're away, I can leave any time. They're not looking for me."

Barzel regarded him sullenly. "How come you're so relaxed?"

"Mine's the easy part. Once the sub surfaces, my equipment can pick up their signals without any difficulty. We're using compressed codes, so there won't be much for the opposition to monitor. Then all I've got to do is contact you via the short-range set, guide you to the landing point . . . and quietly disappear into the night."

Stange clapped Barzel on the shoulder. "You worry too much."

Barzel shook him off. "Can you set up the equipment now?" he asked brusquely.

"If you insist. But every second I'm on air increases the danger. Who do you want me to call, and for what?"

Barzel leaned back against the wall, closing his eyes.

Stange had a point. Somewhere out there, NATO would be closing in on their quarry and they would have radio-monitoring equipment: it was a toss-up who arrived first, the West or the Soviet submarine. So there was no mileage in trying to change their escape plan. All they could do was await the cover of night and hope for the best: showing themselves in daylight would be madness.

Take a chance and radio Berlin?

Why? Barzel knew his orders by heart: Get the file back to base; bring the woman *if possible.*

What was possible, in these circumstances?

Kill Kleist, kill the woman, lock the house, and leave it.

Kill Kleist, stuff the woman in the trunk of the car, hope nobody saw them go on board the submarine.

Kill the woman, take Kleist back to Berlin for trial and punishment.

Kill yourself . . .

"Damn!" Barzel's fist thudded into the wall behind him. "How long have we got?"

Stange looked at his watch. "Another thirteen hours and

twenty minutes to rendezvous. Twelve hours before we're due to leave the house.''

Barzel said nothing for a while. "I'm starving," he muttered at last. "Let's eat."

Stange fried eggs while Barzel made the coffee. They were just sitting down when Gerhard limped into the kitchen.

He did not look at either of them at first. He went across to the sink to rinse his mouth out, before swallowing a lot of water. When he'd done that he slumped into a chair, pouring coffee for himself.

"Why did you beat me up?" he asked Barzel. His lips were puffy, his voice ragged.

"Do you mean that as a serious question?"

"You really thought I was helping her escape?"

"Weren't you?"

"Why didn't I go with her, then?"

Barzel continued to eat without replying. The question was one he had asked himself many times already, without coming any closer to an answer.

"You don't understand shit, Barzel." Gerhard sounded weary; his inflection that of a professor compelled to tutor a dense student for political reasons.

"Why did you encourage those people to take her away on their yacht, then?" Barzel retorted.

"Because if I hadn't, they'd have become even more suspicious than they were already. It would have been a complete confirmation of all that Anna said."

"What if she *had* gone?"

"She wouldn't."

"But—"

"I knew you were both armed. Your plan was obvious enough: once you showed her the gun, it was a foregone conclusion what she'd do."

"How could you be sure?"

"Because I treated her at intervals spanning sixteen years," Kleist jeered. "The reason you came to me in the first place, remember? Give me the sugar."

Stange slid the bowl toward him without a word.

"Will you kill her?" Gerhard asked.

Barzel finished his eggs, mopped up the remains of the yolk with a piece of bread, and said: "Probably."

"Typical response of a stupid man."

"I did warn you, Gerhard. One more chance and then she's dead; that's what I told you, remember?"

"Yes."

"No pleas?" Barzel scoffed. "No begging for mercy?"

"What's the point? You're in command. You can do the killing: no one will hear the shot, not here. Then you can bury her, or you can leave her in the house for Yorgos to find later."

Barzel twitched. Kleist's mind and his seemed to run on parallel tracks. The options were unattractive indeed.

"We'll be away tonight," Gerhard went on. "As soon as the submarine comes, we're safe. Aren't we?"

Barzel looked at Stange, who could not meet his eyes. He knew what the other man was thinking, because he'd been thinking the same thing himself. Suppose the submarine doesn't come . . . ?

It was a Russian sub. The Soviets were helping out a Warsaw Pact ally. Correction: the Soviets *said* they were prepared to help out a Warsaw Pact ally.

If the submarine didn't appear, they would be left bobbing about on the surface in an open boat with nowhere to go except straight into the arms of the NATO forces that even now were homing in on Paxos.

They would be caught.

"Häftlingsfreikauf," Gerhard murmured; and Barzel jumped.

"The buying-free-of-prisoners," Gerhard continued quietly. "Swapping one of ours for one of theirs, on the Glienicker Bridge. Or through the Wartha-Herleshausen border point."

"What about it?" Barzel's voice was unsteady.

Kleist considered him in silence for a long time. "It works better for agents who haven't killed anyone," he said.

"The submarine will come," Stange shouted, half rising from his chair. "Stop this crap."

Barzel and Gerhard stared at him with identical expressions. Stange, reading their contempt, sat down again.

For a long moment no one spoke.

"I see why you became a psychologist, Gerhard." Barzel's tone had become businesslike. "Let's get down to specifics, shall we? What are your chances of resuming control over her?"

"It depends on a lot of factors."

"So suppose we hear them, mm?"

"First, whether she trusts me."

"I don't."

"But your state of mind isn't at issue, is it?" Gerhard's face resembled that of a marble statue: his eyes gave nothing away. "Everything I did on the beach was consistent with my being on her side, yes?"

Barzel reluctantly nodded.

"She'll remember that; a point in my favor. But there are adverse considerations as well."

"Such as?"

"When I brought her here, I implanted a hypnotic suggestion in her mind. I told her not to try to leave this place. Somehow, I have *got* to dig that out of her system."

"What will happen if you don't?"

"Life on the submarine will become . . ." Kleist raised a hand from the table and examined the back of it with a frown, " . . . tiresome."

"Will she let you hypnotize her again?"

"She might. I can promise not to sedate her if only she'll allow me to put her into a trance."

"Would she buy it?"

"She might. She's terrified of drugs. In fact, I don't have any more medication, but she won't realize that."

Barzel sat back, rubbing his tired eyes. He couldn't think straight. He didn't trust either Kleist or Anna one inch, but that scarcely mattered now. What mattered was whether that damned Soviet submarine would make the rendezvous. Because if it didn't . . .

His gaze lighted on the sideboard, where his paperback edition of Nabokov's *Ada* stood propped up against the bread box. He'd bought that in New York, back in '78; it was still banned in Berlin. . . .

"Try it," he said.

CHAPTER 41

Robyn Melkiovicz's memory proved accurate: there was a place called Avlaki on the west coast of the island where Kleist had his villa, and Avlaki did have a landing stage. As David disembarked a thought struck him: if by some remote chance he survived, he would need an escape route. He turned back to Amos, his boatman, and asked, "What are your plans now—will you return to Corfu?"

"No. Mr. Kleist has arranged for me to meet him here later."

David's pulse quickened. "You're expecting him tonight?"

"Yes." The Greek was young, high in his own self-esteem. He did not look inclined to waste time answering importunate questions, but David needed to know.

"Ah, I suppose that means we'll be going for a barbecue. Like last year."

"Perhaps." Amos hesitated; then the desire to manifest superior knowledge won out. "Although Mr. Kleist does not have barbecues on Antipaxos any more. Not after the fire."

"Oh, so it's Antipaxos tonight, is it?"

The man nodded. David paid him off and walked inland for a few miles before coming to a hamlet. There he had no trouble in persuading someone to rent him a moped. After that he did not stop until he reached the outskirts of the larger village, where Robyn had told him she used to buy bread. He bought a box of matches from the main store, at the same time inquiring the whereabouts of the Little House. David was a friend of Mr. Kleist? Indeed yes; was he in residence? He was, together with a few friends. Directions were forthcoming. David thanked the shop keeper and went on his way.

Who were the "friends"? Anna, maybe: but the shopkeeper had plainly spoken in the plural: *filoi.* More than one friend. Be careful. *Count cents!*

He stopped, wiping his brow. Somehow he hadn't expected to be allowed to get this far: what could he possibly hope to achieve, alone and unaided? Nothing. But the only alternative was Albert.

David still didn't know if he'd done the right thing by dunking Albert in the sea. He mopped his forehead again, trying to stifle the fear that hovered never very far from his consciousness. "Cagey" was Broadway's description of Albert; and David never had managed to find out what he really did, or why he always operated alone. But he might have gone on trusting him if it hadn't been for Burroughs's murder attempt. After that, David trusted nobody. Especially nobody who showed as much interest in finding Anna as Albert did.

David was learning how to count cents.

He looked around him. The village had receded into the distance and the light was going. Olive trees grew sporadically in expanses of dry, yellow grass beside the road. Houses were visible here and there, through the branches; all of them stood well back, secluded from the curiosity of strangers like himself. On the road he was too prominent. In this quiet place the phut-phutting engine of his moped invited attention like an ice-cream van's bell.

David knew that Kleist's villa lay off to the right, down a hill, perhaps a quarter of a mile, not more, from where he was now. So he struck off into the countryside to the left of the road, deliberately seeking cover in the opposite direction. Before long he came upon a huge pile of rotting straw, which someone had hollowed out to form a kind of igloo. It was an isolated spot. Hurriedly he stowed his moped deep inside the cavity, and set off on foot.

He kept the road in view wherever possible, anxious to avoid losing himself, even when this meant that sometimes he blundered through nettles or had to climb over barbed wire. At last he felt sure he must have arrived more or less opposite Kleist's house, still on the other side of the road.

David was standing at the top of a slope. Cautiously he began to make his way down, hugging the treeline for as long as he could, until he reached the verge.

Damn! Emptiness yawned on either side of him. Not even so much as a gleam of white wall could be seen anywhere: this stretch was utterly deserted. He waited a moment, checking both ways, then ran across to the other side, where he again lost himself in the obscurity of the olive groves. Here he found a narrow path winding along the foot of an embankment: nothing like the stone driveway to the house that the storekeeper had described. David followed it for a few yards before stopping, certain that he had veered off course.

He flopped down beneath a tree and rested his head on his arms, suddenly tired. For the first time since quitting Corfu he let himself dwell on the case notes Albert had shown him. If they were genuine, every assumption he'd ever made about his wife, every lesson supposedly learned, was founded on falsehood.

Were these notes the real thing? Or were they clever forgeries, concocted by Albert for reasons David couldn't even guess at?

There was only one way to find out. He must ask Anna.

Occasionally Kleist would record in his notes verbatim snatches of dialogue taken from the sessions. One of them had leapt off the page at David when he read it in the taxi.

"My mother always insisted she loved me, but if that was love . . ."

"You didn't want it?"

"And that made me feel evil. Because what good person rejects love?". . .

"My mother . . ." Mrs. Elwell. She must have known about Kleist and the chain of events that had led her daughter to him in the first place. But when he'd asked her about those things, she had lied. Keeping up the front mattered more than Anna's happiness, perhaps even more than her life.

David no longer knew what to think, what to believe. All he felt certain of was that he loved Anna and must keep on to the end of the path he had set himself. Then there would be time for reflection, and truth.

He raised his head. Something was wrong.

For the past few minutes he had been half aware of a curious noise, neither close nor remote. Pods snapping in the heat, perhaps, or rats; but the evening had turned cool and the noise was too loud to be caused by rats.

He stood up and looked around. What should he do? He resolved to push on in the direction he'd been taking before his rest. After a while the path sheered away from the wall and began to zigzag down the hill through dense undergrowth. From the breeze that now refreshed his skin he judged he must be near the sea. Ah, yes: a pale shimmer of molten gold cupped in the V made by two hills, off to his right.

He heard the noise again, louder this time, and looked over his shoulder. At first the dusk defeated his town-orientated eyes, but then his sight sharpened and involuntarily he let out a sharp breath. Twenty yards away, someone stood lighting a cigarette.

Fortunately the stranger was facing in the opposite direction or he could not have failed to see David, who now slowly edged around the nearest tree until its trunk screened him from the other man. He willed his heartbeat into a more regular pattern and tried to think. The person he'd just seen didn't look Greek. He might be a tourist, well off the beaten track, but David didn't think so: this island had yet to be ruined by the summer holiday crowd; tourists were scarce. Kleist, on the other hand, was said to be staying here with *friends*. Bodyguards, maybe. Watchers.

A twig broke, David heard a cough. The aroma of smoldering tobacco entered his nostrils, faintly at first, then more strongly. The man was moving toward him. David jerked his head back to its original position. Should he move? Stay put? He looked to left and right. Trees, nothing but trees . . . Wrong!—up ahead he could see luminous pallor: a wall, maybe, some kind of building . . . Kleist's villa? No, he was way off course. But perhaps he could hide there?

David began to map out a route. At least a dozen olive trees stood between him and the whiteness. If he dodged from tree to tree, moving quietly and fast, he might make it undetected.

He turned to either side, saw nothing suspicious. Then he pushed himself off the tree trunk and went forward at a brisk walk. He was lucky; the earth stayed silent beneath his feet. A few seconds later he had his back to another tree and was peering around its gnarled bole in an attempt to work out if he'd been spotted.

No one.

He took a deep breath and made for the next tree on his route. Now he could see that the whiteness belonged to a small church, its silhouette broken by two powder-blue blocks of sky framing a black bell. It looked deserted. If only he could get inside . . .

The sunset was dissipating swiftly; it would be no easy task for anyone to catch sight of him in the dusk. The smell of tobacco smoke had faded. Not a sound disturbed the evening stillness. While he stood there, indecisive, a feeling of exposure swept over him. On impulse he ran forward to push against the church door. But as he did so, he heard that cough again, very close this time, and the unmistakable click of a cigarette lighter.

"Hey," said a voice. "You!"

David fled into the church, closing the door behind him. He had expected to find the place in darkness, but to his surprise he saw a feeble yellow flame at the far end. He raced down the aisle toward it. The remains of a single large candle stood on the altar, nine-tenths burned away and drooping but still bright enough to show his position to an enemy. David made a lunge. The candle toppled to the floor and went out. As much by luck as judgment the solid brass candlestick was left sitting snugly in his palm.

Outside the church he heard a voice say, "You! I know where you are. Come out!"

The speaker used stilted English; but he didn't sound either English or Greek. David let his eyes stray to the windows, now glowing electric blue in the gathering dusk. Soon night would fall, but there was just enough light left to show him an opening, over which hung a curtain. A vestry . . .

"Who's in there?" The church door rattled.

David's throat had sealed up tighter than a fist. He sidled into the vestry, allowing the curtain to fall across the gap after him.

"You cannot hide!"

A prolonged creak, coupled with a warm breath of air, indicated that the outer door had opened. The stranger walked down the center of the church, disturbing leaves as he approached the altar. *How much could he see?*

"Aah!" The footsteps halted. David's head seemed full of blood, he felt it would explode; surely the newcomer must hear the thudding of his heart? "Aah, show yourself, why don't you? Nothing to be afraid of. I only want to talk."

Another pause. David was standing with his back against the wall that partitioned the body of the church from the vestry, as close to the curtained doorway as he dared. He knew the man was mere yards away from him. How well did he know this church? *How much could he see?*

More footsteps, going away this time. Another creak, followed by a slam. David was alone again. But what would the other man do—wait for him to emerge, or muster reinforcements? *Why had he left the church without searching it?*

By now the gloom had become all but impenetrable. The vestry lacked a window; David could scarcely see his own hand in front of his face.

He came off the wall and turned, preparing to twitch aside the curtain that hung across the doorway. Another second and he would have passed through the gap, into the church itself. But then many things happened at once: someone nearby moved, scattering leaves across the floor; David caught a glint of metal; in a flash he knew that the stranger hadn't left the church, he'd opened the door and slammed it again to fool David and now was mere feet away, ready to strike.

The man growled in satisfaction; David felt the air move; he leapt backward. Hands punched his solar plexus, winding him. A head butted into David's chest, slamming him back against the wall. For a second he merely let it happen, powerless to help himself. Then he remembered what he was holding.

His first blow landed across the other man's shoulders, causing him to freeze with a grunt of mingled surprise and pain. Not much of a respite, but enough. David lifted the brass candlestick as high as he could and brought it down in a vertical stab, aiming just beyond the hands that had been pummeling him seconds ago. Someone groaned. David took the candlestick in a double-handed grip and began to flail it around like a sword, slashing the darkness on either side of him. His third swing made contact: another groan, this time near his feet.

David stepped back a pace, raised the candlestick above his head, and axed downward with all his might.

The sound of brass clanging on stone revealed his mistake. Too late: he was already toppling forward, unbalanced by the force of his own blow. A foot lashed out of the darkness, entangling his legs, and he fell.

Somewhere close he could hear panting. His opponent was still on the floor: it was a kick that had laid David low, not a punch. *So don't let him get up again.* David rolled as far as he could, hugging the candlestick to his chest. The wall stopped him. He managed to stagger up to a kneeling position before hands met around his throat and began to squeeze.

The enemy was behind him, also kneeling. Not a good position, but he was as strong as an ox and clever, too: anticipating the likely reaction he kept his body arched left, away from David's increasingly weakened blows with the weapon still clutched in his right hand.

David's strength was going. Each breath became a nightmare. Purple blotches marred his vision; from the pain in his throat he felt his head must be coming off. Suddenly the right hand on his windpipe fell away and he sensed that the man had made a grab for the candlestick. He missed. Instead of trying again, he moved his left hand from David's throat to his hair, and started to bang his head against the wall.

David cried out. His adversary immediately let go of David's hair and clamped his left palm across his mouth instead. In the darkness, the move was clumsy; his forefinger landed between David's teeth. With whatever strength he had left, David clenched his jaws together and shook his head from side to side.

Until then, the other man had been fighting in near silence— which made his roar of pain all the more gratifying. David managed a half turn, still keeping his teeth closed around his attacker's finger. Through a blur of weakness he realized that his right hand was free. He stabbed to his left with the candlestick and made soft contact. He thrust again—but this time hands stronger than his own managed to grasp his makeshift club, and the next second David was defenseless.

A whoosh of air, frighteningly close, told him that his assailant was trying to duplicate his own move of a moment ago and lay him out cold. He ducked to one side. The next swing caught him on the shoulder, making him howl. That meant the end: his voice would have given away his position.

David fumbled desperately on the floor, seeking purchase. His fingers brushed something spiky and spasmodically closed around it. In the same instant, he heard a clang as the other man threw down the candlestick and launched himself downward. David found himself crouching with his back against the wall, those terrible hands once more around his throat.

This time his opponent was in front of him. *Light going now, can't breathe. Last chance. Go limp. Sink . . .*

As the other man was pulled forward under the weight of the inert body he was holding, David tightened his grip on the spiky thing and drove it with all his force at the two glittering points of light in front of him.

He missed the eyes; but a squeal reassured David that his thrust had done good work. The vice around his throat relaxed, he was free, he was running. As he hurtled through the church's outer door, something made him look down and see that he was holding Juliet's corn dolly. He raised Miss Cuppidge to the light. His hands were shaking. Anna . . . Don't think of that, don't stop, to the right, trees; ahead, a path leading up the hill; on his left, a short drop, then rocks and the sea. A bay.

For a split second he found himself looking across the cove to a house on the hillside opposite. Light streamed out of its downstairs rooms to illuminate a terrace, where two men were standing with their backs to him. David had eyes only for a third figure, seated just inside, but nevertheless clearly visible through the open doorway. A woman. Her pale green V-neck dress with short, white-cuffed sleeves stood out boldly in the artificial light. The dress was Italian, made of cotton, and it zipped up the back. David knew these things because he had bought it for Anna last year on her thirty-eighth birthday: one of his rare and outrageously extravagant declarations of love.

His mission still had a long way to go: all he had done was find Anna, not rescue her. But as David raced up the path, into the trees, his heart sang for sheer joy.

CHAPTER

42

While Stange remained at the house, fitting up his radio set, the others moved fast through the night: Gerhard riding next to Yorgos, who drove, with Anna and Barzel in the back seat.

Yorgos was happy, he explained to anyone who would listen. The olive crop looked like being a good one; there was much to be done. His son would be coming home on Monday, early, thanks be to God.

Somehow Gerhard didn't think so. He wasn't expecting Iannis to show up again. Perhaps his expression hinted at more than Yorgos cared to know, for after a while he trailed off into silence. The atmosphere hardly encouraged social chitchat.

Gerhard knew why Barzel had chosen to ride in the back. That way he could more easily cover him and Anna; because by now both of them were prisoners.

He had tried to hypnotize Anna, with her consent, but his skill had dwindled almost to nothing. The best he could manage was a patient explanation of the arrangements, hoping that would calm her: they were going to a place called Avlaki, there a boat would be waiting to take them on to the small island where they had swum, they would be in the car for so many minutes, on the sea for so many minutes more—but it was useless. The first night on the island, he had told her that David wanted her to be here, so she must stay; now he could not unscramble those instructions. He was afraid to contemplate what the effect might be.

He turned his head slightly. At the start, Anna lay huddled against the door, as far away from Barzel as she could manage within the confines of the car. They had untied her legs but her hands were still bound. She was shivering, sometimes violently, sometimes a mere murmur of the body, reminding him of a very sick animal.

"The submarine," she cried suddenly; and seemed on the point of speaking again but was silent.

"What about—"

"Steel trap. Don't let them." She raised her voice in desperation. "Don't let them do it!"

Barzel shifted onto the edge of his seat. "Can't you shut her up?" he snarled. When Gerhard snapped a refusal, he tossed his head like a man who doubts, but made no reply.

"Don't deserve this. Leaving Juliet. Everyone. Poor David . . ."

Gerhard leaned over to stroke her cheek. It felt wet beneath his palm.

Anna was silent for a long time; she seemed to have fallen asleep. Barzel's short-wave handset crackled into life, making Gerhard jump. Stange's voice emerged over the static. Barzel murmured a few words to test the hookup.

Anna stirred, evidently awakened by the interruption. She looked around, as if surprised to find herself inside a car.

"*Herr* Barzel," she said suddenly. "You really must come around for dinner when we're all living in Berlin. We'll have a laugh about old times, a few drinks. *Lots* of drinks . . ."

No one said anything. Barzel continued to gaze through the windshield as if Anna had not spoken, but Gerhard's professional intuition was already mapping the catastrophe before him.

"You must bring your gun. I want to see you shoot. Can you knock hearts out of playing cards, and things like that? Bet you can."

She was sitting up now, taking interest in her surroundings. When Barzel still did not answer, she bent forward to rest her wrists on the top of the driver's seat—"Sorry, Yorgos, did I bump you? It's this rope"—and say, "Out-of-the-run jobs like yours can be so fascinating."

Her giggle was childlike.

"Anna." Gerhard reached out to touch her arm. "Anna, stop it."

"Mm?" She glanced at him. "Something bothering you?"

"*Anna!*"

She swayed. Her eyes, so intent and alert a second ago, unfocused, and in the same instant her face underwent a subtle change. It was a question of millimeters, nothing more: a sagging of the chin, drooping eyelids, slack mouth . . . countless details emerged to suggest a change of personality, along with the outward show.

"What? Did you say something?" she asked.

"I . . . you weren't quite yourself."

"No. No. What . . . was I saying?"

Barzel broke the barbed silence. "You were inviting me to dinner, Anna; you wanted me to bring my gun and show you tricks."

Gerhard examined her face, what he could see of it in the car's dim interior. No point in asking if she remembered any of that, because plainly she did not. She was tearing apart, severing, in front of him. His dreadful, guilt-ridden handiwork, brought to its logical conclusion at last . . . two Annas. Two separate people. He stared out the window, as if darkness held a peculiar fascination for him.

Anna fell back in her seat. The car cornered sharply. When she lurched against Barzel some hard object ground against her thigh. She knew what it must be. His gun.

Kleist had a gun too, though: she had seen him furtively pocket his Luger while Barzel was still preoccupied with Stange, who had staggered into the house with blood on his face and a long story to tell; but since he told it in German she did not know what was the matter with him.

A tic started at the side of her mouth. She had a sore throat. All her nerves seemed to be at war with one another, right up against her epidermis, suddenly making it impossible to sit still.

You must not leave this place!

They're taking you away. Can't fight them.

David is here. He's come for you. He wants to rescue you.

No, he can't do that. Can't. David's dead.

But it *was* David she had seen, outside the church, a few hours before. They'd left her facing the cove while they argued in German across the top of her head, as if she didn't exist. She did exist, however, and she had seen her husband.

He isn't real. Couldn't be. He's dead.

Before they tied her up again, she had somehow managed to slip his photograph out of her handbag and leave it under a vase of flowers on the window sill. If he found it he would know she'd been there.

Her last message of love.

Fight it!

I can't.

Can't.

Can't.

Do.

This.

Barzel turned toward her. "We are nearly there. Get ready, please."

CHAPTER
43

Albert had told Vassili, "I don't care what color it is as long as it's black." And the Greek replied, "Black is impossible. Gray."

Lindos P.269 was gray, and against a background of mainland mountains the coastal patrol craft became almost invisible, moving soundlessly through the water at twenty-seven knots. But there was a moon, three days off full, and more stars than Albert thought the cosmos capable of holding, so he cursed his luck and prayed for rain.

The worst scenario had, after all and with dreary inevitability, materialized: a sea-borne operation, with one soaking already under his belt and God knew what else in prospect. No matter how often he made an effort to control his shallow breathing, he was left with this unacceptable truth: despite his ability to exercise control over his fear (he had frequently done it before), tonight he was rattled.

No, he told himself for the hundredth time, you are in charge. You are not afraid. You are not *affected.* Fear is not on the list of problems facing you.

Many people now seemed to be involved in the tracking of Anna Lescombe, which gave Albert no pleasure. Half-a-dozen taciturn men clad in black track suits had joined the party before the *Lindos* left Corfu. No one introduced them, they just materialized and stayed. Albert looked at them, raising one eyebrow for Vassili to see, but the Greek merely lifted his shoulders in one of those thespian shrugs.

Competition, Albert thought to himself. Careful . . .

When they reached the island where Kleist had his villa, they found the local policeman waiting on the quay. Albert forced himself to stand with a patient look on his face throughout the involved colloquy that followed. At last Vassili turned to him and said, "He's sure he knows the person you mean. A doctor who sometimes brings his patients to the island for treatment: always beautiful women, never men."

"That figures."

"Something else. A few days ago, the woman he's with this year made some trouble here at the port. From the description, it sounds as if it could be Anna Lescombe."

"Why the devil didn't he report that before?"

"He says no one asked him."

No one does their duty any more! Albert wanted to shout. But he contented himself with saying, "I thought you'd issued an alert?"

"He didn't read it until this evening." Vassili hesitated. "Pay on the islands is low, and perhaps this man is more friendly with Kleist than he should be. But that can wait for later. Right now, we're wasting time."

"What about David Lescombe?"

"Nothing."

"But you did put out an alert on him, too?"

"Of course. As I've told you: a hundred boats go in and out of here every day. Not all of them use the port. There are beaches, coves . . . Lescombe is maybe here, maybe not."

Albert knew already that an air search had failed to locate David's speedboat. Three-quarters of an hour had elapsed between his climbing out of the water and the first chopper taking off, seventy miles away on the mainland. Lescombe could have defected to Albania in that time; he could have *swum* to bloody Albania. . . .

"God damn!"

"Do you want to go up to the villa? It's called the 'Little House,' by the way."

"How charming. Let's get a move on, shall we."

But it took a while to organize enough transport for everyone;

another quarter of an hour lost frigging about, Albert thought savagely. These people wanted to join the Common Market, when all they were fit for was taking long, long siestas. Eventually, however, he was on his way, sandwiched between Vassili and Hayes in the back seat of a Fiat.

"What are you doing about the Coast Guard?" he asked.

"They have been told—"

The car swerved violently to avoid a motorcyclist; for a moment all was cursing and confusion. Albert gritted his teeth at the agony that suddenly boiled through his injured hand.

"We've ordered the Coast Guard to stay on watch, but don't expect too much. When we first put out a description of that speedboat we got three sightings in the first quarter of an hour. Trouble is, they were all in different places."

"But one of them indicated a course to this island, you did say that."

"*En daxi.*"

Got him, thought Albert. Got everyone. Never mind the ifs and the buts, forget about the sea, the watery bit's behind you now, think positive. What idiot drives a motorcycle like that at night? Not a motorcycle, a moped.

At last the convoy slowed to a halt. Everyone got out. The six black-clad newcomers were already in a huddle when Albert and Hayes came up. Albert looked around for Vassili to do some translating, but he had disappeared.

Suddenly there were just three of them: Hayes, Albert, and the policeman.

"We're being set up," Hayes muttered.

"What?"

"They're running this thing for themselves. Although it may have passed you by, we don't figure any longer."

"Then we shall wait," Albert said calmly, "until they collect us again." But Hayes's words jarred him.

He moved away, deliberately distancing himself from the other two in order to listen. He had not experienced such stillness since his last foray into the Empty Quarter, and as for the stars! . . . Albert, enveloped in a velvety darkness that seemed neither moist nor dry, gazed up at them in awe.

How did the inhabitants of this remote place manage for transport, he wondered? Perhaps they all owned bicycles, mopeds . . .

His memory kept looping back to the barely avoided accident

on the road as they were coming out of the port. What sort of maniac rode a motorbike in that way on a hot night *while wearing gray flannels and a long-sleeved white shirt?*

The thump might have been anything, except that Albert's instincts were honed to recognize a stun grenade when one went off. As he crashed down he heard five rounds of automatic fire, muffled by distance, something more than distance. Interior, two o'clock, seventy degrees, *go!*

Less than twenty seconds after he'd risen to the crouch his back was jammed hard up against an outside wall of the Little House. Listen. Wait. *Go!*

Roll around the corner, down, monkey crawl to door, Christ, what a stench! Mayhem . . .

Albert stood up silently, raising both hands above his head. These men were as professional as any he'd encountered, but sometimes the best of us make mistakes. . . .

Vassili was standing inside the hallway. Hearing the Englishman clear his throat he swung around, holding in both hands a pistol aimed at Albert's stomach.

The next seconds seemed inordinately long.

"Come in," Vassili said softly, holstering the gun. "Watch your feet."

A living room, once cozy, now disordered. On the table by the fireplace, two large, empty suitcases and a radio set, powerful, not plugged in. It looked as if someone had been setting up an aerial. They'd interrupted him before he could complete the job, however; he lay on the floor, his legs entangled with the chair on which he must have been sitting when the five rounds drilled through his chest. Face a mess, too: had he been in a fist fight? Halfway between him and Albert lay a Luger, beside that a holster. It had been a case of "No Surrender," then.

"You okay?" Hayes asked as he came through the front door.

Albert nodded. "Too late. Birds flown."

Vassili and his squad were already taking the house apart, aided by the policeman, who had entered as soon as Hayes demonstrated by his own example that it was safe to do so. Nothing showed up, except the radio. Albert wandered about, trying to picture what had gone on here.

Only in the last bedroom did anything attract his interest: a vase of bluebells, now somewhat limp, on the window sill. He went over to look. Then he saw something else. There was a small square of card under the vase: not aligned like a coaster, but slightly askew, as if someone had put the vase down hurriedly to stop the card from blowing away.

Or to hide it.

Albert lifted the vase to one side and picked up the card, turning it over as he did so. A photograph. David Lescombe, wearing a white, long-sleeved shirt—*you moron get after him!*

"Vassili," he yelled. "The guy on the moped, it was Lescombe, out, out, *out!*"

In the car they tried to make sense of it, paint a picture they could all believe in, but nothing worked. If Lescombe was part of the opposition, why didn't he escape with the Germans? If he was straight up, why did he lie to Albert in Corfu? Where was Anna now? Who had her?

Back in the port Albert and Hayes stayed by the car, watching the Greeks fan out. Albert kept his eyes on Vassili, who was on the point of entering the biggest taverna when a woman in the doorway of a nearby boutique said something that made him pause.

Albert, sensing game, drew closer.

Vassili was having an expressive conversation with the boutique lady, who wore large, round spectacles that made her look distinctly owlish. She seemed angry, perhaps a touch scared. Vassili was pushing her too hard. It ended abruptly, with him throwing up his hands in a gesture of despair.

"The man next door," he said to Albert, "runs some kind of travel company. He has boats."

Albert took in the chalked notices. "Yes?"

"This woman saw a foreigner come up to him. The foreigner could speak some Greek. He wanted a boat to go to Antipaxos, right then. The woman got interested: it's forbidden to take a boat to Antipaxos after dark: too dangerous. But the foreigner had a lot of money, seemed really desperate, so in the end they did a deal."

"How long ago?"

"Maybe half an hour, she's not sure."

"What is this Anti-place?"

"A smaller island, uninhabited, due south, one mile."

"Time to go," said Albert.

CHAPTER 44

David had traveled a long way without knowing real fear. When it hit him it came out of nowhere, hard, like an iron force of nature.

Stiff gusts whipped up the channel between the two islands, sending huge surges of sea against the side of the boat, and hampering the Greek helmsman's efforts to keep her on course. The boat was small, powered only by an outboard motor. David sat on the middle thwart, gripping the sides. His hands ached with strain.

He knew he might die out here.

The travel agent had warned him: the strait between the two islands was unpredictable, hazardous even to those with years of experience of Greek inshore waters. Night was worst. At certain times the sea glittered beneath the moon like a millpond, with scarcely an eddy to marble its silver surface; at others it would dissolve into fury at the behest of some whimsical gale or freak tide. If you were caught up in it, there was no going back: all you could do was run before the waves, praying they would not swamp your boat.

In the end, greed overcame caution. The man said he would try a crossing. At £100 for one mile, it made *Concorde* seem like a cheap day excursion.

It had not felt too bad at first. The sea looked choppy, rather than rough; David was an experienced sailor, so this did not daunt him. Shortly after they left the lee of the big island, however, the screw began to leave the water with each pitch and toss. The first wave broke over the prow of the boat. Then another, high enough to soak David's shoes and ankles. He tightened his already painful grip on the planking. If the boat shipped too much water it would founder and sink. He was a strong swimmer, but he was realistic, too, and he was sure he would not be able to survive a sea running this high.

He distrusted the boat's owner. Now he understood the man's cupidity: he was terrified. He kept up a low, monotonous litany; its burden seemed to be not so much that what they were doing was dangerous as that it was illegal, for at night the port police closed this strait to traffic. That didn't worry David: the most welcome sight in the world, right then, would have been an irate harbor master in his cutter.

They were three-quarters of the way across when they started to ship water in alarming quantities.

Cross-currents.

The land mass in front of David lurched from side to side, all scrambled up with black sea and white horses, like a demented television screen. The wind had risen. When David felt the boat smash against the first V of converging waters, he panicked. He could no longer hear the Greek helmsman's chant against the howl of the wind, but the sound of his own voice echoed inside his head like a ghoul's. He was screaming.

He was going to die.

No conscious thoughts. No prayers. Just the fear, the shit inside him welling up in animal protest at the horror of it. The totality of "me." Bottom line: *save me.*

His legs were soaked to the knees; water swished about everywhere, slowing them down, making them unstable. The boat began to rock forward and back, like a swing. Sometimes a wave took her sideways as well, bringing her to a crazy kind of halt, but then the weight of sea on one side would yield, abandoning them to the mercies of the next watery trench. The Ionian, no longer an azure, picture-postcard lake, was black and chill.

This penetrating cold did more than anything else to keep David thinking clearly. The small island lay dead ahead, less than a quarter of a mile off. Anna had already landed. He'd found her.

Triumph. And he wasn't going to let the sea rob him of it now.

He launched himself forward, feeling in the wintry bath for something to bail with. The boat plunged, banging his head against a thwart, and he temporarily lost control, stunned. He was floundering around, soaked to the skin, at the mercy of waves that flung themselves down in a whirl of destruction, of malice concentrated against himself. *God damn,* there must be a bailer somewhere. . . .

He found a plastic pot barely larger than a tooth mug and frantically hurled water left and right until his arms were ready to drop out of their sockets. Useless. Ten, twenty quarts of water landed in the boat for every one he managed to displace. Suddenly the panic he'd conquered earlier had him by the throat. He couldn't draw breath. He cried out, exhausting the last reserves of oxygen inside his lungs. With that, the sea moved in for the kill. The starboard side of the boat slowly sank down, allowing water to pour over its edge. David had no time to take evasive action. His feet kept in contact with wood for a few seconds longer; he felt the boat sink away from him, kicked against the hull one last time, and then he was fighting for his life.

The sea was a mindless creature, home to other mindless creatures. It slaughtered blindly, like justice. And always the place was of the sea's own choosing. By embarking upon it, you accepted its challenge on its own terms. David could not win this struggle.

He swallowed a lot of water and vomited it up. As he surfaced he realized that what he could see was land. He began to swim toward it, hauling himself through the swell about as effectually as if he were already wrapped in his winding sheet.

A wave came down on his head, leaving him breathless. He trod water. The land seemed closer. David struck out once more.

He felt himself weakening. All his effort went into forcing one arm over, left, then right, then left again, but each circle took longer than the last, and cut less of the sea. His legs hardly moved. His clothes hampered him, but it was too late to think about taking them off. Wasted effort. Swim. Left. Right. Left.

David, down to his last breath, opened his mouth, and a wave filled it.

———

The swell that had overwhelmed David Lescombe made little impression on *Lindos P. 269.* By propping himself against the navigator's console Albert was able to read the signal without difficulty.

89/44303/A:SIGINT9 YOUR 56 AND 57 WELL RECEIVED +
COMPSEARCH SHOWS SIG CON GERQUARRY PREV A/R
CASE CABOFFSEC TREATED + GANDERGOOSE GQEQ +
NILCONF + SEETWOENDIT

Albert devoted a lot of thought to deciphering this; for one
thing it distracted his mind from the water around and beneath him,
and for another the word 'Gandergoose' leapt off the paper as if a
highlighter pen had been run through it, making him anxious to
guard against error.

So what did it mean? He knew even before receiving the signal
that the computer had been at work: all of Kleist's patients were
being subjected to scrutiny as Albert left London with Hayes. The
search had apparently thrown up a "Sig Con," or significant connection, between his German quarry (Kleist) and another case where
action had been required (A/R). A cabinet office secretary had been
treated, was that right—"Caboffsec treated"? Albert frowned at the
deliberate obscurantism, which, he realized, had been designed to
confuse "trusted allies" like Hayes and Vassili. Anyway, since he
could not even confirm safe receipt of Shorrocks's cable ("Nilconf"), Gandergoose was up to him.

He folded the sheet of paper and stuffed it into his pocket.
"How much longer?" he asked Vassili.

"That will depend on whether the commander here obtains
clearance from Athens."

"Can't we cut the red tape?"

"I'm sorry. Somewhere close to where we are now there may
be a Soviet sub, probably containing a highly trained Special Operations unit. If it comes to a firefight, our commander cannot just hope
for the best."

"Is that why we're cruising so slowly?"

"Yes." Vassili went across to the chart table. "Let me show you
what we think we are up against."

Albert looked around for Bill Hayes, who a few moments ago
had been standing beside him, ostentatiously trying to read London's signal, but the American was nowhere to be seen.

"Here . . ." Vassili ran a finger north-south ". . . is the Vespuga
Deep. A trench, wide and very deep, as you guess from the name.
If they are anywhere, that's the place. Put yourself in the Soviets'
position. What would you do?"

"Stay down until D minus five, then surface for long enough

to ship the boat that'd be waiting for me up top."

"I don't think so. The sea around here is treacherous, especially at night to those who don't know it. Kleist and the woman would be mad to take such a risk: floating around in a rising swell, with winds and tides against them."

"What, then?"

"We believe the submarine captain will send a boat to make landfall. Whichever option they choose, there has to be a boat, on the surface, at some point and for some time. There's a good chance we'll pick her up. But . . ."

"But what?"

Vassili unwound hands, arms, and shoulders in the finest production Albert had seen yet. "You won't let us help you. Surprise, you tell us. No helicopters; one ship only. It may be *possible;* easy it isn't."

Albert moved to the nearest port and stared out into the darkness. "Kleist and the woman will have gone ahead," he said to the glass. "I can't think of any other reason why Lescombe should be so desperate to get to the small island."

"Unless that was a blind. You have told me already: he's good."

"Not this time. He's getting close to home now. Starting to panic." Albert paused. "I want us to go there too. But quietly. Undetected. Does the captain know where they would have landed?"

Vassili called across to the commander. The man squinted at the ceiling and spoke a few words.

"He says along the eastern side of the island there are many fine beaches. A man could land there if he didn't mind getting his feet wet."

What if the enemy's already in place? Albert thought grimly. Suppose the submarine had surfaced, sent a task force. A German-occupied Greek island; how history does repeat itself . . . He became aware of another voice speaking. The signals officer was at work in his cubbyhole behind the bridge. Vassili glanced in that direction, then back at Albert.

"Orders," he said softly.

Albert nodded. "Where did you stow my bags?"

"Aft. There's a rope locker—"

Shit! Albert thought. Outside, on deck. "I know it. Excuse me."

The breeze had stiffened while they were talking. Albert made his way toward the stern, keeping his gaze firmly on the deck in front of him. One step, two steps, there, you can do it. . . . He opened the lid of the locker and took out a long rectangular case, the sort of thing professional snooker players use to carry their dismantled cues. Then a voice behind him said, "Hold it right there."

Albert obeyed.

"Turn around."

Albert did so. "The thing that's been puzzling me," he said conversationally, "is why you waited so long, Bill."

———

David was lying on sand; and even then he nearly drowned.

A wave, the same one that had filled his gasping, wide-open mouth, met an opponent coming from the other direction. The incoming water proved stronger; it swept him almost as far as the beach. He felt something hard beneath his feet, only to lose it again. His heart seemed to explode and he knew nothing more until he came to, spreadeagled face down on relatively solid ground. Every third wave or so sluiced over his shoulders; if he had taken mere seconds longer to recover, he would have died.

He crawled up the slope inch by painful inch, until water no longer deluged his body. When he finally managed to push himself onto all fours he could see great gouges in the sand. He had clung to the beach as if it were a life raft, trying to become one with the earth, so that he, like it, might become indestructible.

The moon shone brightly, but it provided an ominous, ghostly illumination, which gave more intensity to the shadows than sunlight ever could. He looked out to sea, still in the throes of upheaval, its white horses prancing wildly. Apart from flecks of foam, nothing showed. The boat had gone. So had the boatman.

David sat down heavily. If it weren't for him, another man would even now be alive. No! You can't be sure he's dead yet; suppose another freak wave washed him ashore, further up the coast. . . .

To hell with it. Tomorrow. He could adjust then, fiddling the books of conscience until they came out right. Status check. Nothing broken. No bleeding. A head that ached where he had bumped it against the side of the boat; bruises left, right, and center; stomach, nauseated. But alive, thank God.

He had lost a shoe. *Better take off the other one; you're on sand, it won't hurt your feet. . . .*

The beach was narrow, perhaps a hundred feet long, bounded

by rocks at either end. He could not see a light anywhere. Nor could he hear anything above the wind and the pounding of the sea. *Which direction . . . ?*

He had come down from the north and something told him that Anna was ahead of him. *Go south.*

He kept away from the shoreline, wanting to see if there were any paths leading inland. He knew there were several people involved, because he'd concealed himself to watch while they loaded Anna into the car and drove off; even allowing for the fact that not all of them might have come as far as this, the group would be bound to have left traces. But he discovered only a few false trails, little more than trampled undergrowth leading back to piles of picnickers' rubbish or heaps of ashes.

When he came to the furthest limit of this particular beach he began to climb over the rocks. He was at the summit of the outcrop when something made him raise his eyes. And he saw her.

Anna was standing at the end of the next cove with her back to him, head bowed. She was alone.

David's heart gave a delirious thump of exaltation, but he somehow resisted the impulse to shout. God knew who else might be within earshot. He slid off the rocks, seeking the shadow of the vines, which here came down almost to the sand. He moved slowly, anxious to avoid making the slightest noise. Sixty feet away. Fifty. Forty.

Anna did not move. She seemed to be asleep, suspended upright by invisible puppet strings.

Closer. Thirty feet. Twenty.

As David opened his mouth to speak, something hard thrust itself into the small of his back. "Don't move," said a voice he had never heard before. Anna started to turn; he caught a glimpse of her ghostly face, stagnant, like that of a long-drowned corpse, with two black wounds where the eyes should be. Then his mind filled with darkness and the bitter knowledge that the road he'd followed so tenaciously had at last run out.

CHAPTER

45

W hy did I wait so long?'' The question seemed to intrigue Hayes. He tilted his head to one side, but the black object in his right hand did not waver.

Albert found it impossible to gauge the gun's stopping power by moonlight. "I've been slow," he said. "I admit that."

The shadows did not permit him to see if Hayes smiled, or what expression his face wore. Somewhere just outside Albert's concentration, terror hovered. The pitching of the deck, salt air on his face, the feeling that any second now he might lose his balance and drop over the side were enough to bring on a feeling of nausea that could cripple him. If he once so much as acknowledged its presence he'd be reduced to gibbering impotence. So he did what he always did when faced with water in vast hateful quantities, and kept his entire attention focused on a nearby object: in this case, Hayes's weapon.

Don't let him see you weaken, don't panic, say something! "The real question, I suppose," Albert drawled, "is what shall we do about it all?"

"Do? Tell me, Lieutenant Colonel Albert of the SAS regiment, 'Who Dares Wins' and suchlike crap: what do you believe is going on here?"

"Me? Nothing. I'm only a simple soldier."

Hayes shook his head. "No. You're not. You're a highly complex individual. I've read your Northern Ireland stat sheet. 'Cold personality masked by scrupulous politeness, coupled with significant absence of morality,' isn't that how it goes?"

"I wouldn't be a bit surprised." How insouciant, Albert thought. *Wonderful.* "You can always rely on Army Intelligence to get it wrong."

"No commitment to any one government agency, but held ready at all times for secondment. 'Special operations,' that is to say, state executioner. Freelance."

Albert made a deprecating moue. "There's no money in it."

"That's a lie. But anyway, so what? You don't need money, because you have no life outside your work. Not even a sex life. Relaxations: hunting, painting, long solitary walks, stroking your cat. But oh boy, can you cook! And you're a trained psychologist. Now that really interested us. Why in heck should MI6 need a psychologist?"

"Thinking man's thug, you know the sort of thing."

"No, I don't. I don't understand any of it. I'm just here to do one job."

"Make sure I don't do mine." Albert was struggling with the illusion that someone had flooded the deck with oil, that he would slip and slither and slide. . . . "Yes," he said, his voice almost a shout. "Oh, quite."

"What exactly *is* your job, colonel?"

"I'd have thought that was fairly obvious."

"Pretend I'm stupid."

"My orders are to ensure that the Krysalis file doesn't fall into enemy hands."

"You're to kill the woman, in other words?"

Albert's smile did not falter. Hayes was silent for a long time. No matter how the deck swayed beneath their feet, his stance never changed. That part of Albert's brain not fighting queasiness was busy with spans, ranges, angles, light. Nothing balanced; the lines steadfastly refused to meet. "I'd have thought you'd be rather pleased to let me get on with it," he said. "Why are you so determined to stop me?"

"You know why, Colonel Thinking-man's-thug."

"There's a price on her head."

"On David Lescombe's, too. And whereas you come expensive, me, I'm cheap."

Ah, Albert thought savagely; so Redman *did* hedge his bets. "How much are you in for?" he inquired, not without genuine interest.

"That'd be telling, wouldn't it?"

Albert sighed. "I suppose this explains why you took a free lunch off Vassili, out of my earshot, when you ought to have been staking out the airport with me, if your cover story was true. You wanted to make sure he didn't become *too* efficient at helping me."

"That's right. His orders were to give you everything you asked for. I didn't like that, because I'm going to kill the Lescombes, not you. So I let him think the United States wouldn't be too pleased with his government if your mission succeeded. Unfortunately, I got to Vassili a little late. Like you, I've been slow."

"Oh, I don't know. Unless that submarine actually comes up top, ready to ferry the Lescombes home to Moscow, we're both going to be rather short of excuses for what we've come to do, aren't we? Seems to me Vassili did his stuff: one dead German radio operator meant that nobody could milk him of his codes, send a decoy message, abort the Russian operation."

"Vassili's one of the good guys, yes. Deep down he's anti-British and he's got a lot more power than you think. A pity I didn't get to him earlier; perhaps he'd have persuaded his government to withhold cooperation from you altogether."

"But apart from that, all's well that ends well."

"Certainly. You can relax now, colonel."

"One problem."

"Namely?"

"I'm still holding this case."

There was a moment of silence, of immobility. Then Hayes retreated a step, bringing his back against the rail, which was exactly where Albert wanted him. He heard a heavy click and knew that what Hayes held was a revolver, now cocked, not good, *don't look at the sea, you fool,* not good news at all. . . .

"Put down the case, colonel."

"Going to have to make me, old boy."

Albert's brain was subconsciously counting seconds. The radio officer had been receiving when he left the bridge. So much time to decode. So much time to formulate tactics. So much time to brief. So much time to execute. Now it was D minus nothing. And if the orders said "No," if the game had gone against him . . .

With a sudden surge of power the ship leapt forward, going from five to fifteen knots in exactly the flash of time it took Albert to swing his case up and knock the gun from Hayes's hands. Then the case became a battering ram. It thudded into Hayes's left side, below his breastbone, crushing the pancreas and rupturing his spleen, but before agony could transmit itself through the American's brain, hands grasped his ankles and somersaulted him backward over the rail. Hayes was bleeding to death, internally. By the time he hit the water he had been immobilized beyond any possibility of salvation. He died slowly, in pain, at a great depth.

As Albert thrust his way onto the bridge Vassili turned to him and said, "A boat has already landed on the beach. We are late. What have you—"

"Power, please; make what speed you may. And *no light* until the end. Have you got that?"

"Yes."

"No light at all! I'll be up top."

Only then did Vassili notice what he was holding.

———

"Don't move," said a voice in David's ear. He knew intuitively the voice belonged to Kleist and he raised his hands. "Anna?" he breathed.

She stared straight ahead. He could not tell if she recognized him. "Are you all right?" he asked; and on hearing that, she lifted her chin, but still she did not speak.

"Anna, it's me. David."

For a moment longer she continued to gaze at him in silence; then— "Go away," she burst out. "Please go away. They'll kill you. There's nothing you can do."

David felt the hard object disappear from the small of his back and seconds later a man he'd never seen before walked into his field of vision. So this was Kleist, how strange; he'd imagined someone taller. . . .

Now the three people on the beach stood at the points of an invisible, equilateral triangle, facing inward. David longed to go to Anna, but he felt sure Kleist had a gun. So he was destined to die here without ever holding his wife in his arms again, or telling her how much he loved her.

Anna raised her hands and David saw that they were bound with rope. So she had not gone willingly, then. Despite the peril, his spirits soared. The rope vindicated him. It meant that he'd been right to trust her in spite of everything. She wasn't a traitor.

"Barzel will be back any minute," Anna said. "He's climbed up to the lighthouse, his radio works better there. . . . Gerhard, can't you help him hide?"

But then a new voice spoke from the edge of the moonlight, where sand met trees. "I don't think so," it said. "Your husband and I must have a talk, Anna."

Barzel stepped forward far enough to let David see the weapon he was holding in his right hand. With the left he supported the strap of a cabin bag slung over his shoulder.

"Something's wrong," he muttered to Kleist. "Stange's not answering."

"Why?"

"How in hell would I know?" Barzel turned back to David. "We'll go up the beach," he murmured. "Talk in private."

When David stayed where he was, terrified by foreknowledge of what was going to happen, Barzel gestured with his Luger. "Please," he said softly. "Not here."

"Gerhard!" Anna's shriek made David start, but its effect on Kleist was remarkable: a shudder seemed to pass the whole length of his frame. "He's going to kill David," Anna cried. "Gerhard, *stop him!*"

At first no one moved or said anything. David tried to swallow, but his throat was dry. Then Kleist put his hands in his pockets and stepped to one side, as if conceding a point. Barzel gripped David's shoulder. "Walk," he muttered.

"Jürgen."

But Barzel paid no heed to Gerhard. He continued to march David back along the beach, toward the rocks.

"Jürgen, stay away from him. It's not necessary. We'll be gone in half an hour."

When Barzel did not so much as break stride, Gerhard took his right hand from his pocket. He was holding a pistol. *"Barzel!"*

At that the other man faltered and began to turn, releasing his grip on his prisoner. David's knees gave way and he fell over. Barzel was nearly facing Gerhard, not quite, when suddenly he clasped his hands, bringing the Luger up to horizontal. A shot exploded through the darkness in a spiral of flame, missing its target; then, almost simultaneously, Gerhard returned fire.

Barzel stared at him, not accepting that the reality of his fate could ever be death. He dropped onto his knees and fell forward in two distinct movements, as if at exercise. When David rolled him over his face had left an impression in the sand, like a mold for a death mask.

The Luger had fallen to the ground. Next to it, something lay half concealed by Barzel's body. His cabin bag. The zipper was undone, so that when David picked it up awkwardly the contents fell out: books, mostly, and another object, also of paper, rectangular and white. David stared at it, scarcely daring to believe what he held. But yes—in the top left-hand corner, by the light of the moon, he could just make out a handwritten number amongst typescript; and, centered upon the page, a single word in black capitals.

Krysalis.

Suddenly Anna came to life. "I'm not dreaming," she cried. "Tell me I'm not dreaming, oh *David!*"

As he rushed to take her in his arms, no longer afraid, Gerhard rapped, "Listen! Can you hear it?"

At first neither of the Lescombes understood. Then David caught the sound of a muted engine, still far offshore. He could not see the boat, only its mother ship, visible as a silhouette still far out to sea but already careering toward them. A coastal patrol craft . . .

He swung around to face Gerhard. "What happens now?"

Kleist allowed the gun to slip from his fingers, sinking down to join it on the sand. "The submarine . . ."

"Submarine . . . ?" David struggled to make sense of what Gerhard was saying. Suddenly it all came together. "That boat we heard . . ." He spun around, only to be faced by the impenetrability of night. "It's from a sub. . . . *Anna! Run!*"

But then from out of the darkness by the water's edge a hoarse voice shouted, *"Barzel!"*

———

Perched on top of the bridge, the sling of the FR-F1 tight around his arm, Albert knew that even for this, the greatest sniper rifle ever made, it would be an impossible shot at the best of times, without morbid aquaphobia and an injured hand to worry about. But just as he had to take risks, so it was part of his job to put the bullet where it mattered.

He hugged the Sopelem night-sight nearer to his eye. Range five hundred, closing. He evaluated the ship's movements, counting seconds between troughs and highs and wishing he were dead. Four hundred . . . feed it into the computer along with everything else, let the brain do its own calculations, don't disturb it, trust your instincts . . . how long before Vassili switches on the spotlight, speed, range, movements . . .

The ship lurched into the trough of a wave, and—"Montgomery," he choked out in a last-ditch attempt to distract himself, "the things I do for you . . ."

First the woman, stop the disease from spreading, then the man, that was what "Gandergoose GQEQ" meant, sauce for German quarry, sauce for English quarry. . . .

Closing, closing . . . tight group of three, one of them sitting down, that would be David, a prisoner, of course, thirty thousand pounds' worth of target but he can wait, *what was that beside him, ignore,* what would she do, what would Anna the twenty-grand target do next . . . ?

The Soviet landing party had seen the *Lindos* by now. Some were taking cover behind their own boat. Lights dotted the luminous blue circle into which Albert was peering, automatic fire . . . hold it, Vassili, don't panic, hold your fire while Anna works out what to do.

Albert knew. He had lived with this woman until she'd become a part of him and he of her. He was inside Anna Lescombe's head now. Besotted with Kleist, she would accompany him aboard the submarine; but first she would want to kneel down and hold her husband and bid him look after Juliet. . . .

Range three hundred . . . no light, not yet, not yet, ignore the bullets, Soviet Ping-Pong balls, they never hurt anyone . . . *don't throw up now, don't think about the sea!*

By now the strain of trying to hold an accurate aim was injecting savage bolts of pain through his injured hand. Albert cursed the Japanese man's dogs through gritted teeth, and momentarily relaxed his muscles before realigning the rifle.

She'd hold David, wait, get it right, get it right, three bursts of two, "double-tap," first the woman, then the man, last the husband for Redman, "two for joy," David and Anna, that was the deal . . . don't roll over the side, hold on, Albert, hold it, Vassili, *hold it!* Wait for the Greeks to return fire, make it look like a stray round, there mustn't be any witnesses, *no traces,* Shorrocks had said, *accidental death, act of God, no traces or no deal* . . . what's that on the beach, looks like another man, lying down, ignore, ignore, shoot before the light, *take the first pressure,* range two hundred, *fuck those bloody dogs!* Wave trough, rising, rising, wind gust, second pressure . . .

That's not David sitting on the beach!

Freeze!

Albert nursed the trigger home.

————

The Soviet marines had beached their boat, but even when David pulled Anna's arm she refused to move. She was staring at Kleist, who sat resting his head on his forearms. Suddenly all the feelings that had warred inside her for so long coalesced into a single emotion, and that was pity.

"Quick, Gerhard!" she cried. "Into the trees."

"Anna!"

David tugged her sleeve, but she shook him off. "No! Help him! He tried to save me."

Oblivious of the danger, she bent down to grab Gerhard by the shoulders. At that moment the first fusillade of automatic fire rang out, and David flung himself on top of his wife, dragging her to the ground.

As they fell, a single, tiny, hard object ploughed into Gerhard's left eye, spattering the Lescombes with blood.

Shafts of light burst from the *Lindos,* swiftly raking the beach. David hugged Anna to him and rolled away from Gerhard's corpse. As the Soviet landing party answered a volley of fire from the Greek patrol craft, David grabbed her hand, leapt up and sped toward the nearest trees.

To the Lescombes, lying in the brushwood, the fight seemed to go on forever. In truth, the exchange was a short one, lasting less than a minute. The Soviet contingent, six of them, were both out-gunned and pinned to the beach by the *Lindos*'s searchlight. They made a last stand behind their upturned dinghy but it did not take the Greek machine gunners more than a few seconds to find the range, and then streams of bullets sliced up the flimsy cover like so many chain saws.

The firing stopped as suddenly as it had begun. From his perch atop the bridge of the *Lindos,* Albert scanned the deserted beach, now as dazzlingly illuminated as a football stadium ready for an evening match, and he sighed. Hearing footsteps on the metal-runged ladder behind him, he turned to see Vassili's head come into view.

"All right?" the Greek inquired.

"Yes, thanks. Any survivors?"

"Unlikely. We're sending men to look."

"What are you going to do about the bodies?"

"Lose them." Vassili's smile was friendly, but it did nothing to dilute the quiet authority in his next words. "You can stand down now. You've won."

"Yes." Not *we've* won, Albert noticed. He dismantled his rifle and replaced it in its carrying case, out of sight of curious eyes. The task, which called for meticulousness, came as a welcome diversion from the sea below.

"Where's Hayes?" Vassili asked.

"Haven't seen him for a while. Sorry."

While they spoke, the crew of the *Lindos* had been unshipping her inflatable rubber dinghy. Albert and Vassili stood together on the roof of the bridge, watching its progress toward the shore.

"So much trouble," Vassili said, "for a worthless file."

"Worthless?" Albert's voice was noncommittal.

"Hayes told me many things." The Greek looked at Albert, and for an instant dropped his mask, letting the other man see his resentment at the way he'd been used. "So I say again, yes: worthless to you, to both of you. There will be no further opportunities to carry out your, your 'contract,' do you call it, while on this ship. Understood?"

"Certainly, my dear chap."

"That goes for Hayes, too."

Yes, thought Albert; it certainly goes for Hayes.

On the whole, he agreed with Vassili. It had turned out a pretty worthless operation, one way and another. Shorrocks's orders were very precise: Albert had to make everything look like an accident. With the *Lindos* now lit up brighter than the brashest floating gin palace, there was no longer any scope for an "accident"; and besides, the lady had not, in the end, gone over. Nor had her husband. So no Caribbean hideaway this year, Montgomery, old bean . . . Waste of time all round, really.

Albert found himself looking back along the wedge of moonlight to where Gerhard Kleist still lay on the sand in sepulchral immobility. Not a total waste, perhaps . . .

He pointed. "Here come the Lescombes. What's that David's carrying?"

As Anna's feet touched the deck David slipped a hand through her elbow and she looked at him. Albert heard her say: "You must have learned . . ."

"Everything."

"Even about Juliet . . . at the beginning?"

"Everything, my love," he said, drawing her close; and Albert suppressed a yawn.